D0462360

The Bridge

The Bridge

STAN CRADER

The Bridge

Copyright © 2007 Stan Crader. All rights reserved. No part of this book may be reproduced or retransmitted in any form or by any means without the written permission of the publisher.

Published by Wheatmark®
610 East Delano Street, Suite 104
Tucson, Arizona 85705 U.S.A.
www.wheatmark.com

International Standard Book Number: 978-1-58736-908-7
Library of Congress Control Number: 2007931544

rev20100205

Dedication

THIS BOOK IS DEDICATED TO Nancy Yvonne Dewitt Crader, my mother. She died before this book was written but not before instilling in me the desire to explore new horizons. It's this desire that causes me to enjoy meeting new people, traveling to new places, and trying things that others say can't be done. I've coached sports I never played—not well, but that's not the point. I've reluctantly accepted public speaking invitations and then found myself enjoying the experience. I've ridden my bicycle across multiple states, flown a small plane along the Lewis and Clark trail, and across the Atlantic all the way to Athens, Greece. However, each of these experiences pales in comparison to the work and reward associated with writing a book.

I watched cancer slowly and cruelly take my mother's life before she had accomplished all that she'd set out to do. She often offered advice and encouragement. "Don't wait," she'd say. And, "Just put one foot in front of the other." This advice works in just about any circumstance—whether it's contemplating a flight across the Atlantic or doing something impulsive such as stopping for ice cream during a snowstorm. It's her fault I'm an overachiever and don't always think things through completely.

She was the first one to tell me that I should write a book. Well, she made me promise that I would.

I did it, Mom.

Contents

Contents

Acknowledgments

IT WAS ONLY AFTER YEARS of encouragement from friends and family that I made the commitment to write this first book. Writing a book is hard work, but the feeling of accomplishment after having done so is enormous, almost the same as filling a barn with square bales. I'm forever grateful to all who nudged me along.

Debbie, my wife, told me repeatedly that I needed to get it out of my system. It didn't work. After having written this first book, I can't wait to get started on the next; the story is there, I just need to get it on paper. Writing is now a part of my fiber.

Dave Stewart and Connie Bennett, both successful writers, encouraged me several times to write a novel and kept after me until I started. Those who read this book can decide if Dave and Connie know what they're talking about.

Although it was probably impossible for them to tell, all of my elementary school teachers played a significant role too. They tried to teach me how to spell, introduced me to words, and eventually challenged me to write. I learned the states and capitals in Mrs. Welker's class and how to write while doing reports on South America in Mrs. Scott's class.

Uncle Bob and Aunt Shirley inquired the most about the progress of the book and continued to shower me with encouragement even after reading an early first draft, which was a rather pathetic piece of first work.

The ladies in my writing group, each accomplished writers, were probably too nice to be of as much help as they could have been—they all suffer from chronic kindness. Nonetheless, their input was invaluable and probably made the difference in me getting published or just having a completed manuscript sitting on my desk at home. Thank you Staci, Susan, Ginny, and Jo.

Paul Benton Weeks, a friend I made while attending Mizzou, who was sure I'd never amount to anything, but out of concern has kept track of me, provided a final edit and taught me the proper use of a semicolon. Paul, an attorney, is very thorough. Thanks, Paul.

I owe an enormous measure of gratitude to the people of Bollinger County, Missouri. That's where I grew up, or at least got older. It wasn't until I spent some time away that I realized what a special place and time it was to grow up there. Coming of age in Bollinger County was a privilege that I no longer take for granted. All of the people in this book are fictional, but their characteristics are those of real people.

I thank my grandparents, who raised my parents, who raised me.

Most of all I thank Debbie, Justin, Scott, and Brad for indulging me when a blank look came across my face as I mentally shaped a scene.

Katy, our golden retriever, must be acknowledged. She sat curled at my feet throughout the entire process and never complained.

Prologue

INTERSTATE 55, OR THE "DOUBLE Nickel" as it's called by those with a CB radio, skirts the city limits of Fairview on the west side. State Highway 34 is a winding road from Fairview to Colby that tracks along ridges densely timbered with a variety of hardwoods: sugar maples, oaks, and hickories. Highway 34 dips below the skyline only when necessary—to cross a creek bottom, or two, in search of the next far-reaching ridgeline. There has been talk of the state of Missouri possibly building new stretches of a wide-shouldered limited-access highway to replace the curviest sections. Few believe it will ever happen.

Several crosses, some new and some weathered have been placed adjacent to "Dead Man's Curve." Each one commemorates a family member's death in a failed attempt to beat the legendary speed record for the hairpin section of highway, a record held by a mythic rogue of days past.

A curvaceous hill leading up to Lanagan's Pass often becomes treacherous and impassible during icy conditions. On the steep side, a sign suggests using a lower gear. It's riddled with bullet holes.

The roadside park, built by the Future Farmers of America, Class of 1965, is situated on a precipice just east of town. Cupid-inspired pairs of initials are carved into several of the trees. A giant sycamore, with its soft, thin bark, has been the most popular. Colby, in full view, lies in the Craggy Creek valley below.

The aura of a small town is impossible to describe in a few words. Understanding it requires one to have lived and immersed themselves in the daily life. To truly appreciate the life-lasting gift a small town offers requires experiencing the coming-of-age there.

City dwellers and interstate drivers occasionally exit the concrete national arteries and pass through small towns on their way. From the comfort of their climate-controlled SUVs they use terms such as quaint, charming, and picturesque to describe places that, for an outsider, seem to be paused in time.

Ken and Barbie types, "folders" as I have called them, occasionally flee their gated communities to small towns in search of solace and the prom-ise of a slower pace. Most are fascinated for a short time and then leave before ever learning the name of the checker at the grocery store, or the life goals of their paperboy. Small town intimacy isn't for everyone.

A lucky few transplants have experienced a protracted psychological epiphany and then mentally, as well as physically, joined the ranks of the small town chosen. But even these fortunate few will admit that they feel somewhat short-changed for having not grown up in the ebullient en-vironment. They especially feel this way after hearing the tales of youth from those who experienced it there, no bother that most of what they are told is sufficiently embellished half- or quarter-truth, merely based on fact. Harry Truman has been quoted as saying, "Things ain't like they used to be and chances are they never were." Enhanced memory can be a good thing, if not carried to extreme, especially in old age.

There's something magnetic and curious about rural America which produces the likes of Chuck Yeager from West Virginia, Rush Limbaugh and Ira Biffel from Missouri, and Dan Rather from Texas.

Tommy Thompson wasn't the first person to pierce the sound barrier; doesn't have a grandson who hosts a nationally syndicated radio show; hasn't taught anyone how to fly an airplane, let alone Charles Lindberg; nor has he ever done an evening newscast for a major TV network. He does, however, share an intriguing common bond with those who have achieved such fame: small town roots.

Chapter 1

Popping the Question

ONLY A WEEK EARLIER WE'D missed school for a snow day, typical of the weather in Missouri. That day the temperature had risen to the mid-seventies with snow still evident in a few spots. Booger and I'd decided to make a second attempt at our spring advent ride to the Craggy Creek Bridge. It was February 1967. We waited for Flop to catch up. The creek wasn't far ahead.

This was the first time Flop had ever ridden all the way to the creek with us. We'd started out with him the day before, but he'd gotten a flat tire. Flop rode an English Racer with skinny tires and that, we learned, was often a problem; the gravel punctured them if he rode too fast. Booger and I had big fat balloon tires. We could run over just about anything without getting a flat, including broken windshield glass. Everyone had wanted an English Racer until Flop moved to town. I won't admit to having learned much from Flop except that English Racers weren't worth a plug nickel.

"You oughter ride in 'at center rut," I informed Flop after he'd caught up. It wasn't the first time I'd imparted that bit of wisdom to him. On gravel roads, the center rut was the smoothest. Cars going both ways used it. Anyone with good sense knew that.

"Like-a-said, it's not safe," he argued, too winded to say any more, but nonetheless beginning his sentence with 'like-a-said,' as he often did, even though he'd yet to say anything.

He ignored the advice, as always, and rode on the lumpy side rut. His mom, Mrs. Westwood, who called him "Villiam" with a pious German accent, had told him to always ride on the side of the road. She wasn't from these parts, an unnecessary piece of information she imparted regularly. She didn't know a single thing about gravel roads. Worse than that, she was never around to help Flop fix his stupid flats. Booger and I had been relegated to do that task. But we didn't mind; Flop was easy-going and always had his pockets full of Bazooka bubble gum. We felt a mix of pity and ambivalence toward him.

William Westwood, or "Billy" as we called him in front of his mother, was given the nickname "Flop" less than two weeks after moving to Colby during the fall of 1966. Looking at him from the rear, his head and neck seemed to be smaller than normal; they resembled something akin to a large light bulb flimsily attached to the top of his spinal cord between his bony shoulders. What his head lacked in size his ears more than made up for. It was an odd-looking combination. When he wore a cap it always slid down his head and rested on his ears, forcing them to turn out. If he didn't wear a cap, he could shake his head and make his ears flop around. Uncle Cletus had said that his ears were probably missing some cartilage or something. Since the first time he'd shown us the ear deal, he'd been nicknamed "Flop", a label he carried with pride rather than humility.

Flop's dad had retired from the military. One look at him and the ear mystery was solved. With the help of a realtor, Flop's parents had chosen Colby as their retirement community. The realtor had convinced them that it was quiet, had a good school, and had milder winters than Chicago, where Flop's parents had grown up, which explained a few things.

Flop's mother spoke with a thick German accent, but Flop and his dad had a nasally clipped Chicago accent and occasionally used unusual vernacular. Flop eventually lost his accent but clung to certain strange but discernable word combinations.

It was fairly obvious to anyone with a critical eye that Flop's mom had grown up proper. Flop and his dad were a taciturn pair, the opposite of the mother. Her mannerisms were similar to those of the ladies on the afternoon soap operas. Uncle Cletus once told me he was certain she had German-Italian roots, "the worse kind," he'd assured me.

BOOGER AND I HAD LEFT our bikes lying beside the road just short of the bridge. Flop had to find a flat place so he could prop his delicate racer up on the kickstand. Booger and I ran on up to the center of the bridge and looked down at the creek; the banks were full and the water was crystal clear. Booger and I had known each other since forever. We'd been to the bridge at least a thousand times.

Patches of the previous week's Valentine's Day snow remained on the north-facing bank. It was steep and covered with trees: sycamores, white oaks, northern red oaks, and a couple of sugar maples. Somebody had tapped the maples. Small sap buckets hung on each tree. Uncle Cletus said it took forty gallons of tree sap to make one gallon of syrup. That seemed like a lot of trouble to get syrup. Log Cabin tasted just fine to me.

Just a few hundred yards upstream, the creek had long ago carved its way through a granite boulder field. Water running around and over the boulders, some the size of a house, formed several small pools and waterfalls. It was a fun but dangerous place to swim. Corky Seabaugh had found that out the hard way. Since he'd broken his back diving off the ledge, we were forbidden to go there without an adult. It was a rule that was seldom broken ... at least by anyone who knew Corky. The sound of the water rushing through the boulders was occasionally irresistible.

Booger and I were leaning over the rail making spit strings when Flop caught up. He caught his breath, and then asked, "How long do ya figure this bridge has been here?"

"Since ever, prob'ly," Booger replied. Flop leaned over the railing and stretched a string of saliva almost all of the way to the water.

"No fair, you just put a fresh piece 'a gum in yer mouth," Booger protested.

Flop smiled, chewed, and smacked his lips. Booger lightly slapped the back of Flop's bulbous head, careful not to pluck it clean off of his shoulders.

Mr. Bird beeped his horn before he crept across the bridge in his 1949 Chevy pickup truck. It had a deluxe cab, one with the small windows in the corners of the cab, between the doors and the rear window. He'd seen us on the bridge and was careful not to run over us. We squeezed against the railing as he went by. The door handle hung down at a forty-five degree angle, a common problem with that model. His farm was on up the road another mile and a quarter. It had a cave on it that was big enough inside to ride a bicycle around in, sort of. We hadn't taken Flop there yet, but we would later that summer.

The iron railing on the old bridge was rusty and hot to the touch. The rust meant it was time for the county to paint the bridge; which, by the way, never got done. The warmth meant it was time for our first swim of the season, even if it was still technically winter.

One by one, we squeezed down through the bridge works to the top of the pier. Flop, the cautious one, had to be coaxed.

Booger stood on the pier and pointed at a piece of driftwood slowly bobbing its way downstream. "Think you can hit 'at log?" Booger asked, shortening his words when it suited his need.

I unzipped my fly and got ready to blast it. "Let's see."

Booger and I both guided thin, light yellow streams back and forth across the passing log. Flop couldn't reach it, but I could tell he'd been taking vitamins. Booger may have noticed how dark Flop's stream was but he probably didn't know what caused it. He didn't have an uncle who was a science teacher to explain such wonders.

Booger and I both stuck our hands in the water and commented about how warm it was; Flop did likewise and agreed. We didn't bother to share with Flop the fact that the thermocline was probably less than a foot and a half below the warm surface. He'd find out soon enough, and it's always better to learn through experience.

Uncle Cletus, a high school science teacher and decorated Korean War veteran, had taught me the scientific name for the point where warm surface water meets the cold, deeper layer of water. He had lots of good stories and would expound on any subject so long as he had an audience. That was usually my role. I decided early on that he'd sniffed too much of that rank juice that was in the jar with the rattlesnake. The hair on his head was falling out, but his eyebrows and ears were bushy as a squirrel's tail and seemed to get bushier every year. Something wasn't right about him.

Booger and I stripped down to our birthday suits and tossed our clothes in a crumpled pile next to the I-beam. Flop was neatly folding his clothes when we grabbed him from behind and threw him in. He came up gasping for air, then climbed up on the pier and grabbed his clothes. He probably couldn't have spelled thermocline, but could darn sure have described one just then. I could tell by looking at his privates that he was really cold. I jumped in, putting the pressure on Booger to do the same.

"Feels great," I lied, barely able to get my breath.

Booger took the plunge and came up gasping for air. "Just whadda feller needs after a long bike ride," he said, almost without stuttering. He was good at embellishment too.

The water was so cold my chest wouldn't expand, making it difficult to breathe. About two minutes was all I could stand. I casually climbed out of the water. This gave Flop the impression I wasn't cold, and it also caused Booger to have to stay a little longer in the frigid creek since I was blocking the only place on the pier to climb out. He'd done the same thing to me on the first swim the year before. I dressed slowly because my hands and legs were shaking so hard I couldn't keep my balance.

Flop had gotten dressed and was sitting in the only place the sun was hitting. He was wearing a smirk. "So, Tommy, what does that ungle of yours say causes libs to turn purble?" Flop said, also suffering the effects of the frigid water.

Booger's lips looked like he had just eaten a grape Popsicle. Mine must have too. My first thought was to slap Flop's bony cheeks, but instead I just ignored the question and asked for a piece of bubble gum. He gave Booger and me both one, even though we'd just thrown him in. The thought occurred to me that we had never asked him if he could swim. My jaws quivered so hard I didn't even have to chew.

Booger and I rode slowly on the way back to town, letting Flop keep up with us; he'd earned that much, plus the sugar was almost out of my gum. The swim had done him good. He cruised recklessly along in the center rut like he'd done it all his life. By summer's end, Booger and I had him acting almost normal. We went through a lot of Bazooka in the process.

Flop headed up Maple Street for home. Booger and I headed to Burt's Sinclair, at First and Main, to sit on the dinosaur. It was a ritual in which we found enormous pleasure. I hoped that some of the little kids would have already been playing on it and rubbed the bird droppings off. Dino had become a bit of a target, especially, it seemed, for birds with loose stools.

Booger climbed up on Dino's back and sat facing forward. I sat on the neck facing backward, laying my head on the back of Dino's head. Dino's dark green surface was as slick as a new dime, not a single dropping. The little kids had served their purpose. The plastic skin was warm. It felt good after swimming in the cold creek. Facing each other, Booger and I blew bubble-gum bubbles, watched high school kids cruise by in their cars, wished we could drive, and daydreamed.

From his angle, Booger could see what was going on over at the Houn Dawg. I could see down First Street. A row of trees lined the street between the road and the sidewalk. First and Main streets were the only streets in Colby with a sidewalk on both sides.

The jukebox at the Houn Dawg had an outside speaker. Someone was playing "Penny Lane" by the Beatles. I gazed skyward, imagined standing on a street corner in England, wondered if the Queen actually did anything, and thought about Wendy.

There was once a gigantic tree right next to where the dinosaur sat. I'd heard that the city thought it was a black locust when they planted it. A danged old honey locust is what they got. Every fall it made a big mess with those long, good-for-nothing leaves. The courthouse coots said the leaves were good to feed to cattle, but I never saw anybody collecting them. The leaves mostly cluttered in the street and got ground up by cars driving by. It created quite a stir when they cut it down. I always felt a green dinosaur was a much better use of the space, but letters to the editor indicated that some felt otherwise. Anyway, the courthouse yard had plenty of oaks and maples to go around.

Booger's real name was Randy Burger. He had an older brother, Johnny, who had taken Booger and me fishing a couple of times. He had been the starting running back on the football team his junior and senior years in high school. From Vietnam he'd written Booger a letter saying he planned to buy a Chevelle Super Sport when he got home and that he'd take us both for a ride in it. The letter hadn't mentioned it, but Booger was sure he'd install an eight-track too.

"Hear that?" I asked. Booger looked in the direction the sound was coming from.

"Just sounds like a ridin' lawn mower to me."

"Sound's movin' too fast for a lawn mower."

Something yellow that looked like a miniature motorcycle buzzed around the corner of the station and stopped next to the gas pumps. I slid off of Dino and raced over to investigate. Booger followed.

The driver took his helmet off and I recognized him as Corky Seabaugh's older brother, Dwight. He didn't have a shirt on. His forearms had big veins sticking out and a tattoo stretched across his right biceps. I'd never gotten close enough to make out just exactly what the tattoo was. Rumor had it he'd stabbed a guy at the movies a few years back. Supposedly he'd used a switchblade.

"What is that thing?" I asked, without getting too close and trying not to sound dumb and inexperienced.

"It's a Honda Mini-Trail, made in *Jaypan*," he said, putting too much emphasis on the "jay" part, but that's how most in Colby pronounced the name of the country we'd nuked in the big war.

"Ain't you sorta' big to be a ridin' 'at little thing?" Booger asked.

For a split second, I considered running for cover. Dwight turned around and looked down at us. I noticed then the big scar running from his forehead, down between his eyes, and off to one side of his nose. My mouth got dry. I caught myself looking at his cheek. It was bulging from a huge chaw of tobacco, probably Red Man. I turned my focus back to the Honda Mini-Trail.

"I don't got no driver's license an'nis thing is so small the state rods don't really give a care. It'll run 'bout thirty mollinar," he said, meaning miles per hour. He spat a big wad of black-looking stuff toward the trash can, mostly missing it. I made a mental note not to step there.

"How much you have to give for it?" I asked, thinking that, since you didn't need a license to drive it, I might be able to get one—if Mom would let me, of course.

"Two hunerd'n eighty-nine bucks. I had 'a go all the way t' Fairview t' git it. Only genuine Honda dealers can sell 'em." He then offered to give us both a ride on it but we turned him down since we didn't have permission, more an act brought on by fear of Dwight than obedience to our parents.

Booger and I started home, not talking, just pedaling and thinking. I'd never seen a Honda Mini-Trail before and was pretty sure Booger hadn't either. The pedaling somehow seemed harder now that I'd watched Dwight accelerate down the street with just a twist of his tattooed wrist. We agreed that we needed a Honda Mini-Trail. I turned into my driveway and waved goodbye to Booger. He rode on toward his house, two blocks from mine. I decided before going in the house that I was gonna figure out a way to get a Mini-Trail.

At dinner, Mom handed me the gravy. It was the lumpy kind with bits of shredded beef in it. She gave me an all-knowing look. "You're awfully quiet tonight, Tommy. Is everything okay?"

"Well, I'm a little worried about 'at test tomorrow. I can't never remember the name of the capital of Vermont, Mount Pile or something or other." That wasn't what was really on my mind, but I needed to throw her a bone so she wouldn't keep bugging me and make me tell her about the Honda Mini-Trail.

"You mean you can't 'ever' remember," she corrected. "It's Montpelier. I'll help you study tonight."

I'd heard that fifth graders all across the country were being forced to learn the states and capitals. I wondered if they had to learn to spell them, too. The next day we were being tested over New England. I'd seen a car with Vermont license plates at Burt's Sinclair once. The driver had asked for directions with an accent even more obnoxious than Flop's. He'd sounded like his nose was stopped up or something. I was proud to live in a state with a capital named after President Jefferson and felt a little sorry for kids who had to grow up in a state with a capital like Montpelier.

Marsha, my older sister, and I flipped a coin to see who had to help Mom with the dishes. Marsha lost, so Dad and I went outside to play pitch and catch. Dad and I agreed that dishes were women's work, but it was an opinion that I'd learned long ago was best kept between men. It just seemed only right that Mom and Marsha should be doing dishes while we played pitch and catch. Dad called out a state and I named the capital. It was a man's way of doing homework. I'd work on the spelling later with Mom.

"Don't you think it's about time I started mowin' lawns?" Popping the question was always the hardest part. The look on Dad's face told me that I'd caught him by surprise. He wasn't as quick on his feet as Mom.

"How many lawns you talking about?"

"Booger and I'd like to get four or five yards and mow 'em together." I hadn't really given much thought as to how many lawns we'd need to pay for a Honda Mini-Trail, I just knew that I wanted one.

"What are you going to mow them with?"

"We were hopin' you'd sell us both a twenty-one-inch Lawn-Boy and let us pay for it over the summer." Dad and Papaw had a John Deere tractor dealership and sold Lawn-Boys and other stuff too.

"It sounds like you've given this considerable thought. I'll need to talk to your mom about it." This was the standard reply for more important matters.

"You might see what she thinks about me gettin' a Honda Mini-Trail too."

"A what?"

"A Honda Mini-Trail. It's a little mini-bike. It doesn't go very fast." He got that furrowed brow frown. I kept throwing the baseball back real quick. It'd slow his thinking a little and make him more reasonable.

"I'm not sure I've ever seen one," he said, his face frozen in a perplexed look as he caught a fastball in self-defense.

"Dwight Seabaugh has one."

Dad frowned and said, "That's not very assuring. I don't think I'll share that with your mother." I eased up a little on the return pitches. I was pretty sure that Dad would approve of me getting a Mini-Trail once he'd seen one. He'd been letting me drive a tractor at Colby John Deere all by myself for over a year by then. I don't think Mom knew though. I sure hadn't told her. It sounded like I'd made some progress with Dad. And I had most of the summer to work on Mom.

It was getting dark. Dad went inside to watch TV and read the *Colby Telegraph*. I walked next door to Mamaw and Papaw's house. They had a screened-in porch.

Mamaw was knitting, her fingers working feverishly row after row. "What did you have for dinner?" she asked.

I answered, but didn't mention that the gravy had been lumpy. I sat down in the wicker rocker beside Papaw. I watched him roll a cigarette using Prince Albert canned tobacco. He never spoke when rolling a cigarette, an art I was hoping he'd show me one day.

He snapped shut his John Deer lighter and slipped it back inside his pants pocket, took the first long draw, and exhaled the smoke toward the porch ceiling. He made it look so good.

"This is a habit you best not start, Tommy."

I didn't respond; his admonitions against smoking were recent. I tried to understand why he told me not to smoke when it clearly brought immense pleasure to him.

"Once you start you can't stop," he continued.

The smoke hung in the air until a light breeze carried it through the screen and out toward the garden. It didn't smell particularly good, but Papaw certainly enjoyed it.

"I'm gonna start mowin' lawns this summer."

"You are?" Mamaw asked.

"Gonna gitcha a Lawn-Boy?" asked Papaw.

"Of course," I told him.

"Just wonderin,'" he said, and smiled. Papaw didn't talk much, he mostly just nodded. His gift, according to Brother Baker, was listening. It was a gift I took full advantage of that night and shared my summer plans.

After I finished talking and he listening, we sat there and listened as the night noises started. Papaw finished his cigarette and fell asleep. Mamaw covered him with a small quilt and winked at me. His only movement after that was an occasional cough.

Mom blinked the porch light, signaling for me to go home, just after a whippoorwill sounded off. I gave Mamaw a hug. "Night," I whispered and slipped out the door.

"Night, Tommy," Papaw said softly. He swore he never slept and sometimes I believed it.

I walked home to the sound of a whippoorwill and slipped off my dew-soaked shoes before going into the house. Sleep didn't come easy. A tinge of guilt for tricking Flop lingered as my mind pinballed from mowing lawns to the Mini-Trail and, lastly, Wendy.

Chapter 2

Clyde

MOM DISHED UP SCRAMBLED EGGS, crispy fried bacon, homemade biscuits, and milk gravy. The pork producers' conspiracy to kill us all off with cholesterol hadn't yet been discovered. Dad and I ate together. He read the paper and slurped his coffee.

Marsha, my sister, seldom ate breakfast. She'd reached the age where girls feel it necessary to put a full cosmetic disguise on before being seen in public. Occasionally I'd watch her pluck her eyebrows and remember flinching myself with each pluck. I never told on her for rolling her skirts up at the waistband after leaving the house.

Mom sat down at the table with us. "Did Dad tell you that Booger and I are gonna start mowin' lawns?" I thought I'd try and slip one past her.

"Nice try, little mister. I'll tell you what. You make some good grades and that'll go a long way toward you getting permission to get a lawn mower."

Mom had pretty good sense for a girl. Lots of girls were book smart but most of them didn't have much common sense. Mom was a little different; she was smart, plus what she said usually became the rule.

BOOGER AND CALEB WILFONG WERE having a serious conversation about something when I got to the bus stop. Caleb, ebullience personified, was waving his hands around in the air as he spoke.

"Hey, Tommy, my mom and dad said I could build a potato gun," he announced, his eyebrows bouncing up and down as he spoke.

Booger and I'd read about how to build one and had told Caleb about it like we'd actually done it. In fact, I think I'd even told him all the things he'd need to build one. I looked at Booger and he just sort of shrugged his shoulders. We'd never even seen one, except in a magazine.

"That's great, Caleb. Do you have the stuff you need to build it with?" I was sure he wouldn't.

"I told my dad what you guys said I'd need. He said everything sounded okay to him and that we'd go to Colby Hardware on Saturday and pick it all up. I told him you two knew all about how to build one and would help me." He smiled real big, revealing bits and pieces of what he'd had for breakfast.

Booger and I needed to find that magazine article with the instructions by Saturday. I tried to sound like an expert. "What do you think, Booger? Should we build a long one and see how far she'll shoot, or a short accurate one?"

Caleb beamed. He couldn't have cared less either way, long or short, so long as we helped him build something to shoot potatoes. Booger and I must have made it sound like a lot of fun. Thinking harder, I tried to remember where I'd put that magazine. I hoped that Mom hadn't thrown it out when she straightened up my room.

It was never wise to get on the bus before the older kids, so Booger and I waited. They'd bop you on the top of the head with their notebooks. The seniors would thump the tops of lower classman heads with those big class rings. It never happened to me, but once I saw Flop get whacked hard enough to draw blood. The shape of his head naturally drew attention and, consequently, abuse. His mother had come to the school the next day and talked to the principal and everything. That only made it worse for Flop. He finally started staying back until the bus was loaded, then jumped on and sat in the front seat right behind Miss Barbara, our protector and driver. Nobody messed with Miss Barbara. "Big Bertha" is what we called her when she wasn't around.

Booger and I sat together; we could see Flop's reflection in the wide, all-seeing mirror that hung above Miss Barbara. I should have, but never did, tell Flop that everyone could see him when he picked his nose. Caleb got a seat to himself since he had his tuba with him. The insides of that tuba must be a mess, I remember thinking to myself, watching him licking breakfast remains off of his teeth. I don't think Caleb ever brushed.

Dental visits were surely a painful experience for him, but then again, I doubt that he did that either.

Wendy and Beth Winchester sat in the seat behind Caleb. Wendy was a tomboyish sixth grader, a year ahead of me, and had started taking band already. She played the flute just like Beth. Beth was wearing a letter jacket several sizes too large. Unlike some of the letter jackets adorned with several small medals, making whoever wore it sound like a human wind chime, this one featured only a single letter with the annual stripes. It most likely belonged to some high school football player. He might even be on the bus, sitting in the back. No sense in looking back, though. It was always best to avoid eye contact with anyone in the back. The notion of a girlfriend crossed my mind for the first time when I saw Wendy. I planned to carry her flute for her when I got in band and get an extra helmet so I could take her for a ride on my Honda Mini-Trail, which I planned to have by summer's end.

Miss Barbara waited for everyone to be seated before pulling away. We were the last stop before the school, and the bus was usually full. The sign at the Methodist Church had a new message. It read, "If absence makes the heart grow fonder then people must love church." They might as well have advertised that nobody came to their church anymore. Mom had made me go to Bible school there the previous summer. They only put one piece of ice in each cup of Kool-Aid, and the cookies were store-bought. I wouldn't have time to go this summer since I'd be mowing lawns.

I let Wendy and Beth get off before me. Following them off the bus, I was enveloped in their perfume, Jungle Gardenia; it was the same perfume that Marsha used. Wendy said, "Thanks," and I almost had enough nerve to say, "You're welcome." My pulse raced when she spoke, a physiological response I couldn't control, but one that I mysteriously enjoyed.

EVERYONE GOT TO CLASS EARLY, and most of us had been in our seats for five minutes or longer when the bell rang. Mrs. Enderle, a teacher with a pompous flair, had said that if we were punctual and "a-like-a-that," as she always put it, that we'd get to take the test first thing and get it over with. Everyone got quiet long before she entered the room. I could hear her clomping down the hallway in those high-top shoes. They looked more like Uncle Cletus's army boots than shoes for a lady. After closing the door behind her, she stood at attention and silently scanned the room. Since we had assigned seats, she knew immediately who was absent just by looking for empties; none of this role call business, a horrible waste of time, or so she'd said. Nobody said a word. All eyes focused on Mrs. E.

I could smell the freshly mimeographed tests before she got to my row. It was a very peculiar odor, and the ink that caused it probably came from a special place, or so I thought at the time. All of our tests, work sheets, and spelling words were printed with it. Everyone that already had a test paper was sniffing it.

Mrs. E cleaned out her purse while we took the test. She must have had five pounds of used tissues in there. One time somebody put a Mississippi ringed-neck snake in it. Nobody ever fessed up to it, but I'm pretty sure it was Clyde Goodpasture. He was as ornery as they came and about the only one who was mean enough to do something like that. Much to everyone's surprise, Mrs. E just picked it out of her purse, walked over to the window, and dropped it to the ground like nothing had happened. She didn't even wash her hands after handling the slithering creature. It wasn't much bigger than a night crawler, but I've held her in a little higher esteem since that day.

Melody Hinkebien graded my paper, and I graded Everett Fluegge's. It was Everett's first year in the A class. He'd been in the B class since first grade but somehow he'd gotten moved in with us at the beginning of the year. I'm not sure how they decided who went into which class. The A class was supposed to be smarter, but we used the same books, and the B class usually beat us in the math quiz. It didn't make sense. Everett's dad got promoted to postmaster, and his uncle had gotten elected to the school board the previous fall. That might explain how he'd gotten there. He spelled Montpelier with two l's but I didn't count it wrong. He'd missed enough already.

Melody and I had a secret. One time in the third grade we were walking to the bus stop and old Irma Bordenstein's German Shepherd came tearing after us. Before she'd realized the dog was on a chain, Melody had gotten scared and wet her pants. I saw it running down her legs to her socks and even into her Saddle Oxfords. She ran home crying and embarrassed. The next day she told everyone she'd been sick. I'd never told anybody anything. I'd gone to the bathroom before I left home that morning, or I'd probably have done the same thing. I was hoping she'd remember our secret and give me a break. It would go a long way toward me getting that twenty-one-inch Lawn-Boy.

"Pass all the tests forward," Mrs. E ordered. I sat near the back of the class and wished I had a desk near the front. Kids sitting in the front looked at all of the tests as they came forward, even though they weren't supposed to, and saw everyone's grade. It was against Mrs. E's rules for me to tell Everett his grade or for Melody to tell me mine, but by the end of the morning recess, we'd all know our test scores.

AT RECESS, MELODY CAUGHT ME looking at her and smiled. I took that as a good sign about my test score. Unlike Caleb, her teeth were pretty and white. They could have used her for a Crest commercial. It was almost my turn at the tetherball court when Clyde Goodpasture walked up. "So, who'd you copy off'n, Tommy?"

He sat in the front of Melody's row. He always had to sit in the front since he was such a troublemaker. If his dad wasn't foreman at the shoe factory, he'd have been in the B class, I was sure, maybe even in that other class with the "special needs" kids.

"Nobody." My neck and face got real warm. I didn't want to run but I didn't want to stay, either. Clyde was two years older and about fifty pounds heavier than me, even though we were in the same grade. Caleb had told me that I had gotten a hundred. He sat behind Clyde. Caleb's not a troublemaker; he just can't see very well, that's why he had to sit up front.

"Well, only girls get hunerds. If you didn't copy off'n nobody and you ain't no girl, then you must be a sissy, unless you're some sort 'a Norman Einstein, er somethin'." Clyde was standing real close, and since he was taller than me, I could see up his nostrils. By then a crowd had gathered.

"Oh yeah? Well, meet me at the dinosaur after school and we'll see who's a sissy." It just sort of slipped out before I could think. "And it's Albert, not Norman, you idiot," I continued, totally out of control.

Clyde inhaled and his chest and neck nearly doubled in size. The bell rang. Recess was over. If I'd only waited a few more seconds, the bell would have saved me from making the challenge. After my pulse slowed a bit it was clear to me who was the real idiot.

———

FOR THE NEXT HOUR AND a half, Clyde looked back at me every ten minutes or so and sneered. I guess he just wanted to make sure I was still there. He seemed to be looking forward to the meeting at the dinosaur. I tried to act like I wasn't scared, but deep inside I was imagining going through life with a limp and without the use of an arm. The only positive thought was that if I became a special needs kid, then at least the schoolroom would be air-conditioned. Maybe if he knocked me out cold on the first lick, he wouldn't break any bones or cripple me. On the way to the cafeteria, I asked Booger to stick close in case Clyde decided to settle the score during lunch hour. Booger wouldn't be much help in a fight, but I felt better having him close by. Everett tagged along, too. He was mostly just trying to make friends, probably unaware that he was acting as a bodyguard.

Everett had gotten a good grade on the test and probably sensed I was partially responsible. He was pretty good-sized and could probably whip Clyde all by himself. I told him about his extra *l* in Montpelier just to make sure he knew I was looking out for his best interest. I took my time getting to the cafeteria. Clyde was several people ahead in line; he'd probably cut in front of someone. We were so far back that some of the sixth graders, who were supposed to be served after us, were mixed in with us.

"Tommy, are you really gonna fight Clyde Goodpasture?" I turned around and it was Wendy Winchester. She didn't look happy. Her voice had a stern tone to it.

"I sure don't want to, but I guess I'll have to." Words just didn't come easy. Wendy was talking to me, but all I could think of was Clyde pounding me. It troubled me to think I might not live to carry her flute.

"I heard you were the one that made the challenge." She cocked her head to one side and sounded sort of sassylike.

"Well, that's not exactly how it happened."

"So, you're saying he started it?"

"He called me a sissy and …" Her eyes turned stormy, and she stomped off across the cafeteria before I could finish. She headed toward Clyde; he'd just sat down and was sitting with his back to us. She walked up behind him and slapped him on the ear with a right roundhouse, grabbed his tray of food, dumped it all over his head, and clobbered him with the tray. Then she threw the tray in his lap and ran out of the door and down the hall. The entire cafeteria was so quiet you could have heard a pin drop. It all happened so fast that she was gone before any of the teachers figured out what was going on. Clyde had just received a first-degree thrashing from a sixth-grade female flute player.

For a few seconds I kind of felt sorry for him. He had kettle beef, green beans, mashed potatoes, and Jell-O salad all over his head and shoulders. His right ear was bleeding pretty good too. The principal and the school nurse helped him walk out. That thumping must have made him a little dizzy.

Conversations at each table slowly started again. For most, it was the first time they'd seen a girl beat up a boy. I know it was for me. My mom was always telling me to show girls lots of respect; after that, I knew why.

Caleb chuckled. "Clyde is sure gonna be mad when the nurse tells him it was Wendy that cleaned his clock."

Booger had a more serious look about him. "I'll betcha the nurse takes him 'ome. That'd be embarrassin'. He'll prob'ly be at 'at dinosaur waitin' zafternoon anyways."

My heart sank. Any sympathy I'd held for Clyde instantaneously vanished. Clyde would probably be waiting this afternoon just as Booger predicted.

Everett patted me on the back with his thick hand. "I'll go to 'at danged old dinosaur with you."

My pulse rate started a gradual return to normal, but I was still convinced that only divine intervention would help me survive this thing.

All afternoon, I worried about what had happened to Wendy. She would surely get into some kind of trouble, and the principal would call her parents. I hoped she'd gotten over whatever was bothering her before she found out that I had asked Clyde to meet me at the dinosaur. I didn't want her working me over with a food tray.

I TOOK MY TIME WALKING home from the bus stop. Why couldn't I have just kept my mouth shut a few more seconds? I whispered a prayer.

We had company when I got home. I made out Mrs. Burger's unique laugh. It was engaging. That's probably one of the reasons she was such a good Tupperware lady. From the porch, it sounded like she and Mom were having a good visit, maybe a party. I dragged myself in the door. They were talking Tupperware. Mom always liked looking at the newest Tupperware products. It was beyond me how that could be fun.

Mom got up and gave me a hug. "How was school?"

"Okay."

"Anything special happen?"

"Not really."

Mrs. Burger got up, took her cup to the sink, picked up her purse, and headed for the door. "I need to run, Ellen. Randy's probably home looking for something to eat and wondering where I am. Hi, Tommy."

"Hi, Mrs. Burger." She mussed my hair on her way to the door.

Mom saw her to the door then turned to me. "Are you going to tell me how you did on your test?"

I'd forgotten about the test. Later on I was going to die, or worse, anyway. I wasn't even thinking about the test or the lawn mower. "It won't be official till tomorrow, but I think I got a hundred."

"You don't seem to be very excited about it."

My lip started to quiver. I told her the whole story, including the part about Wendy whooping poor old Clyde. I figured she'd know a way out of this mess. Unfortunately, her advice was to go down to the Sinclair and stand my ground. She was sure he wouldn't do anything because it's always bad form, she said, for bigger kids to pick on smaller kids. She was sure that if I showed up Clyde would back down. But she hadn't seen up Clyde's nostrils like I had. He didn't seem like the backing down type to me. And, I was certain Clyde wasn't worried about his form.

Mom turned and started peeling potatoes. My bottom lip quivered out of control as I backed out the door. She didn't seem to realize it might be the last time that she'd see me alive.

Papaw had just started tilling their garden. I desperately wanted to take my shoes off and walk barefoot in the freshly tilled soil, like I used to. He saw me and waved.

Booger was waiting for me at the end of the driveway. He was finishing off a peanut butter and jelly sandwich. I bit my lip, got on my bike, and we peddled toward Dino. We rode slowly, giving Everett plenty of time to get there. I prayed again, silently.

"Maybe Dwight will be there gettin' gas," I told Booger.

"He might be," Booger agreed. "The gas tank on 'at Mini-Trail was a little 'n."

He built my confidence a bit. Just the thought of one day owning a Honda Mini-Trail and accelerating down the street provided a glimmer of hope which made me feel better.

EVERETT WAS LEANING AGAINST DINO licking a pushup when we got there. I was glad Everett had shown up, but Hoss Cartwright would have been better. I looked around and didn't see Dwight. Uncle Cletus was standing in the service bay door drinking a grape soda. His car was up on the lift. Burt was probably changing the oil or something. A morbid thought crossed my mind; Uncle Cletus had seen death before in the Korean War, so it wouldn't be a big shocker to him when Clyde did me in.

"Clyde ain't showed up yet," Everett reported.

"Thanks for comin', Everett." I really didn't know him that well since he had always been in the B class, but I was glad to see him now.

"I don't think he'll be a problem. Your girlfriend has done and wore him down for ya."

"San Francisco," by Scott McKenzie, was playing on the outside speakers at the Houn Dawg. Right then I wished I'd stuck a flower in my hair and gone to San Francisco with all of the hippies.

I was trying to figure out what Everett had meant by girlfriend when Clyde's mom's big old pink Chrysler pulled up next to Dino. Before the car stopped bouncing, his mom, who was bigger than Miss Barbara, got out and looked hard at Everett.

"You th' punk that done and sucker-punched m' boy?" Her voice had a threatening tone. Clyde got out on the other side of the car, clearly displaying less spunk than he'd had at the tetherball court, and stood there with a big bandage on his right ear. His lip was a little swollen too.

"No ma'am." Everett said. He pointed toward me. She turned, looked at me, then at Clyde; her face turned menacing.

"Don't tell me 'is half pint is th' one 'at sent you home from schoo' early." She pointed at me and glared at Clyde.

By then, several kids had walked over from the Houn Dawg. I was starting to feel a little better. Clyde didn't look like he was up to killing me, but I wasn't so sure about his mom. Uncle Cletus started walking our way. I felt certain he could whip Clyde's mom, what with his Marine training and all.

"No, he's th' one I called a sissy." Clyde had a surprisingly fearful-sounding voice.

She stood staring at Clyde with arms bent, elbows pointing out, and clenched fists resting on her massive hips. "I want 'a know which one'a these boys sent you t' Doc Boyd's fer steetches."

"It was the sissy's girlfriend that done it," Everett told her. He was the only one not shaking too much to talk. He wasn't trying to be sassy, that's just the best way he knew to explain it.

"Like-a-said, it was Wendy Winchester," Booger added, even though he hadn't said anything yet. Everyone seemed to be getting brave at the same time.

"That's right," someone from the crowd yelled. "It was a girl that whooped yer boy."

She glared at Clyde, her fleshy cheeks turned red, and her eyes squinted and got fierce-looking. She took a giant breath, probably using all of the available oxygen for half a block. I thought she was going to explode. Clyde took off running and she followed, swatting at whatever part of him she could reach. We all scattered. Dwight had pulled up on his Honda Mini-Trail sometime during the excitement and was standing by the pumps with Uncle Cletus. They were both holding their sides and laughing. I hadn't yet discovered the humor.

As Booger and I pedaled toward home, I looked back and saw Clyde's mom leading him by his good ear toward their pink car. My mom had been right, again. I didn't know if she'd included Clyde's mom in her calculations, though. Booger and I could hear The Monkees singing "Daydream Believer" on the Houn Dawg jukebox until we were well past the Methodist Church.

Cheer up sleepy Jean …
Oh what can it mean?
To a Daydream Believer and a …
Homecoming queen …

Wendy was probably home studying or practicing her flute. It may have been the first time I was certain a prayer had been answered.

Having escaped certain dismemberment or maybe even death, I started thinking about building the potato gun for Caleb.

EVERY DAY FOR THE REST of the week, Wendy and Beth sat in the same seat on the bus, across the aisle and one back from me. Wendy didn't get into any trouble for clobbering Clyde. None of the teachers had seen her do it and nobody told. Everyone acted as if it had never happened, especially Clyde. Friday morning, I asked Wendy if she was going to the movie on Saturday night, and she said yes. It was our first conversation since she'd whacked Clyde. To me, asking her if she was going to the movie was akin to asking for a date; I started looking forward to Saturday night.

I thought about moving one row back on the bus so that I'd be sitting across from Wendy, but that would put me only one seat in front of Marty Blanken. Marty was a dyspeptic ninth grader, already soured on life, who, being big for his age, had already taken to torturing kids who were smaller than him.

Wilma Bodenschatz usually sat behind me and directly in front of Marty. She was obviously a voracious eater, large for a girl, and seldom smiled except at lunchtime. She was a good buffer between Marty and me and generally protected me from his intractable behavior. He couldn't reach his big fat paws around her. I liked keeping Wilma between him and me just in case he got the notion to flick me on the ear or give me a wet willy. Another thing: he always coughed a lot in the mornings, and her broad shoulders would catch most of whatever hideous germs he was expelling into the air.

In class, Mrs. E acted as if nothing had happened; it's possible that she didn't know, but not likely. Mrs. E, like most teachers, had a way of finding out stuff that even the FBI couldn't have uncovered.

Clyde kept his distance at recesses. He and some of the other kids who lived outside of town mostly messed around by the marsh at the edge of the playground, throwing rocks at anything that moved. Booger and I both wished we'd never mentioned anything about a potato gun to Caleb. He followed us around like a dog-pound puppy all week. His sister had given him an almost empty can of Aqua Net. He said the can probably had enough juice left for two or three shots. How would he know? If he'd told us once he'd told us a hundred times that his dad was going to Colby Hardware early Saturday morning. I'd found the magazine article with the instructions. Thank goodness.

Chapter 3

The Gun

Booger arrived early Saturday morning with coconut brownies. They'd been left over from his mom's Tupperware party the night before. Leftovers at Booger's house were always good.

We each ate two and decided to save the remaining four for later. Booger put the lid back on the Tupperware container and burped it. "Keeps the freshness in," he said, mocking his mom. We'd eavesdropped once on one of her Tupperware parties and watched her entertain the crowd by burping a container. Booger's mom had a knack for lightening everyone's spirit.

Booger and I had just finished the brownies and started looking over the potato gun instructions when I saw Caleb pedaling up the street. It wasn't even nine o'clock yet. The instructions didn't seem too difficult. Just cut the plastic pieces to the right lengths, glue the pieces together, and start launching potatoes. I'd copied them off on a sheet of Big Chief notebook paper and given them to Caleb the day before.

When he got close enough, I could see that he had an excited look on his face. His eyebrows were arched almost all of the way to his hairline.

"We got the stuff!" he announced. He got off his bike and laid it beside Booger's. The sooner Booger and I could get the potato gun built, the quicker we could get back to more important "business" matters. We had to find lawns to mow. We didn't have time to be fooling around with Caleb. We didn't need another friend whose bike we'd always have to be fixing; Flop was plenty.

"Caleb, does your dad have a hack saw and drill?" I asked.

"Sure, but he said he'd cut everything to the right sizes for us. He's workin' on it right now."

"Let's head that way." I folded the instructions and stuck them in my pants pocket. Booger and I grabbed our bikes.

On the way to Caleb's house, I saw Mrs. Whitener picking up sticks in her yard. She was wearing a sunbonnet with an oversized bill. I couldn't see her face, but I knew it was her. No one else except her and Mrs. Gray had a goofy-looking bonnet like that, and Mrs. Gray lived on the other side of town. Besides, who else would be picking up sticks in Mrs. Whitener's yard?

"Hey there," I said from behind her, giving her a bit of a start. She must not have heard me coming, for she jumped a little and stood up straight. She wasn't any taller than me, but quite a bit wider. "I'm Tommy Thompson."

"Where'd you come from?"

"Rode my bike."

"You what?"

I repeated myself. She was obviously hard of hearing or had the bonnet tied too tight.

"You didn't ride in my yard, did ya? Those little tires make marks in the yard."

"No ma'am, I parked on the side of the street. See?" I said loud enough for half the town to hear. I pointed toward the street where my bike was leaning on its kickstand. Booger and Caleb waited with quizzical looks on their faces. Neither one had any idea why I'd stopped to talk to Mrs. Whitener.

"You Ted Thompson's boy? He was in my sixth grade class," she said before I could answer the question.

"Yes, ma'am, Ted's my dad. I'm gettin' a new Lawn-Boy mower this spring and was wonderin' if I could mow your lawn?" She'd been mowing her lawn herself, but when she'd had her mower in the shop the previous summer to get the blade sharpened, she'd mentioned to Dad that she might just start hiring to get it done. He'd told me that when we were making the list of people who might want their lawns mowed.

"How much would you charge me?" She looked at me real seriouslike. I'd never seen her face this close. Shallow wrinkles formed three groups of rings; one surrounded each eye and one enclosed her tiny mouth. It almost looked like she didn't have any lips. She must have taken a real deep breath one day and her lips just stayed curved back over her teeth ... or gums. I couldn't really see any teeth in there.

"Five dollars," I said without thinking. I hadn't given much thought to how much to charge. She didn't have much of a yard, though. It was full of big old maple trees with roots running along the surface. They were the kind that just suck up all of the water. The grass seemed to be losing the battle. She pulled a package of Days Work out of her apron pocket while she was thinking, sliced off a sliver using a Barlow knife, and pushed the chaw way back in her mouth with a dirty finger. It was then that I noticed her hands were bigger than my dad's. In fact, she may have had the biggest hands I'd ever seen. I'll bet she could have palmed a basketball.

"The half-wit twins offered to do it fer four dollars." She talked and chewed at the same time. The Goolsby twins weren't quite right. They mowed a few lawns every summer using two push reel mowers. It was said that the two of them combined might equal a complete thought. I didn't really want to beat them out of a job; they most likely needed the money more than I did.

"Can't see how'd it make much sense fer me to pay you five dollars fer what I can get done fer four." She spat a little Days Work juice, just barely missing her foot.

"Well, you might want to give those Goolsby boys the job." I feigned disappointment and turned to walk away. Looking around a little closer, I'd noticed that the yard was really rough in places. It probably wouldn't have been a good idea to put a brand new Lawn-Boy on it anyway. Being in the lawn-mowing business caused me to look at lawns more critically.

Booger and Caleb were unscrewing both of my valve stem covers, an obvious sign that they were tired of waiting. A few more seconds and I would have had two flat tires. Mrs. Whitener started toward the back of her house with a wheelbarrow full of sticks she'd collected. I said goodbye but she didn't hear me.

"What'd y' stop an' talk t' that ol' bat for?" Booger asked, clearly disgusted.

"I thought we might get her lawn to mow." I screwed my valve stem covers back on. Caleb hadn't waited. His house was next door to Mrs. Whitener's. His garage door was open and he was pacing in and out kind of anxiouslike.

"We don't wanna mow 'at lawn. Look'et all'ose flowerbeds, th' picket fence, an'at danged willow tree. She's got peonies some'rs too; my mom gets 'em from her. Those things are a mess t' mow 'round."

Booger was right. The half-wit twins were going to have a tough job. I hoped they did a good job for her, though. She was a nice old lady and didn't have a husband to look out for her.

CALEB'S DAD HAD GOTTEN EVERYTHING we needed. He'd cut the plastic pipes to what looked like the right lengths. The pieces were all lying neatly on the workbench in Caleb's garage. He even had the hole drilled and the flint ignition installed.

"Hi, boys. I'm Mrs. Wilfong. It's really nice for you two to help Caleb with his little project. His dad had to run to Fairview for some things. He'll be back after lunch. He said he has no idea what you all have planned to do with a potato launcher but he's curious. He said he thought he had everything ready for you to assemble."

Caleb's mom was wearing faded and frayed blue jeans with a goofy-looking T-shirt with all sorts of wild colors in it. I'd never heard a potato gun called a launcher. It sounded a little more scientific and legitimate, though. It was the first time I'd seen his mom up close, but one look at her explained Caleb's scruffy nature.

"Yes, ma'am," I said. "It looks like everything we need is right here. We shouldn't have any problem gettin' it put together." Using the instructions from the magazine, we assembled the pieces in less than thirty minutes. Booger and I never let on like it was the first time we'd ever seen a potato gun. Caleb was too excited to notice that we had to follow the instructions with what I thought was visible uncertainty.

When we were finished, the gun, or rather the launcher, looked like a telescope with a long tube sticking out of the end. It had a piece four inches in diameter and about two feet long glued to an adapter and then to a piece an inch and a half in diameter and about six feet long. The end of the shorter four-inch diameter piece had a screw-in plug; the end of the longer smaller piece was left open. That's where the potato goes. We stood the launcher in the corner to let the glue dry.

"I've got some peanut butter and jelly sandwiches in here if you're interested," Mrs. Wilfong said through the screen door in the garage. Of course we were interested.

"I'll need to call home and ask my mom if it's okay."

"Me too," Booger said. We both called home and got permission to eat at Caleb's house. Caleb's family was new in town, and my mom didn't really know his mom very well. They'd seen each other at the grocery store a couple of times, but that was all.

We washed our hands and sat down at the kitchen table. Mrs. Wilfong had a little vase sitting on the kitchen counter. It had something burning inside of it that smelled bad, but she must have thought it smelled good or else she would've doused it with water.

She sat at the table while we ate. "Tell me what you're going to use that launcher for." I looked at Booger and then at Caleb. I thought it best to let Caleb answer.

"It's good for shootin' at stray dogs and scarin' 'em away," Caleb explained. "You know how they're always peein' on the shrubs and poopin' in the yard."

"It sounds like a nifty gadget. How does it work?"

I was anxious to hear Caleb's response.

"Tommy and Booger are gonna show me after the glue dries." That wasn't the answer I was hoping to hear.

She stood there looking at us, smiling, drying her hands on a dishrag. I noticed she had one of those front teeth with a silver rim just like Uncle Cletus. He'd gotten his in the war. She looked too young to have been in the Korean War and too old for Vietnam. She wasn't wearing a brassiere; I didn't think my mom was going to like her.

The PB & Js weren't quite what I expected. She'd used some kind of weird bread that was sort of brownish-looking and had some little bits of stuff that looked like seeds in it. I took small bites and washed them down with milk, trying not to chew too much. My mouth had started watering when she first mentioned PB & Js; now I wished I'd turned and run the other way.

"It's been thirty minutes, you think the glue is dry?" Caleb had already finished his sandwich. He didn't seem to mind the weird bread. Booger was like me; he still had half of his left. He didn't look hungry anymore. I wasn't either.

"Let's give it another thirty minutes and be sure." Booger and I needed to figure out the next step. I was hoping Mrs. Wilfong would leave the kitchen so I could toss the goofy-looking sandwich out the back door. Surely she'd need to go to the bathroom or something pretty soon, I hoped.

"Can I have a napkin and take this with me?" I asked Mrs. Wilfong.

Booger had just taken his last bite and was still chewing. He probably wished he'd thought of asking for a napkin too.

"Sure, that seven grain bread is a little heavier than what you might be used to. How about I wrap it up and leave it here on the counter? You can finish it when you like."

"Good idea, thanks. Maybe I'll finish it when we get done testin' the potato gun." "Maybe I'll toss it out the window when you're not lookin'" is what I was thinkin'.

"The what?"

"Launcher," I corrected.

After twisting around on the gun a little, I decided that the glue was dry and it was time to try it out. Caleb ran to get the potatoes and the can of hair spray.

Caleb shoved a potato into the barrel. Using a tomato stick, he pushed it all the way down the long small barrel until it formed an air-tight fit near where the small barrel and the short fatter piece connected. I removed the end cap and Booger sprayed Aqua Net into the big fat chamber. I quickly screwed the cap back on.

According to the instructions, the flint would ignite the hair spray and the explosion would shoot the potato out the other end. If everything worked right, it was supposed to send the potato flying about fifty yards. The piece holding the hair spray was about twice the size that the instructions had called for. There was no telling how far the potato would shoot with that much propellant, AKA hair spray. I was anxious to see what would happen.

"Got any duct tape?" I asked Caleb.

"Right there." He pointed to a roll hanging on the peg-board.

"We might wanna wrap tape around this big piece just in case it cracks or somethin'." He handed me the roll and I started wrapping tape around the part of the gun that contained the explosive Aqua Net. The directions hadn't mentioned the tape. It was a personal addition, for good measure.

Caleb was anxious to shoot it. I didn't want to hold it. Booger didn't look any too eager either.

"Let me hold it the first time. You guys have already shot one before," Caleb said anxiously. He picked up the soon-to-be stray dog weapon. His mom heard us talking and came out to watch.

"Can I help?" Mrs. Wilfong asked. Booger started backing up and looked like he was getting ready to run.

"Sure, just twist the knob on that flint and let's see what she'll do." I have no idea why I said it. It just slipped out. She walked over to Caleb, who was holding the gun.

"How far will the potato fly?" she asked.

"It's hard to tell. It depends on the brand of the hair spray, the size of the potato, a lot of things." Once again, trying to sound expert, I'd spoken without thinking.

"Point it out that way, Caleb," his mom said. He turned and pointed the gun toward the backyard. They didn't have a backyard neighbor. Beyond their backyard was an empty field. Caleb held it tightly and pointed the barrel skyward in the direction of the empty field.

His mom gave the flint a good twist. Nothing happened. She looked at me and then at Booger.

"Give 'er another twist," Booger said. I was glad he was starting to chime in a little. I didn't want all of the blame if things didn't go as planned.

BOOM! It sounded like one of those big Fourth of July fireworks. I followed the flight of the potato. It continued to climb for a couple of seconds and got higher than any tree in town. I realized immediately that the potato was going to fly farther than any fifty yards like the directions had said. It wasn't until it started a slow descent that I noticed Caleb had somehow gotten turned around and that the gun was no longer pointed toward the field. The potato was coming down right over Mrs. Whitener's yard.

We could see the water splash when the potato landed smack dab in the middle of Mrs. Whitener's giant birdbath and then bounced out. Mrs. Whitener was still working in her yard. She was leaning over by a forsythia bush that was between her and the birdbath when the potato hit. Being half deaf, she hadn't heard the blast that shot the potato. She must have heard the potato hit the birdbath, though, because she stood up quicklike when it landed. After looking around the bush toward the birdbath and surveying the sky for a few seconds, she leaned back over and continued her lawn manicure. She didn't seem too concerned and never looked our way. She never saw the potato.

Caleb had dropped the gun when it went off. He stood there looking toward Mrs. Whitener's yard with his mouth hanging open. I could see the little hangy-down thing in his throat. The crotch of his pants was wet.

"Far out," Mrs. Wilfong said. "I thought you said it would only shoot fifty yards?"

"It must have been a really good potato or brand new hair spray." I kind of liked the expert tone in my voice. The fact that it had actually worked caught me by surprise, too. It really worked. I'd never seen anything like it before.

"You think that potato could hurt anybody if it hit them?" It was then that I realized Caleb's mom was different than most moms. Instead of running inside and calling my mom and telling her what a lunatic I was and how my parents needed to keep a better eye on me, she was asking me for advice. It felt odd, not quite right. I kind of liked it.

"If it hit you square in the head, it'd probably knock ya silly." Thinking a little more about what had just happened, I added, "But if it was to hit a fat person in the butt it probably wouldn't do much damage."

She looked over toward Mrs. Whitener, then down at the gun, lying on the ground. Caleb wasn't in sight. Booger had run in the garage when the gun went off and never came back out. It was just the two of us.

"And you say this thing is really designed for shooting stray dogs?"

"Caleb is the one that thought it'd be good for that." She looked around for him but he'd gone inside, probably to change his pants.

"I think he's right. Would you mind sticking around until his dad gets home and showing him how to operate it?"

I didn't know what to say, so I just gave her a neutral nod.

Having finished the potato gun, my mind turned to Saturday night and Wendy.

Chapter 4

Johnny

MOM FOLLOWED AS BOOGER AND I headed out the front door for the theatre. "Call if you need a ride."

You Only Live Twice, a new James Bond movie, had just come to town. I was anxious to see it because I'd heard that James Bond masqueraded as an Asian. I couldn't imagine an Asian Sean Connery. We walked, as hardly anybody rode their bikes to the movies. There wasn't any place to park them where people wouldn't bother them. Anyway, parents picked up almost everyone afterwards.

Mickey Murphy's street was on the way to the theatre. He was Marsha's boyfriend at the time. He was in the eighth grade, a year older than Marsha. I'd heard Marsha telling her friends about how he'd gotten a bottle of Jade East. That stuff must have cast some sort of magical spell over girls. They all got dreamy looks on their faces just talking about it.

Mickey had a paper route too. It was a good year-round job with lots of benefits. He got to ride his bike all over town and knew everyone. He'd be the first to know if someone wanted their lawn mowed, plus several customers gave him cookies at Christmas.

Booger was anxious to get to the theatre, but we stopped at Mickey's house anyway. Mickey didn't have any brothers or sisters. He answered the door. I knew he'd be nice to me, since he was sweet on Marsha.

"Hi, Mickey," I said. "Marsha said you got a new Rawlings catcher's mitt." She'd mentioned that, too.

"It's in my room. Wanna see it?"

"Sure. We're on our way to the movie, but I'd sure like to take a quick look at it if I could." Hardly anyone ever got a new baseball glove; they were too expensive, especially a Rawlings. I'd never heard of anyone getting a new catcher's mitt. Marsha had said he'd bought it with his paper route money. We followed Mickey to his room. The mitt was sitting on his dresser right next to the bottle of Jade East.

"What's that Jade East smell like?"

"Put a little dab on." I opened the bottle and poured a tiny bit into my palm and rubbed it on my neck and cheeks.

"Wow, thanks a lot, Mickey." I turned to walk out. "You goin' t' the movie?" I asked.

"Don't ya wanna see the mitt?"

"Oh sure, let me see it." I walked back into the room, held it a few seconds, looked at the stitching, tried it on, hit the webbing with my fist, then gave it back. I already had what I'd come for and was anxious to get to the theatre and start casting spells.

He followed us to the door and said, "Marsha and I are walkin' to the movie later on. We'll see ya there."

"See ya there." He was holding the mitt when we walked out. Booger rolled his eyes.

THE GROCERY STORE, HOUN DAWG, and the theatre shared a parking lot. Because it was Friday, payday for most, lots of people were doing their grocery shopping. Every high school kid with a car went to the Houn Dawg before the movie. Most kids didn't have cars, but those who did filled them up with their best friends. The parking lot was full.

Everyone tuned their radio to the same station and turned the volume up. In the daytime everyone listened to KXOK out of St. Louis, but at night WLS out of Chicago was the favorite.

I'd heard that Mr. Pope, the owner of the Houn Dawg, didn't much care for that part because if people listened to their radios, his jukebox didn't get any business. There wasn't much he could do about it.

From half a block away we could hear Mick Jagger flapping his big lips to "Ruby Tuesday."

Buddy Grover had his '57 Chevy pickup truck there. It had just been painted blaze orange. He must have had lots of friends because the cab and the bed were full of people gyrating to the music. Buddy and Dwight were in front of the pickup licking ice cream cones and talking. Both of them had the sleeves on their T-shirts rolled up. Each had one boot on the bumper of the truck with the elbow of the arm holding the cone resting on their elevated knee. They looked pretty cool. I headed toward them.

"Where y' goin'?" Booger asked.

"I'm gonna go over and talk to Dwight."

"You can't just go o'vair and talk t'em like 'at." Booger was always afraid of something.

I headed toward them; Booger followed. "Hey, Dwight."

"Hey, yourself there tough guy, or is it half-pint?" He'd obviously heard Clyde's mom that day at Burt's. I ignored him, which made Booger even more nervous.

"Truck looks good, Buddy. What she got in 'er?"

He gave me an annoyed look. "She's got a 327 with a Quadra jet, four speed with a Hurst shifter, and headers." He was smaller than Dwight but had more scars. He looked like he'd been drug down a gravel road or something. Neither one of them was chewing tobacco. I figured it was tough to do that and eat ice cream at the same time. I thought about putting my foot up on the bumper but it was too high.

"Will she do a hunerd in the quarter?" I asked.

"Faster'n 'at," Buddy replied. I decided right then and there that he was lying.

I looked at Dwight. "Did you ride your Honda Mini-Trail?"

"No, Buddy picked me up."

Buddy gave Dwight a disgusted look. "Kid's full a questions."

"Well, we gotta go, catch 'a later." Booger had already gotten antsy and started walking toward the grocery store. I involuntarily looked around to see if others had seen me talking to Dwight and hoping that they had.

Gooche's IGA Grocery sat on the other side of the theatre from the Houn Dawg. There was only a small alley between each building. That's usually where the fights after the movie took place. We stopped at the grocery store to pick up some stuff for the movie.

Mr. Gooche was in his office by the front door. He was wearing a green translucent visor-looking deal; he always did. The big windows in the front allowed the sun to engulf the entire store. I guess that's why he wore it. It seemed to me like he should have worn a baseball cap or something and covered his whole head. I knew I would if my head was as bald as his was, and especially if I had a big lump on the top of my head like he did.

I waved as I walked by his office window. "Hello, Mr. Gooche." He looked busy, probably counting all the money he'd made that day.

"Hi, boys. You two yahoos goin' to see the new James Bond movie tonight?" I guess we didn't look like grocery shoppers. I wasn't really sure what a yahoo was.

"Yep, thought we'd pick up some peanut M&M's first."

"I don't think Mr. Arnold likes you carrying candy in, does he?" He half frowned, half smiled, looking up from his work.

"Well, he ought to lower his prices or get used to it, I reckon." I could tell Mr. Gooche was holding back a grin.

"Booger and I have to save everywhere we can. We're buyin' a couple of Lawn-Boys this summer."

"You don't say? That's a smart move. Are you two looking for lawns to mow?"

"Yes, sir. Do you know of anybody that needs their lawn mowed?"

"Well, I've been thinking of hiring mine done. Hey, you might want to post a note on the bulletin board advertising your service."

I'd never noticed the bulletin board before. It was cluttered with thumbtacked notices of all kinds.

"That'd be great, Mr. Gooche. Thanks a lot. We're gonna save up and buy a Honda Mini-Trail too." He smiled suspiciously. He probably didn't know what a Honda Mini-Trail was. Booger and I gave the board a look-see. There were all kinds of notes on there. People selling dogs, cats, and all kinds of used stuff. The Goolsby twins had a little preprinted card advertising their lawn-mowing service. It had a drawing of a man with a lawn mower on it. Booger and I decided we needed a note on the board, too.

"Let us know if you need that lawn mowed, Mr. Gooche. We'll take you up on that offer to post a note, if it's okay with our parents."

"I'll do it. Hey Randy, what do you hear from Johnny?" Adults always called Booger by his real name.

"Well, like-a-said, I got a letter from him this week. He's ready to come home but doing fine. His outfit is based near a town called Khe Sanh. It's in the mountains and real pretty there, he says. He's gonna get a Chevelle Super Sport when he gets out."

There was excitement in Booger's voice. "Mom and Dad bought a watch with the Marine Corps insignia on it for him. They're gonna give it to him when he gets home."

"That sounds great. He started out as a carryout boy and worked his way up. He was one of the best stock boys I've ever had. Next time you write, tell him he's got a job waiting for him when he gets out if he wants it." He paused a second and scratched the lump on his head. "I'd like to train him to be a butcher. He'd be a dandy."

"Like-a-said, he'd love that. He only has a couple of more weeks."

"You boys better get to your movie. Don't let Mr. Arnold catch you sneaking those M&M's in. Randy, tell your Mom that Mrs. Gooche had a good time at the Tupperware party. She spent too much, though."

THE MOVIE WASN'T SUPPOSED TO start for another fifteen minutes, but Booger and I went ahead and bought our tickets and went on in. By getting there early we'd get to see a couple of Merry Melody cartoons. We both got fountain sodas at the concession stand. The sodas at the theatre always tasted better than bottle sodas. Maybe it was the shaved ice.

There were still plenty of empty seats. "To Sir With Love" by Lulu was playing to a blank screen.

> *Those schoolgirl days …*
> *How do you thank someone who has taken you from crayons to perfume…*
> *It isn't easy but I'll try …*
> *I'd write across the sky in letters*
> *"To Sir With Love" …*

I'd told Wendy I'd be sitting halfway down on the right side. We found a couple of seats with no rips or stuffing hanging out and sat down. Every time I tried to hold my soda between my legs and open my M&M's, someone picked our aisle to sit in and needed to get by. We normally sat in the middle and then people never needed to get by. I don't know why I told her we'd be sitting on the right side. We never sat there.

The song was still playing when Wendy and a couple of her friends came walking down the aisle. I acted like I didn't see her until she saw me, and then I looked up and waved. She smiled and sat in the middle, across the aisle, where Booger and I usually sat. I listened to the words of the song and watched Wendy.

Booger saw me looking at her. "If we'd sat in the middle, you'd be sittin' beside yer girlfriend." I didn't know how to respond, so I just ignored him.

Everett Fluegge walked past us after the cartoon had started. He had popcorn and a cup of soda. A bunch of the high school kids were yelling for him to sit down. Somebody was throwing something at him. It looked like peanut M&M's. His eyes probably hadn't adjusted to the dark. He must have stepped on everyone's feet getting to an empty seat, judging by the "ow"s and "ouch"es.

The movie started. James Bond's silhouette moved across the screen. Just as he pointed the barrel of his pistol at the audience, Mr. Arnold tapped Booger and me on the shoulder real hard. He motioned for both of us to come with him.

Surely he didn't think we were the ones throwing those M&M's at Everett! We hadn't even bought ours at the movie theatre. How'd he know we had them? He didn't act mad or anything, just motioned for us to come with him.

Both of our dads were waiting for us in the lobby. Booger's dad took him by the arm, and they left without saying anything. He didn't look happy. Whatever we'd been caught at, it must be bad, I remember thinking. Nobody was talking. I didn't ask any questions and tried to figure out what was up. Maybe Mrs. Wilfong had called my mom about the potato gun after all.

When we got to the car, Dad gave me a big hug. He nearly broke one of my ribs. I'd never seen tears in his eyes since Buster, our old dog, had gotten hit and mashed by a car from out of town. His lip was quivering. He told me how the Marine recruiter had just told Booger's mom and dad that Johnny had been killed in action.

The helicopter he'd been riding in near Khe Sanh had been shot down. Five other Marines riding in the helicopter, including the pilot, had also been killed. People were getting bad news in other places tonight too, I figured.

As we rode along, I realized that lots of Johnny's friends back at the movie were watching James Bond race around in fast cars with pretty girls. Even though 007 would get knocked in the head a couple of times, he'd always be okay. It felt odd knowing that they were having fun now only because they didn't know about Johnny. I wished that I didn't know yet either. I envied them.

When we got home, Mom was talking to Booger's mom on the phone and crying. Booger and his dad must have taken a longer drive and hadn't gotten home yet. I got out a brand new Big Chief tablet and wrote Booger a note. I told him what a good friend he was and how cool Johnny had been and that I was sorry. I told him that maybe someday we could join the Marines and go looking for the guy that shot down the helicopter. Mom gave me an envelope for the note, and Dad took it over to Booger's house.

I fell asleep thinking about Johnny. In my mind I watched him playing football. I imagined how he would have looked in his new Chevelle Super Sport. I wondered if it hurt when he died. I worried about Booger. I prayed. I cried.

By Monday morning, everyone had heard about Johnny. He was the first person from Colby to be killed in action since the Korean War. Eight had died in that war, including Mom's brother, Uncle Clayton. All that the boys at the bus stop talked about was what a good football player Johnny had been. The girls sniffed and sniffled and talked about how good-looking he had been. Booger didn't come to school for a while.

Later that week, on Friday morning, as I approached the bus stop, I heard Caleb telling anyone who would listen how he and his dad had shot an entire bag of potatoes the night before. Most were ignoring him, but the ones who weren't stared as if he'd lost his marbles. Everyone in Colby was mourning Johnny's death except Caleb. It was probably because he was new.

Booger walked up and, out of respect, everyone stopped talking, even Caleb. It was Booger's first day back to school. The only sound was a mourning dove still on roost in a nearby maple tree and an eighteen-wheeler downshifting on the way up Turkey Hill, about two miles outside of town. I didn't know what to say, so I just gave him a one-armed hug. His lip quivered a little, so I stood there with one arm draped around his shoulder, his face buried in my shoulder. Marty Blanken snickered a little; he got a look from the girls.

The bus came and we got on. Miss Barbara patted Booger on the shoulder as he passed by her.

Booger and I sat together. The sign at the Methodist church said, "All of Colby salutes Johnny Burger." I looked over at Wendy and she returned my gaze with a warm smile. I smiled back so big that it felt like my face was going to crack wide open. I licked my teeth and hoped that my nose was clean and felt a tinge of guilt for having happy thoughts.

A familiar voice from the back of the bus boomed. "So, you got a girl-friend *and* a boyfriend." It was Marty Blanken. Wilma turned around and glared at him. He looked the other way, out the window. I wasn't quite sure what to make of him. I didn't look back the rest of the way to school, except to steal a couple of glances at Wendy.

BOOGER SAT QUIETLY AT HIS desk. Everyone left him alone, except for an occasional pat on the back. Mrs. E, who knew all, immediately acknowl-edged that he was back in class. She marched over and put her hand on his shoulder and stood there at attention until all eyes focused on her. She had her Sunday dress on and her boots glistened. She must have expected Booger to be back and had dressed special in honor of Johnny. Her stock-ings only had one little run in them, just above her left boot top.

"In honor of Randy's brother, Johnny, who served this country nobly, and a-like-a-that, we're going to watch a film strip about the Revolution-ary War." That was fine with me, although I always preferred watching them after lunch. That's when I was the sleepiest.

The bell for recess woke me. Booger and I ambled over toward the teth-erball court. My eyes still hadn't adjusted to the bright light, and I was stretching and yawning when Clyde Goodpasture walked up. I was still groggy and sleepy from watching George Washington cross the Delaware one frame at a time and listening to Mrs. E explain the significance of the event, and-a-like-a-that, as she said it.

"Heard you 'n Booger here are sorta sweet on each other." He'd no doubt been talking to Marty. Immediately a crowd started to gather, typi-cal when a fight was coming. Clyde's ear had healed up pretty good. They both looked the same, sort of hanging on his head or sitting on his jaws. It was hard to tell which.

Melody had been taking her turn on the tetherball. She turned toward Clyde and me. "Leave 'em alone," she said.

"So, you're still lettin' girls do your fightin' for you?" Clyde snickered, then stepped a little closer. One thing for sure, he hadn't gotten any smaller. There was a long single strand of hair growing out of his chin that I was pretty sure was new. The crowd moved around behind me.

Booger stepped between the two of us. "There ain't gonna be a fight." He turned toward Clyde and stared. It was out of character for Booger to be that brave. Clyde started laughing and shoved him hard enough to make him fall and almost do a backwards summersault. Booger jumped up and attempted a charge, but was restrained by Caleb and Flop. Everett stepped in front of him. I'd never known Everett to fight.

"It's about time for recess to be over. Let's go on back inside," Everett said, looking at Booger and me.

"Oh, that's great," Clyde announced. "Instead of the Bobsey twins we've got the Tommy triplets."

He stood there with his hands on his hips, rocking back and forth on his heels with a big smile on his face. Everett turned and faced him. Clyde moved toward Everett and shoved him, but Everett didn't budge. Clyde looked really mad then. He was breathing heavy and his nostrils flared with each breath. They were eye-to-eye when the bell rang. Everett backed away.

"That's right, you better back away," Clyde said.

Everett turned toward the school building and started walking. He wasn't walking away in fear, though. Booger and I stayed close to him. The playground monitor was looking our way. She had probably seen the whole thing. I figured she always kept an eye on Clyde.

Mrs. E treated Booger like a pet the rest of the day. I could tell that didn't set too well with Clyde. He was hard to figure. Because of me he got whooped by a girl, but was taking it out on Booger. And somehow Everett had now gotten tangled in the mess, too. That was to my benefit, though.

COLBY HAD TWO FUNERAL HOMES, Willow Wood and Greystone. There wasn't a rule, but usually the Democrats went to Willow Wood and the Republicans went to Greystone. Each funeral home had their own private graveyard, just like many of the churches in and around Colby.

The Marines flew Johnny's body home. Even though the Burgers had always been Democrats, the funeral service was going to be held at Greystone. Some folks figured it was because President Johnson had sent Johnny to Vietnam, so they didn't want his service to be held at a Democrat funeral home. They'd taken their "LBJ FOR THE USA" bumper stickers off when Johnny got drafted.

Booger's mom and dad called and asked if I'd sit with him at the funeral. Dad dropped me off at Booger's house so I could ride to the funeral home with them. Booger looked like he'd had the flu or something. I saw the note I'd written to him hanging on his bulletin board. It was all wrinkled up, like he'd been holding it a lot. There were other cards and notes on his desk. Someone had sent him a helium balloon. It must have been there a few days, because it didn't go all the way to the ceiling, it just slowly floated around the room at eye level.

Booger's aunt Penelope and uncle Norman had driven from Fairview on Saturday night. Aunt Penelope was his mom's only sister. I sometimes called her Aunt Penelope, too. Aunt Penelope had stayed since Saturday. Uncle Norman had gone home and then driven back over the morning of the funeral. The doctor had given Booger's mom some medicine to help her sleep; she still looked groggy.

Mr. Burger kept asking Randy—that's what his mom and dad called him—if he was okay. Mr. Burger thanked me over and over again for sending the note and coming over. Whatever energy Mrs. Burger had lost, Mr. Burger had gained. He kept pacing around until Booger's uncle Norman made him sit down. As soon as he sat down, he started crying. Seeing him cry made Booger cry, and then I cried.

Booger's uncle Norman looked at his watch a thousand times. He constantly did something goofy with his shoulder that made his natural dissonance even more pronounced. Dad called it a twitch.

"It's time to go," nervous Uncle Norman impatiently said.

We headed out the door. Booger's dad thanked me again. He patted me on the shoulder and squeezed my neck so hard that it hurt, but I knew he hadn't meant to.

We pulled out of the driveway. "Ever been t' Greystone?" Booger asked. He and I were sitting in the very back of their station wagon in the small fold up seats.

"No. You?"

"Once. My dad's boss's wife's funeral." He looked out the window. He wasn't smiling, but he wasn't frowning either. "At her funeral they served sandwiches with the crust cut off."

Greystone had a blacktop-covered parking lot. It even had lines that marked the parking spaces. And signs in front of several parking places. A few were marked for family, one for clergy, and a couple for pallbearers. Republicans liked to keep everyone in their place. Uncle Norman pulled into the space nearest the front door by the sign marked for clergy. I don't think he noticed the sign, and probably no one else would either. Democrats didn't pay much attention to such things. That's why they live longer.

Coach Bodenschatz, Wilma's dad, read a eulogy that he and some of the other teachers had written about Johnny. There was an oscillating fan behind the podium. When it blew my way, I could smell Right Guard. Coach Bodenschatz always wore too much of it. He must have had a body odor problem or something. He started crying before he finished, and so did everyone else.

Four people from the community choir sang next. Mrs. E played the piano for them. They sang "Amazing Grace" and "Old Rugged Cross." I'd never been to a funeral yet when they didn't sing both of them.

Brother Baker, our preacher, approached the podium to say a few words. He was a tall, wispy man with a dark olive complexion and a long neck packed full of tendons. Some associated his appearance with that of Ichabod Crane. He asked everybody to turn their Bibles to 1 Timothy 6:12. By the time I found it, he was already reading from 2 Timothy 4:7. He said Johnny had fought the good fight. He'd finished the race. He'd kept the faith. I noticed Dad rolling his eyes and then getting a sharp elbow from Mom. Dad had said at breakfast that Brother Baker always said the same thing at every funeral. I guess he'd used readings from Timothy before.

Some of Johnny's friends, mostly former football teammates, carried the casket out to the hearse. They'd all played together on what many thought was Colby's best-ever football team. The toughest of the tough had each been reduced to freely flowing tears. Booger's mom was crying too, and his dad was holding her. Booger had his face buried in his mom's dress with his arms wrapped around her waist.

Everyone pulled off of the road for us as we drove to the cemetery. Sheriff Omar led the way to the Willow Wood cemetery.

A Marine color guard shot their rifles into the air at the graveside service. A couple of them folded up the flag and gave it to Booger's mom. Her hands were shaking too much to hold it. She sat it on her lap. One of the Marines had walked to a high place in the cemetery while the flag was being folded. After Brother Baker said a closing prayer, the soldier on the high ground played taps. Several commented about how Colby had lost one of their best. All flags in Colby flew at half-mast. Mrs. E had shown us on the globe where Vietnam was, but it still wasn't clear to me why Marines like Johnny were dying there.

I went with Booger to his house after the funeral. He and I fiddled around in his room. Through the bedroom window we saw his aunt Penelope and uncle Norman arguing in the driveway. After a few minutes of fussing, Uncle Norman took his twitch and left.

Lots of people stopped by with food. None of the Burgers felt like eating, but people brought food anyway. There was more lasagna than they could fit in their refrigerator. Booger's mom had taken one of those pills the doctor had given her and was asleep in her bedroom.

Coach Bodenschatz was talking to Booger's dad. If Coach had stayed very long, he'd have had the whole house smelling like Right Guard. Wilma and Mrs. Bodenschatz helped themselves to the food. Neither one of them appeared to have an appetite problem.

When I got home from Johnny's funeral service, Mom told me Mr. Purdy had called. He wanted me to call him back. Mr. Purdy owned a horse ranch at the edge of town. He trained and boarded horses for other folks and had a few of his own. He had a pony named Pokey that he let kids in Colby ride on Saturday mornings.

Normally it's a pain in the butt to get to ride Pokey. You had to get there first on Saturday morning. If you were lucky enough to be the first one, you had to shovel horse poop for about two hours. After Mr. Purdy got a few hours of free work, he'd get around to putting a saddle on Pokey. If he really trusted you, he'd hook up the surrey. The surrey was more fun because it carried two people.

I dialed his number.

"Hi, Tommy. Thanks for calling back. I heard about Johnny Burger. Bad deal, eh?"

"Yes, sir."

"How's Randy doing?"

"He's doin' okay. He's not talkin' much."

"I was wondering if you two would like to take Pokey and the surrey out on Saturday."

My first thought was that it was nice of him to offer, and I was sure Booger would love to ride around in the surrey. But I didn't think he'd want to be shoveling any horse poop, either.

"You won't have to help me with any chores."

It was like he'd read my mind. Some old people have that ability.

"I'm sure he'll want to, Mr. Purdy. It's very nice of you to offer. Let me give Booger a call and make sure."

"Who?"

"Randy. We call him Booger."

"Oh, okay. Well, give the Booger boy a call and let me know, eh." Mr. Purdy had been born in Canada and his family had moved to Colby when he was in high school. His wife's family owned Colby Bank, and he eventually became president of the bank before retiring. He was very proper, still had the Canadian accent, and ended many sentences with "eh." I didn't know much about Canadians except what I'd learned watching Dudley Doright.

I'd heard Dad talk about ice hockey and the Stanley Cup a few times, but I'd never seen a game on TV or anything. Canadians mostly played it. I guess everything freezes in Canada in the winter. Mr. Purdy would know.

I called Booger. He didn't sound too excited about riding Pokey but said he'd go. I called Mr. Purdy back. He said to be there by eight on Saturday morning and that we could help put the surrey on Pokey. I thanked him again.

Sleep would have been difficult if I'd had any idea of the plans Dad, Uncle Cletus, and Mr. Burger had in store for us the next day.

Chapter 5

Old Flame

Mr. Burger, Uncle Cletus, and my dad were waiting for us at the bus stop after school. They'd decided to surprise us and take us to Fairview to look at Mini-Trails. They didn't ask about homework or anything, like our moms would have. I learned later that Uncle Cletus had helped Dad talk to Mom.

Mr. Burger drove. He had the radio tuned to KXOK. Johnny Raven had just started the Top-Ten Countdown. He was always on the radio during the afternoon when we were getting out of school. All the cars at the Houn Dawg would have their dials tuned to 630AM, too. Uncle Cletus sang along to some of the tunes. Occasionally, Mr. Burger would smile. I didn't have to wonder any longer why Uncle Cletus never sang in the church choir. Mrs. E had most likely recommended he sing for the hearing impaired, like she had for me.

The closer we got to Fairview, the better the road was. Leaving Colby it was mostly chip and seal, several layers of chat and oil. Near Fairview, the road turned to new asphalt. It was a lot smoother and quieter. We could hear the radio better; but, unfortunately for us, Uncle Cletus was really getting into the songs.

The only time he wasn't singing was when he was talking about getting a Honda Scrambler. Mom would have told him he needed his head examined if she'd heard him. Mrs. E would have told him his voice had promise, but needed work.

Fairview Honda must have had over a hundred motorcycles sitting outside. There was no way they could get all of them inside the small building because it was full of motorcycles inside, too. I'd never seen so many motorcycles. I imagined that it'd be fun to work at a place like that.

Dad, Uncle Cletus, and Mr. Burger sat on a couple of the Scramblers. They twisted on the throttles and squeezed the clutch levers. A guy with "Farley" on his shirt, a salesman, walked up and started a conversation with Dad and Uncle Cletus. Booger spotted the Mini-Trails; we headed straight for them.

Mini-Trails only came in three colors: blue, red, and yellow. I straddled a red one while Booger sat down on a blue one. Some of them had little luggage racks mounted on the back and were higher-priced. The luggage rack would be handy if we decided to take them camping or fishing and needed to carry a small load. The issue was settled in my mind; Booger and I had to get one.

"Hi, boys, are your parents with you today?" asked an insincerely cheerful guy with "Floyd" on his shirt.

Booger pointed toward our dads. "Yeah, they're o'vair." Mr. Burger, Dad, and Uncle Cletus were still looking at the Scramblers, nodding their heads in agreement with whatever Farley was telling them.

"Are they thinkin' about gettin' a couple of Scramblers?"

"One of 'em is, but they brought us here to look at these here Mini-Trails," Booger told him, almost defensively.

"We're gonna mow lawns and save up. Our plan is to buy a couple of 'em at the end of the summer," I explained.

"Do you know about our layaway plan?"

"Your what?" Booger asked with a frown.

"Layaway." He said it a little louder like that would make us understand. I looked at Booger and shrugged; neither one of us answered.

Mr. Burger, Dad, and Gene Hickam walked up while Floyd was explaining the plan. They'd met Gene in the Scramblers. He worked for a wholesale distributor out of Fairview and sold tires, filters, and spark plugs to Dad at Colby John Deere. Uncle Cletus had taken a Scrambler on a test drive.

Basically, we learned that the layaway plan allowed us to put twenty-five dollars down that day, and then pay twenty-five dollars per month until the balance was paid off. By doing that, we were guaranteed the price wouldn't go up.

We didn't give it much thought. I didn't have any twenty-five dollars and Booger didn't either. We hadn't gotten our Lawn-Boys yet, much less made the first payment. For that matter, we didn't even have any lawns to mow yet. Dad's next comment, though, caught me by total surprise.

"If you boys are serious about getting these things, you ought to put them on layaway and get on with it." I saw him glance at Booger's dad and wink. I knew something was up.

"What about the down payment?" I asked.

"We're willing to loan it to you. Having these things on layaway will give you boys something to focus on and work for," explained Booger's dad. His eyes teared slightly; I felt a little faint. My mouth got dry.

Aunt Penelope walked up. "I can tell by the looks on their faces that I'm too late." She looked at Dad. "I wanted to be here when you told them. I couldn't get Norman to come." She gave Booger a hug and mussed my hair. "What do you think?"

"I can't believe it." I looked at Booger for his response. His bottom lip was quivering slightly. Aunt Penelope gave him a second, extra-long hug.

A new Scrambler came speeding up and stopped beside us. It was Uncle Cletus. He revved the motor before shutting it down and taking his helmet off.

Aunt Penelope put her hand on his shoulder. "You really look cool on that, Cleet. It takes a few years off of you." I guess she knew him as Cleet. She pushed the horn button by the throttle, then stepped back, smiling.

Floyd, thinking they belonged together, said, "You'd look good on it, too. Get on and take a spin with him."

"My husband would *kill* me."

"Oh." Floyd looked embarrassed until Aunt Penelope, her words barely out of her mouth, pulled her skirt up and swung her leg across the Scrambler seat and snuggled in behind Uncle Cletus. It was a loose-fitting skirt, so she was able to maintain a little bit of dignity. Uncle Cletus looked at Dad and Mr. Burger. They just shrugged their shoulders and grinned.

He started the engine, but then shut it down. "We better not, Penny, this doesn't look good."

Aunt Penelope got off. "You're right."

It seemed that Uncle Cletus knew her as Penny.

FLOYD HELPED BOOGER AND ME fill out the papers, and our dads made the down payments. Floyd gave us a brochure with pictures of the Mini-

Trails and all of the accessories available for one. He said our payment books would come in the mail.

As we drove through town on the way home, Booger and I studied the brochures. Uncle Cletus talked about getting a Scrambler. Dad and Mr. Burger kidded him about his old flame, Aunt Penelope.

"Yea, Deloris did her best to keep Penny from marrying that yahoo, Norman, while I was in Korea."

At the mention of Booger's mom's name, the conversation stopped. No one spoke for several minutes. Booger stopped looking at the literature; he was looking out the window with glazed eyes.

After we passed by the Fairview municipal airport, Dad started talking about Gene Hickam. Mr. Hickam had recently started taking flying lessons and had offered to take Dad for a ride. I'd never been in an airplane, and as far as I knew, Dad hadn't either.

We got home in time for me to run over to Mamaw and Papaw's and show them the Mini-Trail brochures. Papaw and I sat on the cistern top and talked. I told him about Dad thinking about taking flying lessons.

"Umph," is all he said, and then he rolled a cigarette.

Chapter 6

Pokey

I SPENT THE NIGHT AT Booger's on Friday night; he had bunk beds. The top bunk was his and the bottom Johnny's. He'd been sleeping in the bottom bunk until Johnny had gotten killed. He'd since moved back to the top, and the bottom bunk was covered with Johnny's things. I didn't feel right sleeping in Johnny's bed, and Booger didn't offer, so I slept on the floor on top of a couple of old sleeping bags.

Booger and I'd both gotten Roy Rogers outfits for Christmas. We'd decided to wear them riding Pokey. My cowboy boots were getting a little small, but we didn't plan on doing much walking, so I brought them anyway. I hadn't brought the spurs since we were going to be riding in a surrey, and besides, I didn't know how to use them. Thinking about the Mini-Trail made getting to sleep difficult. I decided the Roy Rogers outfit would need to be retired when I got the Mini-Trail.

MRS. BURGER FIXED US A farmer's breakfast. We had eggs and sausage links wrapped in buttermilk pancakes. She'd even heated up some maple syrup and melted a whole stick of butter in it. You'd 'a thought we were getting ready to head off with Clint Eastwood on a rawhide cattle drive or something. The orange juice had too much pulp in it, but I drank it anyway.

Mrs. Burger wasn't as talkative as she normally was. I hadn't heard her contagious trademark laugh since Johnny had gotten killed.

Mr. Burger ate with us and asked a lot of questions about Pokey, where we'd be riding, and if I'd ever handled the surrey before. He was worried about everything from Pokey kicking or biting us, to both of us getting hit by a Mac truck and smashed to smithereens. He had a glass of milk with ice cubes in it. I'd never seen anybody except him put ice cubes in milk.

Booger didn't say much, but he did eat several pancakes with the sausage in the middle. It may have been the most he'd eaten in a week. He'd have eaten more if Mrs. Burger hadn't sent us on our way at seven-thirty.

We peddled out of their driveway toward Mr. Purdy's. Booger was pedaling kind of slow. "Is Pokey the horse that bit a hunk out of Corky Seabaugh's arm?" he asked.

"Yeah, but it wasn't that bad of a bite, he didn't need stitches or nothin'." I made a feeble attempt to make light of it.

"How many people has he bitten?"

"Don't know. Most people don't admit to anything that might cause Mr. Purdy to not let them ride him again. Anyway, all you have to do is stay away from his blind side."

Booger slowed the cadence of his peddling to a crawl and gave me a look. "He's blind?"

"It's his right side, the side with the milky-colored eye." I tried to make it sound as if a milky-colored eye was normal.

"So, this Pokey is blind in one eye?"

"Yeah, but he can see really good out of the other one." That didn't seem to relieve him. Once again, I'd spoken too much.

Mr. Purdy's farm was next to my dad and grandpa's John Deere shop, at the edge of town on Highway T. Having a few minutes to spare, we stopped to take a look at the twenty-one-inch Lawn-Boys.

Odie Portman, the parts manager, and the most conscientious employee at Colby John Deere, looked up from his card file. "What are you'ns boys up to so early on a Saturday morning?"

Odie usually got there by six and opened the doors around seven. A Pepsi with peanuts in it sat on the counter where he was working. My dad had told me that Odie drank too many sodas and that his guts were going to rot out someday. He'd never mentioned what he thought pouring peanuts into his soda would do to Odie's insides.

"Mr. Purdy is gonna let us ride Pokey today."

"I figured as much, seeing as how you'ns are dressed." He closed the file drawer and came out from behind the counter.

"Are these the Lawn-Boys that Mr. Thompson is gonna sell Tommy and me?" Booger asked.

"He's been talking about you'ns gettin' a couple a lawn mowers. I s'pect it'll be these or ones like 'em. I don't figure he'd fix you'ns up with self-propelled ones." Odie had been working for my grandpa almost as long as my dad had. Everybody liked Odie.

Odie sort of squinted one eye and asked, "Ain't Pokey 'at pony what's blind in one eye?"

"Yeah, but he can see out of the other one real good, and he's smarter 'n most people think," Booger said enthusiastically. He'd remembered and had even embellished. Odie rubbed his chin and nodded, seeming to agree. Odie was a curious type.

"Stee'yet, be careful with 'at pony. By the way, your dad said you want t' get a motor scooter with the money you make mowin' lawns." Odie looked at me suspiciously.

"A Honda Mini-Trail," I corrected, immediately. "It has big fat tires and you can ride it on gravel and dirt. We went over to Fairview Honda and put two on layaway."

"That so? Well, you won't be a foolin' around with no blind pony once you get 'at scooter."

I didn't like Odie calling a Honda Mini-Trail a scooter. He made it sound like something a mouseketeer or a singing nun would ride.

"We saw Gene Hickam there, too. He said he'd take Dad and me for an airplane ride when he got his license."

"Yeah, uh-huh, and pigs might fly, too." Odie didn't hold out much hope about the airplane ride.

He walked back over to the parts counter. "Let me know if you'ns have any questions." He took a swig out of the Pepsi with the peanuts in it. Yuck!

WE CAREFULLY EXAMINED THE IDENTICAL Lawn-Boys. They were brand-new and had never been used. The tires still had the little nipples attached. The undersides of the decks were just as green as the topsides and didn't have a sign of grass stain. They'd already been started at least once, though; the mufflers had a little bit of oil residue dripping out. All two-cycle engines did that, I'd learned.

"Do not put hands or feet under mower deck" was stamped into the magnesium mower deck. I used to wonder what kind of an idiot needed that warning. According to my dad, there were plenty of people who did, but they mostly lived in the cities and were generally college graduates. He'd told me how once a doctor had picked up a lawn mower and tried to trim his hedges with it, but had trimmed a few fingers instead. The company that made the lawn mower had to pay him millions of dollars. Ever since then they'd been putting the warning on the deck.

I noticed the automatic rewind system. "They've got the new starter cord rewind system," I told Booger.

Odie overheard me and he winked, smiled, and nodded, all at the same time. That seemed to be a sign of approval. Both mowers had the new easy-start system. Instead of having to rewind the starter chord after each pull, it would rewind automatically. Lawn-Boys are known for being easy to start, but they still took several pulls sometimes. This new easy-start feature was something no other mower had.

I looked up at the big green clock with the John Deere deer leaping across it. It was almost eight o'clock. "We'll catch 'a later, Odie. We need to head over to Mr. Purdy's."

"Sure thing, Tommy. You'ns have a good time with 'at half-blind pony."

I suppose we could have survived the day without that parting remark.

Mr. Purdy's barn doors were open, and I could see him shoveling manure out of one of the stalls. Booger and I climbed over the gate and walked across the barnyard, being careful not to step on any fresh cow piles or horse turds.

"Be careful where you step, Booger. There're Republican platforms all over the place." That's what Papaw always called them. Booger knew what I meant and kept a careful lookout. I picked up one of the dry horse turds and hurled it at a chicken.

Mr. Purdy had heard us coming. He came out of the barn wearing pressed Tuff-Nut jeans, a starched shirt, and a grin. "Hello, lads. Looks like it's going to be a nice day, eh? I see you're both dressed for the occasion, eh." He'd noticed our cowboy clothes.

"Yes, sir," I replied, almost adding an "eh." It was catching.

"I was just cleaning out the last stall. These horses sure know how to mess a place up, eh?"

"Can we give you a hand?" I felt obliged to offer even though he'd said we wouldn't need to help.

"Well, I've about got the stalls cleaned out, but you lads can start getting the tack out." We followed him through the barn to the tack room door. Nearly every stall had a horse in it. Pokey was so short that his head didn't come over the top rail like the other horses.

A single, low-wattage bulb illuminated the tack room. The room smelled like an old billfold. He must have saved every saddle and bridle he'd ever had, and it looked like the spiders had claimed a stake on every one. Mr. Purdy grabbed a broom and started sweeping the cobwebs off of a bundle of leather straps and buckles hanging between two old saddles.

"You lads carry all of those out to the hitching post near the gate and I'll be along in a few minutes." He walked out the door and headed toward the stall he'd been working in.

Booger and I stood there for a few seconds; neither one of us wanted to touch anything that had been covered with spider webs. But if Flop or Caleb had been there we could have talked them into doing it.

I grabbed the broom and used the handle to lift the straps and buckles off the bracket and lay them on the floor. Booger leaned over and carefully picked up all he could carry and backed out the door. I warily picked up the rest, vigilant for hiding spiders, and followed him to the hitching post.

While we were waiting for Mr. Purdy, Booger and I started watching a bunch of chickens pecking around on the ground behind and under Mr. Purdy's old outhouse. It was a two-holer. He'd probably stopped using it around the same time we stopped using ours, when the city put a sewer system in, nearly six years earlier.

"Yuck," Booger muttered. He'd noticed them too.

"Poop makes everything grow," I told him. "Put it on the fields to make the fescue grow, feed the fescue to the cows to make them grow, then feed the cows to us to make us grow. Didn't you ever eat a hamburger or meatloaf?"

"So where do the chickens 'n 'at fit in?"

"They eat our poop, then we eat them." I waited for his reply. None. It was all soaking in. He was deep in thought, but at least he wasn't thinking about Johnny.

"I can see why those hippies don't eat meat 'n 'at," he replied circumspectly. I'd never heard that hippies didn't eat meat. It wasn't much of a stretch to believe it, though, seeing as how kooky they acted about everything else.

"Most people put horse or cow poop on their gardens. Any way you look at it we're all eating food grown from poop. Even those hippies out in San Francisco who eat vegetables." He didn't respond. After a moment's thought, I realized how ridiculous I was beginning to sound.

Mr. Purdy came out of the barn and walked our way. "You feeling okay, Booger?" He'd heard the poop speech I'd given Booger. "You look a little pale." I hadn't noticed until Mr. Purdy said something that the color had drained from Booger's face.

He looked at Booger with concern. "The two of us can handle putting the surrey on Pokey. Go on over to the house and sit on the porch swing." It sounded funny hearing an adult call Randy by his nickname. Booger staggered over toward the porch and plopped down on the swing.

Pokey had a halter on and was tied to the hitching post. Mr. Purdy had brought him out while Booger and I were talking about the chickens. He figured out right away that I wasn't going to be much help putting the harness on. I'd never done it before and, anyway, it's pretty much a one-man job. He sent me to get the surrey while he finished adjusting all of the straps. Pokey just stood there blinking and chewing on his tongue or something while Mr. Purdy hooked everything up.

When I returned, Mr. Purdy asked, "Is the Booger boy doing okay?"

"I think so, but he stares into space a lot," I told him.

Booger came back over in time for Mr. Purdy to give us both a few lessons on handling a pony hooked to a surrey. He mentioned that Pokey didn't like to turn to the right, since he was blind in that eye.

"You'll have to pull real sharplike on that right rein if you want to go right, eh." These were his last words of instructions before telling us for the umpteenth time to be careful. Then we were off.

Before we got out of Mr. Purdy's driveway, Pokey came to a standstill. Booger seemed to be feeling much better but still wasn't talking much. I shook the reins and said "gitty-up," but nothing happened. Pokey raised his tail and I thought he was going to kick us, but instead several large dumpling-shaped turds tumbled from their point of origin to the ground. Then, without any encouragement, he started walking again. It was a good thing, too. The air was getting pretty rank. I was glad it was Booger and not Wendy in the surrey with me. We headed for Caleb's house; Flop and Everett were supposed to be there.

Pokey's gait was about the same speed as the old geezers at the nursing home where Great Grandpa Thompson lived, just barely faster than a crawl. On the way to Caleb's, Pokey continued raising his tail on a regular basis. It was mostly gas, in which case he didn't need to stop, but on occasion he purged his system of oat lumps. We could barely hold our breath long enough to get into fresh air. It was looking to be a long day if he didn't work whatever it was out of his system. My dad always had the same problem after eating sauerkraut. I made a mental note to ask Uncle Cletus what made ponies poop and toot so much.

When we reached the blacktop streets, Pokey's hooves made a loud clippity-clop sound. His ears perked up and his gate got faster when we passed Mrs. Bordenstein's house and her stupid dog started barking. Mrs. Whitener, as deaf as she was, heard the clippity-clopping, or she may have felt the vibrations. It has been my observation that when people lose one sense, the others get keener. Anyway, she waddled to the edge of her yard, waved, and gave us a toothless smile as we eased by.

Booger waved to her and then did a double take. He looked at me like he'd just been told he had a dental appointment. "I don't think she's got any teeth."

"Yeah, she does, they're just really small. She can chew the snot out of a plug of Hard Days Work," I assured him.

We stopped at Caleb's house. He wasn't home. His mom said he'd already left with Flop and Everett. They'd taken the potato gun, a bag of potatoes, and some hair spray with them. They'd told her they were going to the school playground to shoot the gun. They'd said something about measuring how far it would shoot; we headed that way.

Handling Pokey in the surrey was a breeze. He'd turn left or right and start and stop just as easy as you please. So far, his being blind in one eye hadn't been a problem.

THE COURTHOUSE WAS LOCATED IN the center of town. State Highways 24 and 65 and County Roads T and TT intersect at the Courthouse

Square. It was sometimes called T-square. There had always been talk of putting traffic lights in, but it hadn't happened yet. People traveling from any direction had to pass through the square, and strangers usually got the Ts mixed up.

Across the street to the north was Burt's Sinclair station and the Colby Telegraph. Gooche's Grocery, Arnold's Theatre, and the Houn Dawg sat on the west side of the square. All three sat back off the street about half a block and shared a huge parking lot.

The Sheriff's office, jail, post office, and city hall were located on the south side of the square. Seabaugh's Shoe Shop, Hinkebein's Dry Goods, Rosolini's Cafe, and Colby Rexall Drug sat on the east side.

Montgomery Fullbright, Solomon Atchison, Benjamin May, and Simon James, known locally as "Monkey", "Fish", "Bem", and "Rabbit", were regulars at the liar's bench. It sat in front of the courthouse on the side with the front door. A new bench made from synthetic wood sits there today.

Montgomery Fullbright, Monkey, had a small but sinewy build. He was a retired logger and tree trimmer, but still worked part-time when he felt like it.

Solomon Atchison, Fish, had retired early with a disability and when not at the bench was fishing on Craggy Creek. He walked bent over slightly at the waist unless he was in deep water; then he miraculously was able to stand straight up. Most believed the disability was trumped up, others marveled at the miracle cure that water and fishing provided.

Simon James, Rabbit, was a fidgety, slightly-built fellow. I always figured "Squirrel" would have been a more fitting nickname, but I hadn't named him. He'd been an All-American high school football player, the only one ever from Colby. The legend of his speed was spoken of every fall during football season. He usually spoke at the football banquet and gave the same speech every year, but football players, not known for their good memories, never seemed to mind.

The bench had been there so long that the names of most of the sponsors were faded and couldn't be read. Rexall Drug and Ex-Lax were the only advertisements still clearly visible. My dad had said once that he thought it only appropriate that those two ads remained, considering who used the bench most of the time.

———————

CALEB, EVERETT, AND FLOP SAW us and stopped their bicycles on the edge of the street. Pokey moseyed up to them and stopped without me even pulling back on the reins. He made good use of the break and tooted and pooped. Caleb had the potato gun strapped across his handlebars. Everett had an empty potato sack in his basket. Flop was carrying the hair spray under his arm.

"We stopped by your house and your mom told us you were at the school." Nobody commented about Pokey's deposit, but Everett was eyeing the lumps of used oats. It only took a few minutes before the flies started swarming around and eating on them. If there had been any chickens around, they'd've been there too. I hoped that Mrs. Bordenstein's dog would get blamed for the mess.

"We've been spearmintin', trying to figure out how fer a potato will shoot with different amounts of hair spray," Caleb said, beaming proudly. "It was actually Flop's idea. His dad used to be in charge of heavy artillery in the military. I timed the number of seconds Flop sprayed the hair spray, and Everett measured how fer the potato shot. We made sure we had the gun at the same angle each time, too."

"It sounds like you've made shootin' a potato gun 'n 'at sort of comp'icated," Booger told them.

"Well, it's bettern' just lobbin' potatoes into the sky. At least now we kin come close to hittin' a target, so long as we know how fer away it is," added Flop.

I could have guessed it would have been his idea to make a scientific experiment, or "spearmint", as Caleb called it, out of shooting potatoes into the sky.

Everett picked up a lump of fresh Pokey poop and held it to the end of the potato gun, comparing the size of the turd with the diameter of the potato gun barrel. It was fresh and still soft. Caleb shook his head. "Don't even think about it."

"We're gonna drop the gun and hair spray off at Caleb's and then head over to the Houn Dawg for a float," Everett said to Booger and me. "Why don't you two meet us there and give us a ride on 'at surrey?"

I tapped Pokey with the reins. "Meecha there." He started slow poking up Main toward the courthouse square.

THEY PEDALED AROUND THE CORNER and out of sight. Pokey maintained his same slow pace. Burt's Sinclair was straight ahead, on the left.

As we got closer, I could hear Burt's bell dinging each time a car pulled through the lot. Burt's bell hose stretched all the way across his lot.

He typically had a high school football player helping him on the weekends. Burt was a jocular guy who liked the football players and rarely missed a game. He always signed off with a "Catch 'a later." Johnny had worked for Burt part-time before he'd gotten sent to Vietnam.

The regulars, Monkey, Bem, Fish, and Rabbit, occupied the courthouse bench across the street.

"It's a good thing we'll be turnin' left when we get t' the station," Booger said as we approached Burt's.

He'd been watching Pokey, too, and had probably noticed Pokey's ears perking up and his head twitch each time a horn honked or Burt's bell dinged. Mr. Purdy had warned us that he might not want to turn to the right, his blind side.

We turned left into Burt's lot and stopped in front of the front-end alignment service bay. Burt was checking the oil for a lady in a station wagon while his pump with the automatic shut-off valve filled her tank. There were a couple of little kids, second graders probably, playing on Dino. Caleb, Everett, and Flop were just getting to the Houn Dawg across the street on their bikes.

Booger jumped out of the surrey and walked toward Burt. "Can we get a bucket or somethin' t' give Pokey a drink with?"

"There's a washtub 'round the side by the water hose. It should be okay, I only use it to ice down sodas with." He nodded toward the other side of the building. Booger headed that way.

The lady with the station wagon was in the lane in front of me, but the lane to the right was clear. I pulled on Pokey's right rein but he wouldn't move. I pulled harder on the right rein and struck him with the left one. His only response was to lift his tail and deposit two huge oat lumps on Burt's concrete. I felt trapped. To the left was a service bay, straight ahead was a car, and Pokey wouldn't go right. My bottom lip started to quiver. Burt started walking toward us.

"Let me help you out there, pard." He grabbed Pokey by the reins, without any hesitation, right where they connect to the bit, near his mouth. Animals seem to know when they're outmatched. Burt had served in WWII as an Army Ranger. He was a part-time deputy sheriff too. Dad said Burt had seen a lot of action in Italy, Greece, and Turkey. Pokey followed Burt right through the pump area until we were clear of the cars. He didn't even flinch when the surrey crossed the air hose and rang the bell.

"Think you can handle him from here?"

"Sure. Thanks a lot. He doesn't like to go to his right, ya know."

"I saw that. Looks like it scared him pretty good." Burt pointed to the pile Pokey had left in front of his wheel alignment bay. "You or your buddy needs to sweep that up before you leave. There's a broom and scoop just inside the door." He pointed toward a side door on the garage, then walked toward a customer who had just pulled up.

Booger had missed the whole thing since he'd been on the other side of the building filling up the washtub. He held the reins while Pokey drank, and I ran back over to clean up the mess.

Burt stopped me on my way back to the surrey. "That's Johnny Burger's brother, isn't it?"

"Yes, sir."

"What's his name?"

"Randy, but we call him Booger."

"Uh-huh," he said and walked toward the pumps wiping his hands with a shop towel.

I ran on back to around where Booger and Pokey were. Booger was standing beside Pokey with a bewildered look on his face. "I filled the washtub to the top; he drank it all."

My thoughts immediately jumped to the consequence of that entire intake. "Well, maybe we can get him back to Mr. Purdy before it works its way through his system," I told Booger.

"Caleb, Flop, and Everett are waitin'," Booger reminded me.

"Let's go then, before Pokey makes any more messes." Booger got in the surrey and I grabbed Pokey's reins and started leading him across Burt's pump area toward the Houn Dawg.

All the kids who had been climbing on Dino and unknowingly cleaning off the bird droppings ran our way and begged to pet Pokey. He didn't seem to mind, so we let them. I guess with all of that water in him, he was too full to care. Pokey stood there and tolerated them with an occasional whinny. Burt, just finished with a customer, started walking toward us. He was probably worried that Pokey was going to poop again.

He looked at Booger. "Sorry to hear about Johnny. Here's a couple of moon pies for you and your buddy." He patted Booger on the shoulder and the two of them just sort of looked at each other for a few seconds, and then Burt headed back toward the pumps.

"Thanks," Booger said.

Burt nodded. "Catch 'a later," he said as he turned to walk back to the station.

I TOOK ADVANTAGE OF A lull in traffic to lead Pokey, the surrey, and Booger across the street to the Houn Dawg. The Houn Dawg had a concrete porch that wrapped around on two sides, sort of an L shape. It was only about three feet higher than the parking lot at the highest point, so there wasn't a railing. Caleb, Flop, and Everett were sitting on the porch, feet dangling off, enjoying their floats. They hadn't waited.

"Don't think I'd be enterin' that pony in no race," Everett said in an unsuccessful attempt at humor.

"We waited until we saw ya havin' trouble over there at Burt's before we ordered," Caleb said with a mouthful of soft-serve. Evidence of an aggressive bite was on the tip of his nose.

I looked at Flop expecting him to add something smart as well, but he didn't. He was too busy enjoying a banana split. He had ice cream and topping dripping from every finger and his chin. He finally spoke. "After that we didn't wait no more. I did order ya a couple a floats when ya started across the roadway, though."

"Thanks."

Booger hopped out of the surrey and headed toward the order window. "I'll get the floats'n'at."

"Wendy," by The Association, was playing on the jukebox.

> Who's skipping down the street of the city?
> Smiling at everybody she sees
> Who's reaching out to capture a moment
> Everyone knows it's Wendy …

Hearing the song reminded me that I'd told Wendy I'd take her for a ride in the surrey.

Booger returned with a float in each hand. He couldn't eat his until I took mine. "You owe me twenty cents." He handed me my float. Everett had finished his and offered to hold Pokey while I ate mine. I gave Booger a dime and two nickels. Since my allowance was only fifty cents a week and we hadn't started mowing lawns yet, I savored every bite.

Caleb, anxious to go for a ride, climbed into the surrey and loosely held the reins. Pokey seemed satisfied to just stand there. One of his rear legs was bent slightly and the hoof was tilted. His blind eye was wide open, but his good eye was half shut. I'd heard that horses could sleep standing up. Pokey might have been asleep, but I knew that it was only a matter of time before a Niagara-like event was going to take place.

"Don't you two look cute." Before looking, I recognized the voice as that of Clyde Goodpasture. He was obviously taken by Booger and me in our cowboy clothes. I turned to look and saw that Marty Blanken was with him. Everett didn't move, keeping his grip on Pokey's reins. Booger walked over by me so we were both standing next to Everett. I hadn't finished my float. Flop was too busy trying to lick his fingers, wrists, and elbows clean to notice our new, unwelcome company.

"It ain't right fer a cowboy to keep 'is clothes so clean," Clyde said, and then shoved Booger hard enough to make him fall. It didn't matter to Clyde that Booger had just lost his brother. Clyde didn't waste any time picking up where he'd left off at school. Fortunately for me, neither did Everett.

Clyde was bearing down on me when Everett punched him square on his left ear. Wendy had clobbered him on his right one. He staggered backward and collapsed smack-dab on top of Flop, who was still sitting on the edge of the porch. Marty dove at Everett and hit him about knee level, knocking him backwards into Pokey. Pokey's good eye opened wide, and he took off in a gallop in the direction of the courthouse. It was the fastest gait I'd seen all day. Caleb had dropped the reins and was holding on to both sides of the surrey.

Marty had Everett on the ground and was trying to hit him in the nose when Mr. Arnold came running out the front door of the Houn Dawg blowing a coach's whistle. Everybody froze. The whistle had the opposite effect on Pokey; his pace quickened.

Caleb was still holding on and looked like a Raggedy Ann flopping around as the surrey bounced its way across the street. Cars stopped and one even honked. The surrey bounced about a foot in the air after it hit the edge of the courthouse square sidewalk. Monkey, Fish, Bem, and Rabbit dove behind the liar's bench as Pokey, Caleb, and the surrey raced by, one tire of the surrey only missing the bench by inches. Mr. Arnold had Marty by the arm, but Clyde was still lying on top of Flop. I grabbed Flop's bike and took off after Pokey and Caleb.

After passing the liar's bench, Pokey headed across the lawn. Flop's racer was in third gear, and I was pedaling as fast as I could, trying to catch them. The cowboy boots were scrunching my toes together; I hadn't planned on riding a bike. I remember thinking how a Honda Mini-Trail could have caught them with no problem. Pokey circled the courthouse and headed back down Main. He knew the way home and was headed for Mr. Purdy's farm.

Less than a block down Main he slowed to a walk. I caught up. He was covered with foam. Caleb was sitting up, looking straight ahead, with a death grip on each side of the surrey. The reins hung loosely and trailed along on each side of the surrey.

Pokey slowed to a crawl before finally stopping completely. He snorted, shivered, tapped the ground with his right hoof, and looked at me with his good eye. I slowly laid Flop's racer down and inched toward Pokey. He didn't try to run away, so I started scratching his nose above his nostrils and petted his sweaty neck. One at a time, I picked up the reins and handed them to Caleb. He didn't want to take them, but I gave him a look, so he did anyway.

Caleb's face was pale, and if he'd opened his eyes any wider, they would've popped out.

I tried to get my breath. "Get out of the surrey slowly," I whispered. He immediately dropped the reins and jumped out, forgetting about the slow part. I'd intended for him to hold the reins while I got in, but when he grabbed Flop's racer and headed back toward the square, I knew my plans had changed.

Holding on to one rein, I worked my way toward the surrey, petting Pokey along his sweaty side. Grabbing the crossbar, I stepped into the surrey, picked up the other rein, and sat down. Pokey shivered from nose to tail, looked back at me, and then started walking slowly toward Mr. Purdy's.

The surrey seat was wet and sticky. Caleb had done it again. That guy needed a diaper.

Sensing that we were headed home, Pokey held his nose high, whinnied frequently, and maintained a quick gate. I could see Mr. Purdy lying in a hammock under one of his big white pines. The limbs had been trimmed high enough to walk under them. I'ed mentioned that he liked the sound the breeze made blowing through the long needles. He raised his head and looked our way when Pokey snorted.

He slowly got out of the hammock and walked toward us. "You're back early." He limped slightly the first few steps. Almost all old people do that after they've been sitting for a while. "Lost the booger boy, eh?"

"He had a little problem." Mr. Purdy petted Pokey on the neck. I saw his jaw clinch when he noticed how sweaty Pokey was. He'd made it clear that we shouldn't push Pokey too hard. I told him the whole story. He said he'd had some dealings with the Goodpastures and understood. I cleaned the seat with Pine Sol and lamented about not having been able to take Wendy for a ride. Mr. Purdy put the tack away in the spider-infested tack room. I walked home wondering how things had been settled at the Houn Dawg.

Chapter 7

Thinker

THE SCENT OF AQUA VELVA meant that Dad had finished shaving. He always took his turn in the bathroom last on Saturday night. Since he was nearly finished, we'd soon be leaving for Rosolini's Café.

My feet felt good soaking in the warm water and Epsom salt that mom had fixed for me. While sitting there I noticed for the first time in a long time the plaque that Mamaw Thompson had given to us as a souvenir after a trip to the Holy Land; it had been made from the wood of a Cedar of Lebanon. I read several times the verse inscribed on the brass plate, Joshua 24:15: "Choose for yourself this day whom you will serve, but as for me and my household, we will serve the Lord." I reflected on the day.

I'd wanted cowboy boots for as long as I could remember, but Dad had always told me they weren't any good for walking. The throbbing pains in the balls of my feet and the blisters between my toes were proof that he had been right, again. I could have sat there soaking my feet for hours.

Flop's mom called, wanting to know who was going to pay for his watch. Mom held her hand over the receiver and told Dad what she was saying. The crystal had gotten broken when Clyde fell on him. Dad suggested she call John Cameron Swayzey, but Mom rolled her eyes and didn't pass the message along. Mom had talked to the other moms and Mr. Arnold, who'd confirmed that Clyde had started the whole thing. Clyde and Marty were banned from the Houn Dawg.

Mom sat my hush puppies next to my soaking feet. "Put your shoes on, Tommy. Your dad will be out of the bathroom in a few minutes, and then we'll be ready to go." My blissful time was up.

She and Marsha helped each other put on necklaces. The soft scent of their perfume struggled with the pungent Aqua Velva. The house had become an olfactory battleground. My feet said stay seated, but Mom said get up. I listened to Mom.

On the way to dinner, Dad mentioned to Mom that he'd been thinking about writing a book.

She gave him a "what planet are you from" look. "You barely passed English in high school. What makes you think you can write a book?"

"I don't know. It's somethin' I've been thinkin' about for a long time." Mom's expression changed from mild shock to certain curiosity.

Dad changed the subject. "Did I tell you about Gene Hickam offering to take us for an airplane ride?"

Mom chuckled. "Yes, at least twice already today." She scooted to the center of the seat, put her arm around him, and patted him on the shoulder. They looked like a couple of teenagers on a date. Marsha rolled her eyes and looked out the window. Dad never mentioned the book deal again.

ROSOLINI'S CAFÉ WAS ON THE northeast side of the square, at the corner of Oak and First. Mr. and Mrs. Rosolini had opened it just after the Depression and still owned and ran it. They'd emigrated from Italy. They both had short and portly builds with low centers of gravity. Mrs. Rosolini had thick hair that had probably once been jet black, but had grayed. Mr. Rosolini was mostly bald, but had a heavy beard that extended well below his shirt collar. They'd both kept their Italian accents and still rolled their r's.

There were only four checkered cloth-covered tables that sat between the horseshoe-shaped counter and the windows that faced the street. The counter had nine stools, but three of them had displays sitting on the counter in front of them.

The daily special was always a meat and three choices, or an Italian-named dish (pronounced "I"talian by most in Colby) that almost always ended with "ini." The featured Italian dish was fettuccini; it had been linguini the week before. Mom was the only one in our family who ever ordered the Italian food. Fried chicken was the only meat on the menu on Saturday night, the only choice being white or dark meat. One of the sides was always lima beans, which nobody with any sense liked. That basically meant to normal people that there were only four choices. I ordered dark meat, mashed potatoes, corn, and applesauce. One time I got a stem in my green beans, so I never ordered them again.

Mr. and Mrs. Enderle and Uncle Cletus were sitting at the other table next to the windows. Mr. Enderle had served in WWII; he was probably too old for Korea. He and Uncle Cletus always marched together with the VFW in Colby parades.

Mr. Rosolini brought their food first. Uncle Cletus had ordered dark meat too. Mrs. E had ordered lima beans. It figured. My stomach began to growl. I hadn't eaten since breakfast. I didn't get to finish my float. I'd probably made a bunch of black ants happy when I dropped it.

From where I was sitting, I could see the Houn Dawg theatre and Burt's Sinclair. Several cars were already at the Houn Dawg. No one was climbing on Dino; most kids were home with their parents.

Wendy, Beth, and Mr. and Mrs. Winchester walked in. Wendy and I made brief eye contact. She smiled. I guess she'd heard what had happened and wasn't mad that I hadn't stopped by her house. It was one of those times that I wished I'd had some Jade East to put on. Wendy sat in a chair with her back to me. I turned and looked toward the Houn Dawg when she turned to look at me.

Mom put her hand on my shoulder. "Do you have an itch, Tommy?" Wendy's presence stirred me in a strange way.

"No," I replied, clearly put out that she asked. I kept looking out the window toward the Houn Dawg and the theatre. It'd only been a week since Wendy and I'd gone to the movies together, kind of. Now we were having dinner together. I figured that Wendy and I were kind of going steady.

Mr. Rosolini brought our food, but I'd lost my appetite. I pretended to be interested in the picture of the whitetail buck over by the counter, but I was really looking at Wendy.

Mr. and Mrs. Gooche came in next and sat down at the table next to ours. Everyone said hello and asked how everyone else was doing.

Mr. Gooche ordered, then looked my way. "You and Booger still thinking about getting into the lawn-mowing business?"

"Yes, sir."

"Well, my lawn mower, hit's shot and I've decided not to buy a new 'un. If you're interested, you boys can take a look at m'yard and let me know how much you'd charge t' mow it."

"Yes, sir!"

"I want the grass clipped 'round my picket fence too. Do you'ns have a pair of clippers?"

"We're gonna get a pair. Yes, sir." I'd seen a pair on the Globemaster display for only $2. I looked up at Dad, and he nodded in approval.

Dad and I had cherry pie for dessert. Marsha and Mom split a piece of coconut cream. Uncle Cletus had gotten the rhubarb pie with a scoop of ice cream. After the dessert, Mom and Dad had coffee. Neither one of them used their cream, so I got to drink the little bottles that came with their coffee. Marsha ate the sugar cubes. I never ate them since they'd given us the polio vaccine in 'em.

MARSHA AND I GOT UP early on Sunday morning. Since Marsha had decided she wanted to learn to cook, we'd started fixing breakfast on Sunday mornings and letting Mom and Dad sleep. It was mostly a break for Mom. Dad never cooked anything.

I stirred the frying bacon while Marsha mixed up the pancake batter. She fixed orange juice with crushed bananas blended in. I grilled pancakes on a big griddle using bacon grease and sprinkled bacon bits in Dad's. Marsha heated up the syrup in a small pan and added a couple of patties of butter and let them melt.

The smell of the frying bacon woke Mom and Dad. We served them pancakes, bacon, and sausage on warmed plates. I didn't give Mom any of the pancakes with crunched-up bacon. The bits hurt her teeth; she had a bridge. We used the new glasses we had gotten free at the grocery store with the proof of purchase coupons for orange juice. When Mom got up, she asked if we'd washed the new glasses. We had, because we knew she'd ask.

She appreciated not having to fix breakfast. Dad enjoyed Mom sitting and having breakfast with him. Marsha and I pretended we owned a restaurant. Dad always left us a tip, usually twenty cents. We always put it in the offering at church.

Marsha washed the dishes while I took my turn in the bathroom. I dried and put the dishes away while she took her turn. Her turn always took longer, that's why she was last. That way I wouldn't be knocking on the door and bugging her. I was never sure what all she did in there. The bathroom was always hot and steaming and smelled like something had been burning when she came out. She had a whole tackle box full of makeup stuff.

Dad, Marsha, and I always left the house for church together. Mom always put a roast on and came later. We got in the truck, Dad started the engine and after saying he'd be right back, returned to the house.

Since Marsha hogged the bathroom, Dad never got a chance to make a serious visit. The urge usually hit him about the time he got in the truck. We always figured it was the coffee. He always made it really strong; at least that was Mom's usual complaint. We waited in the truck with the engine running. It was just like every other Sunday.

The First Baptist Church sat on the highest hill in town. Booger and his mom and dad went there, too. So did Melody and her family. Wendy went to the Methodist Church.

The parking lot was gravel and there weren't assigned places, but it seemed as if there were. We always parked right next to the back entrance. Booger's dad always parked in the front next to the oak tree. Uncle Cletus always drove his Volkswagen to church and parked it between two maple trees near the rear corner. The trees had been planted too close together, and the space was too small to park a normal size car. Everybody parked in the same place every Sunday. Whenever a visitor parked in a regular's place, everything got messed up.

One Sunday, Duke Burk's dad threatened to whip a visitor who'd parked in his regular place. The visitor's car had out-of-state plates and a bumper sticker touting a Republican candidate for governor. That was probably the problem. A couple of the other dads swarmed around and calmed Duke's dad down. The visitor didn't stick around for church. He probably went to the Methodist Church. They didn't care where anyone parked. They clogged up the streets and didn't seem to have any sense at all when it came to parking.

Before Sunday school, all the kids in the first through sixth grades gathered in the big room in the basement to sing praise songs. There were small window wells along one wall; they were usually full of weeds in the summer, but did allow a bit of sunlight to pass through. Mrs. E led the singing and played the piano. Sometimes, she talked about a new Top 10 song and told us how the words described the use of drugs.

There was a drain in the middle of the room, and the concrete floor was always kind of slick with moss or something around it. I saw a big old wolf spider crawl out of it once. Booger and I never sat near it ever again. That's usually where the visitors sat, unaware of the danger. What they didn't know wouldn't hurt them, is what I always figured.

Mrs. E constantly scanned the room, making sure everyone was singing. She always encouraged us to sing as if no one was listening. My lips were usually moving even if there wasn't noise coming out. I'd heard Marsha sing and decided not to take any chances with my voice. Mrs. E had probably recommended her for the hearing-impaired choir, too. Melody had a pretty voice; I always tried to sit next to her in case I did slip and a flat noise came out. That way it wouldn't sound so bad. The two of us singing at the same time sort of evened things out.

Mrs. E's sister from Fairview was visiting. She was a music teacher at the high school there, but had almost gotten famous as an opera singer, or so Mrs. E had said. We sang a couple of extra songs, and Mrs. E's sister sang a solo. Her stentorian voice made my ears throb.

Booger asked for his mom and dad to be added to the prayer list. His mom wasn't sleeping, and his dad wasn't talking much. He said he was doing okay and that was a praise, which could be put on the praise list. Mrs. E made a note of it. By the time Sunday school was over, we all had a new mimeographed prayer and praise list.

Sometimes they asked boys from our class to help with the worship service. Brother Baker came and got Booger and me right after Mrs. E dismissed us to go to our Sunday school classes. We were the only boys in our class who had ties on. I told Brother Baker that mine was a clip-on. He picked me anyway.

"God doesn't look at the tie, He looks at the heart," Brother Baker said.

We'd been chosen to help take up the offering, he told us. He gave us a bulletin and made sure we knew when we were supposed to come forward and get the plates. We'd both be working the center aisle, with a deacon on each side. We'd have to sit on the front pew until after the offering was collected. He told us to sit still and not to be picking our nose, itching, or anything. Everybody would be able to see us.

Next, he took us into the room behind the choir loft, and we helped prepare the communion. Booger and I poured grape juice into the tiny communion cups. Brother Baker cut up crackers using an old paper cutter. He sneezed once and blew a whole plateful of crackers on the floor. He wiped the sneeze jeeze off the back of his hand onto his pants. I was pretty sure we wouldn't get to help hand out the communion. I'd only seen the deacons doing that.

A shoebox full of half-burned candles was lying on the counter. Brother Baker said they'd been left after a wedding and that we could have them. Booger and I didn't have a specific plan for discarded candles but considered them somewhat of a treasure.

Sunday school was letting out, so Booger and I went back out into the sanctuary and took our seats in the front. We'd never helped with the offering before. We'd usually just helped hand out bulletins. It felt kind of weird sitting in the very front. The pulpit was only a few feet away.

Mr. Enderle was the song leader. He stepped up to the pulpit and asked everybody to turn to page nine and sing "Holy, Holy, Holy." I knew that one by heart and didn't need a hymnal. Since I was way up front and nobody could hear me, I went ahead and sang. It felt good. Booger kept looking at me like I'd lost my mind. It was then that I became certain my voice wasn't any better than Marsha's.

Mr. Enderle then gave the report. We'd had sixty-two in Sunday school today and fifty-eight a year ago. The Sunday school offering was $282 today and $268 a year ago. We'd improved on both numbers, and he said we should be thankful.

Brother Baker asked Dad to do the opening prayer; he did that a lot. Dad gave thanks for the rain we'd had recently, the above-average church attendance, and asked the Lord to watch over our boys in Vietnam.

Mrs. E's sister stepped behind the podium and cleared her throat. I'd heard her sing in the sanctuary before, but never while I was sitting on the front pew. Before she started everybody knew she'd be singing "Heaven Came Down and Glory Filled My Soul." That's the only song I'd ever heard her sing in the sanctuary. She'd sung others in the Sunday school opening, but always "Heaven Came Down" in the sanctuary. Mrs. E played the piano.

It had never been made clear why she hadn't gone on to be an opera singer, but it wasn't because she didn't have volume. The Methodists probably heard her two blocks away. The windowpanes rattled on every high note. I was afraid the cut glass window of Jesus holding a baby lamb was going to break to pieces and crash down into the choir. It amazed me how much noise could come out of one person. When she finished, nearly everyone quietly said "Amen." One man said, "Hallelujah, Glory to the Lord." He was no doubt a visitor, maybe a General Baptist or something. His wife had a bunch of hair all wadded up on top of her head.

Fish and Monkey, the two deacons also helping with the offering, approached the pulpit from the outside aisles. People had always confused Solomon with Salmon, which was fitting since he never worked and spent an inordinate amount of time fishing. Booger and I stepped up, too. Monkey gave the offertory prayer. He thanked the Lord for all of our blessings and asked Him to fill everyone with the giving Spirit.

Fish and Monkey each picked up an offering plate and headed toward the outside aisles. Monkey walked erect, almost marching; Fish sort of shuffled, all stooped over. Booger and I walked down the center aisle. Our job was to simply take the plate from one pew and hand it back to the next one. I'd told Brother Baker that it'd go a lot faster if Booger and I had a plate too. That way we could have four plates going at once. He said he'd study on it. There wasn't anything to study on. It'd mean change, though, and change didn't come easy at First Baptist, at least not without ample committee work.

People religiously sat in the same pew every Sunday. You'd think there were assigned seats. It was the same kind of phenomenon as the parking lot. It generally wasn't a problem except around Easter and Christmas, when we'd have lots of visitors.

One time, the pew that Mrs. Whitener usually sat in was full of visitors. She stood at the end of the pew and stared. Brother Baker had to help her find another place to sit. Those visitors had no idea they'd taken the seat of a tobacco-chewing, Barlow-knife-carrying widow lady. I'd heard that she'd spit Days Work juice on the driver door handle of the visitor's car. It was a rumor that was never confirmed, but one most others and I chose to believe.

Everyone at First Baptist had envelopes with their names on them, and some used them for offering. Ours usually just piled up and got thrown away once a year. There was an envelope for each Sunday of the year. Taking up the collection, I noticed that most people were like Dad and just wrote a check and folded it. It was hard to see how much anyone was giving.

Most moms dug through their purses looking for change for their kids to give. All purses combined, I'd say we had about ten pounds of tissue that day. Most likely we were up a little on that number from a year ago, too.

After we reached the rear of the church, Monkey and Fish took the plates and together they marched them to the front. Booger and I had permission from Brother Baker to sit anywhere after taking up the offering. We both sat in the third pew from the rear, on the left side, which is where we always sat. Melody and her family sat on the pew just in front of us. Uncle Cletus sat across the aisle from them. He was wearing his prescription sunglasses. He always did, even at night. Mom said it had something to do with his war wound.

Brother Baker preached on the Fruits of the Spirit from Galatians 5:22–23. He talked at length about love, joy, peace, patience, kindness, goodness, faithfulness, gentleness, and self-control. I worked hard at paying attention, but my mind kept drifting to the Mini-Trail.

Uncle Cletus assumed his regular position: leaning forward slightly, his elbows resting on the tops of his knees, his chin fitting perfectly in the palms of his hands. His left and right index finger tips fit perfectly over his ear canals. He looked a little bit like that statue of "The Thinker," except both hands touched his chin. Uncle Cletus's prescription sunglasses hid the fact that his eyes were closed.

He had that self-control fruit down pretty good, but he needed to work on the patience one. At 11:30 on the dot, he woke up and started looking at his watch. By the time Brother Baker ended the sermon and called the elders to the front to serve communion, Uncle Cletus had crossed and uncrossed his legs a hundred times; he probably needed to take a leak. It was a predictable performance, as if scripted at the Southern Baptist Convention.

Chapter 8

Flapper

MOM HAD INVITED THE BURGERS to our house for lunch. Mrs. Burger brought fruit salad in a large Tupperware bowl. She promptly demonstrated the bowl burping technique even though everyone had already seen it. Mom and Marsha acted as if it was the first time they'd seen the burping bowl demonstration. The three of them worked in the kitchen and talked about cooking while getting lunch ready.

The pot roast had been cooking all morning and the entire house, probably the attic, too, was filled with the aroma of pot roast and baked bread. My stomach growled, and my saliva glands flooded my mouth. Booger and I made several trips to the kitchen to see if it was time to eat. "Just a few minutes" was always the answer given, regardless of how long it was going to be.

Mrs. Burger was in a good mood; her trademark laugh had returned. She told Mom about some new Tupperware products. Mom told her about a new pistachio cake recipe, and Mrs. Burger got tears in her eyes. It was a recipe she was sure Johnny would like, she said, since he loved pistachios. Mom later regretted having mentioned it.

Dad had brought home an owner's manual to one of the twenty-one-inch Lawn-Boys. Booger and I looked through it while we waited. It explained how to mix the gas and oil, adjust the mowing height, and how to clean the air filter. There was also a section in the back on lawn care. We got to thinking and decided to ride over to Mr. Gooche's after lunch and check out his yard.

Mr. Burger and Dad sat out on the patio and talked business. Booger's dad sold Electrolux vacuum cleaners. Mom always said that everyone either had an Electrolux, or they wanted one.

The phone rang. One of Dad's customers was in the hayfield and had broken down. They needed a fan belt for their tractor. Dad told them he'd meet them at the shop in forty-five minutes, allowing time for lunch first. That sort of thing happened a lot during the spring and summer. Booger's dad said he'd ride along, too. Booger and I decided we'd go with them and look at the Lawn-Boys again. I often wondered if the owner of Fairview John Deere got parts for their customers on Sunday.

The pot roast was so tender I didn't even need a knife. The carrots and potatoes melted in my mouth. Mr. Burger asked for salt and pepper before he even tasted it, and then covered his entire plate with a layer of spice. He got a look from Mom, but I don't think anyone except Marsha and I noticed. I ate too much and didn't have room for any fruit salad. I didn't like other people's fruit salad anyway. Some moms didn't do a very good job removing all the seeds from the grapes.

Booger and I rode in the back of the pickup on the way to the shop. Dad turned the alarm off before unlocking the door. An alarm company out of Fairview had installed a projector that shot out a red beam of light, which was guided through the building by a series of mirrors. If the beam got blocked, the alarm went off. It almost always went off if there was a severe lightning storm. Dad never figured out if it was because of the thunder shaking the mirrors, or the flashes of lightning messing up the light beam. The store hadn't gotten broken into since it had been installed, though. I'd also started a rumor that we'd installed shotgun booby traps on every door, too. That probably had more effect than the goofy light and mirror contraption.

Booger and I studied the Lawn-Boys while Dad took care of the customer. It had only been a day since we'd last looked at them. Using the instructions in the manual, we took the air filter off. With it removed, we could see through the barrel of the carburetor into the cylinder. We took turns slowly pulling the starter cord while the other watched the piston move up and down. It had a two-ring piston. According to the sales brochure, the extra ring gave it more power and helped with cooling. Uncle Cletus would know if that was right, or just sales literature malarkey.

On the way home, we stopped at Booger's house and picked up his bike, then pedaled over to Mr. Gooche's yard to take a look. His house was next to Melody's. His yard was mostly flat, but it was big; we walked it off. It was about a hundred yards wide and a hundred yards long—about the size of two football fields, or about two acres, and full of mature old hard maples. The trunks of each one had been whitewashed from the ground to about five feet high. The trunks matched the picket fence, which stretched nearly halfway around the yard.

We estimated it'd take both of us working together at least a half a day to mow the yard and clip the fence, based on the formula we'd come up with. We decided to quote Mr. Gooche twelve dollars. That'd be about a dollar an hour for each of us: fifty cents an hour for the Lawn-Boys, and fifty cents an hour for labor.

"That sounds good to me," he said, standing on his wrap-around porch and looking out at the sprawling lawn. We hadn't asked for enough, was my guess. He'd agreed too quickly. "A new riding lawn mower would cost me over $400," he added, while scratching the lump on his head.

"When do you want us to start?" It looked like it needed to be mowed anytime, but we didn't even have our Lawn-Boys yet.

"You can mow it now. Tomorrow is fine with me. If you can't get it done in one day, be sure and finish up the next." Unless we mowed on Saturday, we wouldn't be able to get the whole thing done in one day, at least not until school was out.

"We'll work you in as soon as we can. It shouldn't be a problem gettin' it done this week." I tried to make it sound as if we had several lawns to do. I extended my hand to shake his, making the deal official. He shook my hand, then Booger's.

WE RODE TOWARD HOME. "How much'r those Lawn-Boys gonna cost us?" Booger asked.

"Dad said he'd sell 'em to us for his cost, about seventy dollars each."

"And he's gonna let us pay for 'em over time?"

"Yeah, he said he'd give us all summer to pay for 'em."

I did some calculations in my head. Mr. Gooche's lawn would probably need to be mowed about twenty times. That would amount to two hundred and forty dollars, more than enough to pay for the Lawn-Boys.

"We'll need t' get a gas can too," Booger said.

"Yeah, and a couple of 'ose hand clippers off of the Globemaster display," I added.

"You think he'd throw in one of 'ose John Deere thermos jugs?"

"We'll ask." Booger kept pedaling and excitedly asking questions. He was having a happy day and so was I. Nobody had forgotten Johnny, but the pain and sorrow of his loss was getting easier to bear, or so it seemed.

Mamaw and Papaw were working in the garden when I got home. I held one end of the string for Mamaw, while Papaw laid out each row exactly straight. Their garden was always a work of art.

CALEB, BOOGER, AND I STOOD together at the bus stop. Marty Blanken hadn't shown up yet. I didn't say anything to Caleb about the surrey seat; it wouldn't have done any good. He still hadn't brushed his teeth, I noticed.

"Dad said he'd have Odie get us a couple of Lawn-Boys ready," I told Booger. He nodded, but didn't say anything. It was going to be a Johnny day.

Beth and Wendy walked up. Wendy was carrying her flute. "Do you have any lawns to mow yet?" Wendy asked.

"Mr. Gooche said we could mow his. He lives over by Melody."

"Ump," she said, and then her cheeks got little red blotches on them. She looked at Beth and rolled her eyes.

"We're gonna get our Lawn-Boys this afternoon. We'll probably mow Mr. Gooche's yard tomorrow." Wendy smiled, albeit weakly.

"Want me to carry your flute for you?" The words just flew out of my mouth. Sometimes I said stuff without thinking.

"That would be very nice. Thank you very much." She handed it to me. If I ever get a letter jacket, I'll let her wear it, I thought.

Marty got to the bus stop just as Miss Barbara opened the doors. I let Wendy and Beth get on first. I should have sat right behind Miss Barbara, but that's where Caleb usually sat, and it'd mean I wouldn't be able to be across from Wendy. I took my chances and walked on back to my regular seat.

"Just keep my flute until we get to school if you don't mind," Wendy said, smiling real prettylike. She looked a little like Dorothy in *The Wizard of Oz*. When she smiled, it reminded me of when Dorothy started down the yellow brick road, skipping along and happy. When her eyes turned stormy that day in the cafeteria, she'd looked more like Dorothy did when she'd figured out that the Wizard was just some old coot. I returned her smile. My mouth was too dry to talk. My tongue felt like it was stuck to the roof of my mouth; that phenomenon was becoming a common occurrence.

Wilma Bodenschatz got on the bus right behind Marty. He knew she'd clean his clock if he did anything to me. I looked out the window as they went by, and hoped for the best. Out of the corner of my eye, I noticed Miss Barbara watching him through the overhead mirror. He might whack me, but if he did he'd be in big trouble. If he made Miss Barbara mad, Wilma would be the least of his problems.

Marty mumbled something as he went by. The only word I made out sounded like "pansy." I acted like I didn't hear it. Wilma gave him a good shove. She must have been standing on the heel of his shoe, because it came off as he stumbled toward his seat. She kicked it under his seat and plopped down across the aisle from him. I turned around and looked at her while Marty was digging around under his seat for his shoe. She smiled and winked at me. Wendy was looking out her window and hadn't seen it, which was good. I turned around quickly and faced forward. My neck felt really warm.

WALKING HOME FROM THE BUS stop, I could see that something strange was on our carport. It looked like one of Mom's old bedspreads. When I reached the driveway, I saw that in fact it was one of her old bedspreads covering something. She'd been watching for me and came out the front door, walked to the carport, and pulled the cover away, revealing two brand-new Lawn-Boys.

"Your dad brought them home during his lunch hour."

Both Lawn-Boys were sitting side-by-side. Beside each one sat a brand new two and a half gallon gasoline can, a six-pack of two-cycle mix, a pair of Globemaster clippers, and a John Deere thermos jug. The gasoline cans said *Colby John Deere* on them. "Tommy" was stenciled on one can and "Booger" on the other. Mom snapped a picture of me looking at them while I wasn't watching her.

"Booger's mom knows, too. She's going to send him over as soon as he gets home." Mom and Dad had thought of everything. I ran to the bathroom so she couldn't see the tears in my eyes.

MOM GAVE ME ENOUGH MONEY to fill the can up with gasoline. Booger's mom had given him some, too. We poured a bottle of mix oil into each can and headed toward Mr. Gooche's house. We stopped by Burt's and filled the cans with gasoline.

Burt came out and looked the mowers over. "You boys got yourselves a couple 'a dandy looking Lawn-Boys there." He gave us each a moon pie. "Who's your first victim?"

I swallowed my moon pie. "Mr. Gooche. His is our very first lawn."

"That's a big-'un to start on. He's been usin' an ol' rider on it. It'll take you a pretty good while to mow it by hand."

"We plan t' start on it today and finish t'morrow," Booger told him.

"I see you got your thermos jugs with you too. Good idea. They'll come in handy, especially after it gets hot. Stop in here anytime you want an' fill 'em with cold water out'a the water fountain." He smiled and said, "Catch 'a later," then walked off to wait on a customer who had just dinged the bell and was waiting for service.

THERE AREN'T THAT MANY LEVEL places in Colby, but Mr. Gooche's yard was one of them. It was bordered on two sides by a street and on two sides by yards, one of which was Melody's. Mr. Thorpe, who owned the *Colby Telegraph*, was the other neighbor.

Mr. Gooche's house sat in the middle of his lot. Booger and I split up. He started on the front, and I started on the back.

I made my first few trips around the yard making right turns. That way, the grass clippings blew into the yard and not out onto the street. After a couple of rounds, I started back the other way, blowing the clippings into the grass that had already been mowed.

Except for the trees and a birdbath, there wasn't much to mow around. Mrs. Gooche had flowers up next to the house and a big square garden in the middle of the yard. Some people, like Mrs. Whitener, had flowers planted all over the place, and Booger and I agreed that it'd be a mess to mow a lawn with so many flower beds, bushes, and trees.

We'd been mowing for a long time, probably two hours, when I began to understand why Mr. Gooche had been using a riding mower. I'd stopped to fill my gas tank twice. I was wearing last year's Converse All Star football shoes; they were at least a size too small, but I'd worn them anyway because I didn't want to get grass strains on this year's shoes. My toes were throbbing.

I turned the Lawn-Boy up on its side and cleaned the grass out from under the mower deck again. Odie had said that keeping it cleaned out would make it run better, or at least cooler. He'd also said that it needed to be cleaned more frequently in the spring, since the grass was so damp. The owner's manual had a section on that, too.

My hands were green with grass stain. "Would you like some lemonade?" I looked up. It was Melody. I hadn't heard her coming. "You've got some grease or something on your chin." She stood there holding two cups of lemonade. "I brought one for Booger, too." I used my sleeve to wipe off my chin.

Her hair was pulled back into a ponytail. She was wearing a white top with red polka dots and red shorts. She had flip-flops on; her toenails were painted red. Her second toes were longer than her big ones; I'd never noticed it before, but they looked weird.

"You gonna take one of these cups of lemonade or stare at my toes all day?" There was a moment of awkward silence. "I get them from my dad." She wasn't embarrassed or ashamed. It was really no big deal, considering the secret we already shared. I took one of the cups of lemonade; it was fresh-squeezed. My cup had a couple of lemon wedges and a cherry in it.

Booger rounded the corner of the house. "Hey, Melody. How ya doin'?" He'd probably seen Melody walking over from her house.

"Hi, Booger. I brought you and Tommy some lemonade."

"Thanks."

"So, are you guys gonna mow lawns this summer?"

"Yeah," Booger said between gulps.

"Saving up for a car?"

"Not exactly. After we get the Lawn-Boys paid for, we're gettin' a couple of Honda Mini-Trails," I told her.

"What's a Honda Mini-Trail?"

I tried to explain what one was, but she didn't seem too interested. She would be when she saw one, I was certain.

"My dad might want you to mow our yard." Melody's yard was about half the size of Mr. Gooche's, but still pretty good -sized. "Want me to tell him you're interested?"

"Only if you promise to bring us lemonade while we're mowin'," I joked. She smiled. It was another one of those involuntary responses I occasionally made.

"Deal! Come by before you go home."

"We'll do it. And thanks for the lemonade."

"Yeah, thanks," Booger said. Melody turned and smiled. Her ponytail whipped around from side to side as she headed toward her house with a bounce in her step.

After she had walked away, Booger pointed toward my face. "You've got a flapper hangin' out'a your nose."

I snorted a little bit, and it came flying out and landed on my mower deck. It'd probably been there the whole time I was talking to Melody. She probably thought we were even now.

We decided to finish the Gooches' lawn the next day. We were both tired, and the sun was starting to set. Mrs. Gooche had said we could leave the Lawn-Boys in their garage. Booger and I scraped the wet grass off of the bottom of the deck. I borrowed a rag from Mrs. Gooche and we shined them up. Booger wiped his gas can off, and I did too. We sat the Lawn-Boys next to each other with a fuel can on each side. The cans still had plenty of gas in them. We took our thermos jugs with us; they were bone-dry.

On the way home we agreed that we hadn't asked for enough money. While lying in bed, I gave it considerable thought until sleep prevailed.

Chapter 9

Negotiating

MELODY'S DAD OWNED HINKEBIEN'S DRY Goods; they mostly sold clothes and shoes, but they had other stuff, too. That's where I always got my Tuff-Nut jeans before school each year. If you bought three pairs, you'd get a free Tuff-Nut pocketknife. I would have bought my shoes there too, except Uncle Cletus was a Mason Shoe dealer, so we always ordered shoes from him.

Mr. and Mrs. Hinkebien were sitting in their porch swing. Somebody was inside playing the piano. Judging by the number of sour notes they were striking, I figured it was Melody practicing.

Mr. Hinkebien stood up – Booger followed me up the porch stairs. "Melody says you two are getting into the lawn-mowing business."

"Yes, sir," we both replied, almost in unison.

"What do you two figure you'd want to charge to mow this yard?" He paused for a second. "I'll have Melody do the clipping."

I visually surveyed the yard, mostly for effect; we'd already decided how much to ask for. "Well, it looks about half the size of Mr. Gooche's."

"Yes, it's exactly one acre. Mr. Gooche has two acres." He paused a few seconds and rubbed his chin. "You have to clip his, don't you? How much are you charging him?"

"He hasn't paid us yet." That wasn't lying, but it didn't exactly answer the question either. "We figured Mr. Gooche's yard was worth about fifteen dollars." That was the truth, even though we were only charging him twelve. "Booger and I need time to study on it." I tried to sound grown-up. We were determined to do a better job of negotiating this lawn.

"We'll do it for eight," I blurted out, almost immediately after saying we needed time to think. Booger gave me a look.

"How about seven dollars and a Tuff-Nut pocket knife?" he replied too quickly.

"Deal," Booger said before I could flinch and ask for more. He obviously wanted in on the impulsive action.

"When can you start?"

"Day after tomorrow," Booger told him.

Melody had stopped playing the piano and was standing at the door. She was smiling at me while Booger and her dad talked. Maybe she hadn't noticed the flapper after all. It was hard to tell what she was thinking, just as it was with all girls.

THE NEXT MORNING, MOM DROVE Marsha and me to school. I was so sore I hadn't wanted to get out of bed. By the time I did, it was already too late to catch the bus. Marsha didn't mind not having to ride the bus. It gave her more time to put stuff on her face. Mom made it clear several times on the way to school that being too tired to get out of bed wasn't getting off on the right foot with the lawn-mowing business. I'd missed a chance to carry Wendy's flute, too.

Booger also admitted he was sore, but he'd caught the bus. His aunt Penelope had gotten him out of bed and fixed breakfast for him and his dad before leaving for Fairview. She worked for a realtor there.

His mom wouldn't have been able to bring him to school, anyway, because she was still taking medicine to help her sleep. He said she sometimes didn't get up until noon on Saturdays. He didn't know when she got up during the week. She was always still asleep when he left for school.

Mrs. E passed out a sign-up sheet for the skating party. Every year, each elementary grade had a roller skating party. It was always near the end of the school year. Fairview was the closest town with a roller rink. The fifth grade was going the next week. If enough people signed up, we took two school buses. It cost two dollars. I signed up and so did Booger and Melody.

I'd gone through the lunch line and was looking for a place to sit when I saw Wendy; she was still in line. She smiled when she noticed me staring at her. I thought about her a lot, even when I was alone. Booger had saved a seat for me, so I sat by him. Flop, Caleb, and Everett were sitting across the table.

"You lawn boys are missin' out on all th' fun," Everett said, between mammoth bites.

"How's 'at?" I asked.

"We've been practicin' up with 'at potato gun."

"Uh-huh," I grunted, with a mouth full of shredded mystery meat.

"Caleb and Flop have it fig'rd out how to hit a target. They can put a potato inside a twenty foot circle from a hunerd yards away." Caleb and Flop weren't saying anything. They didn't talk and chew at the same time, like Everett did.

Flop swallowed his mystery meat and turned to Everett while pointing at his plate with his fork and interrupted him. "Want my Jay-Lo?"

"Sure, watch 'is." Without using a spoon or fork, Everett sucked the cube of Jell-O into his mouth straight off of Flop's plate, swallowed, and started talking again. Brother Baker oftentimes talked about how God puts each of us here for a purpose. Everett's purpose was to eat – of that I was certain.

Others offered Everett their Jell-O just to watch him perform the feat. He never finished the potato gun story. He would have hyperventilated if there'd been enough Jell-O.

AFTER SCHOOL, I SAW WENDY in the hall. I offered to carry her flute. We were walking together toward the bus when Melody stopped me. Wendy made a huffy noise and kept walking.

Melody then asked me, "Are you coming to mow at my house today?"

"As soon as we finish with Mr. Gooche's yard, we'll be right over." She noticed Wendy's flute.

She smiled weakly. "See you then." She hurried off to catch her bus. It seemed to me that she and Wendy didn't like each other for some reason. I got on the bus and handed Wendy her flute. Her eyes had that stormy look again. Somebody had made her mad.

IT ONLY TOOK US AN hour to finish mowing Mr. Gooche's yard. We hadn't clipped the grass around the fence yet. Booger had started at one end, and I started at the other. Almost an hour later, we met near the front side-walk. In that hour, I had learned to appreciate a well-clipped fence and the fact that clippers, like scissors, only worked in the right hand. I also decided that I'd never ever, in a million years, have a picket fence.

Mrs. Gooche inspected our work from the porch. "You boys did an excellent job." She handed each of us six one-dollar bills. "Russell will be very pleased. He needs boys like you two working down at the grocery store."

There was something strange about her tongue. It seemed a little too thick and maybe too long. Speaking clearly didn't come easy for her.

"I thought you had to be sixteen to work there?" I asked, sticking the six dollars in my left pocket. My right hand was too sore to use.

"Well, I think he'll hire just about anybody who will work and be polite to the customers." Her words came slowly. "Is your hand okay?"

"Yes, ma'am. It just seems to have a mind of its own right now." I used my left hand to straighten out the fingers on my right hand. For some reason it just kept cramping up.

"Want us to plan on mowin'n'at again next week?" Booger asked.

"Oh, I'm sure it'll be ready to mow by then, maybe sooner. Russell always puts lots of fertilizer down."

"We'll plan on bein' back in a week. Call if we need to come sooner."

"That sounds good. Are you going to mow Mr. Hinkebien's lawn next?"

"Yes, ma'am," I replied.

"He said Melody was a little sweet on one of you boys."

"It's Tommy," Booger said. "He's got him a girlfriend in the sixth grade, too."

She grinned. "Well, aren't you a lady's man."

"They're not girlfriends really, just friends."

Actually, I was ready to admit that Wendy was a girlfriend as soon as she was ready to call me her boyfriend. Melody was just sort of a, well, I wasn't sure.

"Do they know that?"

"Well, we've never talked about it."

She shook her head and sighed. "That's typical. You boys be careful. I'll see you in a week." She turned to walk into the house. I heard her giggling through the screen door.

MELODY HAD SEEN US FINISH Mr. Gooche's yard and met us at the property line. "Dad said you could put the Lawn-Boys in the garage."

I was too tired to clean the underside of the deck. Booger didn't clean his either. We just pushed them into the garage and sat the gasoline cans next to them. We both had enough gasoline to mow Melody's yard. Our thermos jugs were bone-dry again.

"No lemonade an'at today?" Booger asked.

"Nope, I had other things to do today, sorry," she said to him and glared briefly at me.

"Well, we're comin' back t'morrow. Maybe you'll have time t'morrow," Booger pined.

"Maybe," she said, with a bit of a huff, her hands planted firmly on her hips.

"I sure hope so," Booger continued. I was trying to figure out why she was looking at me so weirdlike.

"I'll close the garage door tonight and then open it tomorrow after school so you'll be able to get the mowers back out. I better go, Mom has supper ready."

Booger looked at me after she'd walked away. "Think she's mad about somethin'?"

I shrugged my shoulders, "Wouldn't know what it could be."

ON THE WAY HOME, WE stopped by Gooche's Grocery. We were thirsty enough to drink from a mud-puddle, but didn't, only because there weren't any. Burt had offered cold water out of the fountain, but we decided to get a carton of chocolate milk. We'd never had any store-bought. The only chocolate milk either one of us had ever had was Nestlé's. It was good, but there was always that stuff left in the bottom of the glass no matter how much you stirred.

We both got a sixteen-ounce carton and paid for it out of our six dollars. I got five pieces of Bazooka bubble gum, too. My fingers still weren't working very well, but I managed to get the carton open. Booger finished his before me. I was almost all of the way home before I drained the last drop out of my carton. My stomach felt like I'd swallowed a watermelon.

"YOU'RE NOT EATING MUCH," MOM said after I refused for the third or fourth time her offer of more meat loaf. "We're going to the fellowship dinner tomorrow night. This meat loaf won't be any good left over until Thursday." She was clearly more than a little put out that I wasn't eating half of the meat loaf, like I normally did.

"That was a waste of money to get that carton of chocolate milk and drink it just before dinner." Now we'd gotten to what was really bugging her.

"I know, and I'm sorry. It didn't seem like that much to drink when we got it. I was just really thirsty."

I shouldn't have drunk that much before dinner. She worked hard fixing dinner, and now some of the meat loaf would be wasted. Maybe Dad would eat it for lunch.

"Your dad will eat it for lunch one day, but not two days in a row." I guess not. She was reading my mind again.

"Do you have any homework?"

"No, ma'am. Mrs. E never gives homework near the end of school. She's nice."

"As soon as you get finished eating, I want you to get cleaned up and go to bed. No more of this not getting out of bed in the morning, Mr. Man." That's what Mom called me when she meant business.

"Yes, ma'am."

"Give me the money you got paid for mowing the lawn, or at least what you have left after gorging yourself on chocolate milk. I'll keep it in a safe place and use it to make your lawn mower and Mini-Trail payment."

"Yes, ma'am." I laid five sweaty dollars and the change on the counter.

"This lawn mowing better not affect your grades."

"Yes, ma'am." I closed the door to the bathroom before she said anything else. Later on she came in my room, woke me from a dream about electric clippers, said good night, and told me she loved me. I lay awake for a long time after that and thought about taking Wendy for a ride on the Mini-Trail.

THE NEXT MORNING I WAS still sore, but I forced myself to get out of bed, ate breakfast and headed toward the bus stop. I was moving slowly down the aisle and hadn't gotten completely in my bus seat when Marty Blanken hip-checked me the rest of the way in. I dropped Wendy's flute, but the heavy-duty case kept it from getting damaged. Marty yelped when Wilma jabbed him in the leg with one of her pencils. I'd noticed before we got on that they'd just been sharpened. He inspected his leg. One of Wilma's pencils had the lead broken off. Marty was a slow learner. Wilma smiled. I don't think she really liked me that much. It was just an excuse for her to pick on Marty.

I GAVE MELODY A PIECE of bubble gum before class.

"You're so sweet," she said, and then fluttered her eyelids.

She didn't say it loud enough for anyone else to hear, which was good, but I was really glad no one had seen her do that thing with her eyelids. She put the Bazooka in her desk.

"Are you going to the skating party next week?" she asked.

"Yep, are you?"

"Uh-huh," she replied softly. We'd both just asked each other a question that we both knew the answer to. I went to my desk and pondered the conversation. Girls caused me to do strange things. I couldn't seem to help myself.

WENDY GAVE ME HER JELL-O. She didn't like Jell-O that had shredded carrots in it. I didn't mind it. Booger and Caleb both kicked me under the table. Everett watched my fork go from my plate to my mouth one bite at a time. It was almost cruel, not offering him the Jell-O. We finished eating, then headed out to the playground.

Melody was standing by the volleyball court chewing the Bazooka bubble gum I'd given her. "Are you going to the fellowship dinner tonight?" she asked.

"Yep, Booger and I are gonna mow until six and then go."

"We're bringing stuff to make ice cream. What are you bringing?" she asked.

"We always bring cobbler. My mom makes the best cobbler in Colby."

"What kind of cobbler?"

"It depends on what gets thawed out. She got some new kind of labels last summer and they all came off in the freezer. She put blackberries, blueberries, strawberries, and rhubarb all in the same kind of container. None of them have labels now, so we won't know until the containers thaw enough to take the lids off."

"What if it turns out the two containers have different fruit?"

"Then she'll just mix them together. Strawberries and rhubarb mixed together is my favorite."

"Yuck!" Her face looked sour enough to curdle new milk.

"That's what most people say. That's okay. There's more for me that way."

Mom cut some small holes in the toes of my old basketball shoes. They didn't look too bad, and my toes felt a lot better.

Except for the willow tree with all kinds of bugs on it, Melody's yard was a lot easier to mow than Mr. Gooche's. Since we didn't have to do any clipping, we got it done before six. Melody brought us both a glass of ice-cold lemonade after we'd put the lawn mowers away.

Mrs. Hinkebien walked out onto the porch while we were drinking our lemonade. "Arnold isn't here. Is it okay if he pays you tonight at the fellowship dinner?"

"That's fine, Mrs. Hinkebien. That reminds me; we need to be goin' so we can get ready fer the dinner." I gave my glass to Melody. She smiled, having gotten over whatever it was that was bothering her.

"Is your family going to the dinner tonight, Booger?" Melody asked.

"My dad prob'ly will, but my mom still doesn't feel very good. She's still taking medicine an'at to help her sleep." I could tell Booger didn't like talking about it, so I didn't bug him like other people did.

We found Mr. Hinkebien at the dinner. He and some other men had gathered in the church basement near the kitchen. He gave us each three crisp one-dollar bills and a 1964 Kennedy half-dollar. "Who gets the pocket knife?"

"Booger gets the first one. We flipped for it on the way home the other day," I told him. "You knew sixty-four Kennedy halves are worth thirty-two dollars, didn't you?" I asked him.

"Really?"

Mrs. Hinkebien interrupted our conversation. "Russell, why don't you ask those boys to help crank the ice-cream makers?"

It wasn't really a question. It was her way of telling Mr. Hinkebien that she wanted him to do something. My mom did the same thing to my dad. Cranking the ice cream maker wasn't so bad. It was better than helping set up those old tables and chairs. They're kept in a dark, spider-infested closet. It was anybody's guess what else lurked in there.

"You heard the boss, boys. Let's get to cranking."

We followed him out the back door to the rear of the church. The ice cream makers were always set up on the concrete slab that covered the cistern. You could still get water from the pump, but nobody drank it anymore since the church had connected up to city water. Ever since everyone had hooked up to the city sewer and water system, hardly anyone got hepatitis anymore.

Monkey, Fish, Bem, and Rabbit were watching the other men crank away. They'd told their wives that they were helping with the ice cream, but they were mostly just chewing tobacco, spitting, and sharing their opinions with anyone who'd listen.

An inmate from the county jail was helping crank ice cream. Sheriff Omar had let him come to church, since he was only in for writing bad checks and wasn't a threat to anyone. He was wearing orange coveralls with "Inmate" written in large letters across the shoulders. I didn't know his name, but figured he was from out near the river. He never talked.

"Did you ever catch 'at runaway pony ov'air at th' courthouse?" Bem asked.

"Yes, sir. I got him stopped about a block from the court house."

"That feller what was a sittin' on the surrey didn't look like he was havin' much fun," Monkey chuckled.

"Whose boy was he anyways?" Bem asked.

"That was Caleb Wilfong. He just moved here. His dad is Mr. Wilfong." I didn't know what Mr. Wilfong's first name was. He was Mr. Wilfong to me.

"Uh-huh," Bem muttered with his mouth full. He stood there for a few seconds, then spat. Monkey, Fish, and Rabbit did too.

"I get it now," Mr. Hinkebien said, looking at me. He'd been listening to us while waiting his turn on an ice cream maker.

"Get what?" Bem asked.

"Sixty-four Kennedy halves are worth thirty-two dollars."

"You don't say." Bem looked at Fish, Rabbit, and Monkey.

"Are you right shore?" Rabbit asked.

Mr. Hinkebien pointed at us. "At's what these two yahoos have been tellin' around." He'd evidently done the math and gotten the joke.

"Well, law me. Here I've been a spendin' them like they was only worth fifty cents," Bem moaned.

By then most everybody was listening. Some of the men were chuckling, while others had perplexed looks on their faces. You could tell by watching the change in their expressions when they'd divided 64 by 2 and gotten the joke. Monkey, Fish, Bem, and Rabbit never did.

AFTER FINISHING THE MAIN COURSE, Booger and I waited for the ice cream to be brought in before we got some of Mom's cobbler for dessert. We'd slipped a piece of tin foil over her cobbler so most people wouldn't notice it. There were plenty of other desserts to choose from. I hadn't eaten much, saving up for dessert. Booger had eaten two plates full of all kinds of food except lasagna. He'd eaten so much lasagna after Johnny's funeral that he'd sworn never to touch the stuff ever again. His mom still wasn't cooking. She hadn't sent anything for the fellowship.

While a line formed by the ice cream, Booger and I got a bowl of cobbler. Somebody had noticed it under the tin foil but had only taken a spoonful or two. It turned out to be blueberry.

Mr. Thorpe saw me taking the tin foil off. "Is that your mom's cobbler, Tommy?"

"Yes, sir."

"Where's she been hidin' it?" Uncle Cletus asked. He'd noticed too, but didn't wait for an answer. Both of them had missed it and immediately got out of the ice cream line and headed toward the dessert table. Several others followed, clearing the way for Booger and me to get in the front of the ice cream line.

Booger and I were almost finished when Uncle Cletus and Mr. Thorpe sat down with their dessert. We were in a hurry to get outside and play kick the can. Melody had asked Booger and me to play.

"Are you boys mowing lawns together this summer?" Mr. Thorpe asked.

"Yes, sir. We're savin' up to get a Honda Mini-Trail," Booger replied.

"Thing of it is, they already have a couple on layaway," added Uncle Cletus.

"Well then, you boys probably need another yard," Mr. Thorpe said.

"Yes, sir," Booger said.

"It looks like you did a good job on the Gooches' and Hinkebiens' yards. What do you get for a yard like that?"

"Mr. Gooche's is twice the size of Mr. Hinkebien's. Isn't your yard about the size of Mr. Hinkebien's?"

"That's right. Mr. Gooche has two acres and Mr. Hinkebien and I have one acre each. How much is Arnold paying you?"

"Mr. Hinkebien is paying us seven dollars plus a Tuff-Nut knife, and that doesn't include clipping. Melody does that." I paused and looked at Booger to see if he wanted to add anything. "Those knives are going to be collector's items someday, so they're worth a couple 'a dollars."

"So you're sayin' you'd mow and clip my yard for nine dollars?" I kicked Booger in the leg in time to keep him from blurting out a yes.

"We looked your yard over the other day after mowing Mr. Hinkebien's. We decided that we'd need at least nine dollars to mow it and three dollars to clip. So, do you want us to mow and clip or just mow?"

Booger gave me a look. His eyes almost bugged out of his head when I asked for a total of twelve dollars to mow and clip. That was as much as Mr. Gooche was paying us to mow and clip two acres. Uncle Cletus leaned back in his chair and winked at me.

Mr. Thorpe flinched a little; it was an old bargaining technique I'd seen my dad use at Colby John Deere. "That sounds a little steep."

He'd finished with his dessert and had started chewing on a toothpick. Booger rolled his eyes and lipped some words, but I couldn't make out what he was saying. I kicked him again. I'd seen Dad haggle with people at the store. I wasn't lowering the price just yet.

"We both have brand new Lawn-Boys with new blades, and new hand clippers too. We'll do a first-rate job. It's bad for your grass to let it get too long before you mow. You shouldn't cut more than one third of the grass blade off at one time, and you should always use a sharp blade."

I'd read that in the Lawn-Boy owner's manual. Uncle Cletus was grinning ear to ear. Booger kicked me and was making a face, but I still couldn't make out what he was trying to say.

"These boys drive a hard bargain, Newt," said Mr. Gooche. He'd been standing behind me. That explained Booger's face-making.

"They're wantin' twelve dollars to mow and clip my yard," Mr. Thorpe told him.

"Good help, it's hard to find," Mr. Gooche told him matter-of-factly.

"What are you payin' them to mow your yard, Russell?"

"Less than what they're worth."

"You don't say," said Mr. Thorpe. "It would be nice to have it done and not have to worry 'bout it." He scratched his balding head and got a contemplative look on his face. "I'll give you boys a shot." Booger let out a sigh of relief and slumped back in his chair.

"When can you start?"

"A couple 'a days. What do ya think, Booger?"

"Fastern'at. We can start t'morrow if we git more gas."

Mr. Thorpe patted me on the shoulder. "You know where the property lines are," he said, then walked off with Mr. Gooche.

Uncle Cletus gently squeezed us both on our shoulders. "Good job, boys. What is Russell payin' you?"

"We're only gettin' twelve dollars from him."

Uncle Cletus chuckled. "Thing of it is, his yard is twice as big."

"You think he'll tell Mr. Thorpe?" Booger asked.

"Not a chance. Thing of it is, Russell spends a lot of money on those ads he runs every week in the *Colby Telegraph*. I'm sure he figures Newt can afford to pay you boys plenty. Besides, Newt's a Democrat and Russell's a Republican. By the way, I'm goin' to do some creek fishin' Saturday. You two want to go?"

"Yeah, that'd be great. Think you can go, Booger?"

Uncle Cletus always did lots of creek fishing in the spring. He knew where all of the good spots were.

"I'll ask my dad, Mr. Thornton. Thanks for askin'." Booger's smile was wider than it had ever been since Johnny had gotten killed. Uncle Cletus had just hit a home run with him.

All that negotiating and thinking about creek fishing had made me hungry. Booger and I both got another bowl of cobbler—not Mom's, her's was all gone. I didn't know whose we'd gotten and hoped it wouldn't give us the runs. There was some ice cream left, but it was mostly melted. It was too dark to play kick the can; besides the mosquitoes had come out, so we ate until we felt sick and then walked home.

"Sure are a lot of far-flies out tonight," Booger said on the way home.

I was glad that he'd noticed.

Chapter 10

Heroes

MRS. E DIVIDED THE CLASS into five groups for the final exam and as-signed each group the task of making a list of all fifty states and their respective capitols. When she wasn't standing in front of the room, as if at attention, with her fists planted on her hips, she walked around the room making sure that everyone in each team participated.

"I want to see everyone helping and a-like-a-that," she said, as only she could. "I have a ten-pack of Bazooka for each person on the team that finishes with the correct list first. After each team is finished, we'll have some individual competition and a-like-a-that. Anyone who wants to may compete for a Bazooka Joe T-shirt." I'd seen them advertised on the comic strips, but had never ordered one. "The first person who makes a list of all fifty states and their capitols gets the T-shirt."

We chose Melody as our group leader. Everyone told her the names of states. A few of the girls started naming capitals. Melody wrote as fast as she could. Most knew the capitals of the central and western states, even the spelling. As we narrowed the list down, only the New England states remained.

Melody leaned close and whispered, "You got a hundred on that test. I remember." She looked at me, smiled, and bit her pencil. It was then that I decided that she'd be okay for a girlfriend, too. Energized by her warm breath, I named and spelled each New England state and capital as fast as she could write. Mrs. E was standing nearby and heard me. Our team finished first.

Melody competed in the individual competition while I doodled in my Big Chief. She won, but after school gave me the Bazooka Joe T-shirt. I took it home and hung it on a hanger in my closet next to my Sunday dress shirt.

UNCLE CLETUS SAID HE'D BE by early on Saturday, so Booger spent Friday night at my house watching TV. *Sergeant York* was on Friday Night at the Movies, but we only watched it until he got drafted. We were both still tired from mowing lawns all week. We'd already seen the part where he killed and captured a bunch of Germans. After Booger and I watched it the first time, we'd made a pact to visit West Virginia sometime and see Sergeant York's hometown and maybe Chuck Yeager's, too.

Mom woke us early with breakfast ready. We finished eating and sat on the porch watching for Uncle Cletus. He pulled up in his blue '57 Chevy pickup truck. "Throw yer stuff in th' back," he said. The bed of his pickup had several cane poles, a minnow bucket, and a minnow seine.

He and Mom had talked on the phone. We were supposed to bring the food. Mom had packed a bunch of sandwiches, some pickles, and Oreo cookies in our ice chest. She made some Kool-aid and lemonade and mixed them together in a thermos. She'd put some cups in the ice chest. Booger and I put our Zebco rod and reels in the back with the cooler. We kept the thermos up front.

"Thing of it is, if a guy'd put a block of ice in 'at chest, the food would stay cooler," Uncle Cletus said. "We'll stop at Burt's and get one. Hop in."

Booger and I jumped in; I sat in the middle. The truck had 'Glass Pack' mufflers and it sounded powerful. He revved up the engine. The gears ground when he pulled the shifter into first. Mom stood on the porch in her housecoat and just rolled her eyes when we roared away. I couldn't hear her, but her lips were saying, "Be careful." Uncle Cletus was her younger brother. She sometimes talked about having to watch after him when he was growing up.

I took all the stuff out of the cooler so Uncle Cletus could put the block of ice in it. He must have gotten the biggest block Burt had. It was a lot of ice for a couple of sandwiches and cookies, I remember thinking.

"Here are a couple of moon pies," he said, tossing me six. I put my arms together and caught five. Booger picked up the other one. "Here are some sodas to put in there, too." He handed me a six-pack carton of sodas. He'd gotten two grape, two orange, and two strawberry. I'd never drunk two sodas in one day. I decided then and there that I liked fishing.

He stopped in the middle of the bridge. We all got out and leaned over the rail and spit. The creek was still clear. The trees had leaves out, and the breeze blowing through the leaves was so loud you could barely hear the water rushing through the shut-ins.

A small plane, probably a Cessna from Fairview Municipal, flew over. I wondered if it was Gene Hickam taking flying lessons. I imagined what they could see and longed to be up there looking down.

"You goin' t' get a Scrambler?" Booger asked Uncle Cletus.

"I think so. I'm going to give it a week or two and see if I still want one. Thing of it is, it's not a good idea to rush into new things." Uncle Cletus was wise.

He opened the door to the truck and motioned for us to get in. "We'll park up stream a bit."

We crossed to the other side of the bridge. He turned off of the main road and started up the little road bordering the strip of woods that separates the field from the creek. He gunned the accelerator just before each mud puddle. We slipped around a little as the truck slid into the ruts made by other vehicles. A couple of times, we bounced out of our seats. The cooler was sliding all over the truck bed, but it hadn't turned over.

"Ever get this thing stuck?" Booger asked.

"Oh, sure, but not on this road. This road is in pretty good shape. If a guy knows where the soft spots are, it's not a problem."

It wasn't much of a confidence-builder. Without warning, he turned the wheel sharply to the left, and we cut through an opening in the tree line. He guided the truck through the narrow gap and onto a gravel bar that was just downstream of the shut-ins.

Before the truck had come to a complete stop, Uncle Cletus hopped out. "First things first." I followed him out on the driver's side. By the time Booger got out and came to the rear of the truck, Uncle Cletus already had the tailgate down, the cooler pulled to the back of the bed, and the lid open. He pulled out three moon pies, gave one to me, laid one on the tailgate for Booger, and opened the third and bit off nearly half of it.

"It doesn't get any better'n this, boys," he said, chewing and looking toward the sky. He chewed with his mouth open. "You want one of 'ose sodas or Kool-aid to wash that moon pie down with?" he asked Booger.

Booger, like me, had probably never had a soda in the morning. I don't think he really knew what to say.

"Uh, I'll just have some of 'at Kool-aid that Mrs. Thompson fixed fer us," he replied. Uncle Cletus laid his moon pie down and took his shirt off. He was a little heavy, but not really fat. He had hair all over the place. Big globs of it grew in patches here and there. I think he had as much on his back as he did on his chest. His right bicep had "USMC" and an eagle, globe, and anchor insignia tattooed on it. He'd gotten that in Korea.

"Grab that seine. Let's catch us some minnows," Uncle Cletus said and started walking toward the ripples. Booger jumped up in the truck bed and handed me the seine.

"Should we bring the minnow bucket, too?" I asked.

"Sure, unless you plan on carryin' the minnows in your pockets, we're gonna need it. There're all kinds of shiners in this little pool below the ripples."

I wrapped the seine netting up so that I could carry it without getting my feet tangled in it. Booger walked over toward Uncle Cletus with the bucket. The two of them standing together looked strange. Booger looked small, pale, and bony next to Uncle Cletus.

Uncle Cletus was wearing his old Marine-issue boots. It didn't look like he had any socks on. His big calves went straight down into his boots. His shorts were Marine issue too—the kind with too many pockets, loops, and snaps. He had a canvas belt with one of those flat buckles. It had a Marine insignia on it, too. He was always cracking jokes and clowning around, but I knew that he could mean business if he wanted to. He had a dent in the back of his head on the right side. He'd gotten that in Korea, too.

He looked at Booger and pointed to the creek. "Take that end and wade out into the ripples."

I'd already taken one end of the seine and stuck it in the water near the bank. I knew the drill. One end needed to be held steady near the bank while someone else took the other end and waded into the cold water and scooped up the minnows. I'd had the good sense to grab the end that stayed on the bank.

Cletus stood there admiring the stream. "Judgin' by the size of those minnows, I'd say this stream is in pretty good shape." We caught more minnows than we needed and threw most of them back. "We'll catch more later if we need to," he said.

———

EVER SINCE WE'D GOTTEN OUT of the truck, a giant green-headed horse-fly had been pesterin' and biting Booger and me. Uncle Cletus had laughed every time we flinched, yelped, or slapped at the flying menace.

"Thing of it is, must be a female. Male horse flies don't bite," he said.

Booger and I grinned at each other when we saw it land on Uncle Cletus's back, right smack between his shoulder blades.

"The females have short piercin' and suckin' mouthparts. Just by watchin' you two, I'd say their bite was PAINFUL." Evidently she'd chomped down good just about then.

His arms were so thick he couldn't reach the center of his back. He finally took his hat off and swatted it away. "That's it! Fishin'll have t' wait a few minutes. That ol' green head just took its las' bite. Tommy, go find a couple stalks o' foxtail. Booger, you're the bait. Just sit there nice an' still and let 'er land on ya."

Uncle Cletus's back was bleeding from the bite. He no longer found the horsefly humorous. I went in search of the perfect foxtail. He'd caught the fly by the time I returned.

"Thing of it is, if a guy sticks a foxtail in their rear end, they can't turn," he was saying to Booger when I returned with a hand full of foxtail.

He was holding the horsefly, and Booger appeared to be examining its hind parts.

"Pick out a stem small enough to fit in there," he told Booger.

Booger picked out a small stalk and handed it to Uncle Cletus. He carefully, almost surgically, inserted the stem of the foxtail into the rear end of the horsefly.

"Watch this."

He gently tossed the modified green head into the air. It flew a straight line upstream over the shut-ins with the foxtail trailing along behind. We watched until it flew out of sight.

"She won't be back. Let's get after them fish now."

Across the creek from us was the bluff that Corky Seabaugh had dived off of and broken his neck. He and Johnny were the same age. They were only sixteen when it happened. He would have been the starting wide receiver on the football team. At least Corky was still alive, Booger was probably thinking.

We made our way through the granite rocks that everyone around Colby called the "shut-ins." The creek was up a little, according to Uncle

Cletus. The water made a roaring sound as it rushed through the granite boulders that tried to block its flow. Just upstream was a long body of water that was always good for catching smallmouth bass, according to Uncle Cletus. Somewhere upstream a little further, a smallmouth had probably just eaten a horsefly with an unusually long tail.

It was too deep to wade up the middle, so we walked along the bank in water about knee deep. We took turns going first. The first person stood the best chance to catch a fish, but they also had to explore the creek bed with their feet. After a few steps, the sediment got so stirred up you couldn't see where you were stepping.

Uncle Cletus pointed toward the bank. "See those coon tracks?"

"You mean those things that look like a small hand print an'at?" Booger asked.

"Yeah, they sort of look like a hand, only with tiny claw marks. If a guy would come out here at night, he'd see coons digging up mussels and eatin' 'em."

"Where do the mussels an'at come from?" Booger asked.

"Are you steppin' on things that feel like small flat rocks?"

"Yeah, they're all over the place." Uncle Cletus handed me his fishing pole and reached down into the water. After digging around a little, he came up with a huge mussel shell in each hand.

"Thing of it is, they're not rocks, they're mussels. They thrive in the sandy creek bed near where the spring empties in."

"Wow," Booger said.

"How'd you know the coons feed on them at night?" I asked.

"I used to come down here at night and just sit."

"By yourself?" Booger asked.

"Yeah, when I first got back from Korea."

He got a faraway look in his eyes, dropped the mussel shells, wiped his hands on his shorts, and took his pole back.

"Let's bait them hooks," he said, changing the subject.

He pulled the minnow bucket in from where it had been floating in the deeper water. Uncle Cletus had tied one end of a cotton line to himself and the other to the bucket. That way, no one had to carry it, except in shallow places.

We got into the fish pretty good and had to seine for more minnows. Booger hooked a nice smallmouth and fought with it for a couple of minutes before pulling it in. Uncle Cletus said it probably weighed two or three pounds. It was about all Booger's Zebco would handle. After that, we waded back down to the truck and ate our sandwiches and more moon pies. I drank a strawberry and Booger drank a grape soda; his lips and tongue turned purple. Uncle Cletus tried the Kool-aid and lemonade mix.

"I was really sorry to hear about your brother, Randy," Uncle Cletus said to Booger after we'd packed up and started back to town.

"Thanks," Booger said. He was sitting next to the door. The breeze was blowing in his face. He looked at Uncle Cletus with tearing eyes. "Tommy's mom said you were a hero in Korea."

"Thing of it is, Johnny would have been a real hero given the chance."

"What do you mean?" Booger asked.

Uncle Cletus turned and faced Booger. "Do you know what a hero is?"

"They're people who aren't afraid to risk their lives doin' really brave things an'at. Aren't they?" Booger looked at Uncle Cletus for confirmation.

"Sort of. Most heroes are ordinary people, who by no choice of their own find themselves in extraordinary circumstances and do what they need to do to survive. There's a few who have gone out of their way to be a hero, but thing of it is, I'm not one of them."

"Were you ever afraid in Korea?"

"All the time."

"What were you most afraid of?" Booger pried. I just listened as the two talked. It was the first time I'd heard Uncle Cletus talk about Korea.

"Gittin' captured. In fact, it was the fear of gittin' captured that caused me to do what I got decorated for. I would have rather died on the battlefield than git captured. If I'd run out of ammunition, I would have been captured. Since the ammo held out, I got decorated. The only thing between me bein' a prisoner of war or a decorated Marine was the amount of ammo I had. Thing of it is, I was scared, that's why I kept fightin'."

"You think Johnny could have been a hero?"

"Johnny was one of those guys who would have gone out of his way to be a hero, the real kind, like my brother Clayton. They're rare." Uncle Cletus looked squarely at Booger. For a second, I thought we might run off of the road.

Booger nodded. He leaned his head out of the window and looked

at himself in the rearview mirror. We stopped on the bridge and ended
our fishing trip by taking a leak off the side of the bridge. Uncle Cletus
gave us both a piece of Clove chewing gum; then he revved up his engine, popped the clutch, and left a big black mark on the bridge planks. I
laughed, Booger hooted, and Uncle Cletus made us promise not to tell.

On the way home, I wondered if, given the chance, I would be coura-
geous, like Uncle Cletus and Johnny, and I hoped that some day Uncle
Cletus would tell me the story about Uncle Clayton.

Chapter 11

Trouble

THE DAY OF OUR CLASS skating party finally arrived. School seemed to drag on forever. The bus left at 5:30 PM, and it only took thirty minutes to get to Fairview. We had the whole place to ourselves.

Everyone stuck close to the side for the first few rounds. That way, they could grab the rail if they started to fall. Most hadn't skated since last year. Some had never skated. Several kept at least one hand on the rail at all times. Everyone gave Clyde and Everett a wide berth. They'd mash you flat if they fell on you.

There were huge speakers in each corner. They blared thunderous music and an occasional announcement. Something by the Kingston Trio had been playing when we arrived. It was some song about a guy named Tom Dooley getting hung or something. I'd seen them singing it on the Ed Sullivan show. Then, the song "Kicks" by Paul Revere and the Raiders came on, and the volume seemed to turn up.

Kicks just keep getting harder to find,
Before you find out it's too late you better get straight,
But not with Kicks

Something about songs like that made everyone, the boys at least, want to skate faster. Mrs. E had told us that "Kicks" was a drug.

"Change direction," boomed the voice over the speakers. Most of us were having enough trouble making left turns; now we'd have to go to the right. Several kids fell as they tried to turn around. Some hadn't heard the announcement and just kept skating the same direction.

Since Mrs. E had talked about "Kicks" at church, I listened to the words. She'd said it talked about taking drugs. I'd never paid much attention to the words until she mentioned it. It was almost impossible to make right turns and listen to the song.

"When a Man Loves a Woman" by Percy Sledge started playing.

When a man loves a woman, can't keep his mind on nothing else
He'd trade the world for the good thang he's found
If she's bad he can't see it, she can do no wrong
Turn his back on his best friend if he puts her down

I was thinking about Wendy and looking for Melody. She'd mentioned doing the "couples" skate together. I was reaching down and scratching a mosquito bite I'd gotten during the fishing trip when it happened. Everett fell down just a few feet in front of me. I tripped over his leg and went facefirst into the hardwood floor. It happened too fast for me to go around him.

"He's going to need stitches and a-like-a-that," I heard Mrs. E saying. Lying on the floor looking up at the stained and ready-to-fall ceiling tiles, I realized I'd been out for a few seconds, maybe longer. The tissue she was daubing my chin with was soaked with blood. I hoped it wasn't one she'd been toting around all year in her big purse.

The chaperone parents were telling the other kids to get back and give me some air. Melody was the only student standing nearby, and she and Mrs. E were looking at me strangely. "Do you think you can walk?" It seemed like a fairly silly question; of course I could walk.

Melody's dad walked up. "I can take him to the hospital," he said. I felt embarrassed. Mrs. E and Mr. Hinkebien both helped me up. It wasn't until I stood up that I noticed the crotch of my Tuff-Nut jeans was damp and warm. The floor was a little damp where I'd been laying.

Mrs. E put her hand on Mr. Hinkebien's wrist. "I'll call Ellen and Ted," she told him. "I'm sure they'll want a doctor to see Tommy."

Melody's dad looked at Mrs. Hinkebien. "I'll take him to the ER."

"I'll go too," Melody said.

Mr. Hinkebien had driven his car from Colby. He had a Ford Galaxy 500. It had cloth seats, so I had to tell him about my pants. He got an old newspaper from the trunk for me to sit on. I got in the back seat and Melody got in the front.

As soon as the engine started, I could tell he had a 390 cubic inch engine in it, not a small block 289. He pulled out of the parking lot and accelerated hard enough to push me firmly against the back of the seat. I heard the secondary of the four-barrel carburetor opening up. You'd think I was dying, the way he was driving.

Melody handed me another Kleenex. "Here." She didn't look back. I noticed her frowning at her dad. He eased up on the accelerator a little.

I took the fresh Kleenex. "Thanks." The one I'd been using was pretty much soaked with blood. My chin had bled quite a bit and was still oozing.

It only took a few minutes to get to the hospital. Mr. Hinkebien pulled up to the emergency entrance, the same one the ambulances used. I didn't want to, but they made me sit in a wheelchair. I didn't tell them about my other "accident." They'd just have to deal with it, since they made me use the chair.

After we'd waited what seemed like forever in the tiny ER room, the doctor finally showed up. "How'd it happen?" he inquired.

At first, I thought he'd noticed my pants. The way his glasses fit on the end of his nose made him appear to be looking down, toward my crotch region. I looked at his eyes and realized he was looking at my chin.

"I was skatin' and fell." My head was throbbing, and talking made it hurt worse.

Mr. Hinkebien cleared his throat. "Another fellow fell in front of him. Tommy tripped over him and hit facefirst." About that time, a nurse came through the door with a tray full of stainless steel instruments and a syringe.

The doctor picked up the syringe and made the obligatory test squirt. He looked me in the eyes. "This is going to sting a little." Any goof knew that, I wanted to tell him.

Before I could say anything, he'd shoved me down on the table and leaned over me. I could smell his breath. He smoked.

In less than an hour, I'd dreamed of skating with Wendy, fallen and busted my chin wide open, wet my pants, and now some doctor I'd never seen before was jabbing me in the chin with a needle.

By the time the doctor finished tying the knot on the ninth and final stitch, my mom and dad showed up. Mom was worried about me having a scar, and Dad wanted to know how my pants had gotten wet. When he got close enough to smell them, he stopped asking questions.

Mom looked at Mr. Hinkebien and smiled. "We can't thank you enough, Arnold."

"No need to thank me. You would have done the same for Melody."

"We came as soon as Mrs. E called," Dad said. "Thanks."

Mr. Hinkebien gave them an acknowledging nod. "Well, we better get back to the rink. Someone else might have cracked their noggin by now." He opened the door and motioned for Melody to follow. The air coming in from the hallway felt fresh, and cool.

Melody leaned close and whispered in my ear. "We're even."

That night my chin throbbed and I fell asleep thinking not so much about Wendy but mostly about Melody.

I AWOKE THE NEXT MORNING and immediately began thinking about Wendy. Both of my eyes were black and my chin was swollen, but Mom made me go to school anyway. She'd said I couldn't mow if I didn't go to school. We'd had rain over the weekend, so the grass had grown. I went to school.

I was a little groggy from the painkiller, but when I saw Wendy and Beth walking toward the bus stop my senses came alive.

Wendy walked straight over to me with a purpose in her step. "Who'd you skate the double with last night?" Maybe she hadn't noticed my two black eyes and bandaged puffy chin.

"I tripped over Clyde on the first skate, didn't make it to the couples."

"Oh," she said, seeming relieved and in a much better spirit.

"Did you cut your chin when you fell?" She'd finally noticed my wounds.

"Yep, had to go the emergency room and get nine stitches."

"Does it hurt?"

"Not too bad. My mom gave me some aspirins to take."

She gently stroked the side of my head. "You poor thing." I became faint and got a tingling sensation. We were halfway to school before normal breathing returned.

By NOON, MY EYES HAD turned dark blue and my chin throbbed. I'd kept ice on my face all night, but didn't have any at school. I'd taken an aspirin at recess and two at noon. Mrs. E let me lay my head on my desk after lunch and take a nap. She made me stay in for recess; I didn't feel like playing anyway. I took my last aspirin and started feeling a little better by the time school was out.

When I got home, Mom put a new bandage and some salve on my chin and fixed me a bacon and egg sandwich. Before I left to mow, she told me she'd have Dad come check on me when he got home from work. I tried to get her not to, but it was no use. She filled my thermos with ice cubes and water.

By the time I got to Melody's, Booger had the lawn mowers pulled out and had started cleaning the grass off of the bottom of his. Melody was watching him.

"I was startin' to think you weren't comin' an'at," he said. Sweat was already dripping from his chin. "I had a lot of grass under my mower deck. You better check yours. It's better to clean it now before the engine and muffler get hot."

I turned my lawn mower on its side and started peeling off the caked-on grass. Booger picked up both piles of mulch and put them in Melody's burn barrel. The thought struck me that our roles had momentarily reversed; Booger was giving directions and taking the initiative. Melody didn't seem to notice.

Melody looked at me with a knowing grin. "Your eyes are really dark," she said, stating the obvious. "Is everything else okay?" she asked.

"Yeah," I said, unenthusiastically. I wasn't sure if she was talking about my nose or wet pants. The grin on her face looked a little devious.

She moved close enough that I could smell her perfume, a little too close actually. "Mom and I are leaving soon but I made a pitcher of lemonade; it's on the porch. Help yourself."

It was odd sharing such a secret with a girl. I wondered how long it would be before I got over the feeling of Melody having something on me. We were supposed to be even now; she had said it herself. Somehow it seemed she had the advantage.

Dad pulled up just as we were finished mowing and ready to leave. We put our bikes and the gasoline cans in the back of his pickup truck, and he gave us a ride home. He offered to fill the cans up with gasoline and drop them back by Hinkebien's on his way to work the next day.

"Are you going to play baseball this summer?" Mom asked. She'd fixed me a plate of fried baloney, fried potato slices, and slaw. I had a mouthful of buttered bread and had to swallow before I answered her.

"Uh-huh," I said, before taking another bite of buttered bread.

"An announcement in the *Telegraph* said sign-ups were this week." She scooted a plate of fried potatoes my way. "Do you think you're going to have time to mow lawns and play baseball?"

I poured ketchup on the potatoes.

"I think so," I said. "Practices don't usually start until school is out." I spread Miracle Whip on the fried baloney.

"I'll leave you alone while you eat," she said, then went outside and sat on the porch with Dad.

Marsha was sitting at the table doing homework. "They think you're trying to do too much," she said. "Mom doesn't think you should be mowing so many lawns. She told Dad he was a complete idiot for letting you put that Mini-Trail on layaway."

"There are only a few weeks of school left. I'll be okay."

Dad came in from the porch carrying two coffee mugs and sporting a grin; the Olefsens, who lived next door, must have been putting on a show. They'd moved in the summer before and endeared the neighborhood to their Swedish customs, one of which was walking around their house nude, with the shades up. They'd moved here from Maine, where they'd lived near a nudist colony. He headed for the coffee pot. "Got any homework, Tommy?" Everyone had decided to worry about my schoolwork.

"A little, I'll get it done as soon as I'm finished with dinner." He flipped me on the ear and filled the mugs with coffee. I could hear the crickets through the screen door as Marsha and I cleaned up.

He started for the door with the coffee mugs. "Mom said to tell you two to stay in here."

I looked at Marsha and she at me. "Olefsens," we giggled.

The phone rang. Mom answered it and after talking quietly, almost secretly, to the caller, hung up and turned to me. "Booger's going to spend the night. His mom needs to go to the doctor. Get your homework done before he gets here. You can watch *My Three Sons*, and then I want you both in bed."

"What's she goin' to the doctor at night for?" I asked.

"She's been having trouble sleeping, and the doctor wants to run some tests."

Dad came in from the porch. "Why can't they run them tomorrow?"

Mom gave Dad a look. "They're running the tests tonight." Then she looked directly at me. "Now, get that homework finished!"

Nobody asked any more questions. Marsha finished cleaning up the dishes while I did my homework. I was watching out the front door when Booger's dad dropped him off. Booger hadn't even gotten to the porch before his dad backed out of the driveway and sped away. I let him in the door.

"He wants to try and catch th' ambulance an'at," Booger said.

"Ambulance? What ambulance?"

"Dad said Mom took too many of her sleepin' pills, and he couldn't get her to wake up. He called the doctor, and th' doctor called the ambulance. Dad said not to worry; she'll be okay."

Mom gave him an unusually long hug. "I'm sure she'll be just fine at the hospital," she assured him.

Booger seemed okay with that. "Put your things in Tommy's room and make yourself at home." He nodded, walked down the hall to my room, and tossed his overnight bag on the bed.

Mom fixed us some popcorn. We shared it with Marsha while watching *My Three Sons*. Marsha liked Chip. He reminded her of Mickey. We waited for Booger's dad to call from the hospital, but the phone never rang.

That night I prayed for two things: the chance to make Booger laugh, and that his mom would get better.

Chapter 12

Laugh

THE NEXT MORNING, MOM TOLD Booger that his dad had called with good news; his mom would be coming home in a few days. Booger and I walked to the bus stop together. Even with the good news, he wore a worried look. By now, 'most everybody knew she was having some problems; news spread quickly in Colby. Wendy and a couple of the other girls stood huddled at the bus stop. As soon as we got there, Wendy turned, smiled, and handed me her flute. She asked Booger how his mom was doing. He didn't seem to mind the question and told Wendy that his mom was doing okay and would be better soon. He also told her that his mom just needed a little more time to get over losing Johnny.

Mrs. E. took Booger out of class an hour before lunch. He rejoined the class at lunch. He told me that a counselor from Fairview had talked to him about his mom. I'd never heard of a counselor coming from Fairview to talk to kids who weren't in trouble.

After school, we rode our bikes to Melody's. On the way there, Booger talked and I listened. "It looks like my aunt Penelope is gonna move in with us for a while." He'd told everyone his mom was doing okay. I was suspicious. "She's probably glad to get away from Uncle Norman an'at for a while anyway."

Aha, now we're getting to it, I thought.

Booger continued. "He's more nervous than a fryin' grasshopper. She's a good cook. He's just a creep. Did you ever notice how he's always scratchin' or diggin' around on himself?"

He clearly thought more of his aunt than he did of his uncle and was definitely looking forward to the meals. It was an assessment with which I agreed.

Our lawn mowers usually ran out of gas at about the same time. As I pushed mine back to the shed to fill it up, I noticed Brother Baker talking to Booger in the front yard. It didn't look like he'd gotten much mowing done.

Melody was waiting with our lemonades. "He's been talking to Booger for almost thirty minutes," Melody said. "I heard him say that all the things that have been happening to his family are part of God's plan."

I started their way. Melody followed with the lemonades. I wanted to see if Brother Baker thought Booger finishing the yard in time to go to church was part of God's plan.

He extended his hand. I shook it vigorously and squeezed it hard, like Dad had taught me. "Hello there, Tommy, Melody. I was just getting ready to come visit with both of you, too. I wanted to make sure you kids would be at church tonight. A missionary who has been serving the Lord in Africa will be there."

"I guess the only thing standin' in the way of Booger and me goin' to church is this lawn." It was a thick hint. "Mom told me about the missionary after I got home from school today and said not to be lollygaggin' around. We're planning on bein' there if we get our work done." Dad had told me that with preachers you needed to be straightforward and forthright. I could be straightforward; I wasn't sure what a forthright was.

"Well then. I look forward to seeing you there." He'd gotten the hint.

"Yes, sir. We'll be there." He tipped his hat and started toward his car.

"I brought you a glass of lemonade, Brother Baker," Melody said, more soprano than usual.

"Oh, no, thanks. I have to get going. No lollygagging, just like Tommy says."

He smiled, tipped his hat again, and trotted toward his car. Booger drank both his and Brother Baker's lemonade. Talking to the preacher must have made him thirsty. He hadn't done enough mowing to work up a thirst.

Melody looked at the unfinished lawn and smiled right at me. "I guess it's no big deal if you don't finish until tomorrow."

"Yeah, you're right," I agreed. "There isn't really anything good on TV tomorrow night. I hope that missionary doesn't go too long tonight, though. I'd like to get home in time to watch *Batman*."

BOOGER AND I RODE OUR bikes to church. Dad said he'd bring us home in the pickup. We were standing under the Osage Orange tree stomping hedge apples when Booger's mom and dad and his aunt Penelope arrived. The hugging and crying started the minute Mrs. Burger stepped out of the car. The men shook Booger's dad's hands and slapped him on the shoulder. The women dabbed their eyes with well-used tissues and slobbered all over each other. It'd be a wonder if everyone didn't catch something the way they went on.

Brother Baker introduced the missionaries, Dr. Artimus and Martha Thomas, or Artie and Marty.

"Rhymes with farty," Booger whispered in my ear. I giggled a little too loud; Mom pinched my arm. Artie was thin and had a long mustache which drooped on each side of his mouth. Dad later described Marty as a little fleshy. She wore a white pith helmet.

Artie did most of the talking. They both had strong British accents. He got everyone's attention, especially mine, when he unrolled a snakeskin that stretched all of the way from the pulpit to the back pew. It must have been at least thirty feet long. It didn't come as a big surprise to me, though. Since he was wearing funny-looking pants like the guy on *Wild Kingdom*, I knew something was up.

The slides we saw were really neat. He showed us the villages they worked in and pictures of people who'd been treated at their clinic. He didn't ask for money, just prayer. He said he knew the Lord would provide for their needs. Dad said later that that's when he knew the guy was for real.

During the question and answer time, Monkey Fullbright raised his hand. "Is it difficult living in the jungle and giving up modern conveniences?"

Artie answered by quoting a former missionary, Jim Elliott. "He is no fool who gives up what he cannot keep to gain what he cannot lose."

This didn't really answer how *he* felt, but it was certainly food for thought. Uncle Cletus later told me that Jim Elliott had been boiled and eaten by a gang of Indians somewhere in the Amazon jungle, which caused mixed emotions on my part. Getting eaten by a bunch of natives seemed a bit foolish.

Booger and his mom and dad and aunt came by our house after church. We got home in time to see the last few minutes of *Batman* and the preview for the next week. The grown-ups drank coffee and ate gingerbread cookies and celery and pimento cheese. Booger and I had once made an oath to never eat pimento cheese. We'd agreed that even chickens wouldn't eat that stuff. Then we did some figuring.

Dad had brought home the invoices for the Lawn-Boys. They had come to just a little under $75 each, including sales tax. We were each making roughly $12.50 a week on the three lawns. If we used all of our money to pay off the Lawn-Boys, it'd take us six weeks. Dad said we should count on about twenty weeks of lawn mowing. That's about the average, he'd said. That meant we'd only have about fourteen weeks left over after paying for the lawn mowers. That would only be $175 each. That wasn't going to be enough to pay off the Honda Mini-Trails, let alone pay for any gasoline or have any extra spending money. We wouldn't be able to get any more lawns until school was out. By then they'd probably all be taken, at least the good ones. Marsha may have been right about men getting to the moon before I got a Honda Mini-Trail. But then, she was basing her opinion of me on her observation of Mickey.

WHEN WE GOT TO CLASS the next morning, the blackboard read, "Mrs. E is ill today. Please make welcome Miss Crawford." "Crazy Crawford" is what we called her amongst ourselves. She'd been an elementary teacher for a hundred or so years. Her best years were behind her; now she just substituted.

According to rumor, she had a panther living in her house. I'd never seen a panther, but she had more cats than I'd ever seen in one place. I doubted she had any problems with mice.

She'd probably started the rumor to keep Milton Merle away. Milton was an old coot who lived next door to her and had a reputation for being a Peeping Tom. I'd seen him around town more than once with a bandage on his head. Mom had seen him stealing her underwear off of the clothesline once, but never told Dad. Milton had been retired since forever. I don't remember hearing what it was he did when he did work, or if he ever did. Dad once used Milton as an example of what a "reprobate" was to Marsha.

Mom said Mrs. Crawford's husband hadn't been from around here, and one day he'd just up and left. Dad said he'd seen him once or twice work-ing at a service station in Fairview, kind of a goofy-looking guy with an overbite and no chin, is how Dad described him.

"Good morning, ladies and gentlemen." That's how she always greeted us. She went on to tell us why she referred to us as ladies and gentlemen. It had something to do with treating us with respect, which is how she expected to be treated. We'd heard it all before.

Her hair was pulled tight into a ball centered on the back of her tiny head. She had a pin of some sort sticking through the ball. Her dress had too many buttons. They stretched all of the way from the bottom to the top. Since they were on the back of the dress, I figured they had to be a pain to get buttoned. She was really thin, hardly big enough to cast a shadow. Her feet were tiny. Her shoes would probably fit inside mine.

"I'd like to start our day by reading a poem by Rudyard Kipling."

She always read to us poems by Rudyard Kipling or Henry Wadsworth Longfellow. I had a copy of "If" framed and hanging in my bedroom, right next to my desk. Mamaw and Papaw Thompson had given it to me for a birthday gift. "Paul Revere's Ride" was my favorite poem by Longfellow. She started with "If." She'd get to Longfellow before the morning was over.

I kind of liked the poems, but kept that small fact to myself. I noticed Everett picking at a scab on his ankle while Miss Crawford read. All of the girls were paying attention. Most of the guys were having a hard time staying awake. Caleb was scratching some chigger bites.

"Please get out your history books," she said, waking the boys and dis-appointing the girls. This meant we were going to read in unison. She always did this, too. If she caught anyone not participating, she'd make them read aloud by themselves. It was always a time of great embarrass-ment for some of the guys.

"I think she's got 'er dress on back'ards," Everett whispered from across the aisle.

"Turn to the beginning of chapter twenty-eight. It's near the end of the book," she said.

"What makes you think that?" I whispered back.

"Well, for one thing there's all of them buttons. It seems like dresses with 'at many buttons have 'em in the front. And another thing, there's them little pointy things stickin' out on th' back. I think they're s'posed to be in the front."

"All together now," she said. Everyone started reading, but not at the same time.

"Stop! Stop!" she said and clapped her hands. "That sounded like several solos. I'm looking for a chorus. Now, let's try it once again." This time, Miss Crawford held her arms up like a music conductor and started us reading. We only read a couple of paragraphs and got saved by the bell.

"Let's ask Melody," I suggested during recess. We walked over to where the girls were. A couple of the other guys had heard Everett and me talking and came with us; even Clyde was interested.

"We were just talkin' about that," Melody said after I'd shared Everett's observation with her. Suddenly, we were all anxious for recess to be over. That was a first.

As we filed back in, the girls were looking at each other and giggling. Melody had given me a confirmation nod. After looking closer, it was obvious Miss Crawford's dress was on backwards. I could see where she'd worn it the right way before and wrinkled it when she'd sat down. The wrinkled area was now in the front.

Miss Crawford saw some of the girls giggling and thought they had been amused because she was trying to teach us arithmetic. She didn't seem to know any more about it than Everett.

"Well, I'm sure Mrs. Enderle is quite capable of teaching you all the fundamentals of the numbers," she said, finally giving up. "Please get out your geography books." We spent the rest of the morning reading in unison about Venezuela, Chile, and Ecuador. She played an album by a group from Ecuador. I didn't recognize any of the songs. It was mostly somebody playing a pan flute.

The word had spread. At lunchtime, girls from the other classes were coming up to Mrs. Crawford, saying hello, and patting her on the shoulder. They'd walk away giggling. I could tell Mrs. Crawford thought they were glad to see her. She had no idea they were making fun of her. I was starting to feel a little guilty about the whole thing until I noticed Booger giggling. We made eye contact, and he busted out laughing. It was the first time he'd belly-laughed since Johnny. We had a good laugh at Crazy Crawford's expense, but somehow it seemed okay.

Chapter 13

Ambushed

THE NEXT DAY WE FINISHED Melody's yard and started on Mr. Thorpe's. I explained to him how we'd had to quit early the night before so that we could make it to church on time. He said he understood and that if we needed to, we could finish his lawn on Friday. He'd been out of town and had missed the missionary show. I told him about the snakeskin.

Not having to push the Lawn-Boys home every night was a break. Dad had filled up our gas cans and put them in Melody's garage. The only thing we had to carry back and forth was our thermos jug. We had it made.

We finished Mr. Thorpe's yard and hustled home before dark. When I got in the house, Mom said Booger's mom had called and asked if I could come over for dinner. Booger's aunt Penelope had fixed beans and ham hocks and cornbread, my favorite. I got cleaned up in record time.

I love cornbread and beans. My mouth was watering so much I had to spit a couple of times on the way over to Booger's house. I tested the light on my bike to make sure it was working. Since the skies were overcast, I knew it'd be pitch dark on my way home.

Mrs. Burger answered the door. "Hello, Tommy. I'm so glad you could come over." She seemed fairly normal, in a good mood. Her engaging smile caused her eyes to twinkle.

Booger's Aunt was in the kitchen. The volume on the radio was turned way up. They were listening to KXOK. I could smell the cornbread. "Randy's in his bedroom doing his homework. Go on in and see if he needs any help," Mrs. Burger said on her way back to the kitchen.

"Yes, ma'am." I watched as she sort of danced her way back to the kitchen.

The bathroom door was open. Mr. Burger was shaving. He had a few hairs in the middle of his chest, nothing like Uncle Cletus. The radio was so loud he hadn't heard me. It gave him a start when he saw me standing in the hall; he cut himself.

"Hey, Tommy," he said. I didn't hear you come in." He grimaced each time he dabbed the cut with his styptic pencil. "Randy's in his room."

Booger's door was open. I stuck my head in. He was hunkered at his desk as I spoke first. "Watcha doin'?"

He looked up. "I'm diagrammin' 'ose stupid sentences." During the time Booger missed school we had worked on diagramming sentences. He was still catching up. It was pretty simple, but they took a long time to do. With Melody's help, I'd gotten a hundred on mine.

"That cornbread is makin' my mouth water," I told him. The entire house smelled like fresh-baked cornbread. I stood at Booger's bedroom doorway. He had a new bookshelf, and all of Johnny's stuff was on it. It looked like he'd been sleeping in Johnny's bed. He was getting better at dealing with Johnny's death. An envelope with "lawn money" written on it was propped up on his desk.

"It's good," Booger said after a moment, without looking up, referring to the cornbread. He laid down his pencil and turned my way. "Aunt Penelope brought some of her homemade strawberry jelly an'at too." His eyes enlarged involuntarily when he spoke.

"Is your Uncle Norman going to be here?"

"Nope, just us."

"Good. I mean, well, there'll be more cornbread for us."

"Yeah, plus he's such a squirrel. Aunt Penelope ought to run 'im off and marry your Uncle Cletus." Booger's mom called us to dinner. Booger's last remark had taken me by surprise. The thought had never occurred to me; they'd make a good pair though, I supposed.

Mr. Burger said the blessing while we all held hands. He prayed for the missionaries and the boys in Vietnam, their families, and thanked the Lord for the food. As soon as he was finished, Mrs. Burger put a Henry Mancini album on the hi-fi. I'd heard some of the songs at the movies, mostly during Pink Panther cartoons. I told them about the album that Crazy Crawford had played.

"Well, that figures," said Mr. Burger.

We had bowls for our beans and ham and a small plate for the cornbread. Mr. Burger put his cornbread in with his beans and ham. Mrs.

Burger put her cornbread in a bowl and poured buttermilk on it. It was disgusting; I tried to ignore it. Booger's aunt Penelope put butter and jelly on her cornbread; she was cool. She smiled and winked at me as she was taking a bite piled high with homemade jelly. She and Uncle Cletus would get along fine. I ate two bowls of beans and ham. Aunt Penelope, Booger, and I ate the cornbread until it was all gone. We ran out of strawberry jelly and finished up the cornbread using some apple butter Booger's aunt Penelope had brought on an earlier visit.

Booger and I helped her do the dishes. She was surprised I knew how. When Mr. and Mrs. Burger went outside to sit on the porch, Aunt Penelope put a Beatles album on the hi-fi. "Penny Lane" was the first song. She moved to the beat of the music. I'd seen Mom do that when she didn't know I was watching. She kept telling us we didn't need to help, but we did anyway. She and Booger's mom were fun.

Just before I left, Mrs. Burger said she'd call my mom and let her know I was on my way home. I flipped the generator down against my tire and headed home. Colby was so quiet I could hear the hum of the generator. It barely produced enough electricity to power my headlight and taillight. The ad in the magazine had led me to believe it would work much better than it really did. My dad had been right when he told me the light wouldn't be as bright as it looked in the advertisement.

I let Mom know I was home, then went over to Mamaw and Papaw's to sit on the porch. Papaw had already smoked his cigarette and was snoozing. Mamaw and I listened to the night noises.

I opened the window in my bedroom before going to bed. Every once in a while, I could hear a car peeling out. Guys with cars that would peel out sat around at Burt's after he closed. I'd seen them there before on the way home from ball games. If Johnny had made it home, he'd be there with his Chevelle.

THE NEXT MORNING, WENDY WAS at the bus stop when I got there. She handed me her flute and smiled. "Good morning, Tommy." Her smile nearly caused me to swallow my tongue.

"Hi, Wendy." I had to concentrate on getting the words out without stuttering.

"Beth is having a party tomorrow night. She invited Marsha. There are going to be boys there, too. My mom and dad are going to be there. They said you could come, too." She said it loud enough for everyone in the world to hear. My mouth got so dry my lips stuck to my teeth. "You feel okay?" I nodded my head yes. I felt a little dizzy. I think I forgot to breathe. I made a gasping noise when my lips finally opened.

"I'll have to ask," I managed to say, barely above a whisper. I looked around. Beth and Wendy were standing together. Their Jungle Gardenia was captivating. I kept moving downwind of them, staying in the scent stream. I'd be able to get a bottle of Jade East now that I had some money, I remember thinking. "What other boys will be there?"

"Beth asked Billy Burke, and Marsha's bringing Mickey." They were both football players. "Mostly she just asked a few girls, and each one may ask one boy. I'm asking you." She rocked back and forth, heel to toe, when she spoke.

"What are we gonna do at the party?" I asked, having already decided to go.

"Play games and records. Dad's going to build a fire, and we're going to roast hot dogs and marshmallows." The hot dogs sounded good, but I'd never seen much sense in sticking a blazing ball of sugar in my mouth. It didn't really sound like that much fun. But there was always the chance that the older boys might do something really stupid if they got to daring each other. That made it worth going to see.

"I already asked. Mom and Dad said you could go," said Marsha. She'd just walked up and heard us talking. "We talked about it last night while you were at Booger's."

I felt like I'd just been ambushed. "Why didn't you tell me about it this morning?"

"Well, I thought it appropriate for Wendy to ask you." She could have at least told me. I could have pretended not to know or something; I felt betrayed by Marsha. The three of them were standing together. I was outnumbered. "You can walk over with Mickey and me."

"It starts at six," said Wendy. I hadn't actually said I'd go yet.

Caleb and Booger were standing a few feet away giggling. They hadn't heard everything, but they'd heard enough.

"You can kiss 'at lemonade goodbye if you go t'at party," Booger whispered to me. We got on the bus. He sat down in the front seat with Caleb. I went on back and sat across from Beth and Wendy. What did my going to Wendy's hot dog roast have to do with Melody giving us lemonade?

I looked up in the mirror as I considered what he'd said. Caleb had one finger knuckle-deep digging away in his nose.

MELODY HAD WORN HER POLKA dotted dress to school. She was wearing Saddle Oxfords instead of sandals. I wondered if her second toes were touching the ends of her shoes. She handed me a note and two pieces of Super Bubble Gum before class started. Super Bubble was a bigger piece of gum than Bazooka, but there wasn't a comic strip inside.

> Dear Tommy,
>
> My dad said that you and Booger are doing a great job on our lawn. He's very happy. I cleaned up your lawn mower. Hope you like the Super Bubble.
>
> Yours truly,
> Melody

She was watching me read the note and smiled when I looked her way. I folded up the note and put it in my pocket. Mrs. E started class. She had her dress on the right way.

AFTER SCHOOL, MOM TOOK ME to the health clinic to get my stitches out. It didn't hurt as much as I thought it might. The worst part was the yellow stinky stuff they put on afterward; the nurse said it was disinfectant. Somebody needs to invent some that's a different color. I suggested red; at least that was our school's color.

Chapter 14

The Truth

SINCE IT WAS SATURDAY, BOOGER and I slept until eight. Marsha had mowed our yard on Friday, so it was my turn to clip; Booger said he'd help. Mom said we could wait until the dew dried. She fixed us pancakes while we watched cartoons. We made paper airplanes and took turns wearing my cowboy hat when *Sky King* was on. Penny reminded me a little of Wendy, and Booger thought Uncle Cletus looked like Schuyler King.

As soon as we finished clipping, we rode our bikes to the drug store. Both moms had given us permission to get a bottle of Jade East. Five-ounce bottles were on sale for $5. That sounded like a lot of money, but Mickey had said a five-ounce bottle would last Booger and me over a year, since neither of us were shaving or dating yet.

They had some new stuff called English Leather. Booger and I used the sample bottles to squirt ourselves with. It had a strong musky odor. We took the bottles of Jade East to the counter. It came to $5.15 with tax. We'd both only brought five one-dollar bills with us. They put thirty cents on my mom's account and told me to be sure and tell her.

On the way home, we ran into the gang. "I could smell you half a block away," Everett said. He, Flop, and Caleb had been hanging out by Dino.

"We stopped by the drug store and squirted ourselves with the samples," Booger confessed. We'd agreed not to tell anyone about the Jade East. They'd all want to borrow it.

"We're gonna shoot the potato gun. Wanna come along?" Caleb asked.

"Sure. We need to run by my house and tell my mom," I said. They hadn't noticed or asked about the brown paper bag in my basket.

"Meet us at Dino," Caleb said.

———————

MOM WASN'T TOO EXCITED ABOUT our plans to shoot the potato gun. "I'm not sure about this potato launcher." The gun had always been called a launcher around her. "Where are you going to shoot with it, or launch, or whatever?"

"I don't know, they didn't say. Prob'ly at the school ground or in Caleb's backyard."

"Well, be careful and be back by noon, and I'll fix you some lunch." She gave us an "I mean business" look. After Booger walked out, she grabbed my shirt collar and told me to be sure and not get Booger hurt. "His mom has all she can handle the way it is." That explained the look.

THEY WERE WAITING FOR US when we got to Dino.

"Where are we gonna shoot it at?" Booger asked.

Caleb gave us an impish look. "That'll be a surprise."

Booger looked at Flop. "I don't know what they've got planned. Don't be a *lookin'* at me," Flop said, defensively. He shrugged his shoulders when I looked at him. "They just told me to meet 'em here."

Something was up.

Caleb got on his bike to lead the way. "Let's go." He and Everett whispered something to each other. We all followed. They rode down the street a ways, turned up an alley, then down another, and ended up behind Burt's. A tall plank fence surrounded his back lot. The gate was locked, but we squeezed through. It was a small area full of weeds, empty five-gallon gear-grease cans, and a big pile of gravel with a willow oak growing out of it. I was surprised that Burt would let his back lot get so grown up.

"Get up on 'at gravel pile and be our spotter," Caleb ordered me with a bossy tone.

"Spotter fer what?" I asked.

"Tell me if you can see 'ose old coots sittin' over at th' court house." I climbed the gravel pile and held on to the willow oak to keep from sliding back down. From there I could see the front and side yard of the courthouse. Monkey, Fish, and Rabbit were sitting on the liar's bench. Bem was pacing back and forth in front of the other three, probably telling a story of some sort.

"Do you see 'em?" Caleb asked.

"Yeah, they're just sittin' there."

"Like-a-said, I don't think this is a good idea," Flop warned. He started creeping backwards toward the gate.

"What's not a good idea?" I asked.

"They're gonna try and hit those guys with a tater," Flop confessed. I'd thought it strange that Caleb had led us all to the back of Burt's. There really wasn't any place to shoot here, yet they'd started getting the gun ready to shoot as soon as we'd gotten there.

Flop was wringing his hands, and his voice had taken on a higher pitch than normal. "They've been talkin' about doing this ever since we started target practicin'. Caleb and Everett had walked off the distance from the liar's bench to a couple of places. They decided this is the best spot. With all of the noise goin' on at the station, nobody would be able to hear the blast." Everett and Caleb ignored him.

"Are we lined up okay?" Caleb asked. He and Everett were squatted next to the gun, holding it at an angle pointed toward the courthouse. Both of them looked at me for directions. Booger was shaking his head and backing toward the gate where Flop was already standing.

I let go of my grip on the willow oak and slid down the gravel pile. "You guys are nuts." Then all of a sudden—Kaboom! They shot it anyway.

Being confined in a small area, the sound was a lot louder and reverberated off the wooden fence and the back wall of Burt's garage. My ears rang. Flop and Booger tried to squeeze through the gate at the same time. Caleb and Everett were scrambling around, gathering their stuff. Everett stepped into an empty five-gallon can, and it got stuck on his foot. Before I squeezed through the gate, he kicked the can off, and it bounced off Burt's brick wall and settled in some weeds. Everett's pants and left shoe had oil and grease smeared all over them.

I caught up with Flop and Booger. We didn't wait for Caleb and Everett.

Booger bopped Flop on the back of the head. "Why didn't you tell us what they were gonna do, ya idiot?"

"I didn't think they'd really do it. Where do you think 'at tater went?" He wore a terrified expression.

"I don't know. With any luck it mighta' landed in some treetops," I said, more hoping than really believing.

It was clearly a case of Caleb, Everett, and Flop having too much time on their hands. Booger and I hadn't helped the matter any by building them the potato gun and, in fact, were probably accessories to the crime, or so Perry Mason might say.

We were near Melody's house, so we stopped and showed Flop the Lawn-Boys. Melody had shined them up; they looked new. Flop talked like he'd like to mow lawns, too, but doubted his mom would ever let him. If she had any sense, she would; at least it would keep him out of trouble.

I knocked on the door to see if Melody was home. Her mom said she was at piano lessons.

"How many times a week does she go?" I asked.

"Twice."

"And she practices on top of that, too?" I asked.

"That's right." She smiled. It didn't seem to help, I thought.

"Do her fingers ever get tired?" I asked.

"She doesn't complain." The smile may have turned to a frown.

"Well, tell her we stopped by and said thanks a lot for shining up our Lawn-Boys."

"I'll be sure and let her know you came by. She'll be sorry she missed you."

BOOGER AND FLOP CALLED THEIR moms and got permission to have lunch at my house. Mom fried up some bologna. She'd gotten it sliced extra thick. Flop had never eaten fried bologna before. He tried one sandwich with Miracle Whip and one with ketchup, just like Booger and me. For dessert, I sliced off several pieces of butter and mixed them together with some syrup and spread it on toast. Flop had never had that either. Mom peeled and sliced each of us an apple. She let us put peanut butter on each slice to help get it down.

After lunch, Booger and I tightened and oiled our chains and made sure the pressure in our tires was perfect. We checked Flop's bike for him. He'd eaten too much for lunch and just sat in the porch swing and watched us. He let us take turns riding his three-speed. The thin tires made the bumps seem worse, but I could tell the extra gears would be nice on the hills. I hadn't had a chance to see how it rode except when I was chasing Pokey, which wasn't a good test.

Booger's mom called and said they were home, so Booger got his stuff together and headed that way. Flop left with him. We hadn't talked any-more about the potato gun deal.

Mom walked out onto the porch after they'd left. She was wearing a smile; something was up. "Don't you have something to tell me?"

I hadn't heard the phone ring. Maybe someone had called while we were riding Flop's bike. Mom had a way of finding out everything sooner or later. I told her the whole story. She frowned several times. The look on her face became more serious. I felt a lot better after I'd finished.

"Well, Tommy, I'm glad you told me about the potato gun. I was wor-ried those boys might be up to something, and I'll have to call their moth-ers, but that's not what I was talking about."

"That's all there is to it, Mom. I told you the whole truth." Whatever she'd been told, it wasn't the truth.

"I was wanting to know if you were going to tell us about Wendy asking you to Beth's party?" I'd forgotten all about the party even though that's why I'd wanted to get the Jade East.

"Marsha said she already asked." I couldn't believe I'd just spilled the beans about the potato gun; my mind started racing; my mouth got a sour taste.

"She told us Wendy was going to ask you and that you could go with her and Mickey. We hadn't heard yet if Wendy had asked you. We were waiting for you to tell us."

I was confused. My neck had gotten warm while I was telling Mom about the potato gun. Now my ears were warm, too. I'd rather have been mowing in knee-deep chigger-infested weeds than having this conversa-tion. Now everybody was going to get into trouble because of my big fat mouth.

"Wendy said I could come with Marsha and Mickey. I told her I'd have to ask. Marsha said you and Dad said it would be okay. I haven't thought about it since then."

"Going to a party like that is a pretty big deal."

"Well, I did think about it. That's why I wanted to get the Jade East. I'm going to wear it tonight."

"Do you think your dad and I should let you go, considering the potato gun thing?" I hated those types of questions.

"I don't know. I didn't really do anything."

"Don't you think you should have told me without me asking?"

"I guess so." I knew I should have, but if I'd said yes she would have asked me why I didn't, and I didn't have an answer for that, either. My stomach was starting to hurt a little. I burped up a little of the bologna and swallowed it back down.

"Well, I'm going to talk to your dad about what we should do. He should be home anytime." She went back inside. I put a piece of Clove chewing gum in my mouth. The gravel on the driveway was messed up a little, so I raked it smooth and was sweeping the carport when Dad got home.

Dad pulled up and got out of his truck. "You in some sort of trouble?" He could always tell.

"Maybe," I mumbled.

He half-smiled. "Well, either you are or you're not. Which is it?" I told him what had happened. He was going to hear from Mom anyway. "Let's go in and see what your mother has to say." He squeezed my shoulder and scratched the back of my head. He took his Mason work shoes off before going into the house. He always did. Sometimes they had grease on them. I took my shoes off, too, hoping to pick up a few points.

Mom was hanging up the phone when we walked in. She gave Dad a hug. She had one hand on her hip, and the other was pointing at me. "He's *your* son."

"Yeah, he told me what happened."

"I just got off of the phone with Everett's dad. He was at the court-house this morning and said that as far as he knew, no one had noticed a flying potato. He said he thought that it had probably landed in one of the big maple trees. I didn't call Randy's mom. I don't think I will."

"Tommy, why don't you run out on the porch, and let your mom and me talk about the situation." I went out and sat on the porch. I was holding my ear to the door, but couldn't hear them. A scab on my kneecap was about ready, so I went ahead and pulled it off. It had been itching. I was squeezing the circle of new skin and watching the blood ooze out when they both came out onto the porch.

"Okay, there needs to be some sort of consequence for your behavior today," Dad said. I could tell Mom had told him what to say. "We'll give you a choice. You can miss the party tonight or go without your bicycle for a week."

"I'll miss th' party." I may have said it too quickly, judging by the looks on their faces. They looked at each other. I gave my kneecap one last squeeze and stood up. "I need my bike t' go t' work. I don't need t' go t' the party. I'd rather miss one party than have t' walk over to Melody's t' mow ever' day." They looked surprised that I had made my mind up so quickly. "What would you do, Dad?"

"I guess I'd choose the bike, too."

"There ya' go," I said with a grin.

"Are you gonna call Flop's mom?" I asked.

"Well, actually, she called here earlier. Billy was complaining about a stomach ache. He told her what he'd eaten, and she called to see if she'd understood him correctly. She'd never heard of eating fried bologna or syrup and butter. I told her that's what we'd had for lunch, and she said, 'Well, it's a wonder,' and hung up. No, I didn't tell her about the potato gun."

"Do you think Everett will be in much trouble?"

"I doubt it. His dad didn't seem too bothered. I doubt he'll say anything to Everett." That was good, I figured.

Missing the party wasn't much of a sacrifice. I had all summer to visit with Wendy, and I could do it when there weren't a bunch of strutting football players around.

Papaw was walking toward the chicken house; I ran over and helped him scatter feed corn to them. I learned that the best way to keep from getting flogged was to throw the corn way out. I told Papaw about the potato gun deal.

"You got to be careful 'bout who you hang around with. Don't fret on it, though. I could tell you a few stories about your dad."

We sat on the cistern and talked politics. LBJ was sending more troops to Vietnam; it was a difficult time to be a Democrat, he confessed. Papaw showed me how to roll a cigarette, but told me again not to start smoking. It was a confusing moment.

Chapter 15

The Party

Our only telephone hung on the kitchen wall next to the refrigerator; everyone in the house could hear what was being said on it. I'd never called a girl on it before and didn't have any plans to start.

"You think I could ride my bike over to Wendy's house and tell her I can't come to the party?" I pleaded with Mom.

"Why don't you just call her?"

"Don't you think this is something I need to tell her in person?"

"I don't know. Why?"

"Well, I'd just feel better doing it in person." Using the phone, centered in the house, was out of the question.

She stopped peeling potatoes, rested her hands on the sink, looked out the window, and seemed to be deep in thought. I hadn't thought it was that tough of a question. We weren't contemplating a trip to the moon or anything.

"Okay, you can ride your bike over, but be back in an hour. Go straight over there and straight back," she said, jabbing the paring knife in the air as she spoke, accentuating every word. The dishtowel that had been hanging on her arm fell to the floor. I reached down, picked it up, and handed it to her. She took it, did a forced exhale, and patted me on the head. Her hands were wet with potato juice, and now so was my hair.

"Thanks, Mom. I'll come straight back." I went to my room and got a hat before heading to Wendy's house. I used the first two drops of my Jade East and, without thinking, put on my Bazooka Joe T-shirt.

I took my time riding over to Wendy's. I practiced over and over telling her I couldn't come to the party.

Breathing in the scent of fresh-mowed grass, I saw the half-wit twins mowing Mrs. Whitener's yard. They had no doubt been working on it all day with their reel mowers. It looked like they were doing a good job for her, and that was good.

As I neared Wendy's house, I could see ribbons tied around the trunks of almost every tree in her front yard. Her front porch had streamers stretching from post to post. I stood at the front door a few seconds before mustering the courage to knock.

Mrs. Winchester answered the door. "Hello, Tommy. I'm so glad you could come to the party. Aren't you a little early, though?"

"Yes, ma'am. May I speak to Wendy?"

"Certainly," she said, too enthusiastically. "They're in the backyard decorating. Come on through the house." She led me through the house to the back door. "You've got company," she announced to Beth and Wendy.

She held open the back door for me. "Thanks."

Wendy and Beth were both wearing cut-offs. Everything I'd rehearsed on the way over suddenly escaped me. My mind was void of any complete thought.

They'd decorated their picnic table and a couple of card tables with crepe paper and streamers. Stuck in the ground off each corner of the patio were tiki lanterns, but they weren't lit. There were two TV dinner stands setting next to the house. One had a vertical paper towel holder, and in place of a role of paper towels was a stack of 45-rpm records; a record player was on the other. "Don't Mess with Bill" by the Marvelettes was playing. Beth's boyfriend's name was Billy.

Wendy came bouncing my way in a half-skip. "You're early, but that's okay; you can help us decorate." She came closer and whispered, "She's been playing that song all afternoon." She leaned closer and sniffed my neck. "Ooh, Jade East!" I got goose bumps the size of red-hots, and a tingling sensation.

I staggered backwards. "I can't come t' th' party." A split second after I'd blurted it out, I realized I hadn't said hello or anything yet. She'd been doing all of the talking. Her shoulders slumped, and the corners of her mouth lost that acute upward curve.

"What do you mean you can't come? You're here!"

"I know. I'm here to tell you that I can't come t' th' party." We walked around in the yard, and I explained.

"You need to stop hanging around with those guys if they're going to get you into trouble," she admonished. That was the same thing my mom had said. "We're about finished here. Let me see if I can ride my bike halfway to your house."

We rode together and talked. I found it easier to talk to her when we were riding. At the halfway point we stopped. She touched my chest and sent a tingle down my spine. "I like that T-shirt. Where'd you get it?"

"It was a prize in the states-and-capitals quiz contest." Not exactly the whole truth.

"Oh, I remember that from last year. Mrs. E is really cool sometimes. That's so neat that you won it." She turned to pedal home. "I'm sorry you can't come to the party. I'll see you Monday."

I didn't start home until she was half a block away. I hadn't said that I'd won it. Why do things always seem to get so complicated? I wondered. I hoped that she'd soon forget about the T-shirt.

MARSHA TOLD ME ABOUT THE party while we fixed Sunday breakfast. A thunderstorm had passed over town just after everyone had arrived, and they had to move inside. The rain had been good for Mamaw and Papaw's garden but had put a pretty big damper on the party. Things worked out. Most of the boys left after they'd eaten all of the food. Beth and Wendy's folks let those who hung around play their 45s on the hi-fi.

"Cecil Becker and Wendy seemed to hit it off pretty good." I got that dizzy feeling again but didn't say anything.

"Somebody called and asked for you."

"Who?"

"I don't know. Beth answered the phone and said she could barely hear what they were saying. She said she thought that it was a girl but couldn't tell; the voice was muffled."

"What did they want?"

"Beth said she thought they'd just wanted to know if you were there." I'd never had a girl call me.

The coffee pot stopped percolating. I called for Mom and Dad and didn't give the phone call much further thought.

"Artie and Marty are going to be speaking to the congregation this morning," Dad said during breakfast. I, surprisingly, found myself looking forward to seeing them again.

Chapter 16

Carnival

ARTIE AND MARTY CAME TO our Sunday school class opening. Artie recognized Booger and me and asked us to help him stretch out the snakeskin. Since there were several kids in church on Sunday that hadn't been there on Wednesday, they showed some of the same slides again. Marty wore her pith helmet for effect.

After the opening, Mrs. E let Booger and me wash our hands before going to Sunday school. The snakeskin stunk, but the soap in the dispenser wasn't much better. During Sunday school, I noticed Booger smelling his fingers every once in a while. Mine still stunk, too.

I fought sleep during the worship service, barely staying awake; it must have been from eating too many pancakes. Brother Baker's sermon was hard to follow, but he got the message across loud and clear. He expected people to be in church on Wednesday night and did his best to convince us that God did, too. He was particularly sensitive because the carnival was coming to town that week. He made it clear he thought everyone ought to be giving their extra money to the missionaries and not wasting it on rides, candy, and games. It was the same message he'd given last year before the carnival, only with a missionary twist.

MOM WAS ALREADY HOME WHEN we got there. She'd left church early, worried about the pot roast. An appetizing aroma filled the house; my mouth watered while I waited my turn for the bathroom.

I knocked on the door. "Hurry up, Marsha."

"Telling me to hurry won't make me go any faster," the voice from the other side of the door replied.

Mom hadn't even changed clothes. She'd gone straight to the kitchen, put on an apron, and started getting lunch ready. Brother Baker had gone about twenty minutes longer than the time published on the bulletin, which was normal; I never understood why people acted surprised.

"I'll just wait in your room and go through your drawers 'till you come out." I heard her scrambling around before the door opened, almost immediately. I rushed in and got to the toilet just in time. When I came out, Dad was waiting to go in and had a newspaper. "There's a new can of air freshener under the sink," I told him.

Marsha was helping Mom dish up and set the table. Dad was going to be a few minutes, so I went in my room and changed clothes. I carefully loosened my tie and slipped it over my head without undoing the knot. It had taken me three tries to get the knot right, so I left it tied. I hung my pants, shirt, tie, and dress belt on the wooden hanger and stuck my dress socks in my shoes and put them in the closet beside my shoeshine kit. Dad came out of the bathroom; I zipped up my Tuff-Nut jeans and headed down the hall pulling my T-shirt on.

Dad waited for Mom to sit down before saying grace. The last thing she put on the table was chocolate gravy. It had been a long time since we'd had chocolate gravy. We usually had milk gravy. Chocolate gravy was a mixture of chunks of chocolate and sugar, melted and mixed together. It was really sweet and had to be eaten while it was hot, before it had a chance to set up. It was really more of a dessert. I put four biscuits on my plate and poured gravy all over them. Pot roast was good as a leftover, but chocolate gravy had to be eaten immediately.

I rubbed the drip that got on my pants real hard, and it just made the smudge mark bigger. The long thin string of chocolate that had gotten on my T-shirt was a different story. Mom made me take the shirt off. She said that it was probably ruined. You'd think I'd poisoned the Colby water supply or something, the way she went on. I didn't understand the big deal since a T-shirt is usually worn under another shirt. It wasn't like anybody was ever going to see it. I dug the Bazooka Joe T-shirt that Melody had given me out of the dirty clothes and put it on. It still smelled like Jade East, with a musty twist.

Marsha and I cleaned up the kitchen and put the dishes away, while Mom and Dad sat on the porch. The pan that Mom had used to make the chocolate gravy was a mess. The chocolate had cooled down and was stuck to the pan like bark on a tree.

Marsha watched me chipping away at the once gravy, now a brown, marblelike substance. "That's why I never eat that stuff. There's no telling what it's doin' to your guts." She had a way with words. Just the thought made my stomach rumble.

AFTER LUNCH, BOOGER, FLOP, AND I rode our bikes to Dino. Burt's was closed, and there wasn't much traffic on the square. We sat there basking in the sun and making carnival plans.

The carnival always came to town during the last week of school. It would be open on Tuesday, Wednesday, and Thursday nights. The teachers always threw a fit and thought the carnival should not be allowed to set up before school was out for the year. Dad always said that Colby was such a small town it was lucky the carnival came to town at all. Tickets were on sale at several businesses, including Gooche's grocery.

"I wish my mom would let me cut lawns," whined Flop, interrupting our carnival discussion.

"Why won't she?" I asked.

"I don't know. Like-a-said, I think she's afraid I'll cut off my foot or somethin.'" Visibly disgusted, Flop leaned back against Dino and found reason to smile. His hands were clasped behind his head. His ears rested against his wrists and stood out even more than normal.

"So, HOW MANY TICKETS AN'AT are you gonna buy?" asked Booger, getting back to the carnival plans.

"Well, like-a-said, if I was cuttin' grass an' had all kinds of money, I'd get a book o' twenty-five," advised Flop, still moping. Tickets were twenty-five cents each in strips of ten, or five dollars for a book of twenty-five. The most I'd ever gotten was ten tickets. Each ticket was good for one ride on everything except the "Bullet," which took two. I'd only ridden it one time, with disastrous results.

An idea popped into my head; they often did, but I decided to share this one. "How about the three of us gettin' two books and splittin' them?"

"That sounds like a good'n to me," said Booger, after giving a moment of thought. "You think your mom'n dad would spring for your share, Flop?"

"I don't know, prob'ly. Maybe I could borrow some money from you guys an' pay it back by cuttin' grass."

Something about Flop owing me money didn't sound good. He might up and move or get hit by a car or something before he paid me back, and there'd go the Honda Mini-Trail.

"Maybe your mom would loan you the money," I suggested.

"How much would my share be?"

"Well, it'd be one third 'a ten dollars," said Booger.

"The tickets will be twenty cents each if we buy them by the book," I said. "How about me and Booger gettin' a couple of books and you buyin' what you can. We can probably sell some to Everett and Caleb."

"The sign said that if you buy three books, you get the fourth one free," said Flop, who didn't have any money. I did the math in my head again, this time a little quicker.

"Each ticket would only cost fifteen cents if we did that," I said. "We could sell them for twenty cents each and make a nickel on each ticket."

"Since you don't have any money, how about Tommy 'n me buyin' the tickets and you sellin' 'em?" Booger suggested to Flop. "You'll make a nickel on each ticket, an' you can use the money you make t' buy part of the left-over tickets."

Flop took his hat off and scratched his head. He seemed to be deep in thought. He was sitting above me on Dino, and the sun was behind his head. I could see the blood vessels in his ears. I didn't know what he was so worried about. It would be Booger and me taking the risk. If we didn't sell most of the tickets, our Honda Mini-Trail savings would be wiped out.

"Like-a-said, I could probably get my mom t' buy a strip 'a ten," he said after a couple of minutes of seemingly deep thought. "She and Dad will probably wanna ride the Ferris wheel together an' the rest can be for me. How many more will I need to sell?"

"I don't really want more than a book of twenty-five. That's over twice as many as I've ever had," I told him.

Booger nodded his head. "Same with me."

Flop squinted his eyes, thinking again. "That'll leave two books for me t' sell or buy."

"Think you can do it?" Booger asked.

"Sure. If I had to, I could sell the tickets for fifteen cents each. Right?"

"Guess so," I said. Booger nodded in agreement.

We decided that we'd stop by Gooche's and get the tickets the next day, since neither one of us had brought any money with us. As we rode our bikes home, Flop started listing all of the people he was going to sell tickets to. We agreed that if we'd had more money, we would have gotten even more tickets and made a bundle on the carnival deal.

THE THREE OF US GOT Mr. Gooche's lawn done in record time. Booger and I used the clippers while Flop took his turn mowing. We headed straight for Gooche's grocery as soon as we finished, not even waiting for Mrs. Gooche to pay us.

Mr. Gooche stood up behind his elevated office. "Hello, boys. Mrs. Gooche said you three left before she could pay you. Is Billy part of the mowing team now?"

"Not yet. We're just teachin' him how to mow right now," I told him.

"Why were you in such a hurry to get over here?"

"We need some carnival tickets and wanted to be sure an' get here before you closed," Booger said.

"It should be a good carnival this year." He opened a drawer full of tickets. "How many tickets do you need?"

"Four books," I said.

"That's a lot of rides."

I handed him the money. I'd told Mom and Dad our plan, and they'd given me some lawn-mowing money.

"They're not all for us. A bunch of us are goin' together and buying 'em by the book."

"That's clever." He grinned and handed Booger the books and counted the fifteen one-dollar bills. I'd kept the money folded neatly in my pocket.

He felt the dollar bills and grinned. "I guess you worked up a sweat mowing. By the way, are either of you gonna be looking for a part-time summer job?"

"Sure," Booger and I both nodded and replied.

Flop got his melancholy look. "Like-a-said, I don't think my mom would let me work at a grocery store."

"I might have something fer you'uns. Stop by when school is out for the summer."

"Yes, sir," Booger and I both said. Mr. Gooche smiled. We turned and headed out the door.

He cleared his throat. "Aren't you boys forgettin' somethin'?" We gave each other blank looks. "What about the yard?" he asked.

"It's finished," Booger said.

"No, I mean, what about gettin' paid?" He handed Booger and me six of the damp one-dollar bills I'd just given him.

"Oh, yeah, thanks," Booger said, taking the money.

He shook his head and sat back down. "Have fun at the carnival."

"Yes, sir." We left.

I made it home in time to watch *The Andy Griffith Show*. A traveling medicine man came to Mayberry and sold Aunt Bee a couple of bottles of elixir. Without knowing it, she'd gotten drunk with all of her friends. Sheriff Andy had to break the news about the contents of the elixir to her. Aunt Bee was embarrassed and ashamed.

FLOP SOLD SEVENTY TICKETS BEFORE the third recess. We had enough money to pay for all one hundred tickets and still had two dollars and fifty cents and thirty tickets left over. Booger and I kept a dollar each and gave Flop fifty cents. We split the tickets evenly. Flop said that he felt that was fair, since Booger and I had put up the money in the first place, and we'd all gotten free tickets out of the deal.

WENDY AND BETH SAT ACROSS the aisle from me on the bus. "Are you goin' to the carnival tonight?" I asked.

"Beth and I plan on going together. There should be a good crowd. Everybody that was at the party said that they were going, too."

I didn't really care about the rest.

"I'll see you there. Maybe we can ride the Bullet together."

"Ooh. That takes two tickets, doesn't it?"

"Yeah." Oh, how I regretted having said it. It took two tickets, and I remembered having puked on it the year before. She smiled. I sunk down in my seat and melted.

Since it was the last week of school and I didn't have any homework, the only thing between the carnival and me was Melody's yard. Flop was waiting for us when we got to Melody's garage. Booger and I didn't waste any time filling the tanks on our Lawn-Boys and getting started. The three of us finished the yard almost thirty minutes quicker than the first time.

"No lemonade today?" Flop asked.

"Guess not," I answered and noticed that Melody's mother's car was gone; evidently Melody was with her. I missed the lemonade, but we had finished the lawn quicker without stopping for it. Anyway, the time seemed to fly by since we had the carnival to look forward to. On the ride home, I realized I hadn't thought about Wendy while mowing Melody's yard.

Chapter 17

The Beast

THE CARNIVAL TOOK PLACE ON the baseball field, and it was usually early June before the grass grew back in some places.

Booger and I rode there with Mom and Dad; lots of parents went on the first night. They seldom rode anything except the Ferris Wheel. I'd decided not to get on that thing unless Caleb and Everett were in clear sight. They'd talked about lobbing potatoes at the some of the bigger rides. The Ferris Wheel seats made for slow-moving targets, and I was sure it looked tempting to them. Caleb and Everett hadn't gotten in any trouble over the courthouse deal, so they didn't have any reason to be careful. Somehow it didn't seem fair.

I walked ahead of Mom and Dad. "Tommy, that Jade East isn't going to last you for a year if you keep putting it on so heavy," Mom said. I ignored her. "You have other shirts you can wear too," she commented. Mom was referring to my Bazooka Joe T-shirt. I was wearing it for the third time in less than a week. I kept ignoring her, which wasn't polite, but it was the best way to keep from getting into a lengthy discussion that might lead to who-knows-where.

Mom and Dad stopped at the cotton candy and corn dog trailers; the fans blowing the aroma out had suckered them in. The fans weren't to keep the people inside cool, but to blow the scent of their goods across the carnival grounds. Uncle Cletus had told me about that trick.

One of the wooden horses on the carousel needed grease. The guy running the Ferris Wheel needed to wash his blue jeans. A little ticket booth sat on the pitcher's mound, and a frail-looking, malnourished, dried-up old man with a thick, bushy, tangled tuft of gray hair was sitting inside.

Booger, Flop, and I had planned to meet in front of the salt-water taffy stand. I got there first and watched the arms of the taffy machine slowly rotate round and round as it made the orthodontic treat. I'd lost a filling chewing the tarry substance the year before. Flop showed up before Booger.

"They've got golden fishes as prizes at 'at softball throw this year," said Flop, visibly excited.

"What are you gonna do with a goldfish?" I asked, emphasizing the word gold, hoping he'd get the hint.

"Don' know. I've heard college kids swallow 'em all th' time."

"See any college kids around here?"

"No, but Everett might swallow one." That thought hadn't occurred to me, but Flop had a point.

Nearby was a trailer with masterfully painted graphics of a well-endowed lady with two heads. "That trailer o'vair has a two-headed lady in it. It cost two tickets to see 'er." Flop had already been investigating.

"Didn't you see that last year? She doesn't really have two heads. She's just a big fat lady with a goiter or somethin' in her neck." He looked a little deflated, and I was instantly sorry I'd said it.

Booger walked up. "Is that the T-shirt that Melody gave you?"

"Yep."

"Why'd she give it to you?" Flop asked.

"I don't know. Maybe she figured it wouldn't fit her." We started walking. Flop took the lead, and we followed him. He walked toward the softball throw.

A skinny midget with half his teeth and probably most of his brains missing was standing behind the counter of the stand juggling three softballs. The sign said one throw for ten cents, two throws for fifteen cents, or three for twenty-five cents. It was a hand-printed sign and looked like something the juggler had made.

"Isn't that s'posed to say three throws fer twenty cents?" I asked.

"What do it say, boy?" He tried to look at me. His nose was pointed at me but his eyes weren't. The left one was close, but the right one had a mind of its own.

"Three throws for twenty-five cents," I repeated and tried to figure out which eye I should follow.

"Well, then, that's what it say." I didn't bother trying to explain my question; he wasn't going to negotiate.

"How many bottles do you have to knock down to get a golden fish?" Flop inquired.

"Just one," the juggler answered, already growing a bit impatient with us. Flop looked away momentarily, just as the juggler tossed a ball his way. The ball hit him in the lip and jarred him enough to knock his cap off. His bottom lip started bleeding immediately. The juggler jumped across the counter and tried to help him; he apologized over and over. The snow cone lady saw the whole thing and brought a paper cup full of ice over. Flop held it to his lip. It stopped the bleeding but not before turning the ice blood red. Flop was a mess. Now he had a swollen lip to go along with his naturally oversized ears.

"You okay, little buddy?" the juggler asked. He was probably a nice guy, just a little on the weird side; well, maybe a lot on the weird side.

"I think so," Flop mumbled. His lip was quivering uncontrollably. He didn't cry but his eyes watered. Sometimes eyes just do that on their own after getting hit in the face.

"I tell you what. How 'bout I give each of you'uns three free throws, and if you don't win, I'll give you a goldfish anyway?" Flop nodded his head yes while holding the cup of ice to his lip. "You go first," he said, looking at Flop. This time he handed him the balls. Both eyes seemed to be looking in the same direction now. Maybe when he really concentrated he could get them coordinated.

Flop's first throw didn't even make it to the racks holding the bottles. His second and third flew between the bottles. Booger and I didn't do any better. It was rigged, we were sure. The Juggler handed Flop a plastic cup with a goldfish in it. Flop thanked him and winced when he tried to smile.

Flop threw his bloody snow cone in a big metal trashcan and a million flies came swarming out. We walked faster. I was looking for Wendy, Flop was probably looking for a college kid to feed the fish to, and Booger was just gawking.

Flop held his cup up. "Whadaya think I should do with 'is golden fish?"

Booger pointed to the rubber ducky game. "That'd be a good place fer it."

The rubber ducks were floating around in a trough full of water. Each duck had a number on the bottom that corresponded to a shelf full of prizes. You paid two tickets to pick up a duck and get a prize from the shelf. One shelf had nice stuffed animals, but the others were just plastic junk, like clickers and fake shark's-tooth necklaces.

"You think he'll be okay in there?"

"Oh yeah, he'll be just fine," Booger assured him. There were lots of kids already crowded around the trough plucking out one duck after the other. Several were walking away clicking their clickers. Click-click, click-click. For a second, I had visions of an Alfred Hitchcock movie in which giant crickets invaded the world.

Flop handed the cup to Booger. "Would you mind doin' it fer me?" Booger took the cup, waited until the rubber-ducky lady wasn't looking, and poured the goldfish in.

CALEB AND EVERETT WALKED UP while Booger was releasing the gold-fish. They had just gotten to the carnival. We told them the fish story. They inspected Flop's swollen lip, and we continued moving through the crowd.

I spotted Wendy. She and Beth were with Billy Burke and Cecil Becker. Billy was Beth's boyfriend and they were getting on the Ferris Wheel. It looked like Wendy had come with Cecil. My mouth got dry, and my tongue stuck to the roof of my mouth again. I regretted not going to the party.

Somebody tapped me on the shoulder from behind. "I'm sorry I missed you." I turned around; it was Melody. I hadn't seen her walking up. "I rode with Mom over to Fairview. I thought we'd be back before you and Booger finished." I still had my eye on Wendy and Cecil. "You feel okay?" She forced eye contact.

"Sure. Ah, yeah, we got finished a little quicker'n usual. We wanted t' hurry up an' come t' th' carnival."

"T-shirt looks good on you." Her smile was engaging.

"Thanks." I momentarily felt faint and had to concentrate in order to keep my balance.

Booger rolled his eyes in disgust. "See ya later." He and the others kept walking.

"Are you wearing Jade East?"

"Uh-huh." My mind had kicked into neutral; I tried hard to focus.

"Wow! That stuff's expensive."

"I bought it with my lawn-mowin' money."

"Smells good." She moved closer. I recognized her Jungle Gardenia.

"I like Jungle Gardenia, too," I whispered, so that no one except her could hear, and was glad my thought process had returned.

"I'm impressed you know what it is."

"Marsha has some." Melody gave me a full-frontal tooth smile, rotated back and forth from heel to toe, and swung her arms back and forth, clapping her hands in the front and back.

She pointed toward the Bullet. "Ever ride the Beast?"

"Not since last year."

Standing there looking at the mass of steel beams and neon lights brought back vivid memories of the previous year's experience. It had been on the last night and, as it turned out, the guy running the machine had planned on quitting anyway, so he let Booger and me take a double ride. We both puked up most of our corn dogs and caramel apple halfway through the second ride. I remember the carnie being really mad and trying to make us clean it up. He finally let us go, but only after Booger suffered a final convulsive fit and completely purged his stomach on the carney's shoes. Yeah, it looked like a bullet, but Melody was right; it was a beast.

"Wanna ride it together?" she asked, snapping me out of my momentary lapse. I was surprised at her eagerness and was still contemplating her having called it the Beast.

"Yeah, I'd love to, but it takes two tickets, you know." It was a weak attempt at hiding my real reason for not wanting to go.

"I've got plenty of tickets. Dad gave me a couple of books. He always buys lots of tickets."

This wasn't looking good. I searched so hard for an excuse that my temples started hurting, but I couldn't think of any.

Standing in line wouldn't have been so bad if Melody hadn't been holding onto my arm. Everett, Caleb, Flop, and Booger had all gone over to get a corn dog so they didn't see us, and I was thankful for that.

"Lettin' the little lady pay, sport?" the tattooed yahoo running the Bullet asked. It wasn't the same guy as the previous year, but many of his features were similar.

"Yes, sir." What else could I say? He was chewing tobacco and spat a big wad of the dark juicy substance on the ground just after strapping us in.

"Gross," Melody said, after he'd walked away.

He pulled a big greasy handle, the engine got louder, and we started to move. Our capsule moved to the top. From there we could see all over the fairgrounds. I saw Mom and Dad and some other parents getting on the carousel.

The Bullet was basically two capsules mounted on opposing arms. Each capsule held two people, sitting and facing each other. I'm sure the operator was in cahoots with the people selling food. His job was to make everybody puke. This, they probably thought, would increase food sales. Although their logic was flawed, the Bullet operator frequently kept his end of the deal. Melody's seat belt had some pink chunky stuff on it near where the seat bottom connected to the frame. She hadn't seen it, and I didn't tell her about it. It was proof that the Bullet had already claimed its first victim of the night.

The capsule started to move again; it gradually sped up. At its fullest speed, we were slung upside-down as we went through the top of the arc. The people in the other capsule were screaming bloody murder. Melody had an evil-looking grin on her face. I'd never seen this side of her. I didn't worry about the drool that was most likely seeping out of my mouth. I concentrated on not getting sick. I kept thinking about her calling it "The Beast."

Finally, we came to a stop; my tongue was floating a little, but I had somehow managed not to puke on Melody. She got off first and missed seeing me stagger with my first few steps. There was a long line of inno- cent-looking people waiting to get on.

"How was it?" some unsuspecting idiot asked.

"Oh, it's a blast," I said and kept walking.

When we neared the end of the line, Melody spun around. "Wanna ride again?" I couldn't believe it. It was as if she was possessed.

"Let's wait until the line isn't so long," I pleaded, trying not to sound too desperate. "How 'bout gettin' a caramel apple?" I anxiously suggested.

"That sounds delicious. It's over by the carousel." She grabbed my arm and dragged me that way, half trotting. I had to double-time every fourth step just to keep up. I heard a little kid telling his mom he'd seen a goldfish in the rubber-ducky game.

"I'm sure it was your imagination," I heard her say back to him.

———

Mom and some other ladies were standing in a circle around Booger's mom and dad. Booger's mom had her face buried in his dad's neck. All of the ladies had their tissues out and were rubbing their eyes. The other dads were just standing there, arms crossed, kicking pebbles with their toes.

I walked up to Dad. "What happened?"

"I don't know. A bunch of kids Johnny's age were riding the carousel at the same time we were, and Booger's mom got upset. She'll be okay," he said. Most of the moms were sniffling and carrying on too. This crying thing seemed to be contagious.

I spotted Booger with Flop and Everett. They were coming out of the two-headed lady's trailer. "We better stick around," I told Melody, and then waved at them. Melody saw them too and whistled real loud. She nearly burst my eardrums. Everyone looked at me. Melody just stood there smiling innocently.

"We were whistling for Booger." I pointed toward the trailer. "How'd you do that?" I quietly asked Melody. She stuck her fingers in her mouth and showed me, only without blowing. She'd whistled louder than my dad ever had.

Dad looked at me and grinned. "I didn't know you could whistle like that." I just shrugged. He thought I'd done it. Melody gave me a sharp elbow to the ribs.

Booger saw that his mom was upset and hurried to her side. He and his dad held their arms around her as they walked toward their car.

Chapter 18

Carnie Smarts

THE NEXT MORNING, I ARRIVED at the bus stop early. Booger was already there. Just like me, he'd worn the same shoes he had been mowing in—the toes were grass-stained. I couldn't tell if he was upset. His Aunt Penelope had probably fixed him breakfast. Judging by the spots on his shirt, it looked like he'd had some of her homemade jelly.

Testing the water, I asked, "You think we ought'a mow Thorpe's yard after school?" It certainly needed to be mowed, but I wasn't sure if he was up to it.

"Sure. You think Flop will wanna help again?" His apparent cheerfulness surprised me.

"We'll ask him when he gets here. Probably so, though." He didn't say anything about his mom, and I didn't know how to ask. She'd probably taken some more of her drugs to get settled down.

Wendy and Beth walked up. With no hint of hesitation, Wendy asked, "How's your mom?" Girls are like that sometimes. They just up and ask questions that they shouldn't. Anybody with half a brain could tell Booger didn't want to talk about it.

"She's doing fine." Surprisingly, he seemed almost eager to talk. "She took some of 'at medicine an'at the doctor gave her an' it made her feel better. She just gets real sad now an' then, but she's okay; she'll get better." He kept looking at Wendy as if she was supposed to ask another question. He didn't act like there was anything wrong. He was probably just hiding it real well.

"How's Cecil Becker?" I asked Wendy, out of the blue, without thinking.

"Okay, I guess." She gave me a quizzical look. "Why? Did something happen to him?"

"Not that I know of." I was sounding really stupid now.

"Why did you ask then?"

"Well, I heard he was dumber'n a bucket 'a coal clinkers is all." My tongue was again outpacing my brain.

"That's not a very nice thing to say about Cecil. Who would have said such a thing?"

"I don't know, one of 'em carnies." The lie was getting out of hand, quick! "Yeah, the softball throw guy." He was as good as anyone to lay the blame on and would most likely never be seen in Colby again.

Booger was shaking his head, grinning. I didn't know what had come over me, but if it made Booger smile then it was worth it. Suddenly a chill came over me, and I momentarily lost my equilibrium. I got on the bus but couldn't force myself to look Wendy's way. She hadn't given me the flute to carry, but then, I hadn't acted like I deserved to carry it.

THURSDAY WAS THE LAST NIGHT for the carnival. About three nights is all the ballpark could probably stand without suffering permanent damage to the grass. Bits and pieces of trash had blown under the rides. The city had spread sawdust chips where people walked. If it stayed down more than a few days, it'd kill the grass.

All the carnies lived in trailers. They weren't supposed to let their sewage drain out, but some of them did. They always parked their trailers on the east side of the park, in the right field foul territory. Since the wind was generally out of the west, the odor blew away from the carnival. The blue mud created from their leaky sewage systems wouldn't be noticed until people started hauling in lawn chairs to watch the baseball games later in the summer. Every year people complained, but by the time the carnival arrived the next year, most had forgotten. Those with good memories sat on the left field side during ball games, and the visitors generally sat in the blue mud. The sun was always in your eyes on the right side anyway.

Booger and I used a couple of our tickets riding the Bullet. It didn't make either one of us feel sick or anything; with no particular risk or thrill, we became bored with it. We sold the rest of our tickets for twenty cents each. I bought a caramel apple; Booger got a wad of cotton candy. We quenched our thirst caused by the carnival cuisine with a couple of grape-flavored snow cones, forgetting that we'd then have purple lips and tongues.

Booger finished his snow cone first. "Let's go over and play 'at softball throw once an' try to win another golden fish."

I felt a dime in my pocket. "I've got ten cents to spare. Let's go."

When we turned to start that way, I saw Cecil Becker and his buddies all standing in front of the softball throw. They looked like they were arguing with the juggler. A couple of other carnie guys had gathered around too. I looked at Booger, he at me. We both grinned and walked the other way.

Flop came bounding through the crowd toward us. He stuck a bobble-headed hula dancer in my face. "Look at what Everett won. He'll win yous guys one, too." He was so excited his ears wiggled when he spoke. "He's over at th' sledge hammer. It's a quarter or one ticket a swing. Everett can ring 'at bell ever' swing. You better hurry, though; I think th' guy 'at runs it is 'bout to run 'em off."

I didn't particularly want a plastic hula girl with a bobbing head, but I thought it might be fun to watch Everett ring the bell. Booger and I followed Flop. We had to see what all of the fascination was about.

Flop kept turning around looking at me. "Yous been eatin' snow cones?"

"Yeah. Why?"

"Yer lips are purple. Ya' look like a couple a vampires or somethin.'"

I wiped my lips on my sleeves and kept walking. Booger's lips looked okay. He'd practically inhaled his snow cone, though.

Everett was standing between the sledgehammer and the weight-guessing-game. He was talking to Caleb and Uncle Cletus when we got there. No one was swinging the hammer. Uncle Cletus had his arms folded across his chest and was smiling about something. Caleb was holding three hula dolls.

"I told you that if a guy would hit that knob on the very front part, he'd ring that bell every time," I heard Uncle Cletus saying to Everett when we walked up. Evidently he'd coached Everett in the art of sledgehammer swinging.

"Hey, Uncle Cletus."

"Hey, Tommy. You missed a good show," he said, punching me lightly on the shoulder.

"It looks like it," I replied.

"Everett would have cleaned that guy out of hula dolls if he'd let him kept on swingin." I suspected they had plenty of dolls or similar junk stuffed in one of their trailers and figured Uncle Cletus knew that too and was just trying to make Everett feel even better.

"How many did ya' win, Everett?" I asked.

"Don't know. Somebody'd pay, I'd swing and win, and they'd take the prize. It was fun while it lasted," he said. Everybody just looked at each other and shook their heads in amazement.

"I hope you boys got your homework finished before comin' tonight." Uncle Cletus winked and then walked away.

"Thanks, Mr. Thornton," Everett told him.

"You're welcome, Everett."

Booger and I soon tired of Flop and Caleb talking about Everett swinging the stupid sledgehammer. Caleb had salt-water taffy stuck to his teeth. It dawned on me, after listening to Flop, how silly these carnivals were. Everyone either ate food that usually made them feel a little queasy, or rode on rides that made them look stupid or feel like puking, or played games and won prizes that are made by people in Timbuktu who probably never washed their hands.

The magic, for me, was gone. The thought that I'd blown money that could have been used to pay off the Honda Mini-Trail suddenly struck me. My stomach started to churn. An even more disturbing thought occurred to me: that the money I'd had on Monday afternoon now belonged to the carnival people, whom I'd been making fun of. I guess that's what Dad had meant by them having carnie smarts. I had one of those acid burps.

Booger and I walked home. The next day was the last day of school and the beginning of summer vacation. Booger and I had big plans: pay off the Lawn-Boys, get the Mini-Trails, go fishing, swim, and sleep in.

I watched a mosquito fully insert his beak into the skin between my thumb and forefinger and start to draw blood. I finger-flipped him and wiped the bloody remains off of my fingernail onto my pants; they were out early this year.

"It's gonna be a great summer," Booger said, cheering me up without realizing it.

"Yeah," I replied unenthusiastically.

"Aren't you lookin' forward to gettin' the Mini-Trail?" he asked.

"Oh sure," I replied with a little more enthusiasm. It was strange how the roles had changed; it was now Booger's turn to cheer up his friend.

Neither of us had any idea how quickly our roles would reverse.

Chapter 19

Interview

SINCE IT WAS THE LAST day of school, Mrs. E gave everyone a chance to tell the class their summer plans. Francis Myers, the biggest wimp in the class, and one who'd never said a word since first grade, decided this was a good day to start talking. He told in excruciating detail his family's plans about going to California on a vacation. The only thing I knew about California was that it had the Golden Gate Bridge and hippies who took LSD. Francis was sure looking forward to going. I figured that if the rest of his family was like Francis it'd be a trip worth missing.

Several kids were going on vacation to Florida. Why anyone would go to Florida in the middle of the summer was a mystery to me. Some of the farm boys talked about how they'd get to drive their dad's tractor picking up hay. Mom didn't know it, but I'd already driven a tractor, pulling a bush-hog.

I told the class about mowing lawns and saving up for a Honda Mini-Trail. I didn't mention the job at the grocery store since I hadn't gotten it yet.

Mrs. E passed out the report cards. I looked at the part where it told if I'd passed or not. I'd had good grades all year, but you could never be sure about passing until you received the last report card. Rumors of people getting held back for little or no apparent reason had been circulating, a typical occurrence near the end of each school year. I breathed a bit easier after seeing that I'd passed.

Melody cracked a big smile and started swinging her feet up and down in front of her desk. She'd gotten straight A's, again.

On the way home, Miss Barbara handed out candy bars on the school bus. Some of them were already soft from sitting in the sun. Most of the high school kids had squirt guns hidden in their book bags; a few had slingshots. I ate a chocolate bar one square at a time and kept my head down.

I leaned over to pick up a piece of candy bar wrapper and saw Wilma's combat boot come down hard on Marty's toes. Everyone was making so much noise I couldn't hear him yelp, but I'm sure he did. I don't remember him doing anything to deserve it. Wilma just did it for good measure. I figured she probably wouldn't see him again until school started next year; it was probably an end-of-school-year boot.

I looked in the mirror at Miss Barbara. She was looking in it too, scanning. We briefly made eye contact; I realized that, for some strange reason, I'd miss her over the summer. Caleb had chocolate all over his chin. Booger hadn't eaten his candy bar. It was sticking out of his shirt pocket. Watching Caleb gobble up his candy bar had probably taken away Booger's appetite.

BOOGER, CALEB, AND I HUNG around the bus stop a few minutes after getting off. Wendy wiggled her fingers good-bye. One thing I knew for sure—her house was the first place I'd go when I got the Mini-Trail. It was one of those lingering thoughts that popped up during mental breaks. After Caleb left, I turned to Booger. "You wanna go down and see what Mr. Gooche has on his mind?"

"Sure. I'll get my bicycle an'at and meet you at your house."

When I got home, Mom was peeling apples for a pie. It was in celebration of school getting out for the summer. I showed her my report card. She smiled and gave me a big hug. She never did put the paring knife down, and I was afraid it was me that was going to get pared before all of the hugging was over.

I told her that Booger was coming by and that we were going to speak with Mr. Gooche about a job at the grocery store.

"You need to eat some lunch. Working men need to eat," she said, half joking, half serious.

"Booger's prob'ly already on his way."

"I'll fix you both a sandwich. Tell him to come on in when he gets here."

I sat on the porch and waited for him. He hadn't eaten anything yet. Booger had a spring in his step when he arrived, which meant that his mom was having a good day. My Mom fixed us some bologna and cheese sandwiches with lots of Miracle Whip on them. Some of the Miracle Whip squirted out on to my hand while I was eating, and I licked it off instead of using a napkin. She gave us each two sweet pickles and some grape juice with lemonade mixed in. I got the pee shakes, chewing on the lemonade pulp.

MR. GOOCHE LOOKED UP FROM his desk when Booger and I walked into the store. "You two didn't waste any time."

"No, sir," I agreed. "School's out. We're ready to work."

"Let me show you around." He stood up and put his Gooche's Grocery apron on. We followed him to the back of the store, through the swinging doors, and into the storage room. It was full of boxes and cases of laundry detergent, paper towels, toilet tissue, canned goods, and all sorts of stuff. Each area had its own scent, depending on what was stored there. Mostly it smelled like damp cardboard and detergent, though. He led us to a large back door.

He stopped in front of a dock door. "Every Wednesday, we get a truckload of groceries. The stock boys unload it here. They make sure the merchandise gets rotated so that we sell the oldest items first."

He raised the door to show us the dock and an old Chevy pickup truck with the bed full of empty cardboard boxes. "The stock boys fill this truck full, and then drive it to the incinerator." He pointed to a concrete block incinerator sitting at the edge of the lot.

He paused for a second, looked at Booger, and said, "I was sure sorry to hear about Johnny. He was an exceptional young man. I'm sure he made a fine Marine."

"Tomorrow would have been his birthday," Booger said, matter-of-factly. We stood there for an awkward moment.

Mr. Gooche took his glasses off and rubbed the lenses with his apron. He cleaned some wax out of his ear with a matchstick, then started walking again. He stopped at the produce section. A well-fed, fleshy lady was cleaning tomatoes, putting them on a cardboard tray, and covering them with plastic wrap. There were fly strips hanging all over the place, and every one of them had already caught several flies.

We followed Mr. Gooche into the walk-in freezer. "You have to wear gloves if you work in here, even in the summertime," he instructed. It was huge, almost as big as our living room. Everything had frost on it. Most items were still in their cases. "We take delivery on frozen items a couple of times a week."

After the tour, we walked back to his office. He sat in his wooden swivel chair and told Booger and me to have a seat. I looked around; there weren't any chairs, just two wooden soda cases. We each pulled one up, turned them on their sides, and sat down.

He eyed both of us carefully. "I need a couple of carryout boys. The hours will be mostly in the afternoon and on weekends. That's when most people shop. You'll need to wear a white shirt and tie."

He was talking like we already had the job. I took it as a good sign. He squinted, leaned forward, and asked, "What do you think?"

I was nervous. "I'll need to talk to my parents." I'd never had a real job before, and I was pretty sure Booger hadn't either

He patted me on the knee. "I understand."

"Can we wear clip-on ties?"

He smiled. "Of course. In fact, they're safer. If you get it caught in something, it'll come off instead of chokin' you."

He looked at Booger. "Any questions?"

"How much does it pay?"

Mr. Gooche leaned back in his chair, scratching the lump on the top of his head. "Carryout boys make one dollar per hour plus tips," he said.

"How many hours an'at will we be workin'?" Booger asked.

"It depends on the week. Probably three or four hours on Thursdays and Fridays and all day on Saturdays." I quickly did the math. That might amount to fifteen to twenty dollars per week, plus tips.

Booger continued with questions. "How long will the jobs last?"

"Whadaya mean?"

"Well, what happens when school starts?"

"Let's see how the summer works out first, but people don't stop grocery shopping just because school starts."

He gave us a form for our parents to sign. It had something to do with us being minors. I folded mine and put it in my back pocket. I didn't sit down on my bike seat on the way home so that it wouldn't get wrinkled.

THE NEXT DAY, THE FIRST day of summer vacation, I headed over to Booger's house. I wasn't sure if he'd be up yet, but I wanted to try and cheer him up; I figured he'd be thinking about it being Johnny's birthday. Booger's mom had gotten Johnny a new watch for his birthday before he'd gotten killed. She'd said something about giving it to Booger when he turned sixteen. Booger hadn't mentioned the watch; I think Johnny was on his mind more than the watch. A ride to the creek was what he needed. I was thinking that maybe we'd sneak up to the shut-ins and dig up some mussels. If we had time we'd go all of the way to Bird's Cave.

When I got to his house, there was an ambulance sitting in front, but the red lights weren't on; the sheriff's car was there, too. I stopped short of the driveway and watched. Brother Baker pulled up and ran into the house. He was so long and lanky that when he ran it looked like he might fly apart. Dad pulled up beside me in the pickup truck. He looked at me like I was in trouble or something.

"What's wrong?" I asked.

"Booger's mom didn't wake up this morning." I could tell something worse than Mrs. Burger oversleeping had happened. He looked out the driver's side window, away from me, and didn't say anything more.

"Is she going to be okay?" I asked.

"No." His bottom lip was quivering. "Booger's Mom has gone to be with the Lord, Tommy. There's nothing the doctor can do. Booger's aunt Penelope called me from Fairview. She wanted me to find you and see if you'd go sit with Booger." He sat there in the truck looking at me. "She's probably right. Booger could use your company."

I could tell he didn't know any more about what to do in a situation like that than I did. "I don't know what to tell you to say to him. He probably doesn't want to talk, but he doesn't need to be alone."

By then, Booger's aunt Penelope had arrived. She had gotten out of her car and started toward the house, but stopped, as if waiting for something, when she saw me. She looked older than she had just a week earlier.

"Your mom doesn't know yet. I'm going home now to tell her. The news will be all over town in less than an hour."

He pulled away; I felt a little faint. My summer plans flashed through my mind. An uneasiness I'd never known consumed me.

Aunt Penelope waited for me on the front porch. Booger's front door opened, and the ambulance guys, with their white uniforms on, came out carrying a stretcher. The body was completely covered. Aunt Penelope took a deep breath when they carried the stretcher by. After they took the body to the ambulance, I followed Aunt Penelope into the living room. She walked over to Booger's dad and started crying. I sat down on the couch beside Booger. He was holding the watch his mom had gotten for Johnny.

He held it up for me to see. "She gave it to me last night."

"She just didn't wake up," I heard Mr. Burger telling Aunt Penelope. "We had dinner and talked about Johnny a little. She gave Randy the watch we'd gotten for Johnny. Everything seemed okay. I guess she just gave up."

He was too upset to talk. Booger walked over and hugged him. It was the saddest thing I'd ever seen. A feeling of helplessness swept over me. I couldn't imagine feeling any worse than I did right then.

Typical of Colby, the news spread instantly. Several neighbors had already gathered and were standing on the sidewalk in front of the house. Most of the women were still wearing housecoats and hairnets. Soon they'd begin to plan and organize an effort to feed Booger and his Dad. Sometimes it's good when everyone knows your business.

Chapter 20

Realization

BOOGER'S MOTHER'S DEATH CAUSED A cascade of emotions to flood my mind. As a Christian, we're taught not to fear death, for it brings a better life. But why, then, do so many people get upset about death? After someone dies, we're supposed to celebrate one's life while lamenting their death; it's a strange and complicated thing, and one I wasn't prepared to understand at the time.

Brother Baker came by the house the next morning to visit with me about Booger. He gave me a Bible verse out of the book of James to share with Booger. We talked about death and the promise of joy that Christians have. I listened, but didn't hear the words that would bring joy to Booger.

Mr. Dittmer, the coroner, was at Booger's house when I got there. Booger's dad and Aunt Penelope were in the kitchen talking to him. Mr. Dittmer was doing most of the talking. Booger and I stayed in the living room. Booger would be doing okay, but then he would look at his new watch and start crying again. It was hard for me to believe that his mom was gone for good. I had no way of knowing how bad he must have felt.

On his way out, Mr. Dittmer turned and looked toward Booger. "I'll be praying for you, Randy." Booger nodded.

Mr. Dittmer owned the Willow Wood Funeral Home and was also a Pentecostal preacher. Last summer, Booger and I'd snuck up next to his church during a revival and sat under an open window listening to him go on and on. The Pentecostals did a lot of standing and waving their arms even while Mr. Dittmer preached. It was one of those nights we were supposed to be camping out in the backyard. I figured his prayer for Booger was going to be a dandy.

The phone rang. Aunt Penelope answered. "Yes, that's right. I'm sorry too. That would be nice." She hung up the phone. "That was Brother Baker. The Baptist ladies are putting together a meal schedule. They'll be bringing you and Randy meals for at least the next week." Mr. Burger showed very little emotion. It had only been six weeks since he'd lost Johnny.

Booger had told me that the Baptists brought fried chicken and that it was good. Nobody from the Methodist church had called yet. They would, but Booger and I both knew they'd be bringing lasagna and other "ini" foods. Mrs. Rosolini belonged to the Methodist church.

Mr. Burger looked at Aunt Penelope and sighed weakly. "I guess I need to give Mr. Baumgartner a call." That meant the funeral would be at Greystone, where the Republicans usually went. Greystone had been in the Baumgartner family since 1902; or at least that's what the sign said.

Aunt Penelope put her hand on his. "Don't you think that can wait until tomorrow?"

"No, I want to get it over with. I'll just dread it until it's done."

He was talking about the funeral arrangements. Booger had told me how tough it was on his mom and dad to make the arrangements for Johnny.

Aunt Penelope stood up. "I'll go with you."

Booger was still curled up, with his face smashed against the back of the couch. He was crying so hard he could hardly get his breath. His T-shirt was pulled up, revealing a row of vertebrae nearly poking through tightly-stretched skin; his ribcage heaved with each breath. He'd heard them talking.

I sat on the couch beside him. "I'll go too." He turned his head enough to see me with one eye and nodded his head, yes.

The doorbell rang. It was Uncle Cletus. I opened the door. He squeezed my nose with his left hand and extended the other to shake hands with Mr. Burger. "I'm so sorry, Jack."

Aunt Penelope came out of the bathroom. "Hello, Penny." Uncle Cletus had caught her by surprise when she walked back into the room, or at least she acted like she'd been startled or something. She hadn't heard the doorbell.

"Hi, Cleet." She brushed her skirt and blouse off and fiddled with her hair. Uncle Cletus acted a little nervous, too.

"I just wanted to say how sorry I am and find out what I can do to help."

"It's just going to take some time," Aunt Penelope told him. They looked at each other for a little longer than what seemed normal, but I dismissed it as how they were responding to the tragedy.

"We were just leaving for Greystone to make the arrangements," Mr. Burger said, breaking their gaze.

"You want me to do somethin' with the boys?"

Aunt Penelope placed her hand on Uncle Cletus's wrist. "No, they're both going with Jack and me to Baumgartner's." Uncle Cletus, or Cleet, as Aunt Penelope had called him, stood there deep in thought. "I'll give you a call if I think of anything. We're heading over to Baumgartner's now."

I was selfishly thinking that a fishing trip would be nice.

"I won't keep you, then," he finally let out. "Let me know how I can help." He backed out the door, but not before flicking me on the ear. Aunt Penelope watched him through the window as he walked to his pickup.

Mr. Burger watched her eyeing Uncle Cletus. "You two would be to-gether if he hadn't gone to Korea." Aunt Penelope looked embarrassed and exhaled forcefully, again.

The phone rang again; it was Mrs. Enderle. She and Mr. Burger talked for a long time. Mr. and Mrs. Burger had both been in her grade school class; just about everyone probably had.

While they were talking, Aunt Penelope started picking up around the house. Since Mrs. Burger had been sick, the house had gotten a little messy, even though Aunt Penelope had been helping out.

I got Booger's Bible from his room and turned to chapter one of the book of James and read verses two and three. "Consider it pure joy, my brothers whenever you face trials of many kinds, because you know that the testing of your faith develops perseverance." I tried to explain perse-verance to Booger but it didn't come out the same as how Brother Baker had said.

By that time, Aunt Penelope had made her way to the living room. She paused for a second with the Electrolux vacuum cleaner hose in her hand and looked at me. "You know how to use one of these, don't you?" Unfortunately, I did.

———

MR. BAUMGARTNER'S OFFICE HAD DARK stained-walnut paneling, the thick expensive kind. His desk was huge and didn't have anything on it except two folders. One folder was lying so he could read it, and the other was lying so that Aunt Penelope and Mr. Burger, sitting on the other side of the desk, could read along. They sat in two overstuffed leather chairs facing the desk. Aunt Penelope picked up the folder. Two people Mr. Baumgartner's size could have fit in the chair he was sitting in. I looked under the desk and saw that his pointed black patent leather shoes were barely touching the floor.

The leather couch Booger and I were sitting on was so slick that if I sat up straight I slid forward, and if I leaned back, my butt practically launched off of the cushion. Booger had the same problem. We both just leaned forward in a C shape. Mrs. E would have told us to sit up if she'd seen us. It was a good-for-nothing couch if I'd ever seen one.

Mr. Baumgartner leaned forward, keeping his back perfectly straight, folded his hands together, and rested them on the desk in front on him. He had cuff links on; they glittered in the light—the diamonds probably weren't real, I figured.

Mr. Baumgartner faked a wince. "I'm really sorry, Jack. I know this must be nearly unbearable for you. We'll do everything we can to make the service special." His lips looked odd when he spoke. It was almost like he was chirping instead of talking.

Aunt Penelope had been looking through the folder. She glanced at Mr. Burger, then looked at Mr. Baumgartner. "It looks like you've already filled out most of this, this, whatever you call it." She had a suspicious, hostile look.

"It's called a funeral plan. We can do anything you wish. I assumed you'd want a service similar in quality to the one the military provided for Johnny. The plan reflects that." He looked at Mr. Burger when he spoke.

"I'm sorry," said Aunt Penelope before another forced exhale; I began to worry about her chest caving in. "This is the first time I've helped 'plan' a funeral. You actually charge for all of these things?" She shook her head and looked around the room.

Mr. Baumgartner had been using his right index finder to accentuate his words, much like ladies do, but at Aunt Penelope's show of disgust he laid his left arm on his desk and propped up his pointy jaw with his right. "And what 'things' would that be?" He no doubt knew what she was talking about. His right index finger continued to tap his jaw, but it wasn't as annoying as before. It was almost like the nerve in his finger was connected to his mouth; they both moved in unison.

The room décor didn't fit his personality. Stuffed wild animals were perched and hanging here and there in his cavern-like office. He didn't look like much of a hunter, but somehow he'd gotten his hands on a collection of stuffed wild animals. About the only thing he didn't have on display was a person. I wouldn't have been surprised to find one of them in a closet or something somewhere.

"Obituaries! Does the newspaper charge to run an obituary? You have down here $75 for an obituary." Aunt Penelope's face was getting distorted.

"That's for a full length obit. The newspapers provide a death notice free of charge, but they charge for obituaries. Notices are very short and just don't do a person justice."

"I think the free notices are fine." Aunt Penelope looked at Mr. Burger, and he nodded in agreement.

"It's really Jack's decision," Mr. Baumgartner said. It was clear he didn't care for Aunt Penelope being part of the meeting. He turned sideways, tilted his head back, poofed his lips out, and looked at Mr. Burger. It was odd how much his face resembled the possum sitting on the shelf behind his desk. It was anybody's guess why he'd have a stuffed possum in the first place.

"You have down here $125 for a hairdresser. That won't be necessary. We've decided on a closed casket ceremony."

"So you're saying we should just bury Mrs. Burger with messy hair. Oh, I just don't think that's copacetic," using a word I'd never heard. It wouldn't have been a big deal if Mr. Baumgartner hadn't said it like that. He made it sound like it would be terrible not to spend a bunch of money fixing her hair.

"Can't you just comb it a little?"

"Is that what you think Deloris would want?" he said, referring to Mrs. Burger by her first name and causing Mr. Burger to flinch. Mr. Burger still hadn't said anything, but then there wasn't much need to with Aunt Penelope present.

"Comb it and make her look good! She doesn't need a hairdresser! Think you can do that?" Aunt Penelope snapped.

Mr. Baumgartner looked at Mr. Burger and raised his eyebrows like my mom did when something wasn't cricket. "Jack?"

"I think Penelope's right. Deloris was her sister, remember." It was the first thing he'd said since we'd gotten there.

"Let's go on down the list. What else do you see that needs to be changed?" He had finally figured out who he was dealing with and faced Aunt Penelope. She challenged him on several more items and got them taken off or the price reduced. He wanted to charge for food, and when Aunt Penelope told him the church ladies would be bringing sandwiches, he wanted to charge for the use of his kitchenette. She just gave him a look, and he dropped that, too.

By the time we left, it seemed Mr. Baumgartner had either gotten smaller, or the chair he was sitting in had gotten bigger. His forehead was covered with beads of sweat and his temples were red where he'd been rubbing them. I was sure his shirt was going to have a yellow ring around the collar; even his cuff links didn't look as shiny after Aunt Penelope had finished with him. He'd probably just gotten as close as he ever would to an aerobic workout.

I SAT ON THE FRONT pew with Booger during the funeral. People waited in line to say they were sorry and that they'd been praying for the family. All of the women gave Booger a hug. Some of them even kissed him on the cheek. I decided right then and there that Mr. Baumgartner should put breath mints on his list of things to sell at a funeral.

The church was full, standing room only. Melody sat with her parents across the aisle and two rows back. Mr. and Mrs. Gooche sat a couple of rows behind her. Mr. Gooche still had his Gooche's Grocery pocket protector full of pens and markers in his shirt pocket. I could make out the impression his visor had made on his head. He'd come straight from work.

Flop and his mom and dad sat about halfway back. Flop's hair was slick and shiny and stuck tight to his head. Mrs. Westwood had made him use Vitalis or something. He looked like Alfalfa from the *Little Rascals*, only with bigger ears.

Flop's mom was surely best friends with the Avon Lady. From over ten feet away, I could see the line on her neck where the makeup stopped. Flop's dad had a fresh haircut. It was really evident now where Flop got his ears.

Aunt Penelope and Mr. Burger stayed together. Booger's uncle Norman hadn't shown up yet. Between hugs, Aunt Penelope kept looking toward the door. She must have been expecting him to show up.

"He said he'd be here," I heard her say to Booger's dad.

Brother Baker stepped up to the pulpit and cleared his throat. Everyone started finding a place to sit down. I looked once more to the rear to see if Booger's uncle Norman had arrived; he hadn't. Caleb Wilfong and his parents crept through the door. His mom had on some weird-looking dress that resembled an old burlap sack sewn together. She was wearing sandals and had a leather headband on. People scooted together to make room. They found a place next to Flop and his parents.

Brother Baker started the service by reading from Ecclesiastes, Chapter 7, Verses 1–3. "A good reputation is more valuable than the most expensive perfume. In the same way, the day you die is better than the day you are born. It is better to spend your time at funerals than at festivals. For you are going to die, and you should think about it while there is still time. Sorrow is better than laughter, for sadness has a refining influence on us." He talked about how each person possessed a God-given gift and how Mrs. Burger's had been the gift of service, doing for others. He never mentioned "fighting the good fight," like he had at Johnny's funeral.

THE SAME MARINES WHO HAD carried Johnny's casket carried Mrs. Burger's to the gravesite. It was covered with an American flag. I'd heard Uncle Cletus talking to Aunt Penelope and Mr. Burger about requesting a military funeral. Since Mrs. Burger had never served in the military, it wasn't possible. He'd been able to get the color guard, though. They didn't shoot their guns like they had at Johnny's funeral, but they did fold the flag and present it to Mr. Burger. Supposedly it was the first time something like that had ever been done.

A tent cost $250, so Aunt Penelope decided we didn't need one. The sun was bearing down; everyone was sweating. I watched drops of sweat drip one by one off of the Marine standing straight across from me, who stood perfectly still. He had probably been one of those kids who always sat still when he was growing up. Watching him made me want to be a Marine.

Brother Baker ended the graveside service by reading Romans 8:17: "Now if we are children, then we are heirs—heirs of God and co-heirs with Christ, if indeed we share in his sufferings in order that we may also share in his glory." He explained by saying that, although people suffer, they can look forward to a time of no suffering and that Booger's mom was at that place and that we should be happy for her.

The realization that Booger's mom was gone for good suddenly gripped me. It would just be him and his dad, sort of like Opie and Andy. I started to imagine how I'd feel if my mom was suddenly taken from me. I tried not to think about it, but thoughts uncontrollably flooded my mind. I was sweating, but felt cold. I started shivering. I turned to run away. Mom had been standing behind me and caught me. I buried my face in her dress. She patted me on the back. My tears tasted salty. I wiped my nose on my jacket cuff and tried not to mess up her dress. Peeking out, I saw that Booger had done the same to Aunt Penelope.

LOTS OF PEOPLE CAME TO Booger's house after the funeral. Mom and Mrs. E took charge of serving people. Mrs. Gooche had dropped off some paper plates, cups, and plastic forks. There wasn't room in the house for everyone, so most people just stood in the yard and visited. Some had thought to bring lawn chairs.

The cups had those little flaps that folded out so that you could hold them like a coffee mug. The ladies used the flaps, but the men just gripped the cup without pulling the flaps out.

Aunt Penelope asked the church ladies to serve the lasagna first and save the chicken for last. There were enough deviled eggs to serve an army. Unfortunately, only four pies had been brought. I hid the best-looking one. Neither Booger nor his dad ate anything. Booger and I played pitch and catch. His dad looked tired; so did Aunt Penelope. Having all of the people around seemed to have made them feel better, but I could tell when they were ready for everyone to leave.

I told Aunt Penelope where I'd hidden the pie. She smiled for the first time since the funeral. One by one, the crowd thinned. Uncle Cletus and I were leaving when Uncle Norman showed up.

Chapter 21

Moving On

On the way home, Uncle Cletus explained how tragedies tended to make a family and a community grow stronger and that he was sure that some good would come of Mrs. Burger's death.

"Thing of it is," he said, "Sometimes the good is just too subtle to recognize at first." I'd never questioned anything he'd ever told me, but found it impossible to imagine he knew what he was talking about now. He quoted Romans 8:28, "And we know that all things work together for good to them that love God, to them who are the called according to his purpose," which surprised me, since he always seemed to sleep in church. If the Bible's true, and it is, then there would be some good. I wondered if I'd be able to recognize it.

There was one thing for sure; it had already brought together people of different religions. People from almost every church in town had dropped off food.

The Burgers were active members of Colby First Baptist. Booger's dad sometimes helped take up the offering and hand out the communion. His mom had always helped with Bible school. They had friends who belonged to other churches too—mostly other Baptists, Methodists, and Pentecostals. The Baptists were by far the best cooks.

The Methodists? Well, Dad had said once that since the Methodists had allowed their women to start preaching, they'd lost their culinary skills. There were still a few Methodists who could cook, but they were getting rare, or so he'd said. I'd never eaten much Methodist food; their ice cream wasn't bad, though.

The Pentecostals were just an odd group all around. They're overly cautious about any sort of excess. Their women don't wear makeup and always do something goofy with their hair, which they never cut. The men travel in pairs and always wear a scowl. Uncle Cletus said they always show up to help when there's a need, though. Anyway, the worst part was, they didn't use enough spice on their food; it probably had something to do with their aversion to excess.

Lucky for Booger and his dad, most of the food was from Baptists. I noticed Aunt Penelope putting it away and leaving the other out for the funeral crowd to eat, except for the dish that Mrs. Rosolini brought; the label read "linguini."

My mind was racing when Uncle Cletus let me out; I don't remember if I said goodbye or not. He was looking in his rearview mirror as he pulled away. I waved; he did too.

Before going to bed, I watched *The Andy Griffith Show* with Dad. I came to grips with the fact that Booger and his dad would be okay. They wouldn't be like Sheriff Taylor and Opie, though. For one thing, instead of Aunt Bee they had Aunt Penelope, and since she wasn't a blood relative, people would start talking; at least that's what I'd heard Mom tell Dad.

Lying in bed, I developed a problem; I couldn't control a really bad thought that kept creeping into my head. "What if it had been Booger's Uncle Norman that had died, instead of his mom?" I guess I thought that because Uncle Cletus and Aunt Penelope seemed like such a good match.

Another nagging question that loomed large was how Booger losing his mom would affect our lawn-mowing business and our plan to get the Honda Mini-Trails. Booger hadn't mentioned mowing, and I hadn't found the right moment to ask him what he wanted to do. I decided to leave him alone and start mowing first thing the next day and see if he showed up. It was a selfish thought, and I felt guilty for thinking it.

Even with all of the problems, there were still things to be thankful for. Melody had never found out that Wendy thought I'd won the Bazooka Joe T-shirt; and since school was out she never would. Imagining Wendy in my letter jacket, when and if I ever got one, stopped the bad thoughts from occurring, and my eyes gradually got heavier.

My last thoughts, however, centered on how things would be different if I was in charge of the world, but then that wouldn't be fair to Booger's Uncle Norman.

THE NEXT MORNING THE DEW was heavy, almost like it had rained, so I took my time riding over to Mr. Gooche's to mow, allowing the sun time to dry the grass a bit. Weekday mornings were somehow different than Saturday mornings. It might have been the traffic; there was less on Saturday, but there was never much traffic in Colby, so that wasn't it. There was something different; a kind of intensity in the air on weekday mornings that wasn't there on Saturdays. People moved with a purpose on weekday mornings. Saturdays were more casual, people moved about more congenially.

It was difficult for me to believe that, to most people, this was just another day. To some, like Booger, it was the beginning of a new way of life. No doubt there were boys in other places who had just lost their mom, too. Booger was my concern, though, not them.

I pulled the mowers out of Mr. Gooche's garage and scraped the underside of my deck with a putty knife and cleaned the muffler orifices with a pipe cleaner. Since the dew still hadn't burned off, I started on Booger's mower.

Booger and his dad pulled up while I was picking up the clods of grass. They both got out of the car. I figured they had come for Booger's mower and to say he was quitting.

"I called your house an'at. Your mom said you'd already left to mow." It still wasn't clear to me what his intentions were. I couldn't read his face.

The thought that not calling him about mowing may have caused him more pain made my heart drop like a glob of lead to my ankles. I attempted a recovery. "Oh, I'm not mowin' just yet, I went ahead and came early to get the mowers ready; I figured you'd be along anytime. I scraped 'em both and cleaned out the muffler orifices like Odie told us to do. As soon as the dew dries, we can get with it."

His face brightened, and he stopped wringing his hands. He looked at his dad as if to ask a question but didn't speak.

His dad squeezed him on the shoulder. "Well, get your thermos jug, and you're in business."

It was the first time we'd mowed early in the morning. The dew posed a new challenge, especially in the areas where the grass was thick. Since we had to stop more frequently to clean out the mowers, it gave us more time to talk. Actually, Booger did most of the talking; I listened, which is what Brother Baker had said to do.

His Aunt Penelope and Uncle Norman had had a big argument. Aunt Penelope had recently caught Uncle Norman with another lady. That was part of the reason she'd moved out of her house and in with the Burgers. Booger said she'd gotten really mad when Uncle Norman told her that moving in with Booger and his dad was just as bad. Booger's dad had made them go outside to argue. After a few minutes, Aunt Penelope came running back in crying and with her lip bleeding; nervous Norman had sped away before Booger's dad could get outside and catch him.

Booger was quiet for a few minutes, then mentioned that they'd watched *Andy Griffith* too. He had Johnny's Marine watch in his pocket and looked at it frequently, but probably not to check the time. We didn't talk about it, but it seemed our mowing business had more purpose now; what the purpose was I wasn't sure of, it was just a feeling.

Part of me wanted to find Uncle Cletus and tell him about Aunt Penelope; I was sure he would have cleaned nervous Norman's plow real good, but I thought better and decided to concentrate on mowing.

We finished Mr. Gooche's yard before noon and moved our mowers to Melody's yard; we planned to mow it after lunch. Melody loaned Booger her bike to ride to my house for lunch. It was a tough time for Booger. Everybody needed to be extra-special to him, but for some reason it bugged me when Melody paid more attention to him than me.

After we got out of the driveway, we switched bikes so he wouldn't have to ride a girl's bike. I successfully fought the urge to rip out the fuchsia-colored streamers that dangled daintily from each handle bar.

The next morning, Mom spoiled my breakfast when she informed me, in one of those ways in which I knew I didn't have a choice, that she'd made arrangements for me to start taking piano lessons. It wasn't like it was totally unexpected; after an argument a few years earlier, she and Dad had agreed to let me wait until I was twelve. My twelfth birthday was nearly a year away, but there was no use arguing. Thanks to Dad, the inevitable had at least been delayed. There was an upside; Wendy's mom was the teacher. And the lessons wouldn't start for a couple of days. My appetite slowly returned.

Booger and I had caught up on our lawns. He had gone with his dad to make an Electrolux vacuum cleaner sales call. He had gone a couple of times since school had been out; his dad had said that Booger helped increase his "kill ratio," a term he used for making a sale. Uncle Cletus had mentioned something about a pity factor, but I wasn't sure what he meant and never repeated it. In any case, Booger and his dad were spending time together.

Uncle Cletus decided to get the Honda 350 Scrambler. Dad and I took him to Fairview, and then stopped off at the airport where Gene Hickman introduced Dad to Dave Blue, a flight instructor. Uncle Cletus stopped too; but probably just so he could pass us again after we got back on the highway. I waited in the parking lot with Uncle Cletus, inspecting the Scrambler, while Dad visited with Dave and Gene.

Before we got started back, he asked if I wanted to ride out to Bird's Cave after we got home. I'd walked the four miles to the cave once and ridden my bicycle there several times. After Uncle Cletus pulled away, I asked Dad about riding to the cave, and he thought it'd be okay. For most of the trip back to Colby, I thought of effortlessly cruising the ridge road and crossing Craggy Creek on Uncle Cletus's Scrambler.

By the time we got back to Colby it had warmed up; Uncle Cletus and I changed into long pants anyway. We didn't tell Mom that we'd done it in case of an accident. Supposedly, gravel wouldn't get imbedded in the skin so bad when wearing long pants versus shorts, or so Uncle Cletus had heard.

Getting on behind Uncle Cletus, I was careful not to burn my leg on the muffler that came up high along one side. Scrambler versions were made that way so that they could be ridden "off-road." I held on to his belt, the one with the Marine buckle. We crept away, barely laboring the powerful 350 CC motor, probably for Mom's benefit.

Out of Mom's sight, Uncle Cletus accelerated much more quickly. I could see the tachometer needle swinging up and down as he shifted through the gears. He turned his head halfway around and said something. I couldn't hear or understand what he was saying, but I nodded yes anyway, just so he'd turn back around—because every time he talked, spit and stuff got sucked out of his mouth and flew back on me. The wind had even washed water from his eyes and back across his temples. When I leaned out from behind him and held my mouth open, the wind puffed my cheeks out like a blowfish. He slowed down near the creek road, but stopped instead of turning and heading down the road toward the cave.

"Jump off," he said.

"Somethin' wrong?"

"No, you said you wanted to drive."

I'd mentioned it back at the airport, but hadn't been serious.

"This is as good a place as any. Let me show you how to work the clutch and shift lever."

He worked the shifter trying to find neutral, somewhere between first and second; I concentrated on getting the look of shock off my face. I guess that's what he'd been asking when he was slinging spit on me.

"Okay, you get on, and then I'll get on behind you. Keep it balanced, though, it's heavy." I was careful not to lean it one way or the other. I knew I wouldn't be able to hold it up if I did.

"You know how to work a clutch, don't you?"

"Sure, it's just like the lever on the tiller."

He laughed. "Well, yeah, but, thing of it is, it's gonna take off a little faster'n the tiller."

He explained how to shift, then threw his leg across the seat. We were ready to go. It took a couple of tries; I learned how to work the electric starter in the process. Finally, I got the clutch out without killing the motor, and we were on our way again.

There was something hypnotic about watching the tachometer needle spin up toward the red line in each gear. I accelerated and shifted through first, second, third, and fourth gears. Who knows what speed we would have reached if Uncle Cletus hadn't squeezed my hip and pointed at the speed odometer. It was right next to the tachometer, sort of a twin instrument, and was sitting on eighty miles per hour.

I shifted to fifth gear and let off of the throttle. The center stripes streaked by so fast it was as if there was a solid white center line. Only then did I become aware of the force of the air on my chest. I momentarily got scared and thought of several consequences if one of my hands slipped from their death grip on the handlebars. Our speed quickly slowed to forty, and I twisted the grip enough to maintain a steady speed. Uncle Cletus eased his grip on my hip. Through the rearview mirror, I saw the grin on his face.

"Pull into that driveway, and let's switch." Had he not said anything, I would've kept going all of the way to Fairview, or further.

We switched quickly. The second we stopped, two mongrel dogs came chasing from behind an old farmhouse and headed our way. "Goodpasture" was printed on the mailbox. A pink car was parked in front of a garage that was overflowing with junk. The Scrambler lurched forward just before the fastest mongrel got a taste of my Converse All Stars, grass stains and all.

I'm not sure how fast we were going on the way back to town. I kept my face buried in Uncle Cletus's back. I didn't dare lean my head out to look around his shoulders at the speedometer for fear of getting swept off by the slip stream.

There wasn't enough time to go to Bird's Cave since we'd gone half way to Fairview and back. We decided to ride by Booger's house and see if he and his dad were home yet.

Booger and his dad weren't there, but Aunt Penelope was. She'd brought a carload of her things from Fairview. It looked like she'd been crying. Her eyes were a little puffy, but nothing else was swollen; it was a good thing, too. As far as I knew, nobody had told Uncle Cletus about her lip. We helped her unload the car. As best I remember, she never said hello. She just started handing us stuff to carry.

"I don't care what people say," she said to no one in particular. "People can talk all they want to," she added, without making eye contact with either of us. I had an idea of what was bugging her, but Uncle Cletus was clueless.

Uncle Cletus looked at me and wrinkled his forehead. A couple of times she stopped, looked at both of us, and blew her bangs up with a puff. She finally looked directly at Uncle Cletus, smiled, and gave him a two-armed, full-frontal-embrace hug. I guess our company made her happy. He looked at me over her shoulder, clearly perplexed, a strange look for Uncle Cletus.

THE HEAVY SMELL OF FRYING bacon and hog jowls greeted Uncle Cletus and me even before we went into my house. Dad had bought a hog from Mr. Bird, and we'd had it butchered and split it with Uncle Cletus. Traditionally, we'd split it with the Burgers and had them over for jowls and beans. It had been recommended to the Burgers that they discontinue some traditions; this was one of them.

Mom was standing over two frying pans. It'd taken Marsha and me two hours to clean up the fat frying mess the previous year. Booger, his mom and dad, and Johnny had been here. We'd done it before Johnny shipped out to Vietnam.

She saw us walk in. "We're ready to eat. We've been waitin' on you two yahoos." Uncle Cletus gave her a hug. She pushed him away. "You've got smashed bugs all over your shirt; your face is covered, too."

We both crowded into the bathroom with Dad, who was just finishing up shaving and was taking a last look in the mirror. I had almost as many bugs as Uncle Cletus, except mine were smeared a little more.

Dad gave us both a "what planet are you from?" look. "You two stink! Here, put some of this on after you wash your faces." He handed me a bottle of Old Spice; it was one of those bottles with the weird top that squirted instead of poured.

Uncle Cletus took a leak while I washed my face. He tooted a little one. We both giggled.

"Are you guys having a party in there?" Mom had good ears. "You'd better be sure and raise the lid," she added.

Drying my face, I looked over and noticed that he hadn't. We switched places. After I finished, I raised the lid and let it fall a few inches. I'm sure Mom smiled when she heard the clunk sound the seat made when it hit the porcelain bowl. Uncle Cletus gave me a wink.

Mom called for Marsha; she and Mickey had been sitting on the back porch. I'd wondered where she was. Mickey didn't have a summer job, except for the paper route. Once, when Mom and Dad didn't know I was listening, I'd heard Dad tell Mom that Mickey was worthless. Mom had told him that he'd no doubt think that all of Marsha's boyfriends were worthless. That was all they'd said about it.

The plates were passed, and everyone took what they needed to build a sandwich. The tomatoes were red but they were store-bought and had probably been picked green, weeks before. They were firm and didn't have much taste. I took several slices anyway.

Black-eyed peas taste good, but they're always a pain to get in a spoon. I liked to use something like mashed potatoes as a backstop to catch them. We weren't having mashed potatoes, though. I noticed Mickey using his knife to catch them. I did the same thing and hoped it wasn't bad manners.

Everyone was enjoying the fresh pork, but Mom couldn't stand the silence. "So, did you two find the cave?"

I knew it was only a matter of time before she or Marsha started asking questions, and then tell me not to talk with my mouth full. I generally put my brain in neutral when I ate, but Mom and Marsha's minds clearly raced at dinner.

I shook my head and glanced at Uncle Cletus, hoping he would explain.

"Really? Well, you need to take your dad with you. He can always find it."

"We didn't look for it," I managed to say after swallowing hard and before she launched into a speech on how I needed to join the Boy Scouts and learn about the outdoors and compasses, or some such stuff.

"You went all of the way out there and didn't even look for it?"

Uncle Cletus wiped his mouth and grinned. "Thing of it is, we stayed on the highway and drove toward Fairview, Ellen."

"Oh, well, why didn't you just say so?" I mentally rolled my eyes.

"How fast will it run?" Mickey asked. Marsha smiled and wiggled in her seat when Mickey spoke. She really acted different around Mickey, sort of stupid and helpless.

"Not really sure, but it'll accelerate all of the way to seventy pretty quick." Uncle Cletus answered and kicked my foot under the table. We'd both just seen ninety, or there about.

Mickey stuck around and helped with the clean up. He'd applied an ample splash of Jade East. I let him scrub the grease off of the oven top. Dad played the piano a while, and then joined Mom and Uncle Cletus on the porch where they drank coffee. Mickey and Marsha went onto the back porch. I studied my Honda Mini-Trail literature.

A CAR PULLED INTO THE driveway; it was Booger, his dad, and Aunt Penelope. Booger and I went out on the back porch to get a couple of chairs and caught Marsha smoochn' with Mickey.

"What do *you* want?" she asked.

"Dad wants these chairs around front." She grunted something and got out of the way.

We carried the two metal lawn chairs around to the front. Marsha and I'd just painted them the Saturday before; it was a traditional spring job. A small scratch on the bottom of one leg revealed several layers and a variety of colors.

Dad told Marsha that she and Mickey needed to come inside since it was getting dark. She probably thought I'd told on her, but I hadn't. They came inside, turned on the TV, and started watching an *Andy Griffith* re-run. It was the one in which Opie accidentally killed the bird with his BB gun.

Booger and I were looking at the Scrambler and eavesdropping on the adults when the phone rang. Marsha came to the door. "It's for you, Tommy. It's Mr. Gooche." I gave Booger a bug-eyed look, shrugged my shoulders, and ran to the phone.

"Yes, sir, we'll be there." Booger had followed me in. "He wants us to start tomorrow. That's okay, isn't it?"

"I think so, I'll ask." He went out on the porch and asked. It was kind of weird. His dad's hands started trembling, he nodded his head yes, and pulled Booger in and gave him a hug. All we were going to do was carry out groceries and stock shelves. You'da thought we'd just been given our draft notice.

Chapter 22

First Day at Gooche's

Booger and I were waiting on Mr. Gooche when he arrived to open the store.

"Good deal," he said, unlocking the door and holding it open for us. "You remembered to wear shirts with collars," he said, shaking our hands. "Welcome to the Gooche's Grocery Team."

He handed us clip-on ties. They were light blue and had "Gooche's Grocery" printed vertically on them in dark blue letters. I remember getting goose bumps putting mine on. We used the mirror on the sunglass display case to get them straight.

"We got our weekly shipment in yesterday and stocked the shelves last night. So, I'd like you two to start in the stock room. I'll show you." We followed him to the back through the swinging doors that only employees can go through. The stock boys had been expecting us; the area was a mess.

"Normally the boys put these boxes on the truck and carry them to the incinerator as they're emptied." He frowned. "Maybe I shouldn't have mentioned you two were coming." He kicked a few boxes out of the way and opened the overhead door.

Booger and I never settled the argument over exactly what model year the Chevy pickup was; I guessed it to be 1950, and Booger was sure it was a '49, because of the door handles. Uncle Cletus had told me how to tell the difference, but I couldn't remember. This one had the kind of knobs that twist. The one on the driver's side was hanging down a little. It had a deluxe cab with the corner windows, similar to Mr. Bird's. On the doors, "Gooche's Grocery" was faded but readable. At one time it had been used for deliveries.

Mr. Gooche opened the driver's side door. "Jump in."

I climbed in, careful to sit on the piece of cardboard that was covering the exposed springs in the bench seat.

"It's got a new batree, start her up."

My heart raced. I thought the collar button on my shirt might pop off as my neck enlarged. The gearshift, starter button on the floor, and ignition-key location were identical to Uncle Cletus's truck. He'd never let me start his, but I'd watched him several times.

"I can do this," I told myself. In the meantime, Booger had jumped in on the other side. I put it in neutral, pulled out the choke button, and pressed on the starter pedal. It came to life instantly; clearly the engine and battery were in better shape than the rest of the truck.

"Good deal. Now, ease it forward a few feet, and then back it back up to the dock." I looked at Booger. He was grinning ear-to-ear, maybe the biggest smile he'd had since before his mom's funeral.

I'd driven tractors enough to know how to use the clutch. It died the first time I tried, but on the second try I got the clutch out without killing the engine, and the truck lurched forward.

Mr. Gooche started waving his arms. "That's good, that's good. Now back it up."

Mr. Gooche stepped back a few feet; he hadn't totally lost his mind. Booger watched and told me when to stop before hitting the dock. I never really got going fast enough to use the brakes.

"Good deal. I figured since you'd been around farm equipment, you'd know how to drive." Booger was still grinning.

He showed us again where the incinerator was and told us we could burn the boxes but not to get the truck too close when there was a fire going. I'd driven all kinds of tractors and a few combines, but never a car or truck. Booger and I'd probably have done the job for free if we'd known about getting to drive.

The AM radio took a few minutes to warm up. At first, Booger thought it didn't work, but our '58 Chevy Bellaire had a radio just like it. The speaker crackled as the radio came to life. A twist of the tuning knob, and the needle spun around to 630 on the sun-faded dial. "I'm A Believer" by the Monkees was already playing—"then I saw her face, now I'm a believer, not a trace of doubt in my mind, I'm in love, I'm a believer I couldn't leave her if I tried, yeah yeah."

"Good Vibrations" by the Beach Boys started playing on the way to the incinerator; it made me want to drive fast, but since I could barely reach the accelerator pedal, we crawled. My view of the narrow alley was through the gap between the dash and the top of the steering wheel, except when we'd hit a pothole, and I'd bounce higher.

One load at a time, we hauled all of the empty boxes to the incinerator. I drove and Booger rode shotgun. Since I'd driven the truck, Booger got to light the fire.

Leon Goolsby, the butcher, and Irvin Enderle, the assistant store manager, were standing on the dock. They'd been watching us a few minutes; I wasn't sure how long. Booger had thought I'd driven the truck a little fast down the alley from the incinerator on the last trip—I did bounce hard enough to hit my head on the ceiling. Swerving to the beat of "Summer in the City" by the Lovin' Spoonful didn't set too well with him, either. Leon and Irvin had probably heard the truck engine racing and came out to see what we where up to. It may have been the fire, too; we'd maybe gotten the incinerator too full before lighting it.

A large, flaming Tide box gently lifted off and drifted toward the building. The hot air rising from the incinerator provided just enough lift to get the box up and into the breeze. All of the other boxes had been crushed or folded and only produced large pieces of flameless ashes floating weightlessly into the sky. The fire in the incinerator died down almost as fast as it started. The Tide box was another story.

Floating weightlessly toward the building, it crumbled when it hit the concrete block wall. As each piece dropped to the dry weeds that bordered the building, small contagious flames sprung up. Booger and I, struck with some sort of momentary paralysis, just watched as the small flames joined together and grew in strength. Leon and Irvin rushed past us and started stomping out the flames. They got the fire out almost as quickly as it had started. Booger and I walked over by them; they were both out of breath.

Leon looked at Booger. "You Johnny Burger's brother?"

"Yes, sir," Booger replied, his voice breaking slightly.

Irvin surveyed the weeds and the block wall. "I don't guess there's any damage."

Leon took his apron off and shook it and eyed us both carefully. "Think maybe you shouldn't burn so many boxes at one time?"

We both nodded.

Irvin looked at his watch. "Mr. Gooche had to leave; he won't be back until after noon." He looked at the two of us. "Think you guys can make it till noon without doin' any more damage?"

We nodded again.

"Well, if you can make it till noon without breakin' anything, I don't see why Mr. Gooche needs to know about this."

Leon gave Irvin an agreeing look. I'd already been trying to figure out how to explain getting fired from my first job before noon on the first day. We'd gotten a break, probably because of Johnny, but at the moment I was just glad to keep my job.

Irvin pulled a piece of paper from his shirt pocket. "Mr. Gooche gave me a list of some things for you'uns to do. Maybe it'd be better if I split you'uns up."

Booger got assigned stocking the paper bag bins at the checkout counters. I was handed an oil mop and instructed to go over everything that was tile, which was basically the entire store.

Halfway down aisle two, in front of the cereals, was Wendy's mom. She gave me a toothy smile; her teeth were like Wendy's, perfectly spaced and straight. "Hi, Tommy. I'm so glad you've decided to take piano lessons."

I smiled and politely kept moving, avoiding direct eye contact. "Yes, ma'am." She was talking loud enough for others to hear, so I thought it best to get away.

"So, are you working here?"

"Yes, ma'am."

"Wendy didn't mention it."

"Well, I'm not sure she knows. Anyway, Mr. Gooche wants me to sweep the entire store, so I better get busy."

"Don't let me hold you back. I'm so looking forward to you starting lessons. Your mother will be so proud when you play in the recital this fall."

Her last statement stopped me dead in my tracks; I dropped the mop handle and stumbled forward. "The what?"

"Recital. All my students play in a fall recital. It's held at the Methodist Church. She didn't tell you?"

I picked up the mop handle and didn't answer; my mouth wouldn't follow instructions from my brain, which was probably best anyway.

"Oh, it's the greatest. There's usually a couple of hundred people there, counting family and all."

"Sounds great," I lied, in a tone that came out an octave or two higher than normal, maybe somewhere in the pitch of a dog whistle. I felt my knees starting to buckle, so I pushed the mop on around to the next aisle. First it was the fire, then the piano lessons; for a moment I felt anxious for school to start again.

Mr. Gooche returned before Booger and I left; we told him about the fire. He was visibly disappointed, but told us we could come back the next day. On the way home, we calculated how much we were going to make at Gooche's and estimated how quickly we'd be able to get the Mini-Trails. Booger looked happy to have something to look forward to.

Chapter 23

Colby Cardinals

"Uncle Cletus called," Mom told me as soon as I walked in the door from work. "You're on his team, the Cardinals. First practice is tomorrow afternoon."

I was desperately in need of some good news; this was it. Mom wasn't finished, though. "Clyde Goodpasture is on the team, too." I fell onto the couch, totally deflated.

Mom gave me a look. "Uncle Cletus doesn't pick the teams, he just coaches. You'll just have to learn to get along."

"What about Everett?" I asked, hoping against hope.

"He didn't say." Everett had signed up at the same time I did; I hoped he'd gotten placed on the same team. I crossed my fingers and called Uncle Cletus.

"No, they put Everett on the Yankees. Thing of it is, all the big guys got split up so that each team would have at least one. Booger's on our team. You two can ride together." He read me the rest of the roster. It sounded like we'd have a good team.

I told Mom about work, including the fire, but left out the part about talking to Mrs. Winchester or driving the truck.

Dad was due home any minute. I found our ball gloves lying on the shelf together next to the leather oil, with a note from Dad. I squirted a dab in the web of both gloves and worked it in, like the note had said to do, and sat on the porch waiting for him to get home.

Mom heard Dad's truck and came out onto the porch to give him a hug. He hugged her with one hand and mussed my hair with the other. "Sorry I'm late. I got held up talking to Gene Hickman." He and Gene had been doing a lot of talking lately.

"Supper will be a few minutes. Cletus called and Tommy's on his team, the Cardinals. Booger is too. Tommy's been waiting patiently to play catch." She smiled and winked at Dad, grinned, and nodded at me. "He had an exciting day at work, ask him about it."

I gave him a chance to get warmed up before throwing hard and trying to sting his catching hand. He tried to act like I wasn't throwing fast, but I saw him grimace a couple of times. After throwing one so high he had to jump to catch it, popping the top button off of his shirt, I brought up the fire.

"What did Mr. Gooche say?"

"He said we'd learned a good lesson."

"How was your first day, other than the fire?"

I told him almost everything.

"Dad?"

He grinned. "What is it, Tommy?"

"Do I have to play in the recital?"

"What did your Mom say?"

"I was hoping you'd talk to her before I asked." We threw a few more pitches before Mom whistled; it was time for supper.

Marsha kept looking across the table and grinning. "Heard you almost burned down the town." I stared hard, hoping she'd burst into flames, or something worse. Seeing no smoke, I settled for a hard kick to her shin.

"Ouch! You little creep!" She threw the ketchup bottle cap, and it hit me in the chest.

Mom grabbed Marsha's arm. "That's enough."

"He kicked me."

"It was an accident, good grief. Sorry."

We both got a look.

"How'd Booger do today?" Dad asked, changing the subject.

"Fine. We didn't talk much; they separated us after ..."

"The fire," Marsha interrupted. She snorted, and then we all started laughing. I was sorry I'd kicked her, even though there was a small ring of ketchup on my shirt.

Dad didn't bring up the recital; he had his own agenda. He'd stayed late talking to Gene Hickam, again, about flying. He would eventually get around to telling us that Gene had offered to take all of us for an airplane ride.

"What would you think about me taking flying lessons?"

"Can we afford it?" Mom asked. She stopped eating and just moved her food around with a fork.

Marsha and I cleared the table while they talked money.

While doing dishes, Marsha started talking about flying. I was surprised at how excited she sounded, since she'd never been in an airplane before. She was looking forward to Sunday and hoped the weather was nice so we could go for a plane ride, too. I finished the dishes so she could go sit on the front porch with Mom and Dad and tell them how excited we were about the airplane ride. I knew Dad needed the help. He owed me.

BOOGER AND HIS DAD HAD an appointment with their counselor. They'd be home by noon, when we planned to mow Mr. Gooche's lawn. I got to the store early and parked my bike in the back near the dock where the truck was parked. I looked inside and saw that someone had left the key in the ignition.

Mr. Gooche was in his office pecking away on his adding machine. Several feet of narrow paper streamed from the machine and down the back of his desk; he'd been there a while. I reported the key in the ignition.

He laughed. "That's where I keep it—don't think anybody's going to steal that old jalopy. It hasn't been licensed for ten years, the tires are bald, and the interior is all but gone. The batree is the only thing in it that's worth anything." He drummed his adding machine fingers on the desk. "Ready to get started again?"

"Yes, sir."

"Irvin's in the back; he's expecting you. He's going to show you what needs to be done."

"Yes, sir."

He grinned. "Don't have any plans to burn the place down, do you?"

"No, sir."

"Booger go to Fairview with his dad?"

"Yes, sir."

"He doin' okay?"

"I think so, far as I know. He doesn't talk much. My mom said it'd be best if he stayed busy. We're gonna mow this afternoon."

"That was going to be my next question. Good deal." He started pecking on the machine again. I headed to the back.

Once a week, an outfit from Fairview came at night and cleaned the floors. They'd been there the night before; I could smell the wax, and my shoes squeaked with each step on the shiny tiles.

Irvin didn't mention the fire, and I didn't bring it up. He and Odie Portman were good friends. They combed their hair the same way—long on the sides and combed back and the top cut short and sticking up like a flat top. It was sort of like they couldn't make up their minds. Following him through the warehouse, I noticed that he had an "Omar Dooley for Sheriff" comb in his back pocket. It'd been a while since he'd cleaned it.

He'd made a checklist of things for Booger and me to do: change the fly strips, run the mousetraps, clean the toilets, sweep the sidewalk, pick up trash on the parking lot, and put sawdust on oil spots.

Working at Gooche's was turning out to be a learning experience. I learned that fly strips become permanently attached to anything that comes in contact with them, including fingers, and that mousetraps need to be checked every day, especially in areas that aren't air-conditioned. I also discovered that Dad and I aren't the only ones that can't hit the toilet, and not everyone had been taught to flush. I found things in the parking lot I'd have to ask Uncle Cletus about.

I didn't get around to putting sawdust on the oil spots. Irvin stopped me and told me to help Leon in the butcher shop. Leon was making individual packages for the meat case. We started with ground beef, but as soon as we'd worked down a huge pile of it, Leon started cutting pork chops with what looked like a band saw. Eventually, we packaged some of everything. My job was to cover the meat and the extra-thick paper plate with cellophane. A hot roller, sort of an iron deal, melted the cellophane and made it stick together; it had some special coating so that the cellophane wouldn't stick to it. Leon weighed the packages and stuck a price label on them.

We didn't take a break all morning. "Irvin says you're doing a good job." He startled me; it was Mr. Gooche. I had no idea how long he'd been standing behind me. "It's 12:15."

"It is?"

"Weren't you supposed to clock out at noon?"

"Yes, sir. I told Leon I'd finish these before I left, though." I only had a dozen or so packages left. Leon was busy doing custom cuts for one of his regular customers. Mr. Gooche squeezed my neck gently, nodded approval, and then walked toward the front of the store. He spoke to everyone he passed.

MARSHA, FEARING THAT I'D SOMEHOW starve while working at a grocery store, had fixed me two sandwiches, one bologna and one peanut butter and jelly. Lava, even with all that pumice stuff they talked about on TV, wouldn't take the meat grease off of my hands. Butcher's hands are either soft from the grease or chapped from scrubbing them. I used a fork to eat my sandwich because my hands still stunk, and I had no idea what all had gotten stuffed up under my fingernails. Marsha didn't make fun; she thought it was cool that I was working at Gooche's. She said that if Mickey didn't have the paper route, he'd probably get a job there, too.

BOOGER WAS WAITING FOR ME when I got to the Gooches' house.

Mrs. Gooche started taking down the laundry from the clothesline when she saw us filling up the gas tanks on the lawn mowers. We split up, Booger in front and me in back. The grass was thick, but dry, and mowed easily. I liked the smell of the exhaust mixed with the freshly mowed grass.

We were a little over half finished when Booger's dad came to check on us. He offered to fill up the gas cans. He returned with full cans and a small carton of chocolate milk for both of us; it was sort of a celebration. He'd just sold a vacuum cleaner to Caleb Wilfong's mom. From what I'd seen of Caleb's house, they needed one.

After we finished with Mr. Gooche's yard, we pushed the mowers to Melody's house where she'd been watching for us and waiting with our lemonade. I couldn't help but notice the tan line on her legs.

She caught me looking. "It's from the iodine." I looked at Booger, standing behind her, for an answer; he shrugged. "It's supposed to make you tan faster," she added.

"Oh." I shook my head, as if to understand, but wrote it off as just another mystery about girls. Uncle Cletus could probably explain it, but even he admitted to being clueless at times about a woman's behavior.

She told us about her babysitting jobs and how she liked taking care of babies. Booger and I listened for a while, and then just before our eyes rolled back into our heads, we told her we needed to go to baseball practice.

Working at Gooche's, mowing lawns, and baseball had left very little time to think about Melody or Wendy; seeing Melody again started my mind working once more.

Uncle Cletus called and said he'd come by and pick me up for practice. I sat on the porch waiting since Mom didn't want me in the house with my cleats on. I heard his '57 Chevy pickup before I saw it, and walked out to the street.

"Whose autograph is that on th' bat?"

"Lou Brock." It wasn't really an autograph, so to speak, since it had been stamped in along with the Hillerich & Bradsby, Louisville Slugger logo.

"Still got that Bob Gibson glove, I see." It had a similarly inauthentic autograph.

"Yep."

"Think Lou will break Ty Cobb's record?"

"I don't know, probably, hope so. Ty Cobb was a jerk and Lou's a nice person."

"How'd 'ja know?"

"Read it."

"Believe everything you read?"

"No."

"Good; it's true what they say about Ty Cobb, though," Uncle Cletus finally confirmed.

He glanced at me. "Worried about Clyde Goodpasture?"

"No, maybe, I don't know." I replied unconvincingly.

"I watched Clyde play last year. Thing of it is, he can hit the ball and block the plate better than any other kid in the league. If a guy would work with him, he'd be a good ball player."

"Will he have to catch when I pitch?"

"He's got a bit of a chip on his shoulder, I know, prob'ly because his dad got killed. You two are just going t' have t' get along; you're teammates now."

"What do ya' mean, his dad got killed? I thought he was the foreman at th' shoe factory."

"That contentious idiot is his stepdad; his real dad got killed drivin' a log truck.

"When?"

"Clyde was only about two. You were too young to remember. His mom remarried fairly quickly. His stepdad legally adopted him, but that's about all he's done. Thing of it is, I doubt he and Clyde have ever played catch. You've met his mom." Uncle Cletus rolled his eyes.

Uncle Cletus kept talking until we got to the ball field. I listened and watched him drive. He was the most insightful person I knew, and he seemed to like Clyde. He'd also mastered a stick shift. I looked forward to the day I could operate the clutch on a truck as good as Uncle Cletus.

No one else was there yet; we were the first team to practice this year. Uncle Cletus unlocked the spider-infested shed. I waited outside and let him hand me the bases. He dumped the equipment out and I inspected it, mostly for spider nests. I put the bases in place on the field and contemplated what he'd told me about Clyde. I noticed that the infield needed to be smoothed out. Winter rains had formed little dirt clumps.

The other players started showing up. Most rode their bicycles and had their gloves and cleats strapped on their handlebars. A couple had bats tied to their handlebars, too. Clyde's mom dropped him off and then left. He didn't have a bat or a glove and was wearing the same shoes he'd worn to school all year. Booger and his dad pulled up.

Uncle Cletus gave us positions to play, and he and Booger's dad took turns pitching while we practiced batting. I took left field; Booger played center. We didn't need a catcher for batting practice, so Clyde was in right field. There was only one left-handed kid on the team and he couldn't hit the broad side of a barn, so Clyde didn't get many balls hit his way. Infield ground balls bounced unpredictably off the winter clumps. A couple of kids got bopped in the face, but nobody cried.

Batting practice order was always infield players first, then the outfield. We used the same balls all practice and they had been in the equipment bag all winter; some of them were solid, but most were soft and mushy. They'd only gotten softer during practice, although no one had shown they could hit well, mostly fouling off or missing the ball completely.

Clyde was the last to hit—the right fielder always was. I was thirsty and tired of standing; we'd been batting for nearly an hour. After fouling a couple off, he hit every ball over the infield into center or right field. A couple went deep on the fly. I was exhausted from chasing Clyde's fly balls by the time Uncle Cletus signaled for us to come in. He'd been right about

Clyde's ability to hit. Clyde no doubt enjoyed watching me chase after his well-hit balls.

At the end of practice, Uncle Cletus talked to the team about discipline. He said that if we were disciplined and practiced the basics, we could compete with any team around. His gaze paused momentarily at Clyde when he emphasized that he wouldn't tolerate "horse play." Uncle Cletus had a reputation for being strict at school; some kids were afraid of him. For most, however, he was the kind of teacher that students wanted to please and impress.

After practice, Uncle Cletus and I waited with Clyde. His mom never came, so after thirty minutes we took him home. It was then that I began to understand him.

Chapter 24

Test Flight

It was the first Saturday of the month and promised to be busy at Gooche's. Many families had just gotten their government checks, and campers on their way to the river for the weekend generally stopped and did their last-minute shopping at Gooche's, too. One of the regular carryout boys went on vacation with his family. So, Mr. Gooche asked me to fill in.

Velma, the checkout lady, gave me some obvious bagging tips: bread and eggs on top, vegetables in their own bag, milk on the bottom.

By 8:30, the store was crawling with customers; most I'd never seen before. Velma gave me the low-down on every shopper. She pointed out one family that lived near the river, about thirty miles away and in another school district. Gooche's was probably the closest grocery store for them. There were eight of them: the parents, four boys, and two girls. They stuck together like a flock of sheep, touching and examining everything before putting it in their cart or back on the shelf—but not necessarily in the same spot where they'd grabbed it.

Mrs. Pope walked in, chose a cart, and smiled. She was older than Mom, thin and statuesque, with naturally graying hair that looked like it had been tinted that way. Velma raised her eyebrows and looked Mrs. Pope's way. "She tips."

"Tips?"

"She'll want her groceries taken to the Houn Dawg next door; whoever does it always gets a nice tip." I tucked that thought away.

Dad tipped a waitress once in Fairview, and Mom chewed him out when we got in the car, but I think it was something other than the tip that had made her mad.

I could bag about as fast as Velma could check. In between customers we talked. It turned out she was Dwight and Corky's mom. She didn't seem too impressed when I told her I was getting a Honda Mini-Trail like Dwight's.

"When he gets his license back, you can probably buy his."

"How'd he lose his license?"

A customer, who looked like a camper, started putting groceries on the counter. "Alcohol," she whispered.

An interesting thing about bagging groceries is getting to see what people purchase. For example, along with several packages of lunch meat and other picnic food, the camper had purchased several packages of cigarette paper but no Prince Albert. Velma knew the scoop, so to speak, on everyone.

THE INSTANT SHE WALKED THROUGH the door, I knew she had to be the "bearded lady" that Leon, Irvin, and Velma had told me to watch for. She was legendary. It was difficult not to stare; I wanted to see the porkchop side burns she was known for. Listening to Velma and bagging at the same time made it almost impossible to get a good look when she walked by.

Velma handed the camper, a hippie-looking guy, his change; I followed him out. He pointed toward a van, one that looked like it had been modified.

"I'm parked o'vair, dude."

When he opened the sliding van door, a pungent odor filled my nostrils. Another guy and two girls were sitting inside, in the dark, on top of camping gear and coolers. They were drinking beer, Pabst Blue Ribbon, and all three were sharing a homemade cigarette. It looked like the kind that Papaw smoked but smelled really different. I handed them their groceries and hurried back inside. They gave me the creeps.

Velma had started checking out the family of eight by the time I got back inside. She had already filled two bags; I took over packing. Their groceries filled four carts, not counting four large bags of potatoes that the dad and the four boys carried. The dad did well to carry his belly. The youngest boy was only half the size of the oldest girl and could barely carry his bag. Our eyes locked for a split second, and he smiled. What teeth I could see looked like little black nubs. I imagined his legs bowing inside his loose trousers under the weight of the potatoes.

They'd come to town in a pickup truck with stock racks on the bed. The adults and two girls rode in front, and the boys all rode in the back. The boys climbed over the tailgate; the dad and I handed them their groceries. The bed of the truck had all kinds of trash in it: oil cans, beer bottles, cigarette cartons, pork 'n bean cans, and other stuff I didn't get close enough to identify.

Once the groceries were situated behind the cab, the boys jumped back out and started pushing the truck. The dad popped the clutch, the engine came to life, and the truck slowed down just long enough for the boys to hop into the back, the smallest climbing in last and barely making it in before the truck sprang to life. He then took a place next to the tail-gate, waved, and smiled. It occurred to me that none of them, except the dad, had spoken.

Velma had almost finished checking out Mrs. Whitener when I got back. She had enough for three bags: eggs, bacon, Spam, cheese, bread, butter, prune juice, grapes, and all sorts of fresh vegetables. She probably made her own jelly.

The backseat of her '57 Chevrolet Belair looked like it had never been sat on. She had it covered with plastic. Supposedly her husband had bought it brand-new just before he died of a heart attack or something. She handed me a buffalo nickel for a tip; a mostly toothless smile spread across her face after I thanked her.

Velma and I worked through lunch; that's when we were the busiest. We finally got a break at 1:30. I'd somehow missed the bearded lady checking out, but Velma told me that she'd bought a copy of the tabloid that featured a photograph taken in Louisiana of a half man, half alligator. Leon fixed us both a sandwich and Esther, the produce lady, made us a salad. Booger had gone to the Houn Dawg at noon with his dad; he'd probably gotten the tip from Mrs. Pope.

Velma and I were sitting in the produce room when Mr. Gooche handed out checks. It was my first paycheck. He asked if Booger and I could work all day; we called home and got permission.

I'd worked twenty-three hours that week and was making a dollar an hour, but only cleared eighteen dollars and seventy-three cents after deductions. Deductions and drought were making the Mini-Trail payments more difficult than I'd planned.

WE GOT OFF AT SEVEN and went straight to the movie. I was still wearing my Gooche's Grocery tie. Booger and I each bought a bag of popcorn and a soda with crushed ice. There was a seat behind Wendy, Beth, and some other girls, so we sat there. I vaguely remember watching the cartoons, but missed the movie starting.

"Tommy, Tommy." Somebody was shaking me. I opened my eyes and it was Dad. Popcorn was spilled on the floor in front of my seat. I'd finished the soda. Dad and Mr. Burger were both standing there, laughing. I'd been drooling. Booger was rubbing his eyes, yawning, and stretching. All the lights in the movie were on, and everyone was gone except for the people sweeping.

"Mr. Arnold called," Dad said. "The movie has been over for thirty minutes."

We'd slept through the whole movie. What a waste of hard-earned money. I had the urge to pee really bad, which was good; that meant I hadn't gone in my pants. We staggered out. My left foot tingled as it came back to life. I waited until I got home to pee; the restroom at the theatre was gross.

THE NEXT MORNING, DAD TOLD me that Mom had agreed to go for an airplane ride. I paid close attention to Brother Baker; I knew Mom would be asking me questions about the sermon on the way to Fairview for the airplane ride. He spoke from John 12:23–25, "Unless a kernel of wheat falls and dies, it remains only a single seed. But if it dies, it produces many seeds. The man who loves his life will lose it, while the man who hates his life in this world will keep it for eternal life."

He told us that in order to live a God-centered life, we had to focus on God's purpose for our life and not on our own plans. We must seek to see from God's perspective rather than our own. I was excited about going for the airplane ride, but I tried not to be anxious, or at least show it, because I had no idea how it fit into God's plan.

We got out of church late; nobody complained, which was rare. After changing clothes, we left for Fairview and ate some sandwiches on the way. We talked about the sermon. Once Mom was satisfied we'd paid attention, she turned the radio on. Petula Clark was singing, "What The World Needs Now Is Love, Sweet Love." Ironically, the song was followed up by a news bulletin on the war in Vietnam. Another B-52 had been shot down over the Ho Chi Minh trail. There was a battle going on for control of someplace called the Central Highlands.

Dave Blue was waiting for us at the airport. He encouraged everyone to go to the restroom before walking us out to a Cessna 206, a six-place single-engine high-wing plane. He explained how the control surfaces worked, checked the oil level, made sure the fuel tanks were full, and then we loaded up.

Mom sat in the back, Marsha and I in the middle seats, and Dad sat next to Dave in the front. The dash was packed with instruments; Dave explained them. Marsha wanted me to sit back so she could see too. I was too enthralled to be anything except selfish.

The engine sounded like a dragster. Dave had warned us that it'd be loud since it had no mufflers. We taxied to the end of the runway. Dave raced the engine and referred to a list and checked some other things.

After getting clearance from the tower, he lined the plane up on the centerline of the runway, pushed the throttle control full in, and the engine came to life with a roar that Dwight Seabaugh could only dream about. The airplane shook and creaked as it accelerated down the runway, then became eerily quiet and smooth once we became airborne.

The ground was divided into squares; the farms looked like giant quilts. I figured this might be the "God's perspective" that Brother Baker had been talking about. The ride was a little bumpy at first; Dave had said something about thermals. Colby looked really different; everything seemed so small and close together. Some people hadn't hooked up to the sewer system yet; the darker shade of green grass clearly revealed their septic tank laterals.

Dave let Dad take the controls. We did some turns and made the plane climb and descend. We flew up the creek over the bridge and shut-ins. I saw Mr. Bird's farm and the hill with the cave. Mom was enjoying the ride now that it had gotten smooth. Marsha stopped looking out and asked about the sick sack. Too quickly, we made a smooth landing, and the first flight was over.

Before leaving town, we swung by Fairview Honda. They were closed, but we could see the Mini-Trails on display. It was the first time Mom had seen one.

"They're kinda small," was her first comment.

I have to admit, her words cut a little. Giving her comment more thought, I realized she might have been saying I should get a larger bike. There was a step-through Trailblazer she thought was "cute." After the airplane ride, the bikes didn't interest Dad at all.

On the way home, everyone was talking at once. Marsha wanted to take the ground school with Dad and get the written exam out of the way; she'd forgotten about feeling queasy. I wanted to fly with him during the lessons and couldn't have cared less about some stupid exam. Mom wanted to know when Dad planned to fit the lessons into his schedule, and for sure that his store would be paying for them.

Looking out the rear side window to the west, I watched the sun. It slowly sank into the horizon. The thin skiff of clouds reflected an orange hue, and the sky became a darker blue. We made it home in time to watch the *Wonderful World of Disney* and *Bonanza*. Mom fixed popcorn; Marsha and I shared a grape soda. It was one of the best days I can remember.

Chapter 25

First Game

OUR FIRST GAME WAS ONLY a day away, against a team from Fairview. We seldom beat any team from Fairview and were all taking practice very seriously. Booger's dad pitched batting practice. He had a good arm. When he tried he could strike out everyone except Clyde.

Uncle Cletus had sorted through our baseball uniforms. They were lying all crumpled up in the bed of his pickup truck. He handed each of us our uniforms. "Take 'em home and ask your mom to iron out the wrinkles." He hesitated a second, looked Booger's way, and then went on. I knew what both were thinking.

Nobody cared about the wrinkles and we changed between parked cars, anxious to wear the uniforms. Clyde's fit him a little tight; his socks looked goofy since he didn't have cleats.

Booger and I'd picked the same two cars to change between. "I'll have Mom iron yours," I told him as he tucked his shirt in. He nodded a yes, but didn't speak. I gave him a one-arm hug and didn't care who saw it.

Clyde caught while I practiced pitching. Uncle Cletus said I'd probably be starting. It wasn't because he was my uncle. There just wasn't anyone else who could throw strikes, which, unless the umpires were blind—and they sometimes were—was a requirement.

Up until then, Clyde seemed to have been avoiding me; I was certainly steering clear of him. I threw a few pitches and he started chattering, "come on baby, rock'n fire, little high, right down the middle," things a catcher says during a game.

I'd worked up a pretty good sweat by the time practice was finished. Booger and his dad were ready to leave. Uncle Cletus took Clyde home again; it was either that or Clyde would have had to walk, since his mom had told him to find a ride. He waved goodbye as they left the parking lot; we still hadn't spoken.

BAD TIMING IS ALL I can figure. My first piano lesson was on the same day as our first game of the season. I wore my uniform to the lesson so Mom could take me straight to the game. Wendy and Beth were lying in their yard on a quilt, sunning, sort of like Melody and her friends had done.

Wendy and Beth both sat up as I walked from the car to the front door. Wendy then said, "Ooh, nice outfit."

"It's a baseball uniform," I told her.

"I knew that," she said defensively. "You're a Cardinal." We made direct eye contact; her smile was captivating.

"Hi, Tommy. You're a few minutes early. That's good." Mrs. Winchester broke my trance, and my pulse slowly returned to normal.

A workbook titled "Prep Course for the Young Beginner" was laying on the piano bench. It had "Tommy Thompson" written in calligraphy across the bottom. Mrs. Winchester picked it up and handed it to me. I was the young beginner.

She patted the bench. "Have a seat." I sat down and we reviewed the book.

The first two pages illustrated the left and right hand with a silhouette and had the fingers numbered. Mrs. Winchester put small stickers with a corresponding number on each of my fingernails. I considered bolting out the door.

She talked about the groupings of black keys. They were in twos and threes. The page illustrating the groups had a frog on it. My life was taking a change for the worse. The other guys were going over ramps on their bikes or shooting potato guns. I was looking at a page with piano keys and frogs. Mrs. Winchester closed the blinds so I couldn't see Wendy and Beth; I was suffocating.

Mrs. Winchester gave me an assignment called "note magic." It was an exercise on quarter notes, half notes, whole notes, and dynamic signs. "Next week we'll start on the musical alphabet," she told me. I looked at the assignment sheet and thought about baseball.

She held my hands and jabbed my fingers at the keys to the tune of "Row, Row, Row Your Boat." I told her I was pitching in the game. She wasn't impressed. Then Mom knocked on the door. To me it was as if the Marines had arrived. I'd been liberated.

Wendy and Beth gave a girly wave, the wiggly finger thing. When I stepped out onto the porch I hid my lesson book and ran to the car.

CLYDE'S MOM HADN'T IRONED HIS uniform, but it fit so tight that, from a distance, the wrinkles didn't show too bad. Uncle Cletus offered to catch my pitches until Clyde got the catcher's gear on. He walked with me to the mound.

"Thing of it is, your grandmother tried to make me take lessons too." I looked around to make sure no one had heard him. "I didn't listen; wish I had." He handed me the ball. "Stick with it." He walked toward home plate. I wasn't sure if he was serious, or if Mom had just gotten to him.

Every Fairview player's parents must have had a brand new station wagon because that's what they had all arrived in. We usually rode to away games in the back of a pickup truck.

It must have been Fairview's first year for their uniforms. They all looked clean and new. We'd never beaten them and usually played them first, just to get it out of the way.

Their first batter was a short, skinny guy. He squatted down, reducing his strike zone to about twelve inches. I walked him on four pitches.

Clyde trotted out to the mound and handed me the ball. "Just like'n practice, Tommy," he said and patted me on the shoulder. I no longer feared him or held him in disdain, but I wasn't exactly ready to call him my friend, either.

The second batter was left-handed. He rubbed some dirt on his hands and glanced at Clyde. "Can he throw a strike?" He had said it to Clyde, but loud enough for me to hear.

"Heard your mom wears army boots," was Clyde's response. The south-paw braced.

"Say what?"

"Yep, heard she howls at th' moon, too." Clyde was looking at me; I could see him grinning through the catcher's mask.

"Batter up," the ump ordered; he couldn't have cared less what was being said between Clyde and the batter.

Clyde gave me a target. "Rock'n fire, Tommy. This guy can't hit." The rest of the infield chimed in, "miss batter batter, miss batter batter …"

The first pitch was inside, but the batter swung anyway, and missed. The next pitch was right down the middle; he let it go by.

"Stee ... rike two." The ump's call only fueled the infield chanting.

Clyde made a sound like a dog howling. "Your mom's callin'," he said. The batter backed out of the box, looked at Clyde, and decided wisely to let it go.

The little runt that I'd walked had already stolen second and third, so I did a full windup. Clyde held up his mitt and gave me a good target, but for some reason the ball left my hand and streaked toward the batter's helmet. I can honestly say it wasn't intentional, although to this day nobody believes me. The batter ducked and hit the dirt, but the ball hit his bat and dropped in front of home plate. Clyde picked it up, tagged him out, and glared at the runt on third. The batter hadn't even gotten up off the ground before the ump called him out. His face understandably had a look of disbelief and frustration emblazoned on it.

The ump had a word with Clyde before the third batter stepped to the plate. Clyde took advantage of the opportunity and pulled his pants up several times. Any higher, and the circulation to a private part of his anatomy would have been cut off. I heard one "uh-huh" followed by several "yes, sir's."

Batter number three was small and wiry, like the first one, but he didn't squat down; he intended to hit. He sent the first pitch into right field and took off like a rabbit toward first.

Balls rarely got hit to right field, so Uncle Cletus had put Timmy Jenkins there. Timmy was facing the opposite direction, watering the grass, so to speak, and didn't see the ball until it bounced past him. Without putting anything away first, Timmy ran to the ball, turned, and hurled it toward second base.

The ball got to second about the same time the batter was rounding third. I'd never seen anyone run that fast. The throw to home was in time; Clyde blocked the plate and, after a collision in which Clyde didn't budge, he tagged the runner out. The runner was lying, apparently dazed, a few inches short of the plate after the collision. He recovered almost instantly, popped up like a cork, and ran to the dugout, surprisingly not fazed at all.

Fairview went on to score five runs the rest of the game. We didn't score any. Clyde was the only one to get a hit. We stranded him on base every time.

Uncle Cletus told us he thought we looked pretty good. It was proof positive that he was an optimist. Timmy Jenkins didn't seem to mind that his pants were wet. Booger had caught every fly ball that came his way. I was happy for him. He rode home with his dad and Aunt Penelope. I rode with Uncle Cletus; we took Clyde home.

Clyde hadn't made any threatening overtures and had actually smiled at me a couple times, but we still weren't buddies. I wouldn't have given him a piece of chewing gum or anything like that. But I was glad he was on my team.

Chapter 26

Duet/Big Win

June was hot and dry. It hadn't rained since Memorial Day weekend. Except for the Johnson grass and several other varieties of unidentifiable weeds, the yards, our primary source of Honda Mini-Trail savings, had gone dormant. The lawn-mowing money wasn't piling up like I'd planned. Mr. Gooche could only give us so many hours, so I'd talked Dad into letting me do janitorial work at Colby John Deere. Getting permission to work there hadn't been a problem; the pay, fifty cents an hour, was what I'd had a challenge negotiating. I got on my bike after dinner and headed that way; I cleaned after hours.

"Be careful not to bump 'ose mirrors," said Odie, referring to the mirror and infrared light beam alarm system.

The alarm system was a series of mirrors mounted throughout the building that reflected and directed an infrared beam in front of the doors and large windows. The mirrors were frequently bumped by customers and knocked out of adjustment. Keeping the mirrors properly aligned was always a problem. Odie was usually the last to leave each day and consequently left with the job of re-alignment.

"I will. Fact is, I won't even get close to them."

"Well, stee'yet," said Odie as he backed out the door on his way home for dinner, "Be careful, they're a job to get lined up." I locked the door behind him.

I turned on the radio, changed the station, turned up the volume, and started my routine. The shop was always first. A huge tractor, a 40/20 John Deere, was getting the bull gear replaced. Under it was a large oil spill. I spread an entire coffee can full of Quick Dry on the biggest area and spread sawdust on the other smaller oil spots.

The next stop was the restrooms. I put Pine Sol in all of the commodes and let them soak, replaced the toilet paper rolls, filled the paper towel and soap dispensers, and wiped off the mirrors. "We Got To Get Out Of This Place" by the Animals came on the radio after I'd started cleaning the commodes. I couldn't have agreed with them more.

"Do You Believe In Magic" by the Lovin' Spoonful played while I swept the display and parts area with an oil mop. It's an upbeat song, and my thoughts changed from self-pity to positive ones. A Mini-Trail dream lasted the whole time it took me to sweep the front—it included riding to Bird's Cave and taking Wendy for a ride.

Sweeping up the shop was always the dirtiest part; I saved it for last. When I finished, there wasn't a speck of dirt or drop of oil anywhere. I wouldn't have recommended eating off of it, but it was clean.

I WENT HOME, GOT CLEANED up, and visited with Mamaw and Papaw over a plate of dinner that Mom had warmed up for me. Mom dropped me off for piano lessons on her way to the grocery store. I'd changed to evening lessons so they wouldn't interfere with my work and baseball schedule.

Mrs. Winchester did her best to teach me about the staff, bass clef, treble clef, and grand staff, but I clearly wasn't a star pupil. When the lesson was finished, she went to the kitchen and took an aspirin; Wendy and I sat on the front porch waiting for Mom.

"I had a difficult time learning to use both hands too," Wendy admitted. I sat on the porch steps and faced the street. She was in the porch swing. I was too embarrassed to talk and was afraid somebody would drive by and see me there. They'd know I was taking piano lessons. I avoided direct eye contact.

"Do you practice at home?"

She waited for an answer. I gave it considerable thought so as not to stutter. "Sometimes."

There was a minute or two of uncomfortable silence. I waited for the next question, unaware, at the time, that girls liked answers longer in length than one word.

"That's the problem."

I looked at her out of the corner of my eye. Her chin was jutted out and her nose pointed skyward. The "I'm right and I know it" look.

"I don't have time to practice. I have three jobs and baseball."

"You could find time if you wanted to."

She walked over, sat next to me on the steps, put a warm soft arm across my shoulders, and faced me, sort of forcing eye contact. For a second, I thought, and sort of hoped, that she might try to kiss me. I tried to remember how the guys on the bus had said to hold your lips.

"You'd find time to ride that Mini-Trail if you had it." The urge to bolt was powerful, but her sweet, honeylike lips froze me trancelike. I couldn't decide if I was being reprimanded or consoled, but I knew for sure I wasn't going to get kissed.

I usually rode my bike to piano lessons, but Mom offered to pick me up on the way home from the grocery store. If I'd ridden my bike, I could have left already, and this conversation wouldn't have taken place. I suddenly understood what they were talking about in those Rolaids commercials.

"How about we practice on a duet for the recital?" She gave me her trademark smile; Jungle Gardenia filled my senses. Thinking about sitting next to her on the piano bench while practicing caused me to momentarily lose my mind. The wait had been worth it.

"Sure!" It was a one-word answer with enormous consequence, and clearly one that satisfied her.

Her smile stretched from ear to ear. "I'll talk to Mom and make sure it's okay. She'll probably have us practice together after your regular lessons."

"Promise not to tell anyone?" I asked.

"They're going to find out at the recital."

"Not everyone goes to the recital."

"Like Booger, Flop, Everett, and those guys?"

"Uh-huh."

She smiled, shook her head, and crossed her eyes. "Okay"

Mom pulled up; Wendy gave me a side-by-side hug, stood up, and extended her hand to shake. "Deal?"

"Deal!" I agreed.

Mom thought the duet was a great idea and was surprised I'd agreed to it. As I gave it more thought, a feeling of entrapment replaced the sense of exhilaration I'd felt only moments before.

MARSHA AND MICKEY WERE SITTING on the front porch breathing on each other when we got home; Dad wouldn't let them sit on the back porch anymore. Mickey helped me carry in the groceries. After we'd finished, Marsha surprised me by inviting me to sit on the porch with them; she said Mickey had something he wanted to ask me.

"Ever heard of Philmont, Tommy?" Mickey asked.

"Yeah, it's that Boy Scout camp in New Mexico, isn't it?"

"That's right." He looked surprised that I knew. "Well, I have a chance go there in July." Mickey had it pretty easy in the summer, no job except the paper route, playing baseball, and now Boy Scout camp.

"Lucky dog," I mumbled.

"How about you takin' care of my paper route for me while I'm gone?" My first impulse was to jump for joy at the chance to deliver papers, but sensing that a negotiation was at hand, I put forth my best stoic face. I figured Mickey thought he was doing me a favor; he knew I wanted the paper route after him.

"I could probably work it in. I'm mowing lawns, cleaning for Dad, and working at Gooche's, you know."

"Takin' piano lessons too," Marsha added, unnecessarily.

"You'd need to go with me a few times to learn who gets papers and how they like 'em delivered." I nodded, without saying anything. Dad had taught me to stay quiet and let the other fellow talk as much as they wanted.

"What do you think, Tommy?" Marsha asked.

"Sounds okay."

"Whaddaya mean, 'okay'? You've *always* talked about getting a paper route."

She rolled her eyes and did a forced exhale. I winked at her when Mickey wasn't looking.

"How much does it pay?" I asked. Marsha grinned at me; she understood.

"I make $102 per month, but I have to collect, too."

"You only deliver Monday thru Friday, right?"

"Uh-huh, the papers are usually ready to be picked up by 3:30."

"So, you make about $5 per day?"

"I have to collect too," he repeated.

"How long will you be gone?"

"Two weeks."

"I'll do it for $50."

"What?" He asked, while looking back at Marsha. She hid her face so he wouldn't see her lip-splitting grin.

"I'm only charging what you'd be making anyway, and I'm throwing in the days it takes me to learn, free." He looked to Marsha for help. She just shrugged. "You know I'll do a good job."

"I'll have to think about it," he said.

"Let me know," a phrase I'd heard Dad say a million times. It usually resulted in a sale. The truth is, I'd probably have done it for free, but I was leveraging his relationship with Marsha. Besides, I was only asking what he was getting paid.

He smiled and tussled my hair. "Get out of here, you little creep."

I went inside. The front door was open and Dad had heard us through the screen door. He winked at me when I walked by. *The Andy Griffith Show* was starting. The aroma of cooking popcorn filled the house.

Chapter 27

Change of Heart

WE'D ONLY WON ONE BASEBALL game that season, against Darby, a tiny town fifteen miles south of Colby. Darby's population was less than five hundred. They didn't even have uniforms, just T-shirts. Colby wasn't much bigger, but at least we had uniforms. I guess we were lucky in that sense.

Uncle Cletus had promised that if we practiced hard, stayed disciplined, and kept our heads in every play, that we'd start winning. I was thinking that it was a good day to start.

We were warming up when the Fairview team arrived in their station wagons for our second game of the season against them. Cumulous clouds to the west looked threatening. The top of the tallest one was starting to take an anvil shape. The breeze had that damp scent, a promise of rain. We needed the moisture, but I wanted to beat the pants off the Fairview bunch first.

I threw a few pitches to Clyde, just enough to warm up; I wanted to save it all for the game. We got our signals straight, not that I could throw a curve or anything. Uncle Cletus called everybody to the dugout and talked to us about winning, memories, and lasting impressions. He looked at Timmy Jenkins and asked if anyone needed to take a leak.

Fairview batted first. The shrimp came to the plate and squatted like before. I walked him on five pitches, an improvement from the first game.

"Runt!" Clyde yelled at the batter as he started toward first base.

We got the next three batters out on ground balls. Their runt didn't score, even though he'd stolen second and third. The breeze had become a gusty wind, occasionally creating little dust devils that moved quickly through the infield.

I'd told Melody about the game; she was sitting in the stands with a couple of friends. I had not mentioned it to Wendy. I didn't want her showing up and spilling the beans about the duet.

Before leading off, I made eye contact with Melody. She gave me a wiggly fingers wave. I heard Clyde clear his throat. He must have seen her too, but he didn't say anything. We'd gotten to know each other better. He wasn't a bad guy and was no longer expressing a desire to kill me, which made him more tolerable. He still didn't care much for Wendy, though; he was difficult to figure.

Their pitcher was left-handed. He was famous for being able to throw a knuckleball. Even Uncle Cletus couldn't explain what made a knuckleball dance around like it does. But, as luck would have it, the wind was in the pitcher's face. So, he kept getting dust in his eyes. After walking me and two other batters, they put in a right-hander. The new pitcher took five warm-up pitches, then the ump called batter up. Our next batter was Clyde.

All year long, he'd been hitting them over the fence during batting practice, but had never hit one over during a game. The right-hander's first pitch changed that. In an attempt to get ahead in the count, he gave Clyde a fastball down the middle. Clyde swung and made solid contact. The ball climbed, and the wind carried it well beyond the outfield fence—grand slam. We took the lead 4 - 0 with nobody out.

The crosswind had gotten so strong that the pitcher had to take the balls well outside and let them drift over the plate. This resulted in a slower and easier-to-hit pitch. Our next two batters singled. Booger batted both runners in with a stand-up double. Aunt Penelope stood up cheering. Timmy Jenkins, who couldn't hit the broad side of a barn, didn't have enough sense to go for a walk, and struck out. The next two batters grounded out, but the second and first basemen both lost their caps making the play.

Between innings, the ump called the coaches to home plate. The ragged cloud bases had turned a bluish purple, and most spectators had gone to their cars for shelter. The wind was howling. The Colby Cardinals had a winner going, and we were ready to play. Uncle Cletus, Booger's dad, the ump, and the Fairview coaches talked.

"Batter up," said the ump after their short meeting. I walked the first batter before figuring out how much to correct for the wind. Widely scattered raindrops the size of quarters began to fall; a large one landed square in my ear. A wave of cold air fell onto the field. I shivered now and then.

The second batter popped up and Clyde caught it, no problem. The third batter watched two strikes go by, but I eventually walked him. They now had two runners on base, and the quarter-sized rain drops were getting closer together.

After throwing two balls to the fourth batter, I decided on a different pitching strategy. I figured that by throwing a little harder, the ball wouldn't drift as much; unfortunately my control wasn't as good when I threw hard. The next pitch was fast and low and actually went behind the batter. Clyde had to dive to catch it. Both runners advanced on stolen bases. I corrected a little on the fourth pitch. Instead of going behind the batter, it hit him square in the rib cage. He glared at me on his way to first. The bases were now loaded with one out.

Uncle Cletus and Clyde approached the pitcher's mound. Clyde tugged at his pants, pulling them up, on his way.

"Thing of it is, if we get out of this inning with the lead, we win," said Uncle Cletus. Clyde didn't say anything, he just stood with his mouth gaping open and motioned agreement to everything Uncle Cletus said.

Uncle Cletus pointed at the next batter. "I've never seen this next guy get a hit. If a guy'd just throw strikes, we might get him out." He tapped the bill of my hat and turned to Clyde. "Give him a target."

The fifth batter was an idiot and swung at every pitch, no matter how bad it was. Their third base coach was beside himself. The batter was probably his son, judging by the way he didn't listen. He struck out on three bad pitches. Uncle Cletus paced in front of the dugout.

At that point the rain was coming down in sheets. The ump called the coaches to the plate. Uncle Cletus told me later that the Fairview coach insisted on finishing the inning. Rainwater mixed with sweat trickled down my face after running through my hair and tasted like salt.

The pitcher's mound had turned into a pile of sticky mud. The ball was wet and heavy. The first pitch to the next batter hit the ground in front of the plate, splashed Clyde and the batter with mud, and then rolled to the backstop.

The runner on third started for home; I did, too. Clyde slid to a stop against the backstop, picked up the ball, and tossed it to me. I turned to tag what I thought would be a sliding runner, but instead caught the full force of his shoulder with my face; it felt like he'd driven my nose to the back of my skull. The salty taste of sweat was immediately replaced with the metallic taste of blood.

I momentarily lost consciousness and came to lying on the ground face up. I felt raindrops pounding on my face. When I opened my eyes, a large drop hit directly on my right eyeball and stung, compounding the pain. It was a second or two before I remembered where I was.

The ump found the ball in my glove. "Runner's out, game over!" he shouted for the few people who had remained.

Booger darted over from the dugout and helped me up. We watched as the disoriented Fairview runner slowly got up and turned toward his dugout. But he was about to learn the hard way from Clyde Goodpasture that sliding would have been better. Clyde's fist hitting the runner's face sounded like a watermelon dropping on concrete. The Fairview runner's knees buckled from the direct blow to his nose. He was out again, in a sense. Booger and I were the only ones who had witnessed it. Everyone else, including the ump, had run to their dugout or car for cover.

A few minutes later, sitting on the dugout bench with my head tilted back to stop the bleeding, I heard Uncle Cletus ask Clyde what he thought was wrong with the Fairview player, the one who was crawling on all fours from home plate toward their dugout.

"Looks like he lost his footing," was Clyde's reply. It wasn't a lie; he had.

Clyde looked my way. "You're tougher than I figured you for."

When I tried to talk, blood ran down my throat; I just nodded.

Booger and I rode with his dad. Aunt Penelope had gotten in Uncle Cletus's truck when it started raining. I don't know how long Melody stuck around. Uncle Cletus pulled out and we followed him to Booger's house, where he dropped off Aunt Penelope and then kept going, probably to take Clyde home. Booger's dad dropped me off at my house.

Over supper I told everyone about the game and how Clyde had clobbered the yahoo from Fairview.

AFTER EATING, I RAN OVER to Mamaw and Papaw's to sit on their porch. The air always smells so fresh after it rains. We sat on the porch and enjoyed the scents.

Papaw started rolling a cigarette and got a look from Mamaw. "You're not going to light up one of those things now, are you?"

Papaw put the can and the paper back in his shirt pocket. "Guess not."

We sat and listened to the night noises until Mom signaled for me to come home.

AT WORK THE NEXT DAY, Booger told me that Aunt Penelope and Uncle Norman were getting a divorce. Three elders from their church had spoken to Uncle Norman, but he didn't think he was doing anything wrong by having a girlfriend. Aunt Penelope felt she didn't have any other choice since he'd joined the "adulterer's club" and had gotten himself a "paramour," as she put it. She'd had him served with the divorce papers. He hadn't hit her or anything lately.

I was filled with mixed emotions. Part of me was glad that Norman might soon be out of the picture, and I felt a twinge of guilt about that but didn't know why I should. But the other part of me anxiously looked forward to the prospect of Aunt Penelope and Uncle Cletus getting together.

Chapter 28

Rolled or Folded

MICKEY RELUCTANTLY AGREED TO THE $50. I asked Mr. Gooche about the paper route, and he'd said it wouldn't be a problem scheduling around it. Mickey had a list of everyone who got a paper and where they liked it placed on their porch. Some people didn't care. Their paper could be rolled and thrown. They were the easiest to deal with.

Others were more particular and preferred their papers neatly folded. Rolled or folded is all I really needed to know, Mickey had told me. As it turned out, Mrs. Enderle and her type insisted that their paper be folded, while Caleb's mom and others like her didn't care either way. Thinking back, it made sense.

Mickey's bike had handlebar and rear saddle baskets. We decided it would be best for me to use his bicycle. During training, Mickey rode my bike, and I rode his. He delivered the papers in two loads. The businesses were first since they were close, and most of them got extra copies to sell.

We loaded ninety papers onto Mickey's bicycle, thirty in each basket. I had to hold the bike up and load the papers at the same time. Loaded, the kickstand wouldn't hold up the bike, and it was more difficult to pedal.

Gooche's was our first stop. I put thirty copies in the *Colby Telegraph* newspaper rack. The rack had a slotted coin box. The papers were ten cents each, honor system.

Pope's Houn Dawg was our next stop. They only got ten papers since their customers were mostly kids. Mrs. Pope kept the newspaper rack inside next to the cash register. She gave us a small ice cream cone for free. Mickey said we needed to keep moving. I thanked Mrs. Pope and ate it in four bites and got an ice-cream headache.

We crossed the street to Burt's. His newspaper rack sat just outside the door and could be easily reached from Mickey's bike; Burt offered me a moon pie while I was putting his twenty papers in the rack, but I told him no thanks and that I'd just had an ice cream cone. He winked at Mickey but didn't know I saw. I suspected he thought Mickey had talked me into delivering the papers for free. It wouldn't be long before I'd be pulling up on a Honda Mini-Trail; then we'd see who winked at whom, I thought.

Before going into the courthouse, we stopped for a minute to talk, well, mostly listen, to Bem, Rabbit, Fish, and Monkey. Monkey was always excited about something. Today it was a new German-made chainsaw he'd just purchased.

"I ain't a kiddin' you," he said. "That Stihl's got more power an's lighter'n any saw I've ebber grabbed holt of." He paused long enough to spit. "It'll start on th' first or second pull ebber time."

"Yeah, it'll start, but will it cut as fast as 'at Homelite?" asked Rabbit.

"Oh, it's faster'n'at, shore is." He nodded several times for affect.

Bem looked our way. "We don't need no paper to tell us the news, we *are* the news, boy." Mickey had predicted he'd say it. Monkey, Fish, and Rabbit laughed at the joke as if it had been the first time they'd heard it, another one of Mickey's predictions.

After taking out thirty papers for Gooche's, ten for the Houn Dawg, and nine for the courthouse, the kickstand worked. Mickey said not to worry about the bike and the remaining papers; no one would steal them. I followed him through the front doors of the county courthouse. Each office doorframe had the name of the office engraved across the top; each office door had a brass plate with the occupant's name.

"Hey there, Mickey," said Mrs. Burk, the Circuit Clerk. She was a Republican and had a reputation for gossiping.

"What's the good news, Mickey Mouse?" asked Mr. Bailey, the Recorder of Deeds, a limp-wristed highbrow type. Mickey gave me a look; I could tell he didn't much like Mr. Bailey.

The county commissioner's office was different than the rest. Although they weren't lawyers and no court was held in their office, each commissioner was called a judge. Mr. Trent, a farmer, was the presiding judge. His desk was the middle one. Mickey gave each judge a paper.

"Who's your little helper there?" asked Judge Trent. Finally, someone noticed. For a few minutes I thought I'd become invisible.

"This is Tommy Thompson. He'll be delivering the paper while I'm at Philmont."

Judge Trent wrinkled his weathered face and studied me a few seconds. "You Ted's boy?"

"Yes, sir."

"Thought so. Haven't I seen you mowin' down at Colby John Deere?"

"Yes, sir. I mow other lawns too, at least when there's enough rain to make the grass grow." All three judges laughed, and then begin talking between themselves about the drought.

Magistrate Judge Grant had his own office. He was a real judge. I'd heard Dad and others talking about him. They called him "$10 and cost." He had a reputation for letting people off with minimum sentences. His office was as big as the one the three commissioners shared, but he had it all to himself, along with his legal secretary. Thin strands of smoke were suspended in the air. A constant supply was generated by a giant cigar protruding out of the corner of his mouth, like some kind of a mutant body part—another thing he was famous for.

"Mighty fine, mighty fine, yes, mighty fine," Judge Grant said. His booming voice filled the office and no doubt spilled out into the court-house hallway, too.

"There's Mickey boy with the news," he said to no one in particular. It seemed he liked to hear himself talk.

"Who's the young man with you there, Mickey boy?"

"This is Tommy Thompson, sir. He'll be delivering the paper while I'm at Philmont."

"Fine looking boy. Yes, yes, Philco. I read the article about you going there, yes, yes. Say, aren't there bears and rattle snakes in those Mexican mountains?"

"There are supposed to be bears, sir, but I think we'll be at an altitude too high for snakes. It's Philmont, sir, and it's in New Mexico."

"Bears and snakes, my my." He looked at me. "Why aren't you going to Philco?"

"I'm not old enough, sir."

"Bears prefer older boys, I guess." He laughed at his own joke and started coughing, probably choking on his own cigar smoke.

His secretary was rolling her eyes. She saw me looking at a tall window that had one of the glass panes covered with cardboard. "Bird," she said.

"Bird?" I asked.

Judge Grant chimed in. "Big bird, yes yes, giant bird. Came crashing against the window and flew away."

"What kind was it?" Mickey asked.

Judge Grant furrowed his brow and walked toward the window. "Mystery, big mystery, you see. We never did actually see it, just heard it, Wap! Yes, yes broken glass everywhere."

"There was something on the sill that looked like a potato peel, but I flicked it off," said the secretary. She was typing something and showed little interest in the giant window-breaking mystery bird.

Mickey and I backed out of the room. The Judge, lost in thought, enjoyed his cigar, while the secretary smiled and nodded a goodbye. A lingering potato gun question had just been answered.

Deputy Fritzenmeyer, Fritz, was standing outside the Sheriff's office, next to the courthouse. We rode our bikes through the grass; I handed him his newspaper. His pistol was huge; the bullets in the cylinder were visible. I always wondered if he'd ever shot anyone.

We left fifteen papers at the bowling alley. I guess lots of people read the paper waiting their turn to play. Dwight Seabaugh was oiling one of the pin-setting machines. He showed me how it worked and was going to let me load some pins, but Mickey said we had to go.

Rosolini's was the last business delivery, except for the funeral homes, which we delivered with the residential deliveries since they were located in neighborhoods. Mrs. Rosolini offered us a small piece of apple pie. Mickey said no; I said yes. I put her fifteen copies in the rack, took the pie, and told her thanks. Standing on the sidewalk, I wolfed it down and realized, too late, that I'd also eaten part of the napkin.

We returned to the Colby Telegraph and loaded up the rest of the newspapers. The residential circulation was only sixty-two; the rural routes got delivered by car. Mickey tried to teach me how to roll a newspaper while I was riding. After nearly wrecking a couple of times, I decided that it was going to take a little practice.

He lectured me on the privilege and art of delivering newspapers. "People depend on you to get their paper to them. When they come home from work, they want their paper to be there. As their paperboy, you can make the difference in them having a good day or a bad day."

I nodded acknowledgement. "It's a lot of responsibility," he said.

He tossed the first few papers and began to explain the rolled or folded concept. "The first and most important thing you need to know is if they want their paper rolled or folded. Rolled people are the easiest to please; just toss the paper in a highly visible and dry place—driveway, porch, sidewalk, even the yard if it has been cut short."

He stopped in front of Mrs. Enderle's house and handed me a list of names. "Here's a list of the people who want their paper folded and where they want it."

I studied the list. He walked up onto Mrs. Enderle's porch and placed her paper between the gridiron Gothic "E" and the screen in the storm door.

Mickey gave me a short lecture about rolled or folded and, in a sense, a lesson about life in general. "If you think about who you're delivering the paper to, remembering rolled or folded will be easy. The folded are the persnickety types, the rolled are the easier-going folks."

"So, the folded folks have plastic fruit baskets and mow and trim their yards, and the rolled folks never trim and don't mow as often as they should," I replied.

"You're getting the hang of it," he chuckled.

"Be careful around dogs. Dogs that have been spanked with a newspaper don't think much of paperboys. You'll see." We didn't have any dog troubles that day.

I was exhausted by the time I got home. The aroma of frying bologna had drifted out onto the porch. My mouth watered profusely before I got inside; I was famished. Mamaw and Papaw had dinner with us that evening. Mamaw brought blackberry cobbler. I ate too much, but it didn't keep me from falling asleep almost before my head hit the pillow. My last thoughts were of the rolled or folded concept and how it applied in other areas, such as how people liked their groceries bagged and yards trimmed. People are different, and I'd just found a new way to view them.

Chapter 29

First Flight

SATURDAY MORNING, DAD AND I met Dave Blue at the airport restaurant at 6:30 AM. I was excited. Dad was nervous—it was his first lesson. Dave recommended we not eat anything greasy. Dave had oatmeal. He was trying to lose weight to get into the army and fly helicopters.

Dave had an 8x10 photograph of the panel of the airplane we'd be flying in, a Cessna 172. The number was N95S, phonetically *November Nine Five Sugar*. It only had four seats. There were gauges and instruments for everything; it seemed overwhelming. Today, Dave wanted Dad to learn how to control airspeed and keep the plane level. "The pitch and power" lesson, he called it. It seemed like a lot to learn. I wasn't sure Dad could do it.

After explaining the lesson to Dad, Dave looked at me. "Think you can remember all of that?"

"Sure," I responded confidently. He gave me a disbelieving grin.

He looked at Dad. "Let's just take it a step at a time. You can't learn it all on the first day." Dave picked up the check. "The first breakfast is on me."

We followed him to the plane. *November Nine Five Sugar* was white with red horizontal stripes on the body and wing tips. Dave walked Dad through the preflight procedure. Dave opened the right side door and looked at me. "Hop in, we're ready to go." I climbed into the rear seat. Dave sat in the right front, the co-pilot's seat. Dad hadn't moved. Dave chuckled. "You gonna stand there, or fly this thing?"

"You want me to sit on the left side?"

"That's where the pilot sits. You better get in before Tommy takes your place." I'd leaned in and was looking at the instrument panel.

I'd never seen Dad so nervous. He looked like I felt the first time Wendy spoke to me. His hands were shaking so bad he had a difficult time getting his seat belt buckled. Dave looked out the window and started whistling. He was trying to help Dad calm down.

With the windows open, Dave had to shout to be heard once the engine was started. "You guide with the rudder pedal brakes, like a combine or Caterpillar." He released the park break, and we started moving forward. "You're driving."

We did a little zigzagging on the way to the runway. A giant red-tailed hawk was sitting between the taxiway and runway, probably watching for a field mouse to cross the vast sheet of concrete.

After setting the park brake, Dave walked Dad through the final run-up procedure, a final check of the engine and flight controls. *Nine Five Sugar* shook and rattled when Dave advanced the throttle and held the brake, making sure the engine would run under full power.

Dad got the airplane pointed in the right direction, and we started rolling down the centerline. After a few seconds, Dave put his left hand on Dad's right and slowly advanced the throttle. As we accelerated, the plane veered slightly to the left, the P-factor, I later learned. We were nearing the left edge of the runway before lifting off.

The second time around—Dad's first attempt without Dave's help—almost caused me to lose my oatmeal. He must have forgotten all about the pitch and power lesson. He jerked the controls back and forth and pushed the throttle in and out. I was sure we'd broken something when we hit the ground, but Dave had Dad immediately take off again; a "touch and go" he called it. The next time, Dave helped him out a little, and the approach and landing were much better. Dad had grin wrinkles that ran all of the way to his ears. I was proud of him.

After the lesson, we had time to drop by Fairview Honda and make a Mini-Trail payment. They'd gotten a new shipment in. The newer ones had a few improvements: larger headlight, more comfortable seat, and a speed odometer. The price on the tag was fifty dollars higher than what we'd bargained for. So long as we kept up our payments, we'd be able to get ours at the old price. But, in order to do that we needed more rain. The downpour that we'd gotten during the Fairview game wasn't enough to make a difference; the lawns were still dormant. I didn't have any savings left after making the Mini-Trail and Lawn-Boy payments.

MOM WAS SITTING ON THE front porch cuffing a pair of Dad's pants when we got home. Dad slumped into the empty porch chair beside her, leaned his head back, and closed his eyes. I had a few minutes before I had to leave for Gooche's, so I sat on the step.

"So, how was your first lesson?"

Dad started rubbing his temples. "I've got a headache."

"Did you take anything for it?"

"No, I thought it would go away."

"I'll get you something for it." She got up and went inside.

"You're not making flying lessons sound like much fun," I told him. He sat up straight and looked at me; he'd gotten the message. It was the first time I remember giving him advice.

Mom returned with a glass of iced tea and a bottle of aspirin. Dad finished telling her all about the lesson with a bit more passion; he just wasn't the animated type. The aspirin didn't take long to work, and once he started talking, it was clear that actually flying the plane was more fun than riding in it and that he couldn't wait until his next flight. He really liked Dave, too.

The phone rang; it was Booger. "Ja'eat yet?"

"No, but I will."

"I'm on my way. We can ride to Gooche's together."

Chapter 30

Miss Anderson

BEFORE CLOCKING IN FOR WORK at Gooche's we parked our bikes behind the trash truck, next to the loading dock, so they couldn't be seen from the street. After hauling the last load of trash to the incinerator, we put the bikes in the back of the truck and laid them down, hiding them from view. We figured they'd be safe there until after the movie. Booger had gotten a generator light like mine, and we'd both gotten permission to stay for the movie after work and then ride our bikes home.

Velma and I talked about flying while she checked and I bagged groceries. She told me about trying to qualify as a pilot during WWII, but after getting rejected, she had never pursued it again because of the expense. She'd taken her first airplane ride in a Stearman when a barnstormer had been in Colby for a couple of days during the late thirties. She was still in high school at the time and had volunteered to help collect money for passengers; for that, the pilot had given her a free ride.

"He tried to give me a kiss, too," she said. "I settled for the ride."

Velma and I were having this conversation while checking out a lady I didn't recognize. There was something incredibly appealing about her; I mentally wrestled to keep from staring. The newcomer was wearing a St. Louis Cardinal's baseball cap with a thick bouncy ponytail pulled through the back. She'd cut the sleeves off of a denim shirt but wore it in such a way that made it look classy. She had a rugged look but somehow looked refined too. Exotic, a word I couldn't remember ever using, but was forced to learn the meaning of in vocabulary class, came to mind.

"Hi. I'm Bridget Anderson. I'll be teaching at Colby grade school this fall." She introduced herself assertively. There was a moment of inexplicable awkwardness for me.

Velma tentatively shook the new teacher's hand. "It's nice to meet you, Bridget. I'd heard we were getting a new teacher. I'm Velma." There had been talk of a new teacher and the talk hadn't been all good. Small towns don't warm up quickly to new people, let alone those who don't conform to the various unstated local rules and mores.

"Well, I've only been in town a few weeks. I'm looking forward to making new friends." "Everyone I've met has been very friendly." Velma gave me a glancing grin.

Miss Anderson then looked at me.

I momentarily lost the ability to speak, then finally blurted out. "I'm Tommy."

She winked. Suddenly I had to remember again how to breathe.

Miss Anderson handed her check to Velma. "I couldn't help but overhear your conversation about flying. My mother was a WWII pilot."

"Really?" Velma fumbled with the check while staring at Bridget, Miss Anderson, as if she was some sort of apparition. Although Miss Anderson didn't know it, she had just broken a major barrier. New people could never go wrong by making a good impression on the checkout ladies or hairdressers.

"She taught me to fly. After she lost her medical, I would take her up from time to time." The bearded lady was waiting to check out; Miss Anderson politely started moving away from the counter.

Velma was visibly moved. In her mind, Miss Anderson had instantaneously gone from simply a new teacher to ultimate admiration status. Standing in front of her was a female pilot, maybe the first one she'd ever seen, and the daughter of a WWII female pilot to boot, something she'd aspired to be.

"My Dad's taking flying lessons," I blurted out, trying to make a relational bridge of some sort.

"See, there's so many cool people in Colby. I know I'm going to enjoy living and teaching here."

Velma smiled and handed Miss Anderson her receipt. "It was really nice meeting you, Bridget. I'd love to hear more about your mother's flying stories when you have more time." Miss Anderson smiled; her teeth were as perfect as Wendy's.

She handed me two bags and grabbed two herself. "We don't need a cart." I followed her out the door and had to walk fast to keep up. "So, your dad is taking flying lessons?"

"Yes, ma'am."

"What grade are you in, Tommy?"

"I'm going into the sixth."

"Then I'll be seeing a lot of you. Aren't you a little young to be working as a carryout?"

"I'm saving up to buy a Honda Mini-Trail."

"Really? That sounds exciting."

"My Uncle Cletus just bought a 350 Scrambler. He teaches science at the high school."

"I'm looking forward to meeting him."

"I have a baseball game on Tuesday night. He's our coach. Come to the game, and I'll introduce you."

"I just might do that." She smiled and closed the door to her car, a red 1966 GTO.

Exotic. The full meaning of the word was forever engraved in my mind's eye.

IMMEDIATELY AFTER WORK, CALEB AND I bought our tickets to *The Blue Max* and got good seats. After seeing the preview the week before I'd been anxious to see George Peppard light up the sky in WWI airplanes. But instead of being enthralled with the flying, I found myself focusing on the uncanny similarity of Ursual Andress and Miss Bridget, both in looks and demeanor. Unbelievable!

Chapter 31

Cave Camping

MONDAY WAS THE FOURTH OF July. Traditionally the Burgers and the Thompsons got up before sunrise and went to the creek, near the bridge, and cooked breakfast. Booger's counselor had suggested something different this year. It had been agreed by the parents that we'd go to the creek but that other families would be invited. Booger and I had talked them into inviting the Westwoods, Wilfongs, Aunt Penelope, and Uncle Cletus. Marsha got permission to ask Mickey, since she wasn't going to see him for two weeks while he was at Philmont.

Mrs. Olefsen overheard Mom talking to Mrs. Westwood at Gooche's and sort of invited herself. Mom had been fretting about it since, thinking they might spring another "Swedish surprise" on us. Learning that they were agnostic was bad enough, but when they started parading around their house in the nude that first summer, without so much as pulling a shade, Mom had nearly tipped her scales. It's a European thing, Dad had told Mom. He didn't seem to mind it as much as she did. Mom felt it was something that should be confined to their nudist colony.

I rode with Booger and his dad. We stopped by the cemetery on the way to the creek. Booger put a flag on Johnny's grave, and his dad set a vase of flowers next to Mrs. Burger's headstone. The sun had just started to rise when we got there, and it turned into a huge orange ball before we left.

Mr. Burger went to the cemetery fairly often, but Booger hadn't been there since Mother's Day. They both stood there, side-by-side, and stared at the graves until the dew completely soaked my shoes.

"Ready to go?" Mr. Burger finally asked, just above a whisper. Booger just nodded. I followed them to the car and felt a little guilty. I'd been wondering who mowed the cemetery and how much they made.

DAD AND UNCLE CLETUS HAD a fire going and hog jowls frying in twin camp skillets by the time we got to the creek. Uncle Cletus's Scrambler was parked on a large flat rock next to the creek. Mr. Westwood and Mr. Wilfong had collected several pieces of driftwood and were breaking them into smaller sticks to burn. Mom, Mrs. Wilfong, and Mrs. Westwood were sitting at the picnic table we'd put there a few years ago, peeling potatoes. Mickey was helping Dad, Marsha was slicing the peeled potatoes, and Aunt Penelope was making camp coffee—a mixture of boiling water and coffee grounds. A thin layer of fog hovered over the creek; the air temperature in the creek bottom was noticeably cooler than it had been in town.

Caleb and Flop had walked downstream a ways. When Booger and I found them, they were cleaning the flint ignition on the potato gun; they had snuck half a dozen potatoes. Both were crouched next to the creek, concentrating so much on the gun that they didn't hear us approaching. Booger hung back. I quietly snuck closer and lightly brushed the upper part of Flop's lily-white leg with the bud end of a sugarcane reed and yelled, "SNAKE!"

"It bit me on the foot!" Flop screamed after he'd leaped out of his sissy thongs and landed on his feet in the creek, splashing Caleb in the process.

The water where he was standing was shallow, and evidently he'd landed on a sharp rock or piece of broken glass. He balanced himself on one foot, held the other one, and watched a trickle of blood ooze from the bottom of his heel. His mom came crashing down the creek bank.

"Who vas bit?" She was frantic. "Vere ist der snake? Vas it a coddon heed?" She paused for a breath and held her hand over her chest when she saw Flop holding his foot. "Villiam!" Her face wrenched; every tendon in her neck was on full alert. She crashed into the water and, in a botched attempt to help Flop, knocked him over. Caleb was looking all around for the water moccasin, or "coddon heed," as Mrs. Westwood had called it.

I nonchalantly laid the sugarcane reed down and glanced at Booger. I hadn't expected such a drastic response. We stood at the water's edge and watched Mrs. Westwood wrestle with Flop. She was determined to examine his foot and had him by the ankle, trying to find the wound. Flop thrashed around and struggled, holding himself up with his hands, in a nearly futile effort to keep his head out of the water. Caleb kept looking around for the moccasin.

"There's no snake," I said, my voice cracking a little.

"Vhy dit you yell den?" asked Mrs. Westwood.

"I don't know, thought it would be funny." By then Uncle Cletus, Mr. Westwood, and Aunt Penelope had gotten there.

"Everyone okay?" asked Flop's dad. He and Uncle Cletus were standing together. It was a picture of polar opposites. Flop's dad was mostly bald and had pasty skin like Flop; Uncle Cletus had color and lots of hair, except on his head.

"Are you blind?" Mrs. Westwood asked. "Villiam has sustaint an inchury to hees fute." She brushed a wad of hair out of her face. She'd let go of Flop's foot by then, and they were standing together, knee-deep in the creek. Mr. Westwood had a blank look on his face.

Uncle Cletus walked to the edge of the water. "Sit down here on the bank and let me take a look." He and Aunt Penelope examined the cut, as Mr. and Mrs. Westwood watched.

Aunt Penelope touched Flop on his trembling chin. "It's a small puncture wound. You probably stepped on a pointed rock." She looked at me. "Tommy, I have some Band-Aids in my purse. How about you and Booger running and getting them for me?"

As soon as we got out of hearing range of the adults, Booger looked at me. "Coddon heed?" We both laughed until our stomachs hurt.

Dad was watching the fire and turning the jowls. "What happened?"

"Flop stepped on a rock and cut his foot a little."

"Bad?"

"No, Aunt Penelope said it was a puncture wound," Booger told him.

"Did somebody see a snake?" Booger told him what had happened while I looked for Aunt Penelope's purse. I found it next to Uncle Cletus's motorcycle helmet.

The Olefsens hadn't moved from their hammock made for two; they were both sleeping. Foreigners don't grow up on a good diet, and consequently they don't have much stamina – that's what Uncle Cletus had told me once.

We took Aunt Penelope her purse. She found a tube of ointment mixed in with a wad of tissue and other women's stuff. She spread a little

on Flop's cut, and then covered the gooey wound with a Band-Aid. Flop
was shivering; his skin had lost the little bit of color that it once had. I felt
sorry for him and regretted having scared him. He would never have done
something like that to me.

Flop's mom helped him up. "Vee neet to take you home and git you
driet off."

Aunt Penelope shook her head. "Oh, don't do that. I've got a pair of
jeans and a sweatshirt he can wear."

Mrs. Westwood looked at Flop; he shivered and nodded his head yes.
By now, his lips were starting to turn purple just like Booger's had when
we'd jumped in the creek earlier in the spring. Through it all, Flop's poor
dad just stood there with his big ol' ears and never made a peep.

THE CAMPFIRE SMOKE DRIFTING DOWNSTREAM with the creek fog
hinted of frying hog jowls. Mrs. Westwood sniffed the air. "Dat camp friet
fute sure does have a nice aroma to it." She cupped her hand under the
back of Flop's head. "I guess we could stay fur brickfist." She looked at
Aunt Penelope. "It's certainly nice of you to offer de driet clothes."

Uncle Cletus gave Flop a hand getting up; Booger and I helped him
hobble back to camp.

Dad prayed before we ate. It being Independence Day, and there being
a crowd, he did it right. He thanked the Lord for a list of things: our country, freedom, forefathers, soldiers, and then, lastly, the food. My neck had
started hurting from bowing so long by the time he finally said "Amen"
and announced that Mr. Burger and Booger should dish up first.

Everyone turned toward Mr. Burger, who was sitting on a driftwood
log, trembling slightly, his head still bowed. Booger left my side and ran to
him. They hugged, and then everyone joined in, even the Olefsens. Uncle
Cletus put his arm around Mr. Burger with a knowing hug and coaxed
him toward the table where the food was getting cold. I put my arm
around Booger, and we followed. It'd become clear that no one was going
to eat until the Burgers did. Uncle Cletus and I took matters into our own
hands, partly out of compassion, but mostly out of hunger.

The grownups sat at one table, where the bowls of food were, and the
rest of us sat at the other. I dished up for Flop, then went back and filled
my plate. Mrs. Westwood rolled her eyes when I put ketchup on my eggs
and potatoes. Mom had fretted all week trying to decide how much food

to bring. As it turned out, there was plenty. I took several strips of hog jowls, and after getting a few stares, I told the grownups that I was sharing with the others. When I got back to our table, I faked a sneeze on my plate that insured that nobody would want any of the hog jowls.

"When are you guys gettin' your Mini-Trails?" Mickey asked, with his mouth full of food.

I was still chewing. "As soon as we have enough money saved up," Booger told him.

By then I'd swallowed. "With the drought an' all, it might be September before we get the money saved up."

"Aren't you makin' payments?" asked Mickey. A piece of egg started to tumble out his mouth, but he caught it with his tongue. Flop, who was sitting directly across from him, laughed. Marsha had seen, too; Mickey got embarrassed.

"The payment is only twenty-five dollars a month, and it's just to make sure we keep the spring sale price." I'm not sure he heard my answer. He was glaring at Flop, who was still giggling. Flop's dad called from the other table.

"Billy, you've got to see this." We each looked; all of the grownups were giggling. Flop hobbled over to see what was going on.

"Like-a-said, it's good," Flop told his mom. Out of curiosity, the rest of us rushed over.

They'd talked Mrs. Westwood into trying ketchup with her eggs, and she'd liked it; she'd poured half the bottle on her potatoes. The real break-through, though, was when she'd tried the syrup and butter on her biscuit, liked it, and then had seconds. Even Mr. Burger was grinning.

I got a chunk of butter, some syrup, and a couple of biscuits before returning to our table. Mom had baked the biscuits the night before and then wrapped them in foil. They'd been lying next to the fire and were still warm.

Mr. and Mrs. Bird crept across the bridge in their pickup. They saw us and waved. It was their property that we were on, but we had permission to use it.

Flop got a perplexed look on his face. "Didn't you guys say somethin' about there being a cave around here?" I guess seeing the Birds had re-minded him.

"Yeah, Bird's Cave, it's just up the creek a ways," I said.

"I thought you said we'd go campin' there when school got out."

Our annual Bird's Cave camp-out had crossed my mind several times, but there hadn't been time to do it. Lawn mowing, Gooche's, sweeping up at Colby John Deere, baseball, and now piano lessons had kept me busy. I'd kind of wanted to wait until we had the Mini-Trails, too. Booger had a contemplative look on his face. The last time we'd camped at the cave, Johnny had been home on leave and had gone with us.

"We need to do it," I announced. Mr. Gooche didn't need us at work until noon on most days, because of the drought the lawns rarely need to be mowed, and Colby John Deere could wait a day. There was no reason not to go.

"Think your mom will let you?" Booger asked Flop.

"I don't know. She put ketchup on her eggs and potatoes. I suspect anything is possible now." He hobbled over to where the grown-ups were sitting.

Mrs. Westwood sat straight up in her lounge chair, took off her over-sized sunglasses, and looked directly at Flop, her lips drawn taut. He must have asked her. Almost as quickly as she'd sat up, she leaned back, put her glasses back on, and the two of them appeared to be having a discussion. Mr. Westwood was listening; Uncle Cletus was looking their way and saying something now and then, too. Mrs. Westwood looked at Uncle Cletus and shrugged her shoulders a couple of times. Flop spun around and started back, wearing an ear-to-ear grin, and barely limping. He stopped after a few steps, inspected his heel, and hobbled the rest of the way, only much quicker than before.

LATER THAT AFTERNOON, THE RINGING doorbell woke me. Still groggy from a long nap, I heard Uncle Cletus talking to Mom.

"People die in bed," he admonished me when I walked into the living room. I yawned and collected my camp gear—too tired to appreciate his feeble attempt at humor.

It was only after his offer to haul our gear and our bikes to the cave that Flop had agreed to go with us, probably relieved that he wouldn't have to ride the four miles in the blistering heat. I figured the camp food had helped, too.

After picking up Booger and Caleb, we swung by Flop's house. Flop got in, and we were instantly overcome with that invasive, menthol odor that Solarcane makes. You'd think it repelled snakes the way his mom had lathered it on him. Uncle Cletus made him and me get in the back; the cab of the truck was too crowded anyway.

At the end of County Road 427, we stopped at the Birds' house to let them know what we planned to do and officially ask permission. Flop and I were covered with dust.

Mr. and Mrs. Bird were sitting in their gliding love seat under a sugar maple tree, drinking lemonade. They seldom got visitors and were always happy when people showed up. Booger and I'd ridden out there a few times on our bicycles and had decided to make the trip frequently on our Mini-Trails. Dad and I had ridden out in his truck a few times and fished in the creek. They always offered visitors something to drink, usually lemonade or a soda. I always enjoyed the way Mr. Bird applied his dry humor to any subject. We each had a soda and listened to Mr. Bird talk politics.

Mr. Bird thought the United States government should take a few lessons from the Israelis and get the fighting in Vietnam over with. "The Israelis beat Egypt, Syria, and Jordan in only six days, you know," he said, referencing the Six-Day War that had taken place in June. He looked at Booger and paused a moment. "It's not'at our boys can't fight, it's just 'at 'r gover'mint won't let 'em do their job. We're losin' too many good boys o'vair."

After getting a look from a normally sweet and submissive Mrs. Bird, he shut up, took off his straw hat, and wiped his balding head with a red bandana. "You shore did pick the hottest day 'a th' year t' camp."

"I'm gonna drop these yahoos off, help 'em set up camp, then head back to town," Uncle Cletus told him.

"Goin' to the fireworks display?" asked Mr. Bird.

"I doubt it, I got up early for the cookout. I'll probably watch the Washington DC mall celebration on television and call it a day. Thing of it is, seems like the mosquitoes get worse at the park every year anyway. You?"

"No, I 'spect not, big waste'a money if you ask me."

"Nobody asked, dear," said Mrs. Bird.

Mr. Bird didn't strike me as the type to sit in a park late at night and watch fireworks. He was a farmer and had more important things to do. He passed a soda carton around; we put our empties in it and got on our way.

The creek crossing near Mr. Bird's house was a wide, shallow, gravel bar.

We stopped and collected some driftwood for a campfire. The air near the creek smelled like minnows. Several pairs of dragonflies cruised by and inspected us. The road led through a stand of birches and sycamores that bordered the creek on one side and a fescue field on the other. We followed the road across the field, away from the creek toward Bird's knob, where the mouth of the cave was. A huge elm, one of the few that had, so far, survived Dutch elm disease, marked the entrance to the cave.

Booger and I drew straws to see who'd go into the cave and check it out. Caleb and Flop had never been there, so we didn't make them draw. I got the short one. I didn't ask, but Uncle Cletus read my mind and went in with me. We crawled through the entrance, me first. Once inside the cave, my damp shirt felt cold against my sunburned skin. The cave opened up to a room larger than our living room; there were three small tunnels leading away into the dark. Using the flashlight, I could see stalactites protruding from the ceiling and water trickling down the walls in several places. It gathered in a small branch that came from under the wall of the cave on one side and disappeared on the other. Outside, the ground was dry as a bone, but somehow the hill above the cave was oozing with water, another mystery that Uncle Cletus could probably explain.

Since I went in first, I came out of the cave first. It was an unwritten spelunking rule at Bird's Cave, at least that's what Uncle Cletus had taught me. Caleb, Booger, and Flop had unloaded everything out of Uncle Cletus's truck and were pulling something out of the bed of Mr. Bird's pickup. He had pulled up while we were in the cave and was standing in the bed.

He spat a pull of tobacco. "I brought the boys an 'ole tarp for 'em to lay their sleepin' bags on. It's bigger 'nuff that they can fold it over and cover up with it too, if it was to rain or somethin.'"

Caleb, Flop, and Booger spread it out under the shade of the elm tree. Unfolded all of the way, it was probably ten by twenty feet.

"I use it to cover my baler in the winter. But I don't need it rat now." He'd brought three old chairs, a coal-oil lantern, and matches, too. "I'll come back in the mornin' and pick it all up. Stop by the house on your way out."

I gave him a hand getting down out of the bed of his truck. "Thanks a lot, Mr. Bird."

Uncle Cletus opened the door of his pickup. "I need to get going. If you all have any trouble, just ride your bikes up to Mr. Bird's and ask him to give me a call."

"Thanks, Mr. Thornton," Caleb, Booger, and Flop said, in unison, just before Uncle Cletus pulled away.

I followed Mr. Bird to the door of his pickup. "Thanks again, Mr. Bird, this tarp is nice."

"No bother. I noticed on your way out that you didn't have a tent or ground cloth. This tarp'ill make for better sleepin' so long as the ticks, chiggers, and coyotes don't git'cha."

"Coyotes?"

"Yeah, they've been doin' a fair bit'o yipping the past few weeks. They won't bother you. They only eat small stuff, like rabbits 'n squirrels."

When Mr. Bird pulled away, I looked across the field and saw Uncle Cletus's truck just disappearing into the tree line. I looked at Caleb, Booger, and Flop. It was clear they'd heard the conversation about the coyotes. "Wanna check out the cave?" Blank stares. "Coyotes don't like caves. It's too damp for 'em." Flop's ears rose almost a full inch when he smiled.

Booger shined the flashlight while I crawled in, then we coaxed Caleb and Flop through the small opening. It was cool inside. Since the mouth of the cave faced west, the late afternoon sun sprayed a thin shaft of light through the narrow slit in the ground, forming ominous shadows on the cave walls. Clogged with the bodies of sweaty boys who took too long to crawl in, the light would be momentarily shut off and the cave become dark as pitch. It was fine with me when Booger handed me the flashlight before crawling in.

Booger and I had brought the candles Brother Baker had given us when we'd helped with communion. The discarded wedding candles, held under our chins, made our faces look spooky. Caleb's hair cast a spiked-looking shadow on the wall behind his head. Flop had a unique shadow of his own. I held the candle behind his head so he could see it. He laughed, covered his ears momentarily with his hands, and then took his candle back. For a moment, we all stood still, holding our flickering candles. The cave had a spooky aura about it. I sensed it, and the dilated eyes looking back at me caused me to believe the others did, too.

Supposedly, during Prohibition, someone had buried a barrel of whiskey in the cave. Dad told me the legend during our first trip there. He'd never seen a barrel of whiskey in Colby and didn't know anyone who had.

He was sure there wasn't anything to the story and that it was just another example of how people with nothing to do will believe almost anything.

Flop listened intently as we filled him in. It was impossible to tell who did or didn't believe it. We all spoke as if the story had been proven beyond any shadow of a doubt. Flop swallowed it hook, line, and sinker, and now he wanted to find the barrel.

Nobody wanted to act like they were too scared to explore the depths of the cave, so it was decided unanimously to make a search for the lost barrel. I crawled back out and retrieved a nylon rope from my camp kit. Since Booger had the flashlight, and he had a brother who had been a Marine, we decided he should go first. He tied the nylon rope around his waist; Caleb and Flop looped it through a belt loop. I brought up the rear and tied it around my waist. We were bound together like a bunch of Bible School Sunbeams. I'd already nearly crippled Flop. It just wouldn't do to get him lost in a cave, too.

Until the ceiling got so low that we had to start crawling, the visibility had been good. The ceiling was a flat, slimy sheet of rock. The walls were dished out and looked sort of like the roof of someone's mouth. The floor was hard packed clay and felt like damp chalk. Once we started crawling, I couldn't see anything except the bottom of Flop's shoes and his rear end. I raised my head a couple of times to see, and hit it on the ceiling. Booger kept shining the light back and forth up ahead, but I couldn't see anything. Heavy breathing was the only sound.

"I found it," Booger announced.

Flop turned. "He found it." The campfire food sitting on his stomach all day and the stress of exploring the cave had combined to produce a nearly lethal breath.

The foul odor, the close quarters, and the sudden realization that I was tied to him made me claustrophobic. Even though the air in the cave was cool, almost cold, I was sweating. My neck swelled with each throbbing pulse. The nylon rope was pulled too tight around my waist.

"It's huge. I can stand up an'at," yelled Booger. He shined the blinding light our way and tugged on the rope. Flop mashed my left hand when he tried to hurry up. I pulled my right hand back before he got it, too. In the process, I hit my head on the ceiling.

We all stood, crouched over, in the small room. My pulse returned to normal. If the ceiling had been six inches higher, we could have all stood up straight. Two other tunnels, about the same size as the one we'd just crawled out of, led off in different directions.

"Somebody has been diggin' an'at o'vair." Booger shined the light at an area where the dirt had been disturbed. We all slowly moved in that direction.

The light and our bodies were giving off enough heat to warm the small room. Out of the corner of my eye, I saw what looked like a lizard or a salamander slither, almost unnoticed, along the edge of the wall and down the tunnel we'd just crawled through.

"What was 'at?" asked Flop.

"I didn't see anything," I lied. The last thing we needed was for everyone to panic.

Booger turned around. "What was what?"

Flop dropped to the floor, pulling the rest of us with him. "Like-a-said, shine 'at light up th' tunnel there."

Booger, already crouched down in order to keep the nylon rope that was connected to Flop and the rest of us from squeezing him in half, shined the light in the direction from where we'd just come. Cheek to cheek, we all looked down the tunnel for whatever it was Flop had seen. There was nothing but a very narrow passage. My claustrophobia was returning.

We sat there motionless for nearly a minute; Caleb's whisper broke the silence. "You think'at's where the barrel is buried?" He was looking toward the dig site.

Because of the way we were tied together, it was difficult to move around. Nobody was suggesting that we untie, though. As a unit, we scooted toward the disturbed dirt and took a closer look.

Caleb stuck his foot out and moved some of the clumps of dirt around. "Somebody could'a buried a body here, too."

"Whose?" Flop asked, as if it mattered.

We stood there in silence a few moments longer. Imaginations were running wild.

Booger shined the light at me. "You wanna go first on the way back?"

"Sure." I took the light and led the way, giving very little thought to slithering reptiles. No matter how fast I crawled, there was always slack in the rope behind me. At the mouth of the cave, I untied the rope and launched myself through the small opening. Everyone else followed using a similar style. We sat for a few moments with squinted eyes. The sweltering heat felt good. We continued to sit there and picked out of our hair what we eventually realized was bat crap.

THE MOSQUITOES CAME OUT IN force about the same time the setting sun disappeared into the horizon. We smeared some oily Avon stuff that Uncle Cletus had given us on our arms, legs, and faces. He said it was a not-so-well-known repellent he'd gotten while fishing in Louisiana. It smelled like something a woman would wear, but it kept biting insects away.

Caleb and Flop nearly had a fight over who was going to light the fire. It's doubtful that either one would actually have hit the other, but they sure-as-a-tick-sucks-blood would have argued all night long. Booger settled it by suggesting they both light the fire. It usually took a couple of matches to do it anyway, he told them.

Flop's entire book of matches caught fire while he was trying to light his first match, and he sat sucking on his singed fingers while Caleb used half his book, one match at a time, to get the fire started. In the meantime, Booger and I cut four sticks to roast the hotdogs. There wasn't any way we were going to let Caleb or Flop use a pocketknife.

Crickets can make a lot of noise when they set their itty-bitty minds to it. One at a time, the bullfrogs in Mr. Bird's pond started to croak. It only took a few minutes until all the woods critters were sounding off. The absence of town noise made the critter noises more noticeable.

"What in the heck was that?" Asked Flop who nearly jumped out of his skin and into the fire when a hoot owl, not too far away, made his presence known. It made me jump a little too, but no one noticed.

"Just an old hoot owl." I said, trying to sound calm.

Booger cupped his hands over his mouth and tried to mimic the night bird. "Who cooks for you, who cooks for you, who cooks for you all?" he said from the back of his throat. He'd've sounded pretty good if we hadn't just heard the real thing.

The owl sounded off a few more times, then nothing for several minutes. Not that it was quiet; there were still the crickets, frogs, and the smacking sound of hotdogs getting eaten.

Caleb stood up and looked around for the owl. "You think he's still there?"

"No, probably flew away after he decided you were too big to eat," I told him.

"You'd think we'd 'a heard 'em if he'd flown off," he argued weakly, visibly curious about the whereabouts of the owl.

"Owls have special feathers on their wingtips that allow them to flap their wings quietly. They can sneak up on critters that way."

"How'd you know 'at?" Flop asked.

"Uncle Cletus told me."

Booger jabbed the fire with his hotdog stick. "Figures."

We let the fire die down, mostly because no one wanted to go traipsing through the weeds looking for more driftwood.

BOOGER SHOOK ME AWAKE. WHAT was once a blazing fire was now only smoldering embers. A full moon straight overhead shed sufficient light to cast vague shadows. Flop was crying and quivering out of control. It was one of those cries when someone sounds like they're gasping for air. Caleb was holding him with both arms.

"How long has he been crying?" I asked Booger.

"I don't know. Caleb just woke me up. Flop wants to go home."

"Now?" I asked, still not totally awake.

"Looks like it," Booger said. We looked at each other; I was hoping some alternate solution would make itself obvious. Nothing.

A pack of coyotes off in the distance yelped for a few seconds, then stopped. Flop tucked his head tighter against his knees and leaned into Caleb. Caleb glanced our way, shrugged, and patted him on his bony back.

"He's scared," said Caleb, a fairly obvious observation.

We covered our gear with Mr. Bird's tarp and started toward town on our bikes. Light from the full moon made seeing easy enough along the edge of the field, but the road cutting through the trees and across the creek was dark. We rode single file.

Once we got past Mr. Bird's house, the road was wide enough that the canopy of limbs didn't cover it completely. A sliver of moonlight shined through. I followed close behind Flop. Some people look good in closely-cropped hair, but on Flop it looked almost cruel. His shoulder blades protruded with each pedal. The rear tire on his bike wobbled so bad it hit the fender braces on both sides with each revolution. Those English Racers just weren't built very sturdy.

We stopped at the bridge for a breather, mostly for Flop. Caleb, Booger, and I carried a few big rocks to the middle of the span and dropped them into the creek. The "ka-plunk" sound they made when hitting the water was fascinating. Later that summer we would dive down, retrieve them, and put them back for future use.

Flop sat silently and watched. Dust had gathered in his tear tracks and below his nostrils. The mosquitoes had stopped biting, but the welts on Flop's forehead reminded me that they had certainly been miserable earlier in the evening. Uncle Cletus would surely know why they only seemed to bite at certain times. Flop had stopped quivering, apologized, and even offered to go back, which we eventually did, but not before the truck ordeal.

SEVERAL TIMES DURING THE EVENING, Booger had mentioned the truck and how he and I had permission to drive it. He'd made it sound like Mr. Gooche had given us carte blanche to do with it what we wanted. The reality was we could drive it from the dock door to the incinerator, a distance not more than forty yards. The enthusiasm was contagious. Even Flop had gotten energized when Caleb suggested we pedal over to Gooche's and start the truck.

The plan, so to speak, was to ride through town on our bikes while Colby slept, start the truck, and then head back to Bird's Cave.

Colby was tomblike. The only sound was a dog barking in the distance. We zigzagged down the middle of the streets since there wasn't any traffic. The only lights were the mercury vapors. I'd never noticed the buzzing sound they made. A cloud of insects and moths swarmed each one. Occasionally a bat would dart through the potpourri, getting his fill.

Several backyards had clothes on the line. Most women hung their undergarments in their basement, but in the summer some would put them on the line at night. At least that's what Mom and Marsha did. Most of what I could see, though, were bedsheets. The moonlight wasn't bright enough to see anything else. The one dog had stopped barking, and now another one had started. The second one sounded close to where the first one had been, maybe a neighbor.

The businesses on the square were dimly lit. A turtle was taking his good old time crossing the road and had almost made it to the middle of the main intersection. Flop picked him up and carried him to the courthouse lawn.

SINCE ALL WE WERE GOING to do was start it, I'm not sure why all four of us had to get in, but we did. Booger pressed on the starter pedal, and the engine came to life.

"Let's take her for a spin an'at," suggested Booger, displaying no reservation whatsoever.

"Yeah! No one will know. Let's just go to th' incinerator and back," added Caleb.

I should have seen it coming, but I didn't. It's a genuine phenomenon how one can look back and realize how obvious the right thing to do should have been.

"I don't think it's a good idea," I cautioned.

Caleb and Booger rolled their eyes at me. Flop wasn't weighing in. "Why don't you guys come down sometime when we're workin', and you can ride along when we dump trash?" Nobody listened.

"That's no fun," said Caleb.

"Why not?" I asked.

"I don't know, jus' ain't."

Booger pulled it into gear and started easing the clutch out. We slowly crept toward the incinerator, bouncing gently through the potholes. Flop and Caleb put their hands on the dash to brace themselves. I held onto the door.

"Let's make a run through th' neighborhood," suggested Caleb. Unfortunately Booger agreed with him, and then Flop exhibited more excitement than he ever had about anything. I was outnumbered.

Booger had never shifted it into second before and didn't know how. Uncle Cletus had taught me how to shift, but I had the good sense not to teach Booger. As we crept through Colby in first gear with our lights out, not having shared that bit of information with Booger was about the only thing I could think of to be thankful for. He'd speed up, then put the clutch in and let it coast.

We were easing the truck slowly down Wendy's street when Flop pointed out someone, a man it looked like, coming out from behind Wendy's neighbor's house. The figure was walking quickly down the street ahead of us. It didn't seem like he'd seen us yet. Booger and I agreed, in a whisper, that we shouldn't use the brakes because they squealed.

"Maybe we'll coast to a stop before we catch up with him," whispered Caleb.

"Who do you think it is?" asked Flop.

"What idiot would be out walking around an'at in the middle of the night?" asked Booger.

"I don't know, everybody just shut up," I said, just above a whisper. The reality of having done something wrong, and the thought of getting caught, losing my job, and not getting the Honda Mini-Trail was taking its toll on me. My mouth got that cotton feeling again. The worst part was how disappointed Mom and Dad and Mamaw and Papaw would be.

"He's carrying something," whispered Flop, pointing, as if we needed to be shown where he was. We were now close enough to determine that the person walking was a man.

I got eye contact with Booger and reached over to turn the ignition key. The engine went dead. The only sound was that of Wendy's neighbor's dog barking from the yard the mystery man had just come from.

I'd hoped to coast to a stop before being seen. Unfortunately, the grade was such that we were actually picking up a little speed. We were going to pass him. Just before we passed him, the items he was carrying became visible: ladies' underwear. As we came nearer to him, he turned and faced the truck. Milton Merle and I had direct eye contact for a split second before he raced ahead of us, cut across the street, darted through a yard between two houses, and was gone.

Booger started the truck. I told him how to shift into second gear, and we headed back to Gooche's.

"That was Milton Merle," said Flop.

"Think he saw us good enough to know who we were?" asked Caleb.

"Well, he sure enough saw the truck," added Flop.

"He looked right at me," I told them.

No one talked the rest of the way back to Gooche's. We parked the truck in the exact spot we'd taken it from and rode our bikes all of the way to Bird's Cave without stopping or talking.

The woods were stone cold quiet, and our sleeping bags were wet with dew. Sleep came easy to the others right away, but I kept seeing Mr. Merle's face.

Chapter 32

Couldn't Wait

"You boys gonna sleep all day?" Mr. Bird asked, standing next to his pickup. The sun, like a giant orange ball, capped the trees along the ridge to the east. "It's gonna be another scorcher when 'at sun gets up." He looked toward the east and rubbed the top of his balding head.

Nobody else was awake. I must have finally fallen asleep, because for a moment I was disoriented, not sure if the truck ride and the visual of Mr. Merle's face was real or a bad dream. Flop's mouth was gapping open, oblivious to the world, coyotes, or anything else. It was a surreal moment. It took me a few seconds to get my bearings. For a few hopeful seconds, it seemed possible that the previous night's episode may have just been an adventurous dream.

"Mrs. Bird is fixin' a big breakfast. She sent me t' fetch you fellers."

It was early, and I was exhausted, but the breakfast sounded good. I woke the others.

"I need to run into town after breakfast. I'd be happy t' give you'ns fell·ers a ride."

"That'd be great," I replied, but didn't say any more.

His truck was nearly the same model as Mr. Gooche's trash truck, but in better condition. I climbed into the cab with Mr. Bird. Booger, Caleb, and Flop were in the back. It hadn't been any trouble getting them awake when they learned that Mrs. Bird was fixing breakfast.

The Bird's house didn't have air-conditioning, except for the window unit sticking out of what was probably their bedroom. The rest of the house was open, including the kitchen. The aroma of frying food was free to escape into the entire valley. My mouth started watering well before we pulled into the driveway.

"Sure does smell good, Mr. Bird," said Caleb. We all made a beeline for the house.

"Not so fast there fellers," said Mr. Bird. "We've got a few chores t' do first." We had expected to do some chores for him, but had hoped that since it was so close to breakfast time we'd get off of the hook.

With spirits slightly dampened and mouths watering, we followed Mr. Bird to the barn. Caleb was given a five-gallon bucket half full of corn and told to feed the chickens. Mr. Bird gave Booger a willow basket and sent him to the chicken house to collect eggs. Flop and I helped him toss bales of hay from the loft down to the crib.

I looked out of the loft and saw Caleb defending himself from a full frontal attack by a very upset rooster.

"Whack'em with 'at bucket," yelled Mr. Bird from the loft. Caleb didn't hear.

By the time Mr. Bird, Flop, and I got down out of the loft, the rooster had Caleb and Booger both chasing their tails. Caleb was swinging the bucket wildly and coming closer to hitting Booger than the rooster. Booger held the egg basket with one hand and swatted at the rooster with the other, while at the same time dodging Caleb's fruitless swats with the bucket.

Mr. Bird launched into a sprint that any varsity football coach would have admired. He then started clapping his hands loudly and chased the killer fowl away. He took the bucket from Caleb and the basket of eggs from Booger.

"Danged bird is gonna come up missin' some day," he mumbled.

We followed him to the house, there being no further discussion of the boys being held at bay by a five-pound barnyard bird.

Mrs. Bird had us all hold hands while Mr. Bird said the blessing. He thanked the Lord for our nation, lifted the boys in Vietnam up in prayer, asked that Social Security taxes not be raised, and that the food would be blessed. We filled up on eggs, bacon, biscuits, and sorghum molasses. After making sure we hadn't found the hidden barrel of whiskey, Mr. Bird took us back to town. The small bit of chores we'd done had been a good trade for the Birds' breakfast.

"You stink!" was how Marsha greeted me after I walked in the door.

"She's been like that all day," said Mom when I asked what her problem was. "Mickey left for Philmont this morning. He brought by his bicycle and a list for you this morning before he left."

I looked at the list. It had the names of everyone on the route listed in order of delivery and an *r* for rolled or an *f* for folded beside each name.

Mom was looking over my shoulder reading the list. "Go take a bath," she said. Her message was essentially the same as Marsha's, only said in a motherly way.

It's a good thing I checked for ticks. I had one in a place that wouldn't have been easily seen and would have given me lots of trouble if not removed. I pulled it and a small bit of flesh off, then let the little devil crawl along the counter long enough to make sure his head was still attached. Once convinced that he was perfectly fine, I sliced his pincher head off with my Tuff-Nut knife. I'd seen my great-grandfather do it a hundred times, sometimes while at the dinner table, which usually got him a look from Mom and Grandma.

I laid down on the couch for a few minutes, and the next thing I knew, Mom was waking me up to tell me that Flop was waiting for me. In a sleep-deprived state of mind, I had to be reminded that I had the paper route to do. I then remembered that Flop said he'd go with me; Booger had to work at Gooche's.

I let Flop ride my bike since I had Mickey's; Flop's tires had gotten dangerously wobbly. He'd been picking at the mosquito bites on his forehead, and the scabs were oozing. My tick bite itched a little, but I was careful to be discreet when I scratched it. Flop was wearing a wide-brimmed straw hat, no doubt his mother's idea of a way to protect him from the sun. It looked a little like the bonnet Mrs. Whitener always wore. It always amazed me how he could wear such ridiculous stuff and not be embarrassed. He held it on with one hand as we rode along.

We delivered to several businesses before getting to Gooche's. I took Flop to the employees' drinking fountain at Gooche's, and we both guzzled cold water until the tops of our heads hurt. We visited briefly with Booger; nobody mentioned the truck deal. It was a secret so sacred it couldn't even be discussed among the core.

After delivering to the Houn Dawg, Mrs. Pope gave us a small ice cream cone. It tasted great, but made us thirsty again. We washed down the ice cream at the water fountain in Burt's shop, drinking long enough that the condenser kicked on. My belly button was about to pop.

Milton Merle's name had an *f* next to it, but I rolled his paper and tossed it from the street. His golf cart was gone, but there was no way I was going up on his porch. He needed some time to forget my face.

Mrs. Enderle was sitting on her front porch knitting; I parked Mickey's bike, walked to the porch, and handed her the paper.

"Who's the boy with the sun bonnet, and-a-like-a-that?" she asked.

"Oh 'at's Flop." Flop heard us talking and took his hat off and smiled.

"Well my stars, it surely is," she said. "I guess his mother dressed him," she whispered to me. Word traveled fast in Colby.

"Have you heard?" Wendy asked when we got to her house.

"Heard what?"

"Some weirdo went through the neighborhood stealing stuff off of the clotheslines last night. Our neighbors said their dog was barking, and they looked out and saw an old truck going by real slow and someone running across the street." My mouth went bone dry again, and my tick bite started itching simultaneously.

"Like-a-said, it was probably Milton Merle," said Flop. I gave him a look.

"That's what we thought too, but according to the Sheriff, Mr. Merle doesn't have a truck, just that silly golf cart looking thing," said Wendy. "My dad is really mad; he said he's going to go talk to Mr. Merle anyway and get to the bottom of it, one way or the other."

"Uh-huh," I mumbled weakly and then noticed my mouth was gaping open. Flop had apparently tuned Wendy out and was cleaning his finger-nails with his Tuff-Nut knife. Wendy's dad didn't seem like a "one way or the other" type, but nonetheless Wendy made it sound like he was bent on talking to Mr. Merle. Milton Merle's face was clear in my mind, and I feared mine was clear in his. "What were the odds he knew my name?" was the thought that I had.

"It's odd," she said.

"What's that?" I asked.

"Well, the neighbor said it looked like the truck was full of people, but as far as anyone knows, Mr. Merle doesn't have any friends with an old truck."

"Might end up being an unsolved mystery," said Flop.

"Well, if Mr. Merle knows anything, I'm sure my dad will get him to talk," said Wendy in an effort to reassure us, oblivious to the fact that it had quite the opposite effect.

"I REALLY NEED TO GO," Flop said for the umpteenth time.

"The Beeker house is just ahead. Mickey said that it's vacant for the summer and that the hedge in the backyard is a good place to go." I was about to bust, too, and my tick bite needed a good scratching, which I wasn't about to do in plain view.

The house looked vacant enough. We followed the path from the car-port, through the open gate, to the patio in the backyard. The hedge hadn't been taken care of and was encroaching on the edge of the patio. We both found a spot and started taking care of business.

I heard the sound of the motorcycle coming up the street, but had put it out of my mind. The sudden shrinking of my bladder sent a goose bump tremor throughout my entire body. The ecstatic moment ended when the motorcycle, which I'd tuned out in my moment of bliss, came roaring through the patio gate. Unable to protect my face because my hands were shielding other parts, the branches of the hedge scratched my cheeks and forehead when I dove through them.

Flop had done the same. Both of his ears had horizontal scratches; the oozing blood looked like war paint. The cavity created by my empty blad-der was now filled with a pounding heart.

"Well, you mentioned that you had a lawn service, but I'd assumed it was more along the lines of mowing, not watering." It was a woman's voice, and she had recognized me. A thousand thoughts pierced my mind. Flop's look of bewilderment combined with his bloody face art provided by the hedge, brought needed levity to the situation. I was able to deduce the source of the voice.

"Miss Anderson?"

"Yes … Tommy?" My head throbbed at the sound of my name, just like it had after drinking the cold water, which seemed, at the moment, like eons earlier. I wanted desperately to move back in time.

"We thought the house was vacant," I said, as I started the slow careful process of explaining our position and negotiating a tactful exit.

"Obviously," she intoned. Her voice wasn't strained, and, in fact, I sensed a bit of humor in her response. I peeked through the hedges and saw her leaning against the bike, fluffing her hair with one hand and holding her helmet with the other one. She was grinning. A feeling of relief filled my senses. Swallowing became less difficult, but my tick bite still itched.

MOM WAS FIXING A LETTUCE salad and Marsha was slicing fruit when I walked in. A barbeque aroma meant Dad was grilling something, probably hamburgers.

"I got another lawn to mow and a new paper route customer."

"That's great. Who?"

"Miss Anderson, the new teacher."

"I don't believe I've met her."

Marsha rolled her eyes, "She rides a motorcycle. All the boys think she's cool."

"Where'd you see her?" Mom asked.

"I carried her groceries out at Gooche's."

"But you didn't work today."

"Oh, uh, today? She's moving into the Beeker house. Flop and I saw her there and talked to her."

"Being able to speak to adults is a good character trait, Tommy. I'm really proud of you." Marsha gave me a look, but she couldn't have known anything; she just didn't like Miss Anderson.

"She said that when Booger and I get our Mini-Trails that she'll go riding with us and let Flop ride behind her," I said to Mom. Then I stuck my tongue out at Marsha and ran out the back door to see if Dad needed any help.

Chapter 33

Cupid

BOOGER AND I MET AT Miss Anderson's house the next morning. After pointing out the property lines, Miss Anderson said, "Oh, and if you feel the urge to water the grass, just help yourself to the bathroom in the basement. It's just inside the door, on the left." It was a subtle reference to the hedge deal the day before.

I'd only made a couple of circles around the perimeter, marked by mature pine trees and ready-to-fall-over poplars, when Miss Anderson motioned for me. I turned the mower off and could hear Booger's mower in the front yard.

"How's Randy adjusting?" she asked. Before I responded, she continued. "I visited with your uncle Cletus at a teacher's meeting. He filled me in about Randy's brother and mother."

"He probably wouldn't mind if you called him Booger."

"That's cool. So, how's Booger doing?"

It was a very uncomfortable conversation for me. She was interested in Booger and asked questions about him, but mostly, it seemed, she wanted to rail against the government for causing the unnecessary loss of life in a hopeless cause. Her eyes watered; I concentrated on not letting my mouth hang open as she went on.

Booger's lawn mower stopped. Miss Anderson snapped back into the here and now when a car door closed. I could hear Booger talking to someone. It was Mr. Burger with our peanut butter and jelly sandwiches and cartons of lemonade.

Mr. Burger smiled and waved when I rounded the corner of the house. But he seemed to stiffen when he saw Miss Anderson. He must have been sucking his stomach in because he had to keep tugging at his pants to keep them up. I'd never seen him stand so straight. Since Mrs. Burger's death, he'd taken to mostly slouching, at least until Miss Anderson. Booger had told me that his dad talked a lot about how much he missed Mrs. Burger. She'd never really been the same after Johnny's death. It seemed like she'd died with Johnny. As for Mr. Burger, he was still in mourning, but Miss Anderson's presence seemed to add a spring to his step.

Years later, I was to learn that his behavior around Miss Anderson was most likely associated with testosterone, a chemical that Flop had way too little of and Clyde too much of. Mr. Burger probably had a normal level.

"Hi, I'm Bridget, pleased to meet you."

"Jack Burger," Mr. Burger replied, noticeably nervous.

It was only a few seconds before they both forgot that Booger and I were there. They became totally engrossed with each other. That was okay with Booger and me; we were starving and preferred eating to talking. It was interesting, though, watching Mr. Burger puff his chest out, hold his stomach in, and talk. Much more of an effort would have caused his asphyxiation. Miss Anderson took on a demure persona, which I found very contradictory, knowing full well she was a Honda Scrambler rider, not to mention pilot. Booger was too engrossed in his peanut butter and jelly sandwich to notice.

WE LEFT OUR LAWN MOWERS at Miss Anderson's and walked over to Mr. Gooche's to get our bikes; we hadn't taken our lawn mowers home for a couple of weeks and had just been moving them from place to place. It hadn't rained for at least three weeks, and our lawn-mowing business was drying up with the grass. It would soon be time to take our mowers home.

The bank was on the way home, so we stopped and deposited the money from Mr. Gooche's and Miss Anderson's yard. The Mini-Trail goal was less than a hundred dollars away. It seemed to me that the closer we came to getting our Mini-Trails, the harder it was for me to pedal my bike. I never mentioned the phenomenon to Booger.

One of those million-dollar rains the farmers frequently referred to this time of year would certainly have helped our effort. Most of the grass had already gone dormant, but the weeds had survived, and a good rain would give them a real power boost. We got paid the same whether we mowed the entire yard or just lopped off clumps of weeds here and there. None of our customers used weed control, and that was fine.

AUNT PENELOPE'S CAR WAS AT Booger's house when we got there. She and Mr. Burger were sitting at the dining room table drinking coffee. How anyone could drink coffee when it was a million degrees outside was beyond me.

"Finished?" asked Mr. Burger.

"Yes, sir," I replied. "Booger's headed for Gooche's Grocery and I'm delivering papers."

"You two are regular money-making machines," said Aunt Penelope.

"Less than a hun'ert to go," said Booger.

Aunt Penelope smiled broadly. "Wow, that's great," she said.

"Aunt Penelope has some good news," said Mr. Burger.

Booger and I both turned and gave her our full, undivided attention. Good news to us usually meant someone was getting a new car or color TV. We were curious.

"I'm moving to Colby."

"Oh man, that's great," said Booger, visibly thrilled. "Now you can come over and cook for us every night."

"Hold on, Mr. Man. I don't think that's what she has in mind," cautioned Mr. Burger. Booger's spirit wasn't dampened, though.

"Where' ya movin' to?" Booger asked.

"That small house next to the Olefsens', just down from Tommy. It's a fixer-upper, but your dad has offered to help."

"You know the Olefsens walk around naked, don't you?" She was still thinking about that when I added, "Uncle Cletus will help you fix it up. He's got a pickup truck and can help you move, too."

I was sure Uncle Cletus wouldn't mind. School wasn't starting for another month, and he liked odd jobs. "I'll call him."

He'd offered to pick up the lawn mowers for us and had said to call when we got to Booger's, so I did. He came right over; I let Aunt Penelope tell him.

After Uncle Cletus got there Aunt Penelope explained her plan. He replied "That's great, Penny. Let me know what I can do to help."

"See, told ya," I said. Uncle Cletus gave me a quizzical look. I quickly added, "If you don't mind, we better get going. Booger has to go to Gooche's Grocery, and I have to deliver papers."

Aunt Penelope winked at me. Mr. Burger grinned, scratched his head, and looked at Uncle Cletus and said, "I'll explain later."

Chapter 34

First Solo

DAVE BLUE HAD FILLED MOM in on his plan to surprise Dad and let him fly solo and that there'd be a small hangar celebration afterwards. Dave and Dad had N95S in the pattern, doing touch-and-gos, when we got to the airport. Mom had baked a sheet cake, and we'd stopped by Colby John Deere and gotten two cartons of sodas. A small hangar celebration was in order, she'd said. Knowing what was going on, as did probably everyone in town by now, Mr. Gooche let Booger off to go with us when we stopped there to get ice.

Mr. Burger and Uncle Cletus had been in Fairview helping Aunt Penelope pack up. Mr. Burger had called Gooche's to check on Booger and had found out what was going on. They were all there, too. Mom was worried there wouldn't be enough cake.

We parked behind the office like Dave had said to do, so Dad couldn't see us from the ramp. After carrying the cake, sodas, and ice inside, we watched from behind the heavily tinted windows as Dave gave Dad some last-minute instructions, then got out of the airplane. It was too hot, which isn't the best time to fly airplanes, but the windsock was hanging limp. According to Dave, that made landing easier.

Dave had trimmed down a lot since the last time I'd seen him. It wouldn't be long before the Army would accept him for helicopter flight school. Once inside the office, he explained what would happen and what to watch for.

"I'm not taking on any more students. Ted's my last one until I get back," he said. He watched introspectively, as Dad taxied N95S out for take off. "I'm just a few pounds short of my goal."

After twice being rejected because of weight, he was finally going to fulfill his dream of flying helicopters in Vietnam. The others were fussing over the cake, sodas, paper plates, and everything. Booger was using the toilet. I was the only one who'd listened to him. He rested his hand on my shoulders and squeezed my neck like grownups did.

Dad and the N95S lifted off right were Dave said they would. The nose pitched up, down, then back up again, just like Dave had said it would. "He's not used to the airplane being so light," Dave informed. "It's also climbing faster than he's used to. I explained it all, but it'll still take a couple of touch-and-gos for him to get the feel of being alone."

"Hey guys." It was Miss Anderson, who'd evidently found out too. "Who's soloing?"

"Ted Thompson," said Dave.

She looked at me. "Your dad?" I shook my head yes.

"Have we met?" asked Dave.

She looked back at Dave, "Oh, I'm sorry, Bridget Anderson."

Dave extended his hand to shake. "Dave Blue."

"Nice to meet you, Dave. I student-taught at Fairview and got a teaching job at Colby. I was on my way there and saw the Thompsons' car and thought I'd see what was going on."

"Do you fly?" asked Dave.

"Sure, in fact I'm an instructor and would like to get a few students. Got any extra you can throw my way?" She half joking, half serious.

"Well, I might. I'm not taking on any more students now and might be able to send a few your way."

We watched as Dad taxied into position for his third and final take off. He'd stay in the pattern and do three touch-and-goes, and then his first solo would be official.

"May I ask why you're not taking on any more students?" Miss Anderson asked.

"I'm going to fly helicopters in the army."

Miss Anderson's face became flaccid. She didn't respond. Her tongue moved around in her mouth between her teeth and cheeks like mine does when my mouth is real dry and I'm nervous. Blinking her eyes more than normal, she turned and looked out the window and watched Dad, occasionally glancing at Dave, who was sitting at a cluttered desk making a notation in Dad's flight logbook.

The N95S bounced on the first two landings, but on the third and final landing, the main wheels chirped as the plane settled gracefully onto the runway. Dad couldn't possibly have heard it, but everyone clapped and cheered. Miss Anderson whistled really loud. Mr. Burger looked at her, grinned, and shook his head.

Dad taxied in, shut the airplane down, and got out. Mom gave him a hug and even kissed him on the mouth; it was too embarrassing to watch. Dave had Dad's logbook in one hand and an oversized pair of scissors in the other.

"Oh, I get it now," Dad said to Mom. She'd insisted that he wear an old shirt that she'd always forbidden him to wear except on fishing trips. Now he knew why.

Dave cut a huge swatch from it, a customary first solo ritual, and also, unknowingly, settled the obnoxious shirt deal once and for all. He wrote Dad's name, N95S, and the date on the swatch. After everyone signed it, Dave pinned it on the "First Solo" bulletin board along with other pieces of material that had been there for over ten years. While the others got their cake and congratulated Dad, I read the names. Dave Blue had signed over half of them.

By now, everyone had heard about Aunt Penelope's divorce and that she was moving to Colby. Since it wasn't too far out of the way, everyone swung by her Fairview place and loaded what they could in their car to take to Colby. She'd insisted that it wasn't necessary, but the caravan, including Miss Anderson on her motorcycle, had headed that way nonetheless. The fidgety jerk wasn't there, which was best. He was probably off somewhere with his paramour, as Aunt Penelope liked to call the "other" woman.

"Does the chair go?" asked Uncle Cletus.

"Oh, that'd be great," said Aunt Penelope with a face-cracking grin.

Uncle Cletus stood there holding the chair looking perplexed. "What?" he asked.

"Well, that's his favorite chair, at least when he's here," she replied.

Uncle Cletus sat the recliner down.

"No, go ahead, let's take it," she said.

"You sure?" he asked. By now everyone had stopped and was listening.

"I'd love to see his face when he comes back and sees that it's gone."

"Don't you guys have some kind of an agreement?" Mom asked.

"Oh sure, the chair is his, but then again we had our marriage vows, that was an agreement. He broke them. Now I'm taking his stupid chair." Everyone saw some humor in the comparison. I didn't quite understand it at the time.

In less than an hour, we'd gotten all of her belongings loaded in the various vehicles. She locked the front door and tossed her door key into the night air. "Hope he has his," she said cavalierly.

Booger rode back to Colby with Miss Anderson on her Scrambler. I rode back with Dad, and we talked about flying. He promised that I'd be his first passenger when he got his license, unless Mom wanted to go. We passed Booger's house on the way to Aunt Penelope's. Miss Anderson's motorcycle was parked in the driveway. Dad's eyebrows rose in an ah-ha kind of look.

Chapter 35

Factory Sold

"SHOE FACTORY SOLD" WAS THE headline. "Fate of 178 Jobs Uncertain" was in smaller but still bold print. Everyone had heard bits and pieces about the sale and was waiting anxiously to get the *Colby Telegraph*. Some had watched for Flop and me and then walked out to the edge of the street to meet us. We were making good time since we didn't have to roll or fold so many papers and place them in specific locations.

Since Wendy's dad was the plant manager, she didn't need the paper to know the details. She'd been telling me what she knew about the sale after each piano lesson. A conglomerate, based in St. Louis, had been trying to buy the shoe factory for a couple of months. Mr. Winchester had tried to talk the owners out of selling, suspecting the conglomerate would most likely close the factory, causing everyone to lose their jobs. He had been fairly certain the conglomerate was only interested in the customer list and not the production facility, since they'd never even asked him about the production; they'd only asked about sales. He was all but certain that if the factory was sold, they'd be shutting it down.

Billy Burke and Beth were sitting in the porch swing; both were pouting. Billy stopped sniveling when he saw me. I was sure that he'd only been doing it to impress Beth. It was a pathetic thing to see the starting tight end for the Colby Cardinals carry on in such pitiful fashion. The football coach would have made him run wind sprints or do push-ups if he'd seen him. The fate of the factory had yet to be determined.

"Well, it looks like you won't have to play in the recital," Wendy said, first thing. She'd already acquired the ability to read minds, or at least mine. I'd already come to that possible conclusion, somewhat selfishly, and had found a kind of comfort there.

"Guess not, and after all that practice too," I replied, trying my best to sound remorseful even though there wasn't an ounce of remorse to be felt. The cancellation of the recital would be cause for rejoicing in my mind.

"Mom's not going to cancel it until we know for sure, though," she said.

"How long do you think that will be?"

"Probably a couple of weeks. We can keep practicing until then."

"You going to register for school?" I asked.

"Oh sure. We'll probably be moving, though."

A plethora of emotions flooded my conscious. I was thrilled that the recital might be cancelled, but the thought of Wendy moving simply wouldn't register. My mind drifted to visuals of giving her a ride on my Mini-Trail and the pleasant memories of all those recital practices. A lemon-scented furniture-polishing rag in her hand almost masked the Jungle Gardenia, but not totally. I realized that Billy Burke's performance in the porch swing might be authentic. I turned and watched a robin probing for worms and fought back the tears.

"Flop's waving for you to go."

"Yeah, I see 'im." I didn't look her way. "See you tomorrow."

I glanced back several times after pedaling away. She never stopped watching me. The visual of her standing by the street watching me pedal away wasn't broken until fifteen minutes later, when Mrs. Bordenstein's dog nearly broke his chain in an effort to take a chunk out of me.

"What'd you jump for?" Flop asked sarcastically from the street. "He can't break 'at chain, at least that's what you tol' me."

I laid the paper under the doormat with only the headlines showing; that's how Mickey had said to do it. Flop had clearly been entertained and was grinning at my expense. The urge to pull his stupid-looking hat off and throw it to the still-barking dog almost overwhelmed me.

He led the way to the next few houses. Noticing again his pencil-thin neck and bony body, my contempt for him waned. Contempt turned to pity when I noticed, for the first time that day, that he'd worn black dress socks with his tennis shoes. Looking like an idiot just came natural to him—a genetic trait, I realized, after meeting his dad. Flop needed sympathy rather than contempt, I decided.

———

THE NEXT MORNING, AFTER DRINKING a cup of coffee with Mom, Uncle Cletus took me to orientation, since he was going to the school anyway. We took his Scrambler.

Miss Anderson's Scrambler was parked next to the building in the teacher's parking lot. Two helmets hung from the handlebars. Uncle Cletus parked beside it. We hung our helmets on the rearview mirrors.

"Come on down to my room when you're finished," Uncle Cletus told me before he walked toward the high school wing.

"Yes, sir. It won't take long."

Booger, Clyde, and a couple of girls were the only others in the classroom when I got there. Clyde and I hadn't become best of friends or anything, but since I'd stood my ground at home plate he was no longer confrontational. He usually looked sad, possibly vexed, but that day his expression was different, maybe one of despair. I motioned a 'hi' to Booger, and then turned to Clyde.

"Hey, Clyde. How's your summer going?"

"Well, purty good, at least till the factory sold."

In an instant it dawned on me. His step-dad was a foreman at the factory and probably not the best employee. I looked in Clyde's eyes, sunken into his puffy face, and saw his mom screaming and chasing him around their car. I saw his fist smashing the face of the base runner from Fairview, and I remembered what Uncle Cletus had told me about his real father.

"It'll be all right," I told him. It was the first thing that popped into my mind, and a lame thing to say. "I'm sorry," would have been better and was what I was thinking, but it didn't come out that way.

The uncomfortable silence was broken when Miss Anderson walked in. "I ley," she said.

I reached a number of conclusions simultaneously: Miss Anderson was going to be our teacher, the town was possibly headed for a major disruption because of the shoe factory sale, and Booger had worn the second helmet on Miss Anderson's motorcycle. I wanted to smile and show my enthusiasm for her as our teacher, but out of respect for Clyde's situation, I didn't act unnecessarily jubilant.

"I'm Miss Anderson," she said and shook hands first with the girls and then Clyde. She pointed at Booger and me. "I know these two yahoos."

Watching Clyde's face, I reached another conclusion: Miss Anderson could make anyone smile. I'd never noticed until then that Clyde had dimples. Clyde, Booger, and I talked baseball while other kids arrived and met Miss Anderson for the first time.

"I heard she rides a motorcycle," one of the girls murmured, with a hint of sarcasm. A group of three was huddled next to the bulletin board, stealing glances at Miss Anderson. It wasn't until then that I'd noticed Miss Anderson was wearing Tuff-Nut jeans. The girls snickered; I fought the urge to kick 'em.

She gave us a mimeographed sheet of paper that had a short note to our parents with her address and phone number. The school's letterhead was at the top, but the bottom had a silhouette of a small biplane. I sniffed the paper, folded it, and put it in my pocket. Fortunately, Mom found it before putting my Tuff-Nuts in the washing machine. Otherwise, the note would have been reduced to bits of white pulp, like so many other teacher-to-parent notes I'd taken home.

Until Melody arrived, I thought about Wendy, who was now in junior high, another wing of the building. Melody arrived later than the rest. The summer sun had made her freckles more pronounced and had lightened her hair, which was put up into what I would later learn was a French braid.

Since her dad sold Tuff-Nuts, I'm sure she didn't mind Miss Anderson wearing them. We talked. She had decided to play the flute, just like Wendy.

"If everybody will take a seat, I'll introduce myself," said Miss Anderson. Everyone took a seat. The girls seemed to have some particular place they wanted to sit and gave each other stares when two or more had decided on the same chair. The boys just sat down anywhere, in the back row, of course. It was only a matter of time before we'd be separated and moved forward.

"My name is Miss Anderson," she announced. "I'd like to tell you about me, and then if you care to do so, I'd like to hear something about you. Anything."

She explained how she'd decided to be a teacher while in grade school and had never considered any other occupation. She also talked about her hobbies. Caleb and Booger were whispering when they should have been listening and had just started to annoy me when Miss Anderson hurled an eraser with pinpoint accuracy and hit Booger in the forehead, leaving a rectangular chalk mark and dispelling any rumor of him being the teacher's pet.

"And that's an example of what happens when you don't listen. I played fast pitch softball too—pitcher." She put on an evil grin, drew a circle on the board, and told Caleb to come to the front of class and put his nose in it. This wasn't new; everyone had put their nose in a circle on the board before, or so it seemed. Caleb complied; he knew the drill.

Looking at Booger, and to the surprise of everyone, she said, "Now, see if you can hit him with the eraser."

Booger looked pleasantly surprised. "Really?" he asked.

Miss Anderson nodded, and Booger hurled a line drive toward Caleb, whose eyes were twitching nervously all the while. Her hand shot up with catlike reflexes and stopped the eraser just inches from the back of Caleb's head. Chalk powder dusted the back of his sweaty neck.

"Caught, too," she said, looking at the class, but mostly the boys. The girls giggled, the boys swallowed and simultaneously stared in both disbelief and admiration.

She looked at Caleb. "We're even, now take your seat."

From that moment on, Miss Anderson was respected and considered armed and dangerous when carrying an eraser.

After the bell rang, Caleb, Booger, Clyde, and I walked to Uncle Cletus's classroom and looked at the snake in the jar. Caleb had never seen it. I'd never been tall enough to read the label on the lid until this year. I got the heebie-jeebies when I saw "Bird's Cave 6/2/61" on the label.

Uncle Cletus took me home. Miss Anderson followed with Booger. The ride made us both even more anxious to get the Mini-Trails. Uncle Cletus left, but Miss Anderson stayed. She drank coffee with Mom and thumbed through Dad's logbook. Since Dave Blue had left for the Army, Miss Anderson had taken over as Dad's instructor. Later on, Mom said she felt better about it after having met Miss Anderson, as if Mom knew enough about flying to be a judge of flight instructors.

On the way to Gooche's house, Booger and I stopped by the bank to make a deposit. We both had less than twenty-five dollars to go. During one of our fuel breaks, Mrs. Gooche gave us ice water and asked if we'd heard about the factory closing. Of course we knew; it was the only thing everyone was talking about, but we listened to her anyway. She mentioned that Mr. Gooche was worried that he'd have to let some people go if the factory closing caused the grocery store to lose business.

We finished mowing, and then we pushed the mowers to Melody's house and were putting them in the garage when she came out with lemonade. "Sorry I missed you while you were mowing. Dad asked me to help him at the store this afternoon."

She had a stressed look about her; it was very unnatural. She was wearing the twin ponytails, only they'd lost their bounce.

"Dad's worried about the factory closing," she finally confessed, her voice a little weaker than usual. "Dad's sure it will affect sales."

Booger's face indicated he was deep in thought, or his mind had gone completely blank, one or the other. The thought occurred to me, for the first time, that the factory closing was going to impact more than just those who worked there. I began to wonder if there was anything that could be done to save the factory.

"Does your dad think everything possible has been done to keep it from closing?" I asked Melody.

"Like what?"

"Well, have they had a meeting or anything?"

"Who?" she asked.

"Well, whoever meets when something like this happens."

She shrugged her shoulders, clueless as I was. I remembered my dad going to a committee meeting once when the city had talked about buying some ground near town and calling it an industrial park. At that time, he'd come home complaining that it was an idea too far ahead of most on the city council.

WE AGREED TO STOP BY Burt's on the way home and get a swig of ice-cold water from the fountain. Mr. Bird was leaning against the bed of his pickup talking to Burt when we rolled in. They were talking about the factory.

"Seems to me we need to find another company to come and make use of 'at building," I overheard Mr. Bird saying.

Burt shielded his eyes from the afternoon sun and nodded in agreement. He moved a toothpick from his mouth and placed it on his right ear; a pencil already occupied the left one. "I guess you're right, Bird," agreed Burt. He always called people by their last name only. "Purdy oughter know how to find out if another company is interested, what with his banking connections and all."

"Aren't you yahoos s'posed to be in school?" Mr. Bird asked when he saw Booger and me.

"Half day the first day," said Booger.

"Oh. Say, when you gonna come and visit again?" he asked.

"As soon as we get our Mini-Trails, we'll be out nearly every day," I told him.

"What's a Mini-Trail?"

Booger and I explained. Mr. Bird smiled and shook his head, then hesitated.

"Haven't I seen Dwight Seabaugh ridin' one of 'ose things?"

"Yes, sir," I said. "That's what we're gittn.'"

He opened the door to his pickup, but before getting in, turned and said, "Sounds like I might need to ask the county to put down some extra gravel."

We were still watching Mr. Bird when Burt said, "I heard that Dwight got his draft notice. He might be selling his Mini-Trail."

Buying a used Mini-Trail didn't have any appeal to either of us, and we didn't give it any more thought. Booger and I drank cold water until our heads hurt.

On the way home, we saw Booger's dad's car at Miss Anderson's, so we stopped. Miss Anderson had called Mr. Burger to help her hook up an extra phone. He'd been helping her a lot lately, but then everyone had said that he and Booger should keep busy.

Miss Anderson was kneeling by the side of the house next to a crawl space door with a flashlight and roll of phone wire. Mr. Burger had crawled under the house and was poking the wire up through a hole in the floor that Miss Anderson was shinning the light on.

"All finished?" she asked Booger.

"Yep, I'm going to Gooche's now, and Tommy has his paper route."

"Could you shine that light on the hole?" Mr. Burger asked from under the house, with a tone of frustration.

"Sorry," said Miss Anderson. She turned her attention back to Mr. Burger and the stuffing of a phone line through a tiny hole.

"Why didn't you have the phone company do this?" I asked.

"They'd run the line for free, but then they'd want to tack on a monthly charge for the extra phone. I don't want an extra phone, just an extra phone jack. That way, I can move the phone to where I am in the house."

"Oh," I said, and then started considering the possibility of putting a jack in my room. That way I could make calls without everyone in the house hearing what I was saying. Marsha would probably want one in the bathroom.

FLOP WAS WAITING FOR ME when I got home. He was wearing a new pair of high top Converse All Star basketball shoes. Even though they were an off-white, it was obvious they were new from half a block away. He'd grown out of his old ones. The new shoes with their pure white soles and thin racing stripe made his feet, which were attached to spindly shins, look even larger and more out of proportion. His ears danced on the sides of his head as he finished chewing the last bit of a Tootsie Roll.

"Where you been at?" he asked, moving the last glob of pasty chocolate around in his mouth.

I was tempted to reply, behind the 'at', but said, "Mowing over at Gooche's."

"Oh," he replied, and then swallowed.

His swallows always seemed painful. Watching his neck left no doubt why the bump under one's chin is called an Adam's apple. In his case, it could have been named an Adam's grapefruit, but then Eve hadn't tempted Adam with grapefruit.

I knew everyone would be anxious to get their *Colby Telegraph* and read about the latest development at the factory, so we didn't waste any time. Flop took one side of a street and I took the other. Some of the older folks who liked their paper folded and stuck in the door were, again, watching for us, and met us at the edge of the street. We kept moving and didn't wait around to see their disappointment in the lack of any news about the factory. The lead article was about the factory, but a historical perspective, nothing new. Nobody was waiting curbside the next day.

Chapter 36

Cross Country

BOOGER AND I'D WHINED AROUND enough that Miss Anderson agreed to let us tag along with her and Dad on his first cross-country.

Having never been in a plane before, Booger was a little anxious. I'd tried to explain how the farmland looked like a giant multi-colored quilt, but he was more concerned about the reliability of the engine. We rode with Miss Anderson to pick up Dad at his shop.

Odie Portman introduced himself to Miss Anderson. "So, you're 'at woman flight instructor," he said, the tone of his voice hinting of suspicion. He was eating his trademark peanuts and Pepsi, which negated any air of authority he was attempting to portray.

"Did they ever fig'r out what caused 'at airplane to crash?" he asked.

Miss Anderson perked up. "What plane was that?"

"Well there was a plane 'at crashed o'vair at Fairview about ten year ago. I heard it was engine fayure."

Miss Anderson was visibly relieved, but at the same time annoyed. "Ten years ago?"

"Yeah, 'bout that."

"I wouldn't have a clue, that's so long ago."

"Stee'yet," said Odie, before taking a swig of soda and peanuts and eyeing Miss Anderson suspiciously.

Dad came out of his office with his flight bag and we left Odie, still wondering about the ten-year-old airplane crash.

"What did cause the plane to crash?" asked Booger after we'd gotten in the car.

"I don't remember anything about it," Dad told him. "I'll ask Gene

Hickam about it sometime. By the way, he was in this morning and said there's going to be a party for Dave Blue at the airport today."

"Dave's in town?" asked Miss Anderson.

"Yep, he's finished with helicopter flight school. Gene said he's shipping out to Vietnam in two weeks."

The corners of Miss Anderson's mouth turned down. Her eyelids drooped noticeably. "Such a waste," she murmured.

WE STOPPED BY FAIRVIEW HONDA. Miss Anderson needed an oil filter for her Scrambler. The Mini-Trail stock was dwindling; it was near the end of the season. Booger and I sat on ours. Just two more weeks, and we'd be back to pick them up. Visions of taking Wendy for a ride on it were so vivid and clear that I momentarily felt a little dizzy and nearly tipped over.

DAVE BLUE HAD LOST EVEN more weight since he'd left for the army. A lot of people I didn't know were at the airport for his party. When we walked in, Gene Hickam was putting up a poster that Dave had brought home. It showed him standing next to a big helicopter. Dave called it a "Huey." Dave had changed; he had a more serious air about him. His body was stuck at attention.

"Sounds like I left you in good hands," I heard Dave say after he and Dad had visited for a few minutes.

Miss Anderson didn't join in on any conversations and after only a few minutes said, "We'd better head out if we're going to get back before dark." She went on out to the plane without visiting.

MISS ANDERSON HANDED DAD THE preflight checklist and followed him around the airplane. "I'm not going to point anything out, but I'll answer any questions you ask," she told him.

Booger and I climbed into the back. Dad and Miss Anderson got in next. Even with the windows open, the cockpit warmed up quickly. Dad did a few more preflight checks, then fired up the engine. The air shooting back from the propeller felt refreshing.

Booger and I were adjusting our seat belts when the engine quit. We both looked up to see Miss Anderson holding a fuel cap. Dad had obviously forgotten to check the fuel caps. They were located on the tops of the wings and were fairly easy to miss.

He got out, stepped up on the wing strut, and replaced the fuel cap and checked the other cap to make sure it was on good and tight.

"You probably won't do that again for a while," said Miss Anderson.

Dad looked at her sheepishly. "I hope not."

"That's enough to cause you to flunk the flight exam," she told him.

She seemed like a free spirit when she was on her Honda Scrambler, but she was all business when it came to flight instruction.

"Okay, let's see if this thing can fly," she declared. Dad visibly relaxed with those words, as if they were some kind of code, meaning there wouldn't be anymore preflight booby traps.

Booger started leaning from side to side, trying to see out both windows as soon as we got off of the ground. The air was smooth; a wing dipped a little each time he leaned from one side to the other. A thin wispy layer of cirrus clouds, "mare's tails," streaked the sky well above us.

Booger's expression was a mix of excitement and fear, but the ear-to-ear smile made it crystal clear that he was enjoying himself. Watching Booger have fun was more of a thrill for me than the actual plane ride.

Dad told us the landmarks he was looking for; Booger and I helped watch for them. Once we leveled off, Dad started noting on his kneeboard the time in which we passed over each landmark. After we'd pass three, he'd calculate our ground speed using the Jeppesen computer. It seemed like you had to be good at math to fly airplanes.

We were getting really close to the Cardwell runway, and Dad added another twenty degrees of flaps, pointed the nose down, and let the airspeed slow to seventy-five knots. It felt like we were going almost straight down; the runway numbers coming at us gave me a sense of speed.

Just before reaching the end of the runway, Dad reduced the power completely and pulled back gently on the stick, gradually bringing the nose up, and slowly reducing the airspeed even further. The tires chirped when they met the ground. "Beginners luck," said Miss Anderson. "Let's stretch our legs, and then get this bird in the air again."

BOOGER RAN INSIDE TO DO his business; I waited outside with Dad and Miss Anderson. They stood near the plane. Dad was stretching his arms over his head and Miss Anderson was looking at herself in a compact mirror.

"Who taught you how to fly?" I heard Dad ask her.

She told Dad about her mother being a WWII pilot and that she'd flown with her while growing up. She hesitated for several seconds; her eyes watered slightly.

"A guy I dated in college was my advanced flight instructor, though."

Something was bothering her, and Dad could tell she wasn't finished talking, so he stood there patiently kicking at pieces of gravel with his toe. Booger returned, and I motioned for him to listen up.

She continued the story. "He was in the Army ROTC program at the university. I was in my freshman year of college when we started dating." She inhaled deeply, threw her shoulders back, and tilted her chin skyward. She struggled to maintain composure.

"I was able to earn my instrument instructor certificate before he shipped out to Vietnam to fly those stupid helicopters. He was so proud."

Dad looked toward Booger and me and made a "guess I shouldn't have asked" face.

"He finished his tour of duty and came home. By then, I was teaching at a local high school and doing flight instruction part-time. He took over a few of my students, but that didn't last long. He missed the helicopters and the Army. So, he reenlisted."

Her eyes had passed the watering point; tears were literally streaming down her face.

"A company of Marines had taken several casualties defending some good-for-nothing, lost-in-the-jungle hilltop. He flew in to do a medical evacuation. The official story is that a grenade fell off of one of the wounded and exploded. Nobody's certain, and there was never much of an investigation. A few hours after the battle, the hilltop was abandoned by both sides anyway."

"So that's why you're so cool around Dave?"

"I guess so," she nodded. "Seeing Dave and sensing his enthusiasm for helicopters brings back too many bad memories."

Booger, crying now, too, had made his way closer to Miss Anderson and reached out to hug her. They embraced and cried. Dad and I patted them both on their shoulders.

Chapter 37

Fire

As FAR AS I COULD tell, the only visible effect the news of the factory closing had was everyone's sour attitude. Bem blamed it on the Chinese. Rabbit was sure it was the Mexicans. They both agreed that the cause was cheap overseas labor. Mr. Purdy, the only person who didn't seem to be blaming someone in particular, said it was a function of cost and competition. Something about the nature of his voice and the words he used caused me to think he knew what he was talking about. Booger said he didn't think anyone had stopped buying groceries. Our lawn-mowing business was slowing down, but that was because the end of summer had been dry. I'd grown the paper route by eight customers since taking over for Mickey. He'd given the route to me permanently after football practice started.

The dreaded recital, which unfortunately hadn't been cancelled, was only two weeks away. Wendy's mom hadn't lost any enthusiasm; I was now going twice a week to practice. Except for the piano playing, practice was a high point of my week. It saddened me to imagine Wendy moving away. I grew anxious for the recital to be over, but knew it meant that sharing a piano bench with Wendy would be over; I was filled with mixed emotions, to say the least.

BOOGER HAD MADE MORE MONEY working at Gooche's than I had delivering the *Colby Telegraph* and already had enough to get his Mini-Trail. It was going to be the end of the month before I got paid for delivering papers again, but Mom and Dad had agreed to advance me the money halfway through the month. Booger agreed to wait, and we'd planned to pick up the Mini-Trails at the same time, on the morning after the recital.

I remember lying in bed and thinking how in no time flat I'd take Wendy for a Mini-Trail ride instead of practicing for the recital. We'd still be sitting together but having a lot more fun.

THE NIGHTS WERE STARTING TO cool down. It had gotten unusually cold, but I'd kept my window open anyway, which is why I heard the siren before Dad did. I knocked on Mom and Dad's bedroom door. Dad had been a volunteer fireman since forever. He was now chief.

"Must be a fire," he said.

"Can I go?" I asked as Dad came through the door tucking in his shirt, headed for the back porch to put on his boots.

"You better not," Mom said, still not totally awake.

I considered a "better not" as something less than a no and followed Dad.

The fire station was only a block and a half from the house; we were the first to arrive. I opened the overhead garage door while Dad called the sheriff's office to see where the fire was. Uncle Cletus had pulled in just behind us and had the fire engine started and warming up. The red lights on top illuminated the firehouse with a red glow.

Dad came out of the office. "It's the Goodpastures' house."

He opened the passenger side door, motioned for me to get in, and we were off. As we were pulling out, several others were arriving and pulled in behind to follow us. The rotating red light on the top of the fire engine made the hood glow with each revolution. A string of cars with blinking blue lights mounted on their dashes followed us.

"Probably the water heater," said Dad.

"Yeah, that's usually the case this time of year," Uncle Cletus said in agreement.

We weren't speeding, but it sounded like it. The one-thousand-gallon water tank and the rest of the firefighting gear made the engine strain to accelerate after we slowed for each curve. Dad had to downshift to second gear going up Turkey Hill.

A mercury vapor light mounted on a pole between the burning house and the barn illuminated thick columns of smoke boiling out of the windows. Flames flickered inside. Clyde's mom was standing in the driveway, pointing at the house with one hand and covering her face with the other. Uncle Cletus rolled down the window to speak to her, but Dad didn't stop. He pulled the truck up closer to the house. She looked haggard and hollow, much different than the imposing mountain of a woman I'd watch chase Clyde through Burt's parking lot.

Clyde was directing a thin stream of water from a garden hose through one of the windows; it clearly wasn't doing a lot of good. His hair had been singed off on one side; he was holding a small picture frame in one hand. The two mongrels that had given chase to me and Uncle Cletus were sitting at his side, apparently in no mood to fight.

Blinking blue lights lined the highway. Everyone was there or on the way. I recalled Dad coming home after the volunteer firefighter meetings talking about doing the training exercises. Watching the men take their places was evidence they all took the volunteer firefighting service seriously. Even though they were volunteers, everyone seemed to know exactly what to do, and they were doing it with speed and precision. Uncle Cletus was positioning a ladder on the side of the house. Coach Bodenschatz and Mr. Thorpe were putting on fireproof gear. Mr. Burger and Mr. Gooche were dragging the large water hoses off of the truck toward the house.

Monkey Fullbright started up the ladder that Uncle Cletus had put up. Uncle Cletus steadied the ladder while Monkey literally ran up the rungs carrying a pickaxe. He ran up near the ridgeline and started hacking away.

"He's going to vent the house so it won't explode in flames," said Uncle Cletus. He later explained the venting procedure.

Mr. Gooche and Mr. Burger blasted away at the broken out windows with their hoses. The pressure was so great that an extra fireman had to help hold each hose. I approached Clyde, cautious of the dogs, and together we watched the contents of the thousand-gallon tank pour into his home.

"Get burned?" I asked.

"Yeah," he replied and held up the picture frame. "I went back inside to get this."

He held it up for me to see. It was a picture of a man standing beside a log truck and holding a small child.

"It's me and my dad."

Giant turtle tears edged slowly down Clyde's chubby cheeks. The left side of his face was red: his hair, eyelashes, and eyebrows were badly singed.

I knew the volunteers were doing their best, but it seemed to me that whatever might have survived the fire couldn't possibly survive the firefighters. It wasn't until Uncle Cletus found the gas line and shut it off that they were able to fully extinguish the blaze.

I stood next to Clyde but didn't know what to say. I remembered a passage from Romans that Brother Baker had preached about that said God knows our prayer even when we don't know how to pray.

"They may as well let it burn," he murmured.

"Surely saving something is better than nothing," I assured him.

He looked at me with glazed eyes. His face was smeared with black. An ample amount of belly hung over the waist of his shorts. "Nothin' worth savin' in there."

Clyde's mom and stepdad stood in the shadow of a hollowed-out hard maple and watched as their home was invaded, first by fire, and then by the Colby volunteer fire department. The fire was under control, but what didn't burn was going to be soaked.

I laid my hand on Clyde's thick shoulder. His hurt resonated throughout his body. A stench similar to that of a burn barrel just after a rain filled my nostrils.

On the way home, Uncle Cletus said he figured that there had been a problem of some sort with their water heater and that the fire had most likely started when it kicked on.

CLYDE DIDN'T MAKE IT BACK to school until Friday. He and his family had temporarily moved into the basement of the church. Clyde was wearing secondhand clothes. They were nice enough, but I'm sure he would have preferred his own. Secondhand clothes are okay if you know who owned them before, but I'm sure he felt strange wearing a stranger's castaways. If he'd been smaller, I could have given him some of my stuff. I'm sure he wouldn't have minded wearing clothes given to him by someone he knew.

His desk was next to mine. He leaned across the aisle and whispered, "We don't got no 'surance."

The gravity of the comment didn't sink in immediately; I gave him a quizzical glance.

"Dad figured we were gonna be short on money, what with the factory closin' an' all, and didn't pay th' last premium."

I just stared, unable to comprehend the total consequence.

"Guess he didn't fig'r on th' house burnin' down," Clyde continued, a little louder.

Miss Anderson gave us a look. Clyde's disposition had switched completely from predator to prey. I gave Miss Anderson my physical attention, not wanting to be the target of an eraser, but was mentally hung on Clyde and his family. His situation plagued me the rest of the day.

Chapter 38

Recital

TIME HAS A WAY OF dragging along ever so slowly as a favorable point draws near, but it sure does fly at lightening speed as events such as dentist appointments, spelling tests, and piano recitals approach. I'd looked forward to the recital day with mixed emotion, since it was also the Mini-Trail day. That day finally arrived, but the gloom was tempered by the plans we had for after the recital—picking up our Mini-Trails.

Everyone in the world would soon learn that I hadn't been going to Wendy's courting, but to take darned old piano lessons. And the days of sitting next to Wendy on the piano bench would end. I clung to the hope that I'd be able to take her for a ride on my Mini-Trail.

I'd been led to believe that the only people who attended a recital were the students and their families. Over time, I'd learned who the other students were and found comfort in the fact that few people I knew well would be in the audience. It was this peace of mind that allowed me to enjoy the practices relatively stress-free and to savor every moment sitting next to Wendy.

As we waited our turn, my heart sank until it settled somewhere in the vicinity of my belly button as I watched the auditorium slowly fill to capacity. I scanned the crowd. To my horror, everyone I knew by name and a lot I knew by sight were filling the pews.

"It may be my mom's last recital," said Wendy with a joy-filled tone. Her eyes sparkled. "Everyone's going to be here." Our emotions were at opposite ends of the joy meter.

It was only because it had been made clear to me that boys didn't hit girls under any circumstance that Wendy didn't get a sharp elbow to the ribs. She was thrilled at the honor that was being bestowed on her mother; I was horrified.

She gave me a look. "You scared?"

"No, I just hadn't planned on everyone on planet Earth finding out I've been taking piano lessons."

"Good grief," she said. "What do they think you've been doing at my house every week all summer long?"

Not having the nerve to attempt an explanation that might expose my crush on her, I logically replied, "I don't know." She appeared to believe me and didn't pry like my parents did when I gave them the same response to questions with forbidden answers.

All of the students sat in the front two rows. Wendy and I were listed last in the program. We sat in the second row at the end of the pew, next to the wall aisle. My skin felt cold and clammy; I was hot but shivering. Breathing became laborious. Then it happened.

Wendy put her hand on top of mine. I'd been constantly rubbing the sweat off of my palms, and my kneecaps were soaked. Her hands were soft and dry. We made eye contact, she leaned toward me, and I was too slow to dodge a tap kiss on the cheek. If my tongue hadn't been stuck to the top of my dry mouth, I would have swallowed it whole, which would have been really embarrassing. I'd heard of people having convulsions and wondered if forward girls were mostly to blame.

A calmness swept over me. I decided that any amount of ridicule I would receive was worth it. I looked around to see who had seen the tap of grace and dry choked when I made eye contact with Clyde, sitting only two rows behind me. He was wearing one of Odie Portman's old shirts, which was a tad small for him. It said "Odie" above the right chest pocket. Odie was well-known and highly respected, so Clyde wore it with pride.

Wendy squeezed my hand, then released it. I turned back around. The first soloist had just finished. Wendy clapped; I did, too. I glanced back at Clyde; he was grinning. The fire had taken a toll, but Clyde hadn't let it get the best of him.

I wore a new pair of Wellington boots and Wendy wore flats, which caused me to appear a little taller than her. When it was finally our turn, we walked up together and took our place side-by-side on the piano bench. The room became deathly quiet. Wendy's Jungle Gardenia entranced me;

I had the sensation that we were alone. She started playing her part, and I joined in with the accompaniment.

We neared the end of our third and final song. We never missed a note, the result of hours of practice or answered prayer. It didn't matter. My desire to continue to play was overwhelming; I didn't want the moment to end. The crowd started clapping, and Wendy stood to bow. Instead of springing off the bench and jumping for joy that the miserable recital was finally over with, my legs felt like I'd been mowing lawns all day. I mustered the strength, took my place next to Wendy, and bowed.

After the recital, there was a potluck dinner in the fellowship hall. Caleb's mom had brought sandwiches made with the weird bread; I steered clear of them.

Wendy motioned me her way. "Here, try these." She had a tray of cupcakes. Everett, Booger, Caleb, Clyde, Flop, and I all took one. I bit into mine; the cake part was dense, dry, and tasteless.

She stood there smiling. "We didn't have any eggs. Think it made any difference?"

"They're great," I lied and mentally marked her off of my potluck list. The others had already stopped chewing and waited for Wendy to walk away so they could spit the remains into their napkins.

Clyde surveyed the room. "I hope we get a crowd like this at the auction," he said.

"What auction?" asked Caleb.

"The church is havin' a fund-raising auction for us. People are donatin' thangs to be auctioned off t' raise money."

"When?" asked Booger.

"Next Saturday."

"How much money are they figurin' to raise?" asked Caleb.

"Enough to fix up the house; it's gonna take a lot, and we can't start until we raise the money."

"Where you living at now?" asked Caleb.

"In those two rooms o'vair." He pointed to the two rooms that the church had fixed for them to live in until they found somewhere to go. They'd been living there since the fire.

Suddenly, a crowd rushed out the door; we followed. Wendy and Beth were crying. Burt and Sheriff Omar were restraining Mr. Winchester and talking to him. Mrs. Winchester was standing next to him crying.

"What happened?" I asked Monkey Fullbright, who was standing in the bed of a pickup truck and had a better view.

"It looks like'at Harold Winchester done and punched Milton Merle square in th' nose."

"Really?" asked Caleb.

"Yep, I guess Milton is still lookin' where he shouldn't be a lookin' and a grabbin' what he shouldn't be a grabbin."

I hopped up into the bed of the pickup. Most of the men were amused by it all. The women were herding up the children and telling them to get back inside. Milton Merle was leaning against a car with his head tilted back, holding a handkerchief on his nose. He saw me standing in the truck, above the crowd. We had momentary but piercing eye contact. He blinked slowly, then looked skyward and applied pressure to his nose. He had to have recognized me.

THE RECITAL AND RECEPTION LASTED longer than expected. We wouldn't have been able to make it to Fairview Honda before they closed, so picking up the Mini-Trails had to be postponed until the next day. Anyway, looking forward to getting them helped me get through the recital.

Mamaw and Papaw had attended the recital, but left before the excitement. They were sitting on their porch when we got home. I filled them in. Mamaw gave Papaw a look.

"Papaw got a bad report from th' doctor t'day."

I looked at Papaw. "Doc says I need t' stop smokin."

"Why'd he say that?"

"Said it's bad for my lungs and heart."

"Well, stop smoking then."

"It's not that easy. I've tried." He explained to me about the addictive nature of nicotine and how he'd been trying to stop for several years. He stopped talking, and we listened to the night noises. I noticed the can of Prince Albert was missing from his shirt pocket.

"Tell ya what," he said after several moments of silence. "When you turn eighteen, if you haven't taken up this dadgum habit, I'll give you a hunert dollars." I looked at Mamaw. "We've talked about it," she said. "He's gonna make Marsha the same offer."

I thought about it for a few minutes. "Why eighteen?"

Papaw grinned. "No particular reason. Why?"

"Oh nothing, just wonderin.'"

He eyed me carefully. "Shake on it?" he asked.

I got up to shake his hand. "Sure."

After sitting back down, I watched a spider build a web and thought about something that had been bothering me; I shared it with them. They suggested a solution, but it had no appeal to me at first.

We sat there for nearly an hour longer before Mom blinked the time-to-come-home light.

Mamaw touched my wrist as I started to leave. "Let Papaw tell Marsha."

I walked home contemplating Mamaw and Papaw's suggested solution to my problem. It was clearly the right thing to do, but ...

Chapter 39

Change of Plans

THE NEXT MORNING, THE MOMENT Booger and I'd been waiting for and working toward all summer had finally arrived. I'd hardly slept at all. We went into the bank together to withdraw enough money to pay off the Mini-Trails; my account was left with less than five dollars. Clyde and his parents were seated in the lobby, waiting to see a loan officer. We saw each other and nodded, but didn't speak. Banks are solemn places.

I'd looked forward to this moment since spring, but for some reason, now that it was at hand, I didn't feel like I thought I would. I had an unsettled sense. I played Mamaw and Papaw's suggestion over and over in my mind.

Booger, Miss Anderson, Mom, and Dad rode with Mr. Burger in his car. Uncle Cletus had offered to haul the Mini-Trails back in his pickup. I rode with him and Aunt Penelope. It was a perfect late summer, fall preview day. The milky haze of summer had given way to evenly scattered puff-ball clouds and a sea blue sky. I hung my head out the window, caught the wind in my face, and reflected on all that had happened since putting the Mini-Trail on layaway.

Since our quest for the Mini-Trails had begun, many things had changed. Booger had suffered losses that had created a void that it seemed could never be filled, at least until Miss Anderson came along. Uncle Cletus had always been the most jovial of my relatives, and he'd recently become even more so, and the reason was sitting between us. Dad was fulfilling a dream and learning to fly. We'd beaten Fairview in baseball, and I was getting a Mini-Trail. Yet, when I glanced in the passenger side rearview mirror, the face I saw looking back at me didn't look as happy as it should have been. The answer to my dilemma had been made clear, but I wasn't yet willing to accept it.

We topped Turkey Hill, but Uncle Cletus didn't accelerate. He drove slow past Clyde's house and let Aunt Penelope see the damage caused by the fire. She looked but didn't say anything. Seeing the house again brought back vivid memories of that night.

"It doesn't look that bad from the road," she said.

"Thing of it is, there's more damage than it looks like," he assured her and went on to explain about the structural damage caused by the fire and the interior damage caused by the water.

"You know, in many cases when a home catches fire and the fire is contained, the water damage can be almost as bad as the fire. Sometimes, at least with older homes, it'd probably be better to let them burn."

"You mean just let them burn and collect the insurance?" she asked.

"Yeah," he confirmed. "In fact, in some cases the insurance company will declare a 'saved' house a total loss and recommend burning it the rest of the way and rebuilding."

"Think that's what they'll do with Clyde's house?" she asked.

Uncle Cletus shook his head, not in disgust, but sympathetically. "Thing of it is, they didn't have insurance." He explained to Aunt Penelope how Clyde's dad hadn't paid the last premium, and why, and that they'd have to foot the bill for the repairs.

She frowned. "I knew there was going to be a fund-raising auction, but I had no idea they needed to raise enough money to repair their house. I thought it was going to be primarily for things not covered by insurance." She rubbed her temples. "That almost makes me sick to think about it."

Sometime during the conversation, I came to grips with the situation, found peace, and shared my plan with Uncle Cletus and Aunt Penelope.

"Are you sure you want to do this?" asked Aunt Penelope.

"It's the right thing, Tommy," Uncle Cletus assured me. "But it's more than anyone would expect you to do."

"You think Booger will go along with it?" asked Aunt Penelope.

"I hope so."

The rest of the way to Fairview Honda, we discussed the plan and the consequences. I hoped Booger would understand and that I'd be able to get my deposit money back, but I'd decided to do it either way. I'd struggled with an emptiness that was completely filled when I'd made the choice to help Clyde.

Before Uncle Cletus got out of the truck he said, "I'll talk to the people here and let 'em know what you have in mind. It shouldn't be a problem gettin' the deposit back, considerin' the situation."

Both Mini-Trails were sitting outside when we got there.

"I'll bet it's been a long summer for you two boys," said Floyd. He'd seen us pull up and was waiting with the papers.

"You'll need to decide who gets which one before I finish filling out the title applications." Floyd stood there waiting for an answer.

"Booger and I need to talk about it."

Floyd reached into his pocket. "Oh, sure. Want to flip a coin?"

Uncle Cletus put his hand on Floyd's shoulder. Floyd winced a little when Uncle Cletus squeezed hard enough to get his attention. "I think they need some privacy."

Booger and I walked out into the Scrambler display while the others stood near the Mini-Trails.

"Booger, I've decided not to get a Mini-Trail."

"What?" His eyes nearly popped right out of his head.

"Yep. I've already made my mind up. I'm going to spend my Mini-Trail money at Clyde's benefit auction. His family needs the money worse than I need a Mini-Trail."

He kicked the tire on a Scrambler and squeezed the clutch lever several times.

"I think Clyde would do the same for me," I told him.

I saw Uncle Cletus talking to Floyd and started to turn that way, and then Booger's eyebrows started dancing.

"How about we go halves on one?"

At first, I was shocked at his suggestion, just as I thought he would be at mine. I listened while he explained how he thought it could work. In less than five minutes, we had a new plan, which included not telling anyone why we'd decided to do it. We figured Clyde would be embarrassed if he knew what we were going to do for him. For a few minutes, I felt ashamed at having ever doubted Booger's heart. I should have known that if anyone could understand, it would have been him.

———————

THE OWNER OF FAIRVIEW HONDA was so moved that he gave us each a helmet and the deposit money back on the Mini-Trail we weren't buying. We thanked him, and then loaded the single Mini-Trail onto Uncle Cletus's truck and headed for Colby.

Booger and I rode in the back of the pickup with it. We decided to flip to see who got to drive first. I flipped a nickel, but the wind coming over the cab caught it and carried it out the back. Booger flipped a '64 Kennedy half-dollar, careful to keep it out of the wind.

WE HAD EASILY AGREED THAT Bird's Cave would be our first destination. We were finally on our way. Booger had won the toss, so he drove going out. We stopped and visited with Mr. and Mrs. Bird long enough to be polite. The Mini-Trail barely had enough power to make it up the hill leaving the Bird farm, but it was still better than pushing a bicycle any day.

Booger dropped me off so I could start delivering the papers. Riding my bike was a chore and seemed childish after having ridden the Mini-Trail.

We'd spread the word for everyone to meet at the bridge after church on Sunday. Booger and I took turns giving Clyde, Everett, and Caleb rides. It was strange, but no one questioned the fact that we'd only gotten one Mini-Trail. Everyone was thrilled just to be getting a ride on one.

Booger and I almost had our first argument when I wanted to take it to give Wendy a ride. I agreed to sharpen the blade on his lawn mower and scrape the underside of the deck in exchange. He was happy with that, and I left the bridge as they started singing "Tommy and Wendy, sitting in a tree ..." Anticipating the thrill of taking Wendy for a ride on the Mini-Trail easily outweighed any ribbing they could offer. I sped away without giving their remarks a second thought; my mind was on Wendy. I stopped by the house long enough to put on a dab of Jade East.

Wendy was waiting on her front porch.

"Sorry I'm late."

"That's okay."

She circled the Mini-Trail and said, "Kind of small isn't it?"

I don't remember having any expectation of what she'd think about the Mini-Trail, except that she'd be impressed. "Kind of small," however, wasn't the desired first impression comment I'd hoped for.

"It'll run," I said, without thinking. Every time I talked to her about going for a ride, she'd made me promise not to drive fast. I could tell by the look on her face that my words, "it'll run" weren't very reassuring to her.

"You promised not to go fast."

"I know. Get on." I was anxious.

I folded the rear foot pegs down. We almost fell over when she got on. She'd never ridden a motorcycle and didn't know to keep her weight balanced.

"Slow down," she yelped every time I got going fast enough to shift into high gear.

Slow speeds made it a challenge to keep the Mini-Trail balanced. After a few minutes, she got used to the speed, and I was able to go a little faster, but still not fast, but at least fast enough to shift into high gear.

We rode to the creek and sat on the bridge; Booger, Clyde, Everett, and Caleb had already left but not before scraping Wendy's initials and mine in the gravel leading up to the bridge.

Fall was just around the corner. Spider threads drifting in the breeze reflected in the setting sunlight. The only sounds were the Craggy Creek ripples, birds whistling, trees bending in the breeze, and the crackling sound a cooling Mini-Trail engine makes. Wendy at my side made the trees seem more colorful.

It was only a short ride on a gravel road, but the sensation was akin to heading off to California on a Harley; a more satisfying sensation was impossible to imagine. In my mind, owning the Mini-Trail had moved me up a notch; I had hoped that Wendy felt the same. Had it been a little bit cooler, she might have asked me to put my arm around her to keep her warm.

All too quickly, an orange band across the horizon was all that was left of the setting sun. By the time we returned to Wendy's house, it was well after dark; I was probably going to be in trouble when I got home. The darker it got, the tighter she held on. After she'd gotten off, I reached to help her with the helmet clasp. She'd mistaken it for an embrace and slowly moved closer. Before I knew it, I'd gotten my first real kiss. I was halfway home before I got the ear-to-ear grin off of my face. It was never clear to me if I'd kissed her or she'd kissed me, or how long the kiss had lasted, but it probably hadn't lasted long enough to exchange germs; I'd have to ask Uncle Cletus. But it had been a real kiss because I could still taste her Clove chewing gum. It was then that I wondered, and sorta worried, if I should have chewed some gum before going on the ride. It was a moment I would remember forever; the piano lessons had finally paid off.

MAMAW AND PAPAW WERE SITTING on the porch with Mom and Dad when I got home.

"It's a little late, isn't it?" Mom asked.

"Kind of lost track of time," I replied.

"We were worried. Please don't do this again," she told me. I could tell by her tone that she wasn't upset with me, just worried.

"We're very proud of you, Tommy," said Papaw. Mamaw was beaming; so were Mom and Dad. I connected the dots and realized why I wasn't in too much dutch. I guess doing a good deed for someone pays off in lots of ways, or as Brother Baker once said, "Be a blessing to someone and get blessed tenfold." Anyway, I was beaming too, but for a different reason.

I stopped in front of Mamaw's chair. She cupped my neck with her hand. "It feels good when you know you've done the right thing, doesn't it?"

"Uh-huh." And it really did. But the kiss would have had me feeling good no matter what.

Papaw flipped me a 1964 Kennedy half-dollar. "Ninety-nine dollars and fifty more cents to go." He grinned.

It seemed like the sun was starting to rise before I fell to sleep that night. I tossed and turned and tore the bed apart. I couldn't get the Mini-Trail, Clyde, Wendy, or the kiss off of my mind.

Chapter 40

Full Circle

So many items had been donated for the auction that it had been moved to the baseball field. Booger and I got there an hour before it was supposed to start, and people were already thick as flies.

"You yahoos figured out what you're gonna bid on yet?" asked Uncle Cletus. He and Aunt Penelope were standing by the ladies auxiliary stand drinking coffee.

"Not yet," I told him.

Aunt Penelope looked at Uncle Cletus and then at me and Booger. "Look around, you'll find somethin." She smiled one of those "I know something you don't know" smiles.

Several men huddled nearby. Mr. Purdy had their attention. Booger and I walked over and eavesdropped.

"You right shore about 'at?" Bem asked.

"Well, it's certainly not carved in stone, but that's what my sources are sayin."

"What kind of hats?" asked Monkey.

"Can't say, they just said that the folks who are buyin' the shoe factory want to start makin' hats instead and are considering Colby for their first plant."

"Who ya think they'll hire on?" asked Bem.

"Look, everything I know is secondhand, but I'd 'spect they'd start with the people who are workin' at the shoe factory."

Booger and I kept walking; I had a bit more of a spring to my step in light of what Mr. Purdy had said and, of course, the kiss, which I hadn't told anyone about. I contemplated the consequence of Wendy not moving and was torn. On the one hand, I'd get to see her, but then on the other, piano lessons would continue. I momentarily wished for another recital; I was really losing my mind.

The auction company had combined small things, such as old tools, into single cartons. All the small hardware stuff was in one area. We spent a little time browsing in each area.

We saw a most surprising thing in the area where they'd put the refrigerators, stoves, radios, and electrical things. It took my mind completely off of Wendy. Wilma Bodenschatz and Marty Blanken were walking around together and holding hands, a far cry from her stabbing him with a pencil, or stomping his toes. When we got closer, I noticed that Wilma was leading and Marty was following. They walked by, paying no attention to us.

Old riding and push lawn mowers were in another area. Most of them had seen better days. Some people were using the auction as a way to get rid of their junk. That was aggravating. Something by an old Lawn-Boy was covered with a tarpaulin; I figured it must have been something completely worthless, but we were curious. Booger lifted it up. I couldn't believe my eyes.

"Dwight left for basic training last week. His mom donated it," said Uncle Cletus, who had been following us. "I brought it over for her early this mornin.'"

He and Aunt Penelope had known all along and had followed us around until we'd found it.

Aunt Penelope was smiling. "I couldn't wait to see the looks on your faces."

"How much ya think it'll go fer?" Booger asked.

Uncle Cletus gave us both a pontiff look. "I doubt many grown-ups will be interested in it, and I only know of two kids that plan to spend a wad of money."

Booger and I looked the Mini-Trail over, unable to believe our good fortune. We covered it up, bought a couple of caramel apples at the ladies auxiliary booth, and waited for the bidding to begin. Uncle Cletus was going to help with that part, too. He warned us not to scratch our heads or wave at anybody when in the bidding area, or we might end up buying an old doll house or something.

———

Dwight's Mini-Trail had several miles on it, and the seat had a small hole in it, but it ran just fine. We only gave $95 dollars for it and spent the rest of the money on some tools for Uncle Cletus; a used telephone for Miss Anderson; an old, possibly antique, Electrolux vacuum cleaner, according to the auctioneer, for Mr. Burger; and an old refrigerator for Clyde's mom.

A few days later, after we'd helped work on Clyde's house, his mom gave us a ride home in her big pink Chrysler. Booger and I took Clyde and Flop for a ride on the Mini-Trails to the bridge. We leaned over the rail and made spit strings. Since we'd had several cold nights, the leaves on the trees were already turning colors and had started dropping into the creek. The reflection of the sky mixed with the floating leaves would have made a beautiful painting. The sky was clear, and the air was unusually warm for late October.

Booger grinned at Flop. "One last swim?"

"Sure, like-a-said, let's check the water and see if it's still warm," Flop chimed in, with a snicker.

Clyde had already started climbing down through the bridge works to the pier.

"Like-a-said, stick your finger in 'at water and check th' temp'achure," Flop told Clyde.

Clyde was on his way to learning, by experience, his first lesson about a thermocline. Flop, the former student, had learned well and was now the instructor or rascal, as it were. Being the "rolled" type, they'd both tossed their clothes in a crumpled heap next to the pier. Before Booger and I had a chance to take off our clothes, Clyde unknowingly took the plunge, and cold water from below the thermocline drenched us. Flop stood there naked as a jay bird, every rib clearly outlined on his pasty white spoon-billed chest. He was grinning ear to ear, having just pulled a prank on Clyde.

It wasn't until several years later that I realized the value of the friends I made that summer.

About the Author

STAN CRADER WAS BORN AND raised in Bollinger County, Missouri. Coming of age in rural Missouri provided him the material for many of the rich characters in his books. He credits the variety of jobs and the people he worked with for providing him his creative foundation. While growing up, his jobs included paper routes, mowing lawns, grocery store carryout, farm equipment set-up, sawmills, and janitor.

After graduating from high school, he attended the University of Missouri, where he fully realized the uniqueness of his hometown. He met his wife Debbie at a Missouri / Nebraska football game, in which Missouri won. Some believe that Debbie considered Stan a project; most feel she still has much work to do. Stan and Debbie live near Bollinger County where they raised three boys and a golden retriever.

Stan's favorite hobby is writing, but he's passionate about flying and also enjoys biking, hiking, scuba diving, snow skiing, snow-shoeing, maple sap collecting, and photography.

He regularly flies a number of planes ranging from pressurized turbines to a small fabric-winged two passenger aerobatic model. On a typical Saturday morning, he can be found flying the fabric-winged plane at low level over the Mississippi River looking for bald eagles. He and a couple of friends once flew the entire Lewis and Clark trail at low level. His longest flight was from Missouri to Athens, Greece, in a small Cessna, just to see if he could do it.

While growing up, he couldn't wait to get his driver's license and discard his bicycle; after turning forty, he got back into bicycling and has made a number of long, cross-country rides, including the famed Katy

Trail that runs along the Missouri River across Missouri, and a ride across Montana including Glacier National Park.

On a whim, Stan and his youngest son, Brad, got dive certified at Branson, Missouri. Like his other hobbies, he immediately immersed himself in it, purchased all of the equipment, and started looking for the best dive spots. He met the pilot, with whom he flew the trans-Atlantic trip, while scuba diving in the Bahamas. His favorite dive spot, however, is Cozumel.

During the month of February, you can find Stan looking for maple trees to tap. He collects the sap, then boils it down into pure maple syrup and shares it with family and friends.

His photographs are mostly for private use, but a number of them have been used for calendars and university literature and websites. His favorite place to take photographs is while hiking or snowshoeing with Debbie in the Rocky Mountains, but he's taken some of his best from the cockpit of an airplane.

Stan is known for the unusual. For example, most settle simply to catch a baseball at a Cardinal game; Stan once caught a thrown bat that made its way into the lower deck. It was Father's Day and the game was televised. By the time he got home, several had called and wanted to confirm that it was Stan they'd seen on TV. His grandfather once filmed him jumping a small creek on a motorcycle. So it's evident where he got the daring gene.

His professional life is that of a business executive. He's president of a small family business that sells Stihl chainsaws and power tools. As a businessman, he won a Silver Quill for business writing and once qualified as a finalist in Ernst & Young's Entrepreneur of the Year. He's quick to credit his success as a businessperson to those with whom he works.

He was once elected city councilman of Marble Hill, the town where he came of age. He discovered a new respect for those who serve as volunteers in small towns in this capacity. The mayor he served as councilman for was also his former elementary school music teacher, which made for an interesting dynamic.

He applies his Christian principles in every walk of life, and it's his hope that others recognize Christianity as the root of his success and the source of his creativity and drive.

Favorites:

Song: "House At Pooh Corner" by The Nitty-Gritty Dirt Band
Place to be: Home
Holiday: Christmas
Book: Bible
Food: Wib's Bar-B-Q